Book 2 of the KAZUCHIYO series

KAZUCHIYO
THE BREAKING OF THE SIEGE

BY
MELANIE SCHOEN

Cover illustration by Erion Makuo
Typography by Natalia Junqueira
Edited by Jessica Hatch of Hatch Editorial Services

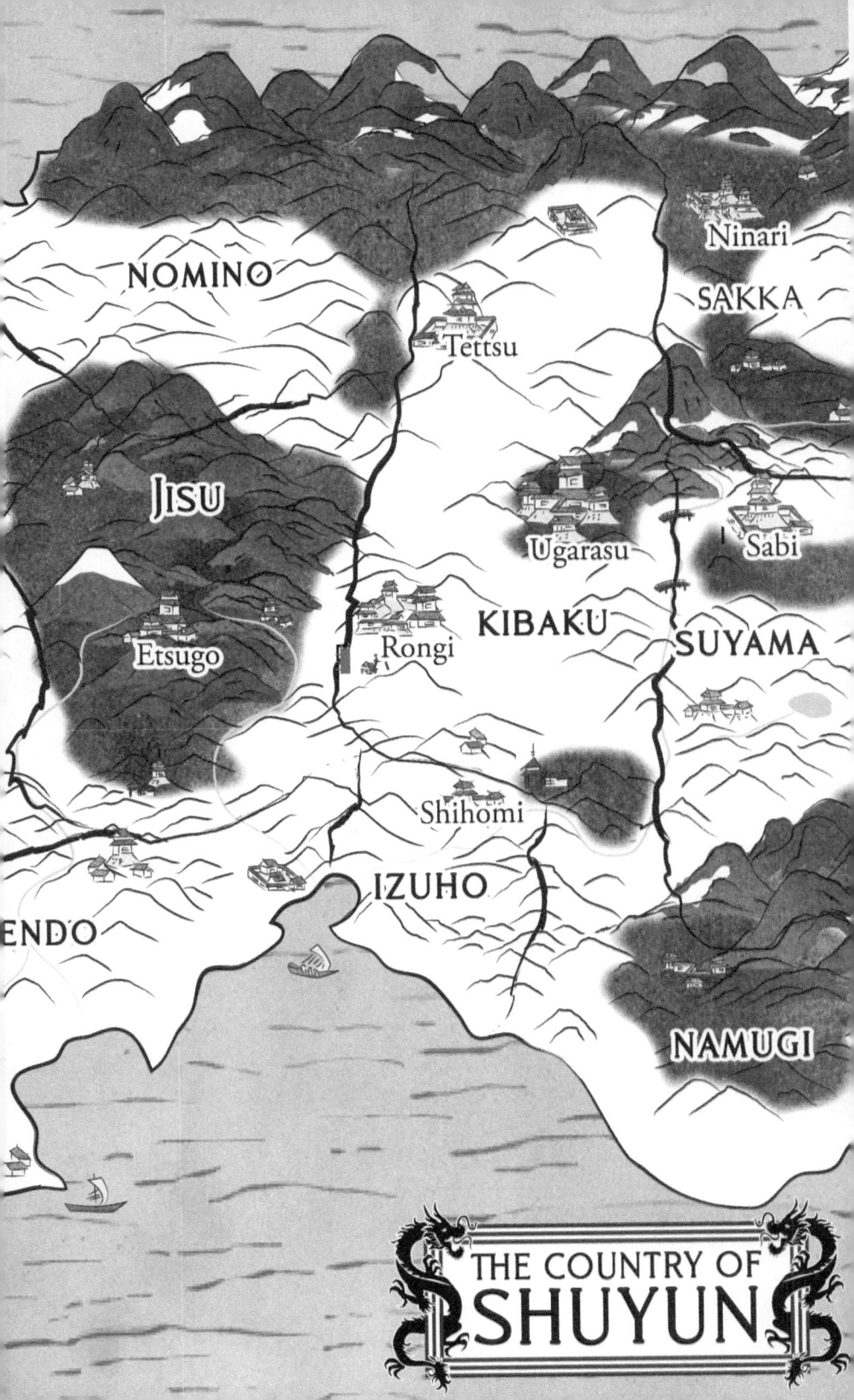

THE COUNTRY OF
SHUYUN

THE CLANS OF SHUYUN

Sakka Province
Lord Aritaka Souyuu
Aritaka Kazumune also known as Kazuchiyo
Commander Ebara Motonobu, also known as Yagi-douji
Amai
Aritaka Mahiro
General Rakuteru
Commander Rakuteru Ginta
General Hosoda
Tomoto
Master Iomori no Jun

Kibaku Province
Lord Koedzuka Danzou
Lady Koedzuka Anisha
Koedzuka Danmaru
General Oihata Naoya
General Sasahara Beihou
Lady Purnima

Izuho Province
Lord Watarizume

Jisu Province
Lady Dada Tangiku
Commander Chikakuni Okiaki

Tendo Province
Lord Umafusa
General Umafusa Kusagao

CHAPTER ONE

In the final throes of the sweltering, overlong summer of 1488, an army of three thousand Sakka and Kibaku soldiers marched south into Izuho Province. Their aim was to capture the fledgling province's latest stronghold, Shihomi Castle.

Izuho Province was not very large or very rich. It did not boast any warriors of particular renown and was not even very old, having only ten years previously separated itself from the mountain-dwelling lords to the southeast. It did, however, boast the unfortunate distinction of lying along Kibaku's southern border, and allied itself with the inner territories to the west. The mouth of the grand Fukugawa River met the sea along its shores, and the great roads that led to the capital passed through its gates. No general of even mediocre wits would overlook the strategic value of owning that small, diamond-shaped land.

It would, however, take a general of superior wit to claim it. Thus, it should come as no surprise that at the head of those three thousand men rode the heir to Sakka, Suyama, and Yaefu provinces, heir to the Great Bear Lord Aritaka, and the hero of Nodo Bridge, Aritaka Kazumune. To those, like us, who know him better: Kazuchiyo.

He spurred the army from its camp before dawn, and by the time morning sunlight crested the hills, his troops had surrounded the compound in a precise and compact curve. Shihomi Castle, built partially into the jagged and rocky mesa to the south, could not be encircled entirely. Its keep was long and narrow, peculiarly rectangular, with handsome, sloping eaves topped with gold figures meant to dazzle rather than defend. The walls had a bit more effort put into their function at least: stone brick and mortar, with many holes for archers and oil, and guard stations dotting the length.

These stations were heavily manned by the time Kazuchiyo and his army arrived. There had been no intention of stealth in the approach after all; certainly the samurai of Izuho had known for weeks that they had carelessly provoked a fearsome enemy, with plenty of time to prepare. Even the master of the castle himself, lesser daimyo Lord Watarizume, stood close at hand atop the northernmost gatehouse, watching the enemy form their lines. All along the wall his soldiers readied their bows in tense anticipation of the coming siege.

Kazuchiyo urged his horse forward. He had been outfitted in new armor since his campaign in the previous year, with indigo plates woven together with gold cords, and a broad helmet bearing the Aritaka crest at its temples. With three of his companions beside him, he approached Shihomi's gate and raised his voice.

"I am Aritaka Kazumune," he declared, "son of Aritaka Souyuu, Lord of the North and of the East. I seek an audience with Lord Watarizume."

Lord Watarizume, clad in his audaciously white coat over black armor, did not move any closer to the fore. Instead, the squat, bushy-faced general at his side marched across the gatehouse roof to glare out over their invaders. "What you seek isn't an audience, boy," he said. "It's an assassination, and the samurai of Izuho will not relent to your bullying!"

Positioned at Kazuchiyo's right, General Oihata Naoya bristled. "The samurai of Izuho are cowardly brigands!" he retorted with sonorous outrage. "Traitors to their lords and murderous thieves! You dare to think our march unprovoked?"

"A beast, whether from the north or south, can find provocation wherever they wish to," the general said in kind. "Your insults hold no more weight than passing wind!"

Naoya shifted atop his horse, red in the face, but he reined in his tongue when Kazuchiyo gestured him to quiet. "Do you deny it, then?" Kazuchiyo said, looking past the huffing general to the stony-faced Lord Watarizume. "A month ago, the village of Mitake along the border was attacked and looted by soldiers bearing white banners. Was this not your doing, Lord Watarizume?"

The general glanced back to his lord. Even at such distance their guilt could be easily detected, and the men at their stations tightened their grips on their bows. Kazuchiyo held his breath. Now was his chance to take the measure of the man that would determine his course.

At last, Watarizume himself strode forward. Not unlike the land he ruled, he was not in any way outwardly remarkable— not especially tall or strong, not old enough to be distinguished but not young enough to be considered green. His lovely white coat and lacquered armor were well crafted but had never seen use. "Mitake Village falls within Izuho's borders," he said, with every effort to match Naoya's grandiosity. "It was ours to take."

"There are *children* living in that village older than Izuho's borders!" Naoya protested, but again he yielded to Kazuchiyo.

"Those borders can be discussed, but not in a setting like this," said Kazuchiyo. "Grant us an audience, or we have no choice but to assume your refusal is an acceptance of your guilt and act accordingly."

The lord and his general coiled tight beneath his gaze. "Do you think we're frightened of you, boy?" goaded the general. "It will take more than this lot to tarnish the Jewel of Izuho!"

"You needn't be frightened of *me*," said Kazuchiyo. "But you are familiar with General Oihata Naoya, son of Naoatsu, of a thousand victories." Naoya puffed himself up with the introduction, and Kazuchiyo continued. "And I'm certain you also know who stands to my left."

To his immediate left was his sister, Mahiro, mounted atop the most celebrated warhorse who had lived or ever will. She was armored in her father's colors at last, though still boasting striped tiger fur draped over her thigh guards and at her neck. The mane of her helmet shone pure white in the early light, and the blade of her freshly polished naginata flashed.

Beyond her, and more imposing still, was Ebara Motonobu, better known to all as Yagi-douji, the oni warrior said to have slain two thousand men at what they now called the Bloodstained Bridge. He, too, had been redecorated following that campaign, the chest piece of his armor now bearing the snarling face of a fearsome oni, his helmet topped with a pair of reaching horns.

Yagi dismounted from his horse. He held out his hand, and one of the soldiers behind them broke from the line and dashed up to offer him a spear. In practiced pageantry Yagi hefted the weapon, took three mighty steps, and heaved it in an arc toward the gatehouse. Lord Watarizume and his men could only stare in shock, too stunned to order counterfire, as the blade struck one of the gold ornaments and wrenched it from its post. The heavy clang of it splitting open against the courtyard below echoed up and down the walls.

Mahiro snorted loudly atop Suzumekage. Her bravado might have dispelled some of the awe over the displayed feat, if not for the weakness of Watarizume's nerves. He gazed out over Kazuchiyo and his generals, over the three thousand men, and at last took in the empty post. "I will hear you," he said.

"I am glad of it," replied Kazuchiyo, relaxing in his saddle. "Our shinobi will have already infiltrated your chamber in the keep." Watarizume and his men tensed. "They've left instructions on the time and place for our audience this evening. We look forward to seeing you there."

Lord Watarizume was speechless while his general scoffed and sputtered nervously. But when Kazuchiyo bowed his head, they had no choice but to respond in kind, and they watched in silence as the army turned and departed.

The soldiers returned to camp, some discouraged to have been thwarted in their hopes of claiming enemy heads, most of them relieved to have avoided armed conflict entirely. Kazuchiyo related the particulars to his generals and captains, and most particularly, Master Iomori no Jun, his father's advisor and onmyouji.

"I'm certain it's not quite what my father had in mind," Kazuchiyo concluded, "but I am very glad to have avoided a siege here. Though between our army's might and your sorcery we may have taken the castle with relative ease, any effort not expended now will aid us in the campaign to come."

"Relative ease, you call it," said Iomori. She tilted her folded straw hat against the sun, looking particularly uncomfortable in the heat given her thick, dark kariginu. "Don't think *too* highly of yourself, young lord. You have never engaged in a siege, and you have yet to obtain Watarizume's surrender."

"Yes, you're right. I must apologize for getting ahead of myself."

"Hmm. Well." Iomori turned her gaze to the south, where Shihomi's eaves were still visible. "You do have every reason for confidence, thanks in part to my own prognostications. Long have I predicted you would have no difficulty claiming Izuho. Even so, I'll remain here during your negotiations if you permit it. To keep my eye on them."

"I'd appreciate it," said Kazuchiyo. He returned to his entourage and rode off again with only fifty men, following the Izuho border a mere hour's ride eastward to Hioka Temple.

The temple was nestled in the slopes of a bamboo forest, the stalks tall enough to blot out the worst of the summer sun yet narrow enough to allow some wind to pass through. The compound itself, built in years past to house the immortal soul of a long-dead emperor, was well known for its auspicious layout and seclusion. It made for a pleasant refuge as Kazuchiyo and the others prepared for their audience.

"Do I have to keep wearing this?" Yagi asked, his manners blunt and gruff as ever, as he and Kazuchiyo paced the grounds.

"The armor?" Kazuchiyo loosened the cords securing his helmet but did not remove it. "I doubt Watarizume will try anything, but no one knows him well enough to say for sure. Better to stay prepared."

"But it's so…" Yagi's face screwed up in boyish distaste, and he prodded at the ghoulish oni on his breastplate. "It's embarrassing."

Kazuchiyo could not stop a smile. "Yagi-douji is the most famous warrior this side of the capital," he said. "The armor lets everyone know it."

"It's silly," Yagi insisted. "They'll all know it's me with or without it." He forced himself to stop fussing with it. "They're going to keep spreading rumors that I'm really an oni."

Kazuchiyo drew them to a halt behind the shrine so he could face him and his concern seriously. "If it truly bothers you, there's plenty of other armor. I won't force you to wear it." His smile turned wistful. "To be honest, it reminds me of the heroes of old. I think you look dashing in it."

Yagi scrunched his reddened cheeks. "You do?"

"I do." Kazuchiyo stepped closer and pressed his hand to the armor to cup the oni's face. "It symbolizes your reputation, which is a great boon to us. It's because of *you* that we avoided a siege this morning. It may seem silly, but there's great value in a little pageantry."

Yagi sighed, but he covered Kazuchiyo's hand with his own. "Well, if you put it that way, I'll manage."

Kazuchiyo stood up on his toes to press a kiss to Yagi's lips. Their helmets clacked against each other, and he chuckled. "You can take *all* of it off later," he promised.

"Good," said Yagi, his eyes heavy with anticipation. They continued on with their tour of the grounds.

Lord Watarizume and his retinue arrived, as scheduled, in the waning hours of daylight. The heat of the afternoon had broken, leaving coolness in the swaying shadows of ancient bamboo. Kazuchiyo greeted him in the temple courtyard, joined by the aging monk who managed the grounds and many of his disciples. He kept his manners affable despite the paranoia of his guests. After a brief exchange of pleasantries, they were all seated in the hall to begin negotiations.

"We all know what's brought about this meeting," Naoya began, his righteous anger from the confrontation that morning now tempered. "The white banners of Izuho have been spotted encroaching on Kibaku land for over a year now. We will not suffer these trespasses any longer."

"Izuho's borders extend to the valley north of Mitake," replied the stocky general, also making a visible effort at maintaining decorum. "As was the case when it was still part of Namugi Province."

Naoya puffed his chest indignantly. "We took that land back from Namugi sixteen years ago. I remember very well, as it was my first time taking the field, and before that, Namugi had stolen it from Lord Koedzuka's grandfather."

"If conquering a land means owning it, by your own admission it belongs to us now," the general insisted. "So, what pretense will you next invent with which to besiege us?"

"My lord Watarizume," Kazuchiyo interrupted gently, focusing entirely on Izuho's governor. "We understand your position very well. Your land is very valuable, and you are surrounded by envious neighbors." Naoya cast him a sideways glance but did not interfere. "You feel you must be courageous to keep hold of what is yours, and you're not mistaken. Your boldness is commendable."

Lord Watarizume's face was calm and unmoved as he fanned himself. "Go on," he said.

"However," Kazuchiyo obliged him, "you are aware that Kibaku Province has allied with the great Lord Aritaka, who himself rules three domains. You know the fortitude of the samurai who follow him." His gaze flickered to Yagi at his other side, successfully drawing Watarizume's attention to him. Yagi played the part of stoic deterrent quite successfully. "Your neighbor to the east, Namugi, is already being besieged on my father's order, and will soon be his as well. Your neighbors to the west stand in the way of my father's ambition. Now is not the time to bicker over a village; there are better uses for courage such as yours."

"You flatter me," Watarizume said, a weariness creeping into his tone to suggest he did not think the praise was warranted. "But our courage comes from necessity, young lord. I must tend to my people before your father's ambition."

Kazuchiyo nodded. "I understand. You had hoped to secure Mitake so that you could claim their harvest once the season ends. I imagine your coastal fishing has produced poor yield this year, and you're eager to make up the loss to feed your people."

The general scoffed mightily. "Did your crow spies tell you as much?"

"One need only ask a passing merchant to know the state of your food stores," retorted Naoya. "If Izuho was in need of assistance, you ought to have come to Lord Koedzuka. He is magnanimous and would have aided you willingly if not for your paranoia and pride."

Watarizume and his general shifted uncomfortably, having at last taken Naoya's chiding to heart. Seeing this, Kazuchiyo placed his final piece. "Lord Watarizume, let us come to a mutually beneficial agreement. Let us aid you and your people through this difficult season, and in turn let us have your reassurance that you will support my father's campaign in the west. He asks no servitude, only what men you can spare, and access to the river and coast if need be."

"Unfettered access to our lands and soldiers *is* servitude," said the general, his nostrils flaring. "And he'll only ask for more if he does manage to become shogun."

Kazuchiyo shivered; he was still unaccustomed to hearing

8

his father's ambition stated so unambiguously. Even at this stage every battle Aritaka ordered was carefully explained away as necessity rather than warmongering, an open secret to leave unvoiced. He could not help but respect the gruff general for speaking it so plainly.

"What else are you going to do?" said Mahiro, and everyone looked to her in surprise. "Telling our father no won't stop him from being shogun. He'll just send us back here without any offer of help."

"You resort to threats?" the general said, his fingers flexing in want of his sword.

"It's what will happen," Mahiro replied simply. "You'll either take the offer now, or you'll be fed a worse offer later. Everyone here knows that."

Kazuchiyo kept his face impassive, withholding any emotion toward Mahiro's intervention until he had seen the outcome. Watarizume and his general exchanged long, measured looks. Then Watarizume met Kazuchiyo's gaze once more.

"Very well," he said. "We will accept your aid and grant ours in return."

"You honor us," said Kazuchiyo. He bowed his head low, and everyone else did the same.

The monk brought them saké, and they poured cups for each other to symbolize the union. Dinner was simple rice and vegetables, and as they ate Kazuchiyo prompted Watarizume to describe more of the particulars of Izuho's situation. As he had suspected, unruly seas had hampered their fishermen, and the steaming heat was rotting crops in the fields. Reassurances from Naoya that Kibaku's northern lands were expected to overproduce and were eager for trade helped put them at ease. Over the course of the meal, the reserved Watarizume relaxed, and even his overprotective general shared an extra drink with Mahiro.

As the party prepared to depart, one of Watarizume's soldiers came forward bearing a spear, its blade wrapped in tanned leather. He bowed so low with the weapon offered before him that Kazuchiyo worried he might tumble off his balance. "Please allow me to return the spear of Ebara Motonobu," he said, each word crisp and rehearsed.

It was only one of the foot soldiers' spears, but Yagi stepped forward and accepted the weapon without attempting to correct him. "Thank you," he said gruffly, and the soldier hurried back to his companions, who looked upon him with envy.

At last Lord Watarizume and his entourage left to return to Shihomi Castle. Kazuchiyo stood at the temple gate with Naoya for a while, watching their horses disappear into the bamboo. Only once they were long out of sight did he allow himself a relieved sigh.

"I daresay that could not have gone any better than it did," Naoya congratulated him. "Your gifted tongue won us a valuable ally without any need for conflict. However." He gathered himself up stiffly. "I do believe you misspoke when you described my Lord Koedzuka as 'envious.'"

Kazuchiyo managed to tuck away a tiny smile before he turned to face Naoya. "I'm sorry that I spoke offensively. It cannot be considered accurate to say a man is envious of land that is rightfully his own. My only intent was to get Lord Watarizume talking ahead of his loyal defender."

"And you were right to do so," Naoya admitted, "but you know my honor won't allow me to let pass any slight against my lord."

"Certainly." This time, Kazuchiyo did smile, and with sincerity. "You do him proud."

Naoya took the compliment very seriously, and it prompted him to continue as the two of them walked back to the temple proper. "Thank you. For that and for your efforts on my behalf. My temper sometimes makes a fool of me, so it is a great comfort to have your guidance. I appreciate it dearly."

Kazuchiyo felt his cheeks redden; Naoya's sincerity was sometimes overwhelming to even him. "I'm glad to hear it. I was worried that I overstepped."

"Not at all! Your equanimity is a great boon to me, to this campaign, and to our country. It will serve you well as shogun."

Kazuchiyo stopped in his tracks, right in the center of the temple courtyard. He looked to Naoya in surprise. "Shogun?" he repeated, his voice little more than a breath. He swallowed. "Me?"

Naoya viewed his confusion with amusement. "Of course!" he declared, but then he became mindful of his friend's demeanor, and he leaned closer to lower his voice. "It's been your father's design all this time, hasn't it? Who would that title fall to after his life is spent if not to you?"

"Y-Yes," Kazuchiyo stammered. All his composure over the course of hours flitted away like feathers through his hands. "Of course, but I don't… That's not my aim in all this."

Naoya's expression stretched into a grin, and he clapped Kazuchiyo soundly on the shoulder. "It is, though," he said with wise patience. "It takes a great strength to bend the mighty wood and draw the bowstring taut."

Kazuchiyo swallowed before rejoining, "And yet only the arrow will ever strike the target."

Naoya nodded, trusting his meaning was clear. He gave Kazuchiyo another clap, this time on both shoulders, and then stepped back. "The men have their watches, and the guesthouse has been prepared, so let us retire for the evening. There'll be even more to discuss come morning."

"Yes, of course." They bowed respectfully to each other. "Good night, Sir Naoya."

"And you, young lord."

They separated, and as Kazuchiyo returned to the temple, he was relieved that Iomori had not been present to hear Naoya's declarations. Though she had been his ally almost since his coming into Aritaka's home and service, her motives were ever a mystery to him. He did not know what she would say or think if he expressed too much interest in his father's claim to the shogun's seat.

Kazuchiyo found Yagi and Mahiro already in his room, sharing a drink. Though Mahiro was still clad in her full armor, Yagi had already shed his; Mahiro teased him as he tipped the cupful of saké to his mouth.

"You ought to leave all the grandstanding to me from now on if it twists your loincloth so much," she said. "I could have struck that ornament too. And looked better doing it!"

Kazuchiyo smiled as he removed his helmet. "There will be plenty of feats for you to impress Shuyun with during the campaign," he promised her.

"Kazu!" Mahiro waved the wine jug at him. "Have a drink!"

"Thank you, but I've had enough tonight." Kazuchiyo placed his helmet aside, and before he could go any further, Yagi pushed to his feet and came toward him. He was given no choice but to stay still and allow Yagi to begin removing the rest of his armor for him. The arch of Mahiro's eyebrow as she watched them made him blush. "You shouldn't drink too much either," he cautioned her. "There is still much work for us left to do, and I need you by my side."

"Of course," said Mahiro with a sliver of dry amusement. "We really should rest."

She stopped the jug and climbed to her feet. "I'll leave you to it," she teased, but as she moved past Kazuchiyo, she paused to fix him with a more serious expression. "You're not mad at me, are you? For interrupting during the talk?"

"Of course not," Kazuchiyo was quick to reassure her. "It was the push they needed." He caught Yagi's hands for a moment to still them so that he could impart greater seriousness of his own. "You're just as much our father's child as I am. You have every right to speak up."

Mahiro smiled, relieved. "Then you haven't heard the last of me," she promised, and with a laugh she moved on and shut the sliding panel behind her.

As soon as the door was closed, Yagi drew Kazuchiyo into a kiss. As always, his lips were heavy and possessive, and

Kazuchiyo melted happily into him. They fumbled over the remaining cords on Kazuchiyo's armor, too distracted to easily loosen the knots, until another set of hands took hold of Kazuchiyo from behind.

"Getting started without me?" teased Amai.

Kazuchiyo tried to turn, but between Yagi gripping his shoulders and Amai untying his belt, he could only manage to crane his head toward the familiar, slender figure of the troublesome shinobi. "There you are. I was starting to worry."

"A bad habit, that," Amai scolded him playfully, and he pushed Kazuchiyo's hakama down. "I told you these upstarts wouldn't be any trouble."

"And yet you're only getting back now?" retorted Yagi who, not to be outdone, stripped Kazuchiyo out of his robe. "Did you get lost?"

Amai laughed. "Never. Not with my shining lord to guide me."

He leaned against Kazuchiyo's back and pressed a long, wet kiss to the now naked crook of his shoulder. Kazuchiyo squirmed, reaching back to touch Amai's peach-round cheek. Before he could even release a sigh, Yagi took him by the chin and held him still for another deep kiss.

"Mm—both of you—" Kazuchiyo chuckled breathlessly as he tried to urge each man back. "One of these days you're going to smother me!"

"Don't pretend you wouldn't enjoy that," Amai teased. He stepped back, and Yagi finally allowed Kazuchiyo to turn so he could watch his undressing. His every movement was so smooth and effortless it almost seemed as though his robe shed itself without any intervention on his part.

Kazuchiyo reached behind him to loosen Yagi's robe as Amai swayed into him once more. "I suppose there are far worse fates," he admitted, and he welcomed Amai's mouth on his as he blindly fumbled Yagi out of his robe.

The three of them sprawled out across the mats together. Though Kazuchiyo tried to keep them mindful of the fact that they were far from alone on the temple grounds, even he struggled many times to stifle his voice. They had spent so many nights in this trio congress, and yet there was still so much to learn and explore in the dynamic of eager, grasping limbs, in Yagi's strength and Amai's flexibility. To relay greater detail than this would perhaps embarrass the dear sweet monks of Hioka Temple hosting them, so suffice it to say each of them thrilled the other into utter satisfaction.

Afterward, as they lay panting in the sweltering heat, Amai finally saw fit to give his report of what he had seen in Shihomi Castle.

"They were just as easy to infiltrate as I told you they would be," he boasted. He reached across Yagi's chest to draw forward a lock of Kazuchiyo's hair, which he then used as a brush to draw symbols on Yagi's skin. "The Jewel of Izuho has many cracks."

Yagi pursed his lips as if determined to show no reaction to Amai's teasing strokes. "How hard could it be when you've got Oihata's witch leading the way?"

"I'll have you know the lady Purnima didn't have one spell to offer me," Amai retorted, swirling Kazuchiyo's hair around Yagi's right nipple. Yagi's nose twitched, but he didn't flinch.

Kazuchiyo leaned into Yagi's ribs and watched their play with a fond smile. "And how fares the lady Purnima? I know Mahiro was disappointed not to see her at supper."

"She's as pleasant and accommodating as ever, though not half as keen as she thinks she is." Amai grinned with triumph as he rolled away from the pair to root about in his shed robe. "I know she didn't bring back any prize for her master that comes close to what I have for you."

He pulled from his robe a long cylinder of lacquered bamboo, which Kazuchiyo recognized immediately to be a scroll case of some substantial importance, given the hand-painted embellishments on either end. Kazuchiyo sat up, afterglow forgotten as he accepted and pored over the handsome case.

"I found it in Watarizume's chamber," Amai explained as

he nestled into Yagi's other side once more. "Are you impressed?"

Kazuchiyo rubbed his thumb against a delicate engraving of cranes along one side. His heart began to thud, and he was grateful for Yagi stretching his wide palm against the small of his back. It kept him centered. "Craftsmanship like this didn't come from anywhere nearby," he said.

"Open it."

Kazuchiyo held his breath as he tugged the stopper off and turned the cylinder on its head. Nothing came out, but Amai was still watching expectantly, and so Kazuchiyo checked the underside of the lid. There he found a family crest engraved, of a narrow triangular shape piercing another.

"It's empty," said Yagi with disappointment. "What's so special?"

Kazuchiyo showed him the crest, but Yagi only continued to frown up at him, awaiting an explanation. "It's the family crest of the Oomiyari clan," he obliged. "This case once held a message from the shogun, or one of his family." He looked eagerly to Amai. "And the scroll?"

"I couldn't find it in the time we had," said Amai, "but if the case is still here, it probably means Watarizume never answered."

Kazuchiyo continued to inspect the case for clues, but finding none, he set it aside. "The last time Aritaka received a message from the shogun, it was to announce the ascension of Lord Ryousai, following the death of his father. Could there have been another death?"

"Another assassination, you mean?" suggested Amai. "You don't have to receive messengers from the capital to know that it's every bit as lawless as we are out here."

Kazuchiyo frowned deeply as he stretched out at Yagi's side. "Unless the Oomiyari have heard of Aritaka's ambition," he murmured, pillowing his head on Yagi's chest. "Maybe they thought to remind Izuho of where their loyalty ought to be."

"Then they should have offered food and aid, like you did," said Yagi, and he wrapped his arm around Kazuchiyo's shoulders. "It's not hard to buy the loyalty of hungry men."

"Oh, but it is," replied Amai, "when you've got more pride than sense, that is."

Kazuchiyo trailed his fingertips back and forth across the familiar scar on Yagi's hip. His true concerns bubbled up, and he said, "Sir Oihata thinks I should be shogun."

Amai hummed. "He may be melodramatic, but he's not stupid."

"I'm being serious," Kazuchiyo scolded him.

"So am I." Amai propped himself up on his elbow to smirk down at him. "You're already fighting Aritaka's war for him. Take his prize while you're at it."

"A country is not a prize for the taking," said Kazuchiyo. "To kill and conquer is Aritaka's nature—like he did to my father. All I've wanted since then was for our family's land to be ruled in our family's name again, nothing more."

"We could take it," Yagi suggested with all the easy bluntness Kazuchiyo loved him for. "You're Aritaka's heir, so if anything happens to him, everything he owns is yours. When he dies, you'll own your homeland."

Kazuchiyo closed his full palm over the scar as if it still bled as it had that fateful autumn day at Shimegahara. By killing the Red Dragon on that rainy plain, Lord Aritaka had claimed everything he owned: his lands, his generals, even his eldest remaining son—Kazuchiyo himself. It was only fitting that treachery and death find him, and wrench everything from him in turn.

"Yes," Kazuchiyo said carefully. "That's true."

"So let me kill Aritaka for you." Despite the nature of his words, Yagi's broad fingers were tender as they combed through Kazuchiyo's long hair. "Neither of you would have to be shogun then. With the fox's help you could even blame it on someone else."

He smacked Amai's buttock; Amai startled ungracefully and then rolled his eyes. "You'll have to ask more nicely than that."

"If you can't do it, I can handle it myself," said Yagi.

"A scheme from you? I'd sell my ears to see it."

"Please," Kazuchiyo interrupted, but then he sighed, unsure what to say. So often he had been lauded for his cleverness, and yet he could not get his mind to focus. "It's probably what he deserves, but it would have to be perfect to avoid detection. There are still too many men loyal to him. And who can say if the generals of Suyama would accept me even then? I've fought all this time under Aritaka's banner without any complaint…"

"There he goes again," teased Amai. "He worries so much."

Yagi gave a quiet hum as he continued to stroke Kazuchiyo's hair. "Well, we're a long way from Aritaka now," he said. "We're here to help the crows, so let's just focus on that."

"Yes, you're right." Kazuchiyo nestled more deeply into Yagi's welcoming embrace as Amai settled in opposite him. "Securing Kibaku's borders will be challenge enough. I suppose there's no point in fretting about Aritaka yet."

"Either way, I'll support you," Yagi added.

Amai smirked at Kazuchiyo across Yagi's chest. "That goes without saying. Aritaka, Oomiyari—just say the word and I'll gut one or both for you."

"You shouldn't throw those threats about so lightly," said Kazuchiyo. "Though I do thank you. Both of you."

Nightfall offered very little relief from the oppressive summer heat, yet even so, Kazuchiyo and his two devoted lovers stayed close together, wrapped up in each other's limbs, through to morning.

CHAPTER TWO

I f one were to rate the provinces of Shuyun by the envy of
its neighbors, by almost anyone's estimation Kibaku would
be chief among them. It stretched north to south nearly the
entire length of the country, neatly separating the then-bitter
warlords of the east from the interior domains cluttered about
the capital. Its borders were sheltered with mountains, forests,
rivers, and other natural deterrents to invaders, and it had for
many generations boasted the rulership of the clever and even-
tempered Koedzuka clan, which was blessed with good fortune
and loyal retainers.

These would be reasons enough for any ambitious daimyo
to consider campaigning against the famous Kibaku crows, but
more tempting still was the land itself: rolling plains from one
edge of the province to the other, fertile and well-watered by
rains crushed out against the eastern mountains. It is said that a
hundred thousand bales of rice sprang from its flooded paddies
every season. If the true heart of any army is its stomach, in
that regard Kibaku could again be counted among Shuyun's
finest.

Thus, Lord Aritaka of the east, having failed in his
half-witted attempt to conquer the valuable Kibaku, had no

alternative but to seek their trust and camaraderie if he were to have any hope of marching on the lands beyond theirs. To this end he sent his children to their aid when called upon, in the late summer of 1488, when the heat was fit to smother even an emperor.

After securing the peaceful partnership of the small but advantageously placed Izuho Province, Kazuchiyo, Naoya, and the armies under their commands continued westward along the Kibaku border. There were tales of small incursions from every corner of the emerald plains, and Naoya was as keen to cast out any and all trespassers as Kazuchiyo was to see his fabled countryside. This, as we well know, was once again only another of Lord Aritaka's artless pretenses; even a small conflict discovered along the border could mean the perfect excuse for yet more war.

Even so, Kazuchiyo was determined to take advantage of the panorama while he could. He rode with Naoya at the center of the column of soldiers marching along, up and down the gently sloping hills, gazing in shameless wonder at the expanse of green that swayed around them as far as he could glean in any direction. The lands to the east where he had come from were no less beautiful, but due to their mountains and forestry he had never before seen such large stretches of unblemished farmland.

"The sweet-smelling wind, bends each tiny blade of grass," said Kazuchiyo, "over and over."

Naoya straightened in his saddle, and after only the briefest consideration, he replied, "Like waves of the deep ocean, unmatched in magnificence."

Kazuchiyo smiled. He could well imagine that Naoya had memorized a thousand verses in praise of his homeland for just such an occasion. "And atop those waves, a mighty warship plows on, far into the west."

Naoya took a breath to continue, only to be spoken over by Mahiro as she spurred Suzumekage to their sides. "Bearing dragons, crows, and the best lay in all of Shuyun!" she finished, smacking the handle of her naginata against her armor.

Kazuchiyo couldn't bring himself to admonish her or even to hide his smile. Naoya, on the other hand, fixed her with a glare as his cheeks burned red. "Bearing *warriors*," he corrected her through a second verse, "of the utmost dignity, aiming for glory."

"To cast out all invaders," Mahiro happily followed, "and pleasure their lovely wives!"

Naoya sputtered in embarrassment amid Mahiro's cheers at her own lewdness. A few of the nearby soldiers could be seen hiding smirks and chuckles against their gloves. Kazuchiyo expected Naoya to chide her, and could see it brewing in the clenching of his jaw, but instead he remained silent. She had not, after all, blatantly broken the theme or the rhythm of the renga verse.

"Mahiro," Kazuchiyo said, hoping to deliver only a mild rebuke for the sake of his host's favor.

"C'mon, little brother, give me another," Mahiro goaded him heedlessly. "I'm just as good a poet as you are!"

Kazuchiyo sighed, though he was rescued by an unlikely source; just behind him, Yagi cleared his throat and asked, "How do you know what to say?"

Kazuchiyo turned in his saddle just enough to see him. "What do you mean?"

"You're making them up, right?" said Yagi. "How do you know what the words are?"

"Well, you… think of them," Kazuchiyo replied. "The first person chooses the theme, and the second person tries to continue it, but using a certain number of syllables."

"What's a syllable?"

Mahiro threw back her head and laughed, which earned her a much swifter rebuke from Kazuchiyo. "Mahiro, enough." He looked back to Yagi, though the man's sour, distracted expression convinced him it was better not to attempt an explanation then and there. "If you'd like to learn, I can teach you," he offered. "Though we should probably start with reading and writing at all before you graduate to poetry."

"I don't need to read," Yagi grumbled. "Haven't had to so far."

"There are many fine tutors where we're headed," said Naoya, seemingly relieved to have been rescued from Mahiro's humor. "Rongi Castle is lorded over by the wise and mighty Sasahara Clan. They would be honored to accommodate your education in between campaigns."

"I don't need that."

Mahiro laughed some more. "Better to leave well enough alone," she teased. "Who knows what kind of poetry an oni would write?"

Yagi scowled at her back, and Kazuchiyo squirmed in his saddle, eager to find some change of topic to occupy them. "I'm looking forward to meeting General Sasahara," he said. "To earn such compliments from you, Sir Oihata, his must be a skilled governance indeed."

"Yes, indeed!" Naoya declared. "He is a dear friend of mine, though I know you won't take that to mean that I've leveled any unwarranted praise. He is the best sort of man, and you'll certainly get on very well."

Naoya continued to sing his friend's praises as the march continued, though as they went Kazuchiyo could not help but feel somewhat anxious. The name Sasahara was familiar to him, though he could not place straight away if they had ever met in person during the battles against Kibaku. It wasn't until he glanced back toward Yagi again that the answer came to him: Sasahara Enkichi, second general of the Kibaku vanguard, had died on Yagi's spear their second day at Sabi Forest. He did not know what relation the lord of Rongi had to that unfortunate soul, but he braced himself for the meeting.

On the third night after leaving Shihomi, the armies reached Kibaku's western border without incident. They camped outside a small village graced by a stream, allowing the soldiers the chance to bathe and wash the sweat from their clothes. By morning everyone was clean, well fed, well rested, and eager to march the remaining distance to Rongi Castle.

It was as the column was reforming its ranks for the day's march that they were approached by a rider from the north: a familiar samurai in green and gold armor bearing a full-moon crest on her helmet. She rode unimpeded through the troops straight to Naoya.

"Sir Naoya," Purnima greeted him, and she dismounted so that she could offer him a proper bow, which he returned. Her face was mostly covered by a snarling mask, but Kazuchiyo very well remembered the sharp gleam of her dark eyes and, even more obviously, her foreign accent. "News from the north: two armies skirmishing within our border, at Chouwa Valley. Their banners are violet and aqua."

"Within *our* border?" Naoya repeated, and Kazuchiyo could see the righteous fervor welling up in him. "Have they not border enough of their own to squabble over?" He motioned for his bannermen to hurry in preparing his horse. "Let us go at once, and put an end to them both!"

"Just a moment," said Kazuchiyo. He turned to Purnima. "How far of a ride is it to Chouwa Valley? Can our entire army reach it before the skirmish is decided?"

"Hard to say," Purnima admitted. "The Jisu samurai struggled, and it took me an hour to ride here from there."

Kazuchiyo stared into the north, but the fabled Kibaku plains were famously wavelike, and he could not glimpse any of the conflict at such a distance. He scoured his mind for the lessons he had absorbed of Kibaku's western neighbors: violet and aqua indicated provinces Jisu and Tendo, vicious rivals who sat north and south along Kibaku's flank. They were less than a day's march from Tendo's border even then, but his knowledge did not span deeply into the current area politics.

"Sir Naoya," he said, "if you were pressed to side with one over the other, who would you choose?"

"Neither can be trusted," Naoya replied immediately, "and both are trespassing now. Jisu is a land of mountain hermits,

22

Tendo of unscrupulous pirates. I would not seek an alliance with either if I could help it."

"Then let us hope they've given us that option." Kazuchiyo took in a deep breath. "I recommend we fly with fifty riders to the valley and see for ourselves. By the time our soldiers arrive I'm certain we'll have divined the proper course."

Naoya nodded enthusiastically. "Yes, I agree! I will pass on the orders."

Naoya marched off in the direction of his senior commanders, and Kazuchiyo turned to do the same, only to realize that Yagi and Mahiro were already approaching with their horses in tow. Upon seeing Purnima, Mahiro's expression contorted into one of violent glee, and she shoved Suzumekage's reins at Yagi so she could hurry forward. "Purnima!" she declared proudly, as if she expected the woman to be shocked she had learned her name. "There you are! Weeks we've been marching now, and you finally show up." She thumped the butt of her naginata against the earth in a confident pose. "You've been hiding from me."

"No, I have not," Purnima replied, and she likewise stood tall and poised, her hand on her scabbard. "The lady Aritaka is merely dull."

Mahiro laughed mightily. "Take that mask of yours off so you can say that again face to face!"

"Come take it from me, if you can," said Purnima, and though her tone was forged of iron, there was no mistaking the happy anticipation in her narrowed eyes.

Mahiro looked well eager to make the attempt then and there, and might have if not for Kazuchiyo's intervention. "They will be plenty of time for that at Rongi," he told them, taking one step between the pair. "For now, let's save that competition for the field."

"I'm going to take the general's head before you even draw your sword," Mahiro promised, and she hurried back to Suzumekage. "Just you wait!" Purnima scoffed loudly as she mounted her own horse.

Kazuchiyo feared they might race off to their contest immediately and was glad to see that Purnima only moved to the front of the assembly. Mahiro joined her, and they continued to exchange barbs while the rest of the riders gathered.

"That could be trouble," said Yagi as he offered Hashikiri's reins to his master. "She's even wilder when her father isn't around."

"Maybe," said Kazuchiyo as he accepted them, "but she's also happier."

He pulled himself into the saddle and turned Hashikiri about. "I'm going to pass the order to our commanders. I'll want you at the front with me when we depart."

"Of course," Yagi replied, clearly offended at the idea that Kazuchiyo would want anything less.

Kazuchiyo rode toward the rear, where Iomori had taken it upon herself to remain among the commanders. She stood considering a piece of paper in hand, which bore creases as if it had been recently unfolded. She was quick to tuck it into her sleeve as Kazuchiyo approached. "Is there some issue, my lord?" she asked. "I expected you to remain at the fore."

"There's some conflict ahead between two of Kibaku's neighbors," he explained. "I intend to ride ahead with a small force and see what part we can play in the outcome. This may be a good opportunity to judge our next quarry. Would you care to join us?"

A captain approached with Iomori's horse; she thanked him and pulled herself into the saddle. "Unless you object, I believe I'll stay with our forces," she said. "I have every faith in your judgment on the matter."

"Very well." Vowing to ask her later about whatever message she had been reading, Kazuchiyo turned his horse around. "Continue north and we'll meet in due time."

With the plans set, they spurred their fifty riders north along the border. Among them was the freshly promoted Commander Rakuteru Ginta, the most accomplished of Sakka's riders. He stayed close behind Kazuchiyo as they made their way toward Chouwa Valley.

"If only the stream stretched farther north," said Ginta as they rode, "we could repeat last year's great victory."

Kazuchiyo smiled, though he wondered if Ginta remembered their bold crossing of the river differently. To his mind it was an act of desperation he hoped not to have to rely on again. "Whatever we find at the valley, we'll make it a whole new victory for Sakka," he replied, and Ginta grinned with confidence in him.

After an hour of riding, the group arrived at a hilltop overlooking Chouwa Valley. As Purnima had described, two armies lay scattered across the sloping, grassy fields, one bearing the violet banners of Jisu Province, the other, the aqua banners of Tendo. It was clear that the fighting had already gone on for many hours judging by the number of bodies cooking in the summer heat. Kazuchiyo had to struggle not to grimace at the choking stench. Only one of the contingents was still fighting: not more than thirty men stubbornly trading spear blades at the center of the field while the majority of both forces stood back, struggling to regain order.

"A thousand troops on each side, at least," Kazuchiyo mused aloud. "Both with heavy losses."

"It'd be a simple thing to take them both," Amai drawled, and Kazuchiyo startled to find the man standing at Hashikiri's shoulder, as easily as if he'd been there for hours. "They're all exhausted, and they're not defending their east flank."

"It's what they deserve," Naoya agreed. "There's a small temple village not far from here." His fists clenched around the reins of his horse. "Our own neighbors, squabbling over the privilege of corrupting our borders. Disgraceful!"

Suzumekage's great hooves pawed the earth, and all along the line the riders shifted eagerly for the call to charge. Kazuchiyo's gaze swept over their intended victims below, and he saw the formations of soldiers as if they were tiles on a board, well positioned for their ambush. The Jisu soldiers were marginally closer but better protected, their command unit well-guarded on all sides, while the Tendo soldiers were brazenly reforming their line for an all-out assault. Their superior momentum might allow them victory against the Jisu, but their formation would not repel a cavalry charge with Yagi and Mahiro at the head.

"Wait them out," suggested Purnima. "In the time that our soldiers come, there will be only one side left."

Mahiro gave a great snort at that, sounding very much like her horse. "Yes, sit here and wait! Leave both commanders' heads to me!"

Kazuchiyo looked down to Amai. "Have you been watching them all morning?" he asked. "Do you know how it started?"

"The lady Purnima and I scouted ahead at dawn," Amai replied. "They were already at it when we found them, so I imagine it started overnight with some kind of ambush."

"Racing to plunder our land," Naoya surmised. "As always."

Kazuchiyo nodded grimly. "Yes, I'm sure you're right. Whoever started it matters little now." His gaze caught on Yagi, who was watching him with stoic patience. It helped to harden his conviction. "Ginta, do you have your oxen horn?"

"Yes, my lord."

"Let them know we're here."

Ginta urged his horse forward as he freed the horn from his belt, though every eye was on Kazuchiyo. "It's a straight shot now to either of their camps," Amai warned. "As soon as they see us, they'll reposition."

"That's what I'm hoping for," replied Kazuchiyo, and he nodded to Ginta one more time.

Ginta blew a long, clear note from the horn, as if to announce the arrival of supportive troops. Even considering the distance they could see the soldiers in the valley turn their heads toward the unexpected intrusion. More horns sounded, fans and banners were raised, and the exhausted troops struggled to adjust. The Jisu forces to the north were already focused on defense and had an easier time repositioning to the east; the Tendo forces were spread farther, and their soldiers at the front were too interested in pursuing the enemies in front of them to appreciate the threat to their flank. Their commanders struggled to maintain order.

"If my father holds any hope of attacking the capital eventually, our armies will need to pass through one of their provinces to reach it," Kazuchiyo reasoned. "One must be a true ally, not a conquered foe, for us to trust we have safe passage. If that choice must be made now, it might as well be as informed as possible."

Naoya sighed, his pride likely wounded to have to seek favor from either side. "You're right, of course, and as long as reparations are made from both of them, Kibaku will honor your choice."

A trio of mounted riders broke from the embattled Jisu camp: an officer, judging by the gold character fastened to his helmet, and two bannermen bearing violet flags. They cut a swift path up the side of the hill toward Kazuchiyo and his band. As they approached, he was able to make out the white chrysanthemum sigil embroidered on their banners.

Yagi had remained stoic during the discussion, but as the Jisu soldiers approached, he urged his horse a few steps forward and brandished his spear. The sight of him did much to prevent their guests from venturing too close.

The commander dismounted from his horse. He had a slighter build than most samurai of his rank, but he moved with easy grace despite the exhaustion evident in his sloping face. The character fastened to his helmet in gold leaf read *duty*. With calm determination he removed the swords from his belt and placed them in the grass before him as he bowed over his knees.

"Honorable Sir Oihata," he said, "it shames me to have our first meeting be in this sorry state. You are right to stand in judgment of our trespasses, and I have no excuses to offer, though I do offer you my life, such as it is, if you will show mercy to my soldiers on the field below."

Kazuchiyo leaned back, startled and impressed by the young commander's bravery. Even the righteous Naoya seemed moved, and he asked, "What is your name, and whom do you serve?"

"My name is Chikakuni Okiaki, sir. I serve Clan Dada of Jisu."

That a Jisu samurai would claim service to the Dada family was no surprise at all, powerful as they were, but Naoya was taken aback all the same. "Chikakuni," he repeated. "Heir to Okiharu?" When the man nodded, Naoya hummed thoughtfully. "I was not aware that Okiharu had a son."

Chikakuni dared to lift his gaze then. His eyes were very tired. "I stand before you, Sir Oihata."

"You *kneel* before him," interrupted Purnima. "As you should."

Chikakuni lowered his head again, and Naoya resumed his questioning. "Is your father down in that valley?" he asked. "He sends you to make his amends?"

"My father is in the valley," Chikakuni replied, his gloved fingers digging into the soil beneath them, "but he did not send me. He's already made his amends."

Naoya considered, and Kazuchiyo watched his face, hoping to catch a glimpse of his decision before it came. Though it was not his place to intervene, he could not help the impulse to do so. The movements of the troops had already convinced him that Jisu presented the greater opportunity for allyship, thanks to their more restrained and responsive tactics, and Chikakuni's honorable conduct even more so. He prayed that Naoya would see as much or, if not, then see it in his own anxious countenance.

"Kazu," said Yagi, and a motion from his spear drew Kazuchiyo's attention to a second group of riders making their way up the slope from the Tendo camp. Chikakuni's two bannermen shifted atop their horses, but the man himself did not stir as he awaited Naoya's judgment.

"Let's hear from the fish, too, then," quipped Mahiro as they watched the approach of the Tendo's carp-sigil banners. "A little late on the uptake, aren't they?"

"I'll hear them," said Naoya. He sounded hungry for it.

It took several minutes for the riders to make their way up the hillside. Kazuchiyo could not judge much about the soldiers by their bearing, so he split his attention between the continuing battle and its commanders. Though the fighting had slowed, some of the Tendo forces continued to press their advantage where they could and were gaining ground. Given time, their brutish efforts would be successful. As for Chikakuni, much like his men in the valley below, he held his ground, despite how evidently his hands shook against the earth.

The Tendo commander arrived: a wiry, angular man who dragged his horse to a cruel halt just beyond the rough assembly. "Sirs of Kibaku!" he declared as he dismounted. "It's good you've come!" He marched into the space alongside Chikakuni and bowed over his knees, though not nearly as far or for as long as his rival. Kazuchiyo could feel Naoya's hackles rising at the vast difference in their manners.

"My name is Umafusa Ran," he introduced himself. "In just a short time, I'll have slaughtered this Jisu rabble for you."

"For me?" Naoya replied, and he seemed to grow in size upon his horse. "This amateurish brawl you fling upon Kibaku's lands is for our own sake, you say?"

Umafusa blanched. He seemed to realize all at once, staring up at Naoya's gold-winged helm and the men and women beside him, whom he was addressing and how dearly he had miscalculated his approach. "Honorable Sir Oihata," he tried again, "my men and I spied these honorless curs encroaching on your lands and moved to intercept. Let us join together and have them slaughtered!"

Chikakuni shot him a look of exasperation and contempt, but he ground his teeth and remained silent. Kazuchiyo was not inclined to let him remain as such, though, and he cleared his throat. "Sir Chikakuni, you look as if you have more to say. Do you disagree with Sir Umafusa's account here?"

"I do," said Chikakuni with great effort toward restraint, "but we're already in the wrong. I dare not squabble in front of you, or..." He hesitated, his face screwing up. "Arguing now will just make me look like an asshole," he finished with resignation. "I already said I'd cut my belly open for you; all that matters now is if you'll spare my soldiers."

"Ha!" crowed Mahiro. "Well said. Let's kill the other ones."

She hefted her naginata threateningly toward Umafusa, who turned pale. "Wait," he said. "It was General Chikakuni who crossed the border first—we've killed him for *your* honor, Sir Oihata! If we need to repay you for trespassing, I..." He glanced behind him to his bannermen, who were suddenly looking back at him with dread. "One of us will honorably—"

"Enough," snapped Naoya. "Say the word 'honor' again, and I'll cut your tongue from your head before I display it! Your rotten mouth is unworthy of the word."

Kazuchiyo shot a significant look at Yagi, who nodded and then dismounted from his horse. The heavy rattle of his oni-plate armor had both kneeling samurai shuddering. Umafusa started to rise, his face going from pale to red very quickly. "Kill me if you want!" he shouted. "These fifty riders of yours won't be enough to break our line! The samurai of Tendo are stronger than—"

Yagi put the blade of his spear in the man's throat before he fully made it to his feet. With a twist of his wrists the head squelched free and tumbled to the dirt. As Umafusa's body collapsed in a bloody heap, his bannermen turned their horses to flee. Yagi hefted his spear and heaved a smooth arch directly into one man's spine, armor be damned.

Mahiro gave a holler, and she spurred Suzumekage on to give chase to the others, with Purnima just behind. Together they made quick work of the fleeing cowards and sent their horses tearing off in wild directions.

Chikakuni and his bannermen remained rooted in place, eyes wide with the gruesome spectacle. Chikakuni's hands were still shaking, but his jaw was set. He was not a samurai who fled. Kazuchiyo judged then that he would make an ally of this man, whatever the cost. It was to his great relief when Naoya turned toward him.

"The general Umafusa's reparations leave me unsatisfied," Naoya declared. "For my lord Koedzuka's sake, I will see Tendo punished more thoroughly than this."

"Commander Rakuteru and his riders will see it done," said Kazuchiyo confidently. "But what about Sir Chikakuni?"

"As he said, he's offered his life." Naoya frowned thoughtfully for a moment and then nodded, as if having come to a decision he was proud of. "What say you on the matter, Kazumune?"

Kazuchiyo's mind was well made up, but he did not answer too eagerly. "I'm not of a mind to see a family line ended on this hill," he said. "One servant of Dada has already given his life for this mistake. Let it be the last, so that this one may live to pass on greater wisdom to *his* heir."

Naoya nodded again, pleased. "So be it," he said, and he drew his nodachi, the metal hissing all along its superior length. "Samurai of Kibaku and Sakka, follow me!" he shouted to their riders as he guided his horse to the side of the speechless Chikakuni. "Let us sever the neck of this cowardly fish!"

The ranks replied with eager war cries, and already at the head of them, Yagi retook his horse. Mahiro and Purnima circled back to become twin prongs leading the charge, and within moments the lot of them swarmed down the hillside in a thunder of hooves. Kazuchiyo remained behind, Amai at his side, along with half a dozen of his and Naoya's bannermen. He watched as the calvary split the ragged defensive line of the Tendo soldiers and passed entirely through their forces, taking heads and other limbs as they went. The Jisu forces took full advantage of the unexpected attack and hurried forward, reestablishing their own ranks and pressing ahead. The tide had turned, and it did not take a tactician as keen as Kazuchiyo to see the outcome long in coming.

Kazuchiyo climbed down from his horse so that he could crouch in front of the stunned Chikakuni. "I haven't introduced myself," he said. "My name is Aritaka Kazumune."

Chikakuni blinked at him, dazed but with growing clarity. Within a few beats he grasped the significance of the introduction and swallowed. "You spared my life," he said, with all the gratitude, and also all the caution, that such a revelation warranted.

Kazuchiyo was very pleased with both. "I did," he said, confirming the implication that his mercy was not without its consequence. He offered his hands, and after some hesitation, Chikakuni allowed him to pull them both upright.

"You don't need to worry about it too much," said Amai with a half-smile. "No one who owes Kazumune their life has regretted it so far."

Chikakuni was quick to release Kazuchiyo's hands, even though he wasn't all that steady on his feet yet. When one of his bannermen brought him his horse, he was eager for the animal's reins to grip. "I'm grateful," he said, "but I can't offer you my full loyalty. I'm promised to someone else."

"I know," Kazuchiyo reassured him. "When the time comes, I want you to be the one to introduce me to them." He softened his tone. "In the meantime, I'm sorry for the loss of your father. I'm sure he fought bravely."

Chikakuni's mouth betrayed him with a bitter curl. "He did," he said, and he bowed his head. "Thank you."

They watched the rest of the battle play out. Back and forth the calvary ravaged the Tendo lines, cutting the chain of command at every opportunity. Mahiro's flashing mane may have called the most attention to her feats, but Kazuchiyo's focus was drawn continuously back to the bold figure of his mighty Yagi. By the time Iomori arrived with the rest of the combined Sakka-Kibaku army, the Tendo forces had long surrendered. It was no victory for Jisu either, though, and as the day wore on into evening, the invading armies set their camps at opposite ends of the valley to lick their wounds and hope for mercy.

Kazuchiyo and Naoya meanwhile camped their army on the hilltop, where they held a supper ceremony for the battle. They ate and drank and set a display out for the heads claimed in the fighting: Chikakuni Okiharu, Umafusa Ran, and several more on either side of the conflict. Though Kazuchiyo's words to Chikakuni regarding his father had been merely well-meant platitude, it was evident to all that they had been true, as General Chikakuni's dying expression was one of powerful wrath, uninhibited by the horrific goring of his left eye. He had certainly died in the throes of a violent resistance against his fate.

"It was my father's idea to attack the village," Chikakuni confessed to the assembly. Still in his armor but freed from his helm, his full features were on display: cheekbones high, hair dark and coarse, eyes pale. He was joined by a much older man who had been his father's second-in-command, a distant relative of the powerful Dada clan who seemed too overwhelmed by their circumstances to speak. "For years our lord has been trying to forge an alliance with the Umafusa clan in Tendo so that we could unite against Kibaku. We struck a deal: they would help us in a campaign against Kibaku if in the aftermath we'd split the lower half in two, allowing them to take Izuho as well."

Naoya huffed mightily. "You thought you could challenge all of Kibaku with this paltry force?"

"It was only meant to be a test." Chikakuni glanced to his father's head, and conflict came into his face that Kazuchiyo had much sympathy for. "My father wasn't a great strategist, but he wasn't an idiot. We were going to take the village as a foothold, and to goad General Sasahara out of his castle. The real fight would come after."

"But your new Tendo allies betrayed you," Kazuchiyo supposed. "They must have found out that we were already in

Izuho."

Chikakuni reacted with surprise to the news. "You were?" He exchanged a glance with the aged general beside him, who could only sigh. "Well," he said, again with that sliver of grim humor, "I guess that explains it, then. They must have attacked us in the middle of the night because they heard you were coming."

"Cowards," spat Naoya. "Cowards betraying brigands. You are lucky indeed that Kazumune stayed my hand, or both your armies would be soil for the valley."

Kazuchiyo winced; as grateful as he was to have Naoya taking up his causes for him, he did not want to see it overdone. When Chikakuni bowed his head low, he was quick to encourage him upright again. "It is finished now," he said, "and no harm came to the village. You and your soldiers will be sent home with your dead. All I ask in return is that you convey a message to Lord Dada."

"*Lady* Dada," Chikakuni corrected him, though he then caught himself, unsure of his manners. Kazuchiyo bowed his head briefly.

"My apologies," Kazuchiyo said. "Lady Dada, then."

Beside him, Mahiro looked up from her wine. "Jisu's daimyo is a *woman*?" she declared, and she cast Chikakuni a sly smirk. "Is she *pretty*?"

"Beautiful," Chikakuni replied confidently. "Intensely so."

"Ha!" Mahiro slapped her knee and then leaned back so she could see Naoya around her brother. "Oi, Oihata! Do we even need to go to Rongi? I've got somewhere else in mind." Naoya's face turned red, and he tried to avoid her gaze by drinking his wine.

"There'll be time for that," Kazuchiyo promised her. He looked to Chikakuni and allowed his manner to grow serious once more. "In the meantime, tell the lady of Jisu all that's happened here. Kibaku will not forgive any further trespasses, and they have the full support of Lord Aritaka and his armies. Now is the time for her to give up any ambition she has for owning this land. Is that understood?"

Chikakuni bowed deeply. He even seemed glad of it. "Perfectly so, Lord Aritaka," he said. Hearing that title ascribed to him gave Kazuchiyo a chill.

After the meal had concluded, Kazuchiyo took a few minutes to write a letter to Lady Dada directly. Though the contents of this letter were only ever to be known to the pair of them, do not think me too lacking in propriety if I share them with you here:

To the head of Clan Dada and venerable lord of Jisu Province,

Please excuse any offense at the informality of this first correspondence, but I could not wait until our proper introduction to write you this letter. While traveling with Sir Oihata Naoya of Kibaku Province, it was my fate to stumble upon a skirmish involving your forces on Kibaku lands. Sir Chikakuni will no doubt relay to you the particulars of the conflict, though I think it important that you know it was the good sir's strength of character that motivated our intervention to take the form that it did. Though the samurai of Sakka cannot boast the reputation for chivalry enjoyed by Kibaku, I am no less moved by displays of intelligence and duty.

I tell you this not to curry favor on Sir Chikakuni's behalf, or to boast of my own character, but only so that the truth of the matter be known. It is my honest hope that you and I will have the opportunity to meet on this and other topics before the days grow much shorter, as the sun already sets very early in the evening now, though it does very little for the heat.

We travel now to Rongi Castle, where I pray I will soon receive your favorable reply and an invitation to further conversations, in text and in person.

Respectfully,
Aritaka Kazumune

One can easily imagine Yagi's frustration with "samurai doublespeak" if he were able to read this letter, but even he would be forced to admit that explicitly stating, "I hope you will throw your lot in with me before answering any letters from the capital in the west," would be too bold at this stage, even for clever Kazuchiyo.

Thus, armed with this invitation, Chikakuni and his aged companion returned to their camp in the valley. Kazuchiyo watched from the camp's perimeter, contemplating his decision. Though he was confident that he would rather have Chikakuni as an ally than the Umafusa they had dispatched, he was very aware that he could not judge an entire province and its lord by a single soldier. He could not help but wonder how many allies he might forge in the west who would judge Aritaka incorrectly through him.

"Lord Kazumune," called Iomori.

Kazuchiyo turned, and he was surprised to see Iomori approaching in her full travel garb with her horse saddled and supplied. "Master Iomori? You're leaving us?"

"I'm afraid so." Iomori stopped in front of him, though, as usual, her long face was unreadable. "I'm going to return to Shihomi. There are a few things I wanted to confirm for myself before we leave them to their own devices." She tilted her head. "With General Oihata and his sorcery among your army, you hardly have any use for me after all."

Kazuchiyo did his best to hide a moment's apprehension; he had not shared with her the scroll case that Amai retrieved from Watarizume's chamber, and he wondered if she had found a way to intuit it. "That's not true at all," he said, and just to test her, he added, "Without you here, who will receive my father's messages for me?"

Iomori's lip quirked just slightly, and without breaking eye contact, she reached into her sleeve and produced the paper Kazuchiyo had caught her reading earlier. "Your father assumed we would be assailing Shihomi for some time," she said as she allowed Kazuchiyo to read over the brief note written in Aritaka's blunt handwriting. "He's sending someone to deliver a message best not left to a lone shiki. I'll alert him to your swift victory and wait for them to arrive."

The letter confirmed as much, and Kazuchiyo frowned, mulling the revelation over as he passed it back to her. "It's addressed only to you," he noted.

"I prepared this shiki for him before we departed," Iomori replied easily. "It's *meant* for me; that's how the magic works. You needn't be concerned."

"Curiosity rather than concern. You will inform me once the full message has been delivered?"

"Naturally." Iomori tucked the paper back into her robe and then offered Kazuchiyo a bow. "Fear not, Kazumune. As I have always said, yours is a celebrated fate. Whatever new challenge awaits you, I have every confidence that you will succeed."

Kazuchiyo bowed his head in return despite his doubts. "Yes, as you've always said," he echoed. "And likewise, I am ever grateful. Travel safely. We hope to see you at Rongi before too long."

"You shall," Iomori promised, and she took to her saddle. Kazuchiyo watched her ride into the south, his mind full of questions.

Had Aritaka deemed their progress too slow? It was already late in the season, with very little time left for campaigning. Perhaps he had sensed, even from days of travel away, that Kazuchiyo lacked conviction to warmonger in his name. It was little more than a year ago, as we recall, that Kazuchiyo himself had driven two provinces to war, with civilians among the many casualties. Only a master as impatient and cruel as Aritaka would hold it against him if he hesitated to be that headstrong again.

"Brother!" Mahiro stomped across the hilltop toward him, still happily clad in her armor and mane. She jutted her chin toward the retreating figure of Iomori. "The hell is she going?"

37

"Back to Shihomi," Kazuchiyo related, curious to see her reaction. "Our father thinks we're still there and is sending a messenger, so she hopes to intercept them."

As he suspected, Mahiro scowled. "Checking up on us, huh?" she muttered. "If he didn't think we could handle it, he shouldn't have sent us. Or did he think he could march down here just in time for us to take the castle so he could take credit for it? Ha!" She turned about with a toss of her mane.

Kazuchiyo fell into step beside her to return to the camp. "This campaign is being fought in his name," he said, testing the words as he spoke them. "I don't blame him if he wants to see the results himself."

"It's not like it makes a difference. Anything you win belongs to him until he drops dead, and then it'll be yours. So there's no reason for him to be paranoid."

Kazuchiyo frowned as they continued toward their tents, reminded of his conversation with his lovers at Hioka. Whether he waged war or whether he was patient, he had much to gain and only his conscience to lose. "Yes, you're right."

CHAPTER THREE

The armies arrived at Rongi Castle in the late afternoon, when the sun was at its most sweltering, and soldier and beast alike were eager for rest. The castle's construction was as impressive in its function as Kazuchiyo had anticipated, built for defense more so than ornamentation. It boasted no gold tigerfish on its gatehouses, no clever engravements, only tall, green banners bearing the wings of the Koedzuka family crest and fortifications fit for a border garrison. It stretched out across the top of a tall, sloping hill, each guard station manned and each wall built upon an imposing barrier of stone.

Kazuchiyo could not help but marvel as they passed through the immense gates to the interior. Much like in Castle Ninari, which at the time had seemed like the pinnacle of defensive engineering, the march to the center of the complex was a maze of walls, towers, and baileys, with rough stairs and long-stretching eaves to cast each courtyard in jagged shadows. He did not envy the general who chose to make war on such a fortress.

General Sasahara Beihou himself greeted them just inside the central courtyard, and Kazuchiyo could see at once why Naoya had spoken so highly of him. He was a man of considerable size, nearly as tall as Naoya and twice his girth, his well-worn armor stretched to its limits across his muscular shoulders and round belly. His mustache was very thin but very wide, and it seemed to touch his ears when he smiled. As soon as the procession was within the walls, Naoya dismounted from his horse, and he and his old friend embraced mightily.

"It's been too long," said Beihou, his voice deep but gentler than expected given his great size. "Much too long since I had the honor of hosting you, dear friend."

"The honor is mine," Naoya replied as they separated. "Ever more so, because I have fine guests in need of your hospitality."

"If they're guests of yours, I have hospitality enough to overwhelm them."

Beihou signaled for his attendants to come forward, and they assisted their guests in dismounting and relinquishing their horses. Kazuchiyo accepted their help and then moved to Naoya's side so he could offer his host a bow as deep as was acceptable given his greater status over the man. "General Sasahara, thank you kindly for accepting us as your guests. I am Aritaka Kazumune, son of Lord Aritaka of Sakka."

Beihou bowed in return. "Sasahara Beihou," he introduced himself, and when he straightened up, he fixed Kazuchiyo with a fatherly smile. "Though the introductions aren't that necessary. I'd recognize you anywhere."

Kazuchiyo blinked at him in surprise, though an explanation came to him a beat later. "You were at Nodo Bridge."

"Aye, I was," he said, and he motioned for Kazuchiyo to follow him toward the keep. "And the forest before that."

"It was General Sasahara who severed your chain of command at the river," Naoya explained, and from any other man it may have seemed a boast. "His riders are experienced and fearless."

"Not so fearless," Beihou confessed wistfully. "Not when I watched a young samurai and *his* riders cross the bridge to my lord's flank, when there was an entire battlefield keeping me from him." He fixed Kazuchiyo with a wise look. "That you spared his life that day is a debt I'll never be able to repay to you."

"Nor I," Naoya hastily agreed. "Kazumune's captain from that day is with us as well, if you'll admit him to your audience tonight."

"Of course, but what about…" Just before reaching the step up to the keep, Beihou turned, and his smile pressed thin as he spotted Yagi among the approaching ranks. "Ahh, there he is," he said.

Kazuchiyo took in a long breath and reluctantly motioned for Yagi to join them. Though he had had the foresight to warn Yagi about this encounter, he was still uncertain how it might play out. "This is one of my lord's samurai, Commander Ebara Motonobu," he said while Yagi dutifully bowed.

Beihou returned the courtesy. "Another unforgettable face," he said. "Rongi is glad to have you."

Yagi regarded him stoically a moment, perhaps trying to recall a script Kazuchiyo had suggested to him the evening before. Instead of reciting it, he bluntly said, "I killed some relation of yours in the Sabi woods. Sasahara Enkichi. I hope you won't be angry with Lord Kazumune because of it."

Both Beihou and Naoya reacted with surprise, and Kazuchiyo tried to ready some balm of words, but then Beihou's smile returned. "I would never," he reassured them, resolute and proud. "To die on the spear of Yagi-douji isn't any fate to sneer at, and you even remembered his name. I'm sure he's thrilled."

They resumed their progress into the keep, Kazuchiyo breathing a quiet sigh of relief. "He fought very well," he said. "Was he a very close relation of yours?"

"My elder brother," said Beihou, and he gave a chuckle. "Someday, when they recount the victims of Yagi-douji, the list will begin with 'Sasahara Enkichi.' I'll have to work much harder to get anywhere near that level of immortality."

"I think we all will," said Kazuchiyo. Seeing Yagi frown deeply and look away, he changed the subject to prevent Beihou from noticing. "We've been a long time at travel. If you'll excuse us for an hour or so, I'd like to prepare for more formal introductions."

"Of course, of course." As they all gathered on the broad engawa surrounding the keep's main hall, Beihou gestured again to the attendants. Each was rougher at the edges than Kazuchiyo was accustomed to, likely soldiers unfamiliar with their current domestic tasks. "I have chambers prepared in the main keep for you and your sister, and a very fine room atop the lesser keep for Sir Ebara and your other commanders."

"I'll stay with my lord," Yagi said immediately.

Kazuchiyo could not help a blush as several eyes and a few raised eyebrows were aimed his way. Before he could offer some explanation, Mahiro laughed and thumped him on the back. "I'll take Yagi-douji's room in the lesser keep," she declared. "I do better among the soldiers anyway."

"As you wish," said Beihou, and he cast Naoya a look that bordered on sly.

Naoya cleared his throat loudly. "I trust my usual accommodations are prepared?"

"Naturally, but I'll show you the way, just in case." He nodded to Kazuchiyo. "My men will take you to your room, and we'll meet for supper this evening."

Kazuchiyo nodded in return, relieved. "Thank you, General Sasahara."

The soldier led them to a small but handsome room at the center of the keep. Though Kazuchiyo would have been most pleased with an exterior window, he supposed that the governors of a castle meant as a border fortress preferred their guests to be well guarded. As soon as they were in private, he and Yagi helped each other out of their armor and, using a basin of water left for them, mopped up the worst of their sweat.

"It's a small room for two," said Kazuchiyo, though he

was not displeased with the arrangement. "We'll have to keep a panel open through the night to get any amount of air in this heat."

Yagi grunted an acknowledgement as he thumped down in the center of the room and stripped out of the upper half of his underclothes. He seemed to be in a sour mood, scraping the lukewarm water across the back of his neck in an effort to ward off the sweltering heat. Kazuchiyo let him be for a moment just to see if he would speak on his own, vain as that hope might have been. At last, he took it upon himself to kneel behind him, and he blew across the back of Yagi's damp neck.

Yagi startled as the small hairs on his neck stood on end. He looked to Kazuchiyo over his shoulder. "What?"

"I know it's uncomfortable, but you seem unhappy," said Kazuchiyo. It was too hot to stay pressed together for very long, so he contented himself drawing idle patterns across Yagi's bare shoulders with his fingertips. "What's on your mind?"

"Nothing," Yagi grumbled, but he didn't manage to keep that lie for very long. Slowly he relaxed beneath Kazuchiyo's trailing hands. "I don't like that Sasahara."

"No? I thought he was charming."

"I don't like him." Yagi stewed quietly for a moment more until the soft drag of Kazuchiyo's fingernails drew the rest from him. "I don't understand how you can thank someone for killing your brother."

Kazuchiyo stopped. He was only just then reminded of Yagi's downturned expression during the conversation earlier. "Did you ever have a brother?" he asked.

"No. At least, I don't think so." Yagi wet his rag again and wrung the excess out, his knuckles white. "I just don't understand samurai. Flinging themselves on each other's swords as if that's hard to do. If they want to line up in front of my spear, I'll gut them and be done with it without any battle at all."

Kazuchiyo leaned back on his heels, uncertain of how to respond. "That would certainly make things quicker," he said, aiming for levity, but Yagi's quiet snort was proof he had not hit that target. He wet his lips as he groped for something more sincere. "I know it's... strange," he tried again, "but if you absolutely could not escape your fate of death on the battlefield, wouldn't you feel better knowing that it was someone powerful who ended up defeating you? That people would remember your name for generations to come?"

"It's only my name because you gave it to me," said Yagi. "I don't care who kills me or who remembers me." He turned again to look at Kazuchiyo over his shoulder. "I just care about you."

Despite having received such a declaration many times before, Kazuchiyo's heart still thudded over every syllable. He leaned into Yagi's strong back and met his lips for a welcomed kiss. "Then I'll have to live a thousand years, like *my* name says," he replied, "so that your fame will live just as long."

Yagi snorted again, but he already sounded less surly. He didn't stop Kazuchiyo from plucking the rag out of his hand. "That's not what I meant, but all right."

"I suppose it doesn't feel so strange to me because it's what I grew up with," Kazuchiyo said as he scrubbed Yagi's back. "The tales of battles past, the samurai who fought in them— they're part of our history, of our clan. That history and those memories are important. They help us remember who we are and where we came from."

Yagi was silent for a beat, and only then did Kazuchiyo realize how arrogant his words must have sounded on the ears of a man who had no family or history of his own. Before he could apologize for speaking carelessly, however, Yagi asked him, "If you knew which of Aritaka's generals took your father's head, would you thank him for it?"

Kazuchiyo once again was struck still. A trail of water seeped from the rag beneath his fist. "No," he said, and with a deep breath he forced himself to continue. "My father was killed by treachery. That's different."

"Same for that Chikakuni, I guess."

44

"Yes." Kazuchiyo drew his finger along Yagi's back as he spelled out the man's name, trying to imagine which characters might be used. "You liked *him* at least, didn't you?"

"Well enough. I know *you* did." Yagi craned his neck again to look over his shoulder. "You said you wanted more allies for marching on the capital, but I thought you said before that you weren't sure about being shogun."

Kazuchiyo blinked, and a bubble of incredulous laughter tumbled out of him. "Well, the heat has certainly loosened your tongue," he teased. "You're very talkative tonight after all."

Yagi blushed in embarrassment and turned forward again. "I'm trying to pay attention," he mumbled.

"And I appreciate it," Kazuchiyo said quickly. Feeling the need to prove it, he set the rag down so he could wrap his arms around Yagi's shoulders. "I'm grateful for *all* the ways you've supported me." He pressed a kiss to the nape of Yagi's neck. "You're right. I did say that, but I also need to keep up appearances. Better to have as many allies and as many open paths as possible moving forward."

"All right." Yagi reached up to squeeze Kazuchiyo's arm. "Whatever you want to do, I'll follow you."

"Thank you," said Kazuchiyo, and with one more kiss they finally pulled apart to prepare for supper.

The meal was not lavish, but it was impressive: simple foods served in larger portions than Kazuchiyo was accustomed to. There was certainly no mystery as to how Beihou had reached his great size, to speak nothing of his four equally burly children. He thanked Naoya and Kazuchiyo for intervening in the valley battle, which he and his scouts had only become aware of after it was nearly over. Despite its advantageous position on the hill, even Rongi Castle had its blind spots with regard to the land's topography.

"Though I wouldn't have been put out if you did accept

Chikakuni's full surrender," Beihou finished. "That entire family has been a fly on our hides for too long already. I thought we might have gained some peace when Okiharu's wife was killed at Uragaoka this last year, but no such luck it seems."

"His wife?" Mahiro echoed with interest. "Was she on the field?"

"She was," said Beihou with wary amusement that spoke to a long history. "At the vanguard, even. That woman had the fight of a boar in her."

Mahiro grinned and motioned for an attendant to refill her cup with saké. "We should ally with Jisu as soon as possible," she declared. "I like everything about it so far."

"Aside from their sneaking across our borders to ransack a temple?" said Naoya disapprovingly.

"*Of course* aside from that."

"It's too soon to know what we can accomplish with Jisu," said Kazuchiyo, "but I am eager to know more about them. I hope Lady Dada will consent to a meeting."

Beihou looked doubtful. "If she does, consider postponing it for a few days. You'll have numbers by then to turn her hair white."

"Lord Koedzuka is sending more men?" asked Naoya.

"Not ours," said Beihou, saving the bulk of his attention for Kazuchiyo. "A messenger arrived barely a day before you did, cut straight across from our eastern border. Lord Aritaka's foray into Namugi Province was a great success, and he's sending three of his generals our way with their soldiers."

He motioned to his eldest son, who conveyed to Kazuchiyo a scroll case bearing the Aritaka's coin-shaped family crest. Kazuchiyo already assumed Generals Rakuteru and Hosoda to be among those sent and was not disappointed to see their names listed. The third was not named, but Kazuchiyo's heart was set aflame nonetheless: the letter explained that an army of a thousand men commanded by "an obedient general from Suyama" would be among their numbers.

"Was this the only letter sent?" Kazuchiyo asked, trying

not to sound as anxious as he suddenly felt. Though Aritaka had conquered Suyuma years ago, he had resisted deploying its soldiers on the field. Kazuchiyo could barely begin to guess which "obedient" general of his former homeland it could be.

"I'm afraid so," said Beihou, and Kazuchiyo realized that he and Naoya both had sympathy in their expressions, as they were very aware of his family's circumstances. "The messenger did not name the third general."

"Will my father be coming?" asked Ginta.

Kazuchiyo was all too happy to let Ginta's enthusiasm for the news override his trepidation. "Yes, he and General Hosoda will be joining us. With such numbers and talent, we could very well conquer Jisu and Tendo both."

Beihou laughed, and his children smiled at him knowingly. "Let's not get carried away," he said. "You're going to make me and this fortress obsolete!"

Dinner continued with pleasant conversation and more speculation as to Jisu's mysterious daimyo. Beihou was more than willing to share all manner of tales of battles past against the different clans dotting Kibaku's borders. As when Kazuchiyo was a boy, he drank in every detail, treating each story as a textbook from which to learn.

Kazuchiyo finished his evening with a short, cooling trip to the bathhouse and then retirement to his and Yagi's guest chamber. Even long after sunset the summer heat persisted, and as anticipated there was little choice but to leave the panels cracked open to allow for airflow. Though Yagi managed to fall quickly asleep, Kazuchiyo tossed, sweating and anxious from the day's news.

When the moon was high, Kazuchiyo crept from his chamber. Despite the unfamiliar layout of the castle, he followed the jagged corridors until he found an exterior wall, hoping for a few breaths of fresher air and a glimpse of rolling plains to ease his mind. He found both, and he also found Amai.

He was sitting propped in an open window, his robe

hanging loosely about him, his hair tied high on his head. He must have heard Kazuchiyo approach, but he pretended not to, only turning his head when they were a few paces apart. "Aha," he said quietly. "You've found me."

Kazuchiyo stopped to lean against the window frame near Amai's foot. He hadn't left his room in search of his slippery friend, but seeing him here made him wonder if that had been his unconscious motive all along. "I was wondering what had become of you since we arrived," he said. "Acquainting yourself with the castle?"

"I have to admit, I'm impressed with it," replied Amai. "The crows know how to build a castle for shinobi, that's for sure. The lady Purnima was showing me how to come in and out without impaling myself."

Amai drew his knees in, one foot dangling outside the castle, the other in. Kazuchiyo accepted his invitation, climbing up into the sill. It was cramped, but the faintest of breezes blew across Kazuchiyo's sweat, and he sighed with relief.

"It's good to hear you're getting along with Purnima," he said, pushing his long bangs away from his forehead. "She's just as much a valuable ally as Sir Oihata, given her many skills, but I had my doubts you'd work together after how much you teased her last year."

"She's as easy to read as her master and just as easy to manipulate." Amai smirked with triumph. "I pretend to be inept, and she is very eager to correct me. Works every time."

Kazuchiyo chuckled; he could very well imagine Amai's faked earnestness egging Purnima on. "Did you learn about more than the castle itself?" he asked.

Despite his attempts to sound casual, Amai saw straight through him. "You mean, does she know which Suyama general is on his way here?"

"Sometimes I wonder if you don't know me better than I know myself," said Kazuchiyo, shaking his head.

"Oh, you're not so tricky." Amai bumped Kazuchiyo's knees with his own. "I'm sorry to report that she doesn't know, and neither do I. The messenger didn't say, and there was only the one letter."

Kazuchiyo frowned with disappointment and looked to the east. Past Rongi's sturdy walls the plains rolled on in all directions, and beneath the full moon he could see the shapes of distant villages sweating the night through. Though it was much too soon then, within a few days' time they would be able to spot banners making their way up Kibaku's sloping roads. What symbol would he see cresting those distant hills? What house of Suyama would heed Aritaka's call to war?

"Do you want me to go?" Amai offered. "I could ride out to them and back before they arrive."

Kazuchiyo was tempted, but only for a moment. "At most it would mean a single day for me to prepare," he reasoned, "and knowing who it is won't tell me what I want to know most."

Amai raised an eyebrow. "You mean, if it's someone still loyal to you?"

"Yes…" Kazuchiyo loosened the collar of his robe further. "Most of my father's retainers were killed during or immediately after Shimegahara. It could be General Waseba, but I doubt he'd be eager to leave his castle now that he has it, and I'm certain Aritaka doesn't trust Kibaku enough to leave our border without him to guard it. It must be some house of Suyama that survived the battle, but then…"

"You're going to worry yourself into knots at this rate," Amai scolded him gently. "Whichever of your two fathers the man is more loyal to, that loyalty will *have* to extend to you. You'll be fine."

Kazuchiyo smiled, wishing his concerns could be soothed so easily. "What about you, Amai?" he asked, and he nudged Amai's hip with his foot. "What's got you so contemplative that you're out here in the middle of the night?"

Amai scoffed. "In case you haven't noticed, this heat is insufferable. Rongi has too many interior rooms for my liking." He fanned himself with his collar for a moment and then

49

added, "I thought about joining you, but I can't imagine it's easy for two men in that little chamber, let alone three."

"You don't have to imagine," said Kazuchiyo. "You've already caught me out here." He softened his tone. "You're still welcome, all the same. You can't very well sleep on the roof."

"I can do whatever I like," Amai retorted, seemingly purely for the sake of it. A beat later he must have realized how ridiculous he sounded. "Don't worry about me. There are plenty of normal places for me to sleep once I've had my fill of fresh air."

Kazuchiyo thought to press him; as uncomfortable as it would be to crush the body heat of three grown men into a stuffy chamber, he didn't care for the idea that Amai was playing martyr for his and Yagi's sakes. Faced with Amai's careless smirk, however, he couldn't bring himself to complain. "All right," he said. Though it seemed the conversation had run its course, he was slow to climb down from the sill. "You'll keep me informed of what you learn about the castle, won't you?"

"I'm at your service," Amai replied, and despite his good humor, the words left Kazuchiyo uneasy. Still, there was nothing to do but bid Amai good night and return to the room.

As soon as Kazuchiyo stretched out atop his futon again, Yagi dragged him closer. His huge body, which was such a monument for Kazuchiyo, was hot, almost stifling, and Kazuchiyo had to squirm to keep a bit of distance between them. Nevertheless, he stayed at an easy distance, occasionally carding his fingers through Yagi's hair to soothe him.

CHAPTER FOUR

The two armies spent the next several days at Rongi Castle preparing for battles to come. General Sasahara was an unparalleled host, offering not only fresh supplies for whatever campaign drew them next, but also training and entertainment for the travel-weary and combat-starved soldiers. The Rongi garrison was especially fond of sport, it soon became apparent; the border soldiers were eager to test their mettle in archery and horsemanship, even more so in wrestling, and in any other competition their guests acquiesced to. Yagi found himself in high demand to exhibit, and though the attention seemed to wear on his nerves, he could not hide from Kazuchiyo that he enjoyed the challenge and the exercise.

One morning in particular, a hard wind sent large clouds racing across the sky. However ominous, the reprieve from torturous sunlight and the promise of a storm bearing cooler air had all the men of the castle turned out in the lower bailey, where the bravest of Rongi's commanders challenged Yagi to various contests of strength. Though it ought to have been below his station as lord of the castle, General Sasahara Beihou himself joined in, and they competed side by side as the soldiers cheered, racing to see how many times each could overturn a great oak beam end over end.

Kazuchiyo was very content to watch, amused by the raucous spirit of the assembly and even more so appreciative of Yagi's impressive physique. It reminded him fondly of nights spent back in Gyoe when he was a boy, fantasizing about Yagi's efforts in helping fortify Ninari Castle. Visions of ropy muscles flexing beneath sweat-dampened skin had filled his adolescent imagination for years, and he felt a kind of triumph at having the real thing to view now.

In the end it was Sasahara's technique that offered him the victory, though even his most stalwart supporters had to admit that in strength alone Yagi was clearly an equal if not his better. Each was met with congratulatory shouts and laughter.

"Any wood-brain can push over a log," Mahiro complained at Kazuchiyo's side. "Let's go back to wrestling."

Before she could make that suggestion to more than her brother, however, the festivities were interrupted by a shout from the westerly guard tower. The higher ranking of Beihou's men hurried to re-instill order to the exuberant soldiers while the contestants pulled their robes back over their shoulders.

"That didn't sound urgent enough to be a call to arms," Mahiro remarked, disappointed, as soldiers hurried to relay some kind of message from the tower. "A messenger?"

"A messenger coming from the west will have news from Jisu," Kazuchiyo replied hopefully.

Beihou and Yagi returned to them, each still a bit winded from their contest and only partially dressed. "We have a visitor approaching from the west," reported Beihou. "A violet banner escorted by two of our scouts. They could have picked a better time."

"I'll fetch Sir Oihata," Kazuchiyo suggested. "He and I can accept them in the lower keep until you're presentable."

"You have my thanks."

Beihou and Yagi moved on, and though Kazuchiyo was disappointed that he couldn't congratulate his champion on his prowess just yet, he and Mahiro hurried to their task. He had high expectations of a favorable reply from the Lady Dada meant specifically for him.

Kazuchiyo, Mahiro, and Naoya received their guest in a meeting chamber in the lower keep, as arranged, and from the first instant Kazuchiyo knew that his expectations had been excessively answered: the Jisu messenger brought before them was none other than Chikakuni Okiaki. He looked very much like he had the last time Kazuchiyo had seen him, his manners harried and exhausted, and in fact his armor had very blatantly not been cleaned or repaired since the battle at Chouwa Valley. Rongi's guards watched him very closely as he placed his helmet aside and lowered his forehead to the floor.

"Sir Chikakuni," Kazuchiyo greeted him. "When I encouraged you toward further correspondence, I did not intend for it to come so soon, nor so personally. Is your business here so urgent?"

"It is," said Chikakuni, and Kazuchiyo could see a great strain in his face as he chose his words. "I know how inappropriate it is of me to come to you like this, but I have no other allies to turn to."

"We are not your allies either," Naoya reminded him matter-of-factly. "Why have you come?"

Chikakuni straightened up, though he kept his head respectfully lowered. "I bring you a message from Lady Dada," he said, reaching into a sack at his belt to remove a small scroll case. "I don't know how much she was able to explain, but..."

He offered it up, and one of the scouts that had escorted him in conveyed it straight to Naoya. Kazuchiyo watched patiently as Naoya emptied the paper contents into his hand and read over what appeared to be a very short message. With every effort to hide his reaction, he passed the message to Kazuchiyo.

"I assume this is meant for you," he said. Kazuchiyo was not able to hide his surprise nearly so well when he read the single line of hasty script, signed with the Dada crest:

Help me reclaim Etsugo and I won't stop you from becoming

shogun.

Kazuchiyo then passed the message to Mahiro, who gave a mighty snort and shook her head. "I like her," she declared.

The rear of the chamber opened, and in walked Beihou and Yagi in more formal attire. Though Beihou had served as a generous and charming host to Kazuchiyo for the past several days, his smile was noticeably lacking in warmth as he seated himself directly across from Chikakuni to head the assembly. He, too, greeted the letter with a snort, though he did not share Mahiro's humor.

"What about the rest of us?" he asked, relinquishing the letter back to Kazuchiyo. "Am I not also invited to Etsugo?"

Yagi thumped down next to Kazuchiyo and asked, "What's Etsugo?"

"Etsugo is a fortress high up in the mountains," Kazuchiyo explained to him, "and the ancestral home of Clan Dada, as I understand. The largest in Jisu Province."

"Dengoro." Beihou motioned to the elder of the two scouts. "I hope you can enlighten us."

The man bowed his head crisply. "Sir. We followed the Jisu army back into their own territory, and soon discovered that in General Chikakuni's absence, Tendo had sent its armies against Etsugo. The castle is under siege."

Chikakuni's fists clenched against his knees. He looked so ready to speak but also so uncertain, and Kazuchiyo was again overcome with sympathy for him. His homeland suffered betrayal and assault, and here he kneeled, begging for aid from sworn enemies. It was enough to turn Kazuchiyo's stomach.

"It's clear now that the Umafusa never meant to adhere to our alliance," said Chikakuni. "They encouraged us to prepare for a fight against Kibaku so that our defenses at Etsugo would thin. The castle itself won't fall easily, but they're surrounded, and our armies can't get there without greater numbers."

Once again Chikakuni pressed his forehead to the tatami mats. "I beg of you, please send your army to assist!"

"This peril you face is your own doing," said Naoya, his

54

manners devoid of pity. "Your greed for Lord Koedzuka's land made you weak, and now you reap your bounty. Why should the armies of Kibaku fight on your behalf?"

"I'm not asking for the armies of Kibaku," Chikakuni replied. "I am asking the young Lord Aritaka of Sakka."

Naoya and Beihou bristled, and Kazuchiyo himself wished that he could draw the man aside from them. Brave though Chikakuni was, his was not a temperament for the politics Kazuchiyo had spent his youthful years training in. Though all three rallied a response, it was Mahiro who beat them to it. She leaned forward against her crossed knees as if hungry for the room's mounting tension.

"Are you asking for us because you think we're the safer bet?" she challenged. "Because we have less history?" She gave a bark of laughter. "What makes you think we won't save your precious Etsugo only to claim it for ourselves? It must have a very pretty view of the capital from that high up."

"On the contrary; I know there's nothing safe in inviting the Aritaka into our lands." Chikakuni risked lifting his head again, and this time, he sought Kazuchiyo's gaze. "I'm asking *because* safety won't save us now, and we need allies of strength and honor *both* to defeat Tendo."

"Sir Chikakuni," Kazuchiyo said quickly, as he could see the heat rising in Naoya's cheeks at what was certainly an implied slight against him. "You flatter me, but if you think so highly of me, allow me to correct you." He sat up straighter and fixed Chikakuni with a serious eye. "I and my soldiers are here in service to Lord Koedzuka, to honor our hard-forged alliance. If you seek assistance from this army, you must seek it from Sir Oihata and me both."

Chikakuni must have gleaned everything from that look as Kazuchiyo intended, for he forced his shoulders to relax and replied, "I understand, Lord Aritaka, Sir Oihata. Please excuse me if I offended. I am not..." He ground his teeth. "If we don't expel them before the harvest, they'll make off with our yield and salt the earth. People are dying even now while we—"

"All the more reason for you to take responsibility," interrupted Naoya. "Tell us why *our* people should fight and die for yours, when they have already claimed so many of our lives?"

"He's already offered you his life," Yagi spoke up, to Kazuchiyo's surprise. "He's literally begging for your help. What more do you want from him?"

Naoya frowned at him severely, and again Kazuchiyo rushed to intervene, suggesting, "Perhaps we should reconvene after supper. I'm sure Sir Chikakuni is in need of rest, and we have much to discuss."

"Excuse me, my lord, but I'm very well," Chikakuni said, thwarting him. "I came here prepared to answer for myself, and I'll pay whatever payment Sir Oihata demands of me."

Beihou hummed thoughtfully. "It's not the Chikakuni line alone that has to atone for three generations of war," he reminded him, like a father delivering a rebuke that left Chikakuni flushed. "If Lady Dada if offering only to ignore Sakka from now on, I can't imagine she has anything satisfying to offer *us*."

"The lady Dada is—"

Chikakuni clapped his jaws shut. He glanced to each member of the assembly as his fingers clenched, white with restraint. The fear and anger battling in the muscles along his jaw reminded Kazuchiyo very much of when he was a young boy, bowing his head to the cruel Lord Aritaka so that he might live. As Kazuchiyo strained to think of something that would placate the Kibaku generals, Chikakuni at last forced himself to properly calm, and he dropped his head.

"Forgive me," he said. "I'm not... in a fit state of mind for this. I'd like to take Lord Aritaka's offer to rest, if it stands."

"Yes, I think that's best," Kazuchiyo reassured him. "We would all benefit." He looked to Naoya and Beihou and was relieved to see them also unwinding. "Shall we reconvene in a few hours? I'd like to hear a more detailed account from Sir Dengoro here."

"Yes, that's fine," said Beihou. "We'll confirm Chikakuni's account in greater detail and discuss what's to be done." He motioned to the second scout. "Escort him to a room and make sure he's tended to."

The scout bowed. "Yes, sir!"

"Thank you," said Chikakuni, though he then hesitated. "If it's confirmation you need, I do have something to offer you."

He reached again into his pouch and then opened his palm to his hosts. His gift was so small that Kazuchiyo didn't see it at first: a small, lacquered bead threaded around a length of twine. Recognition made his own small bead seem to grow heavy against the inside of his wrist.

It was Naoya, however, who reacted most strongly to the offering; he took in a long, slow breath, and his irritation shifted to some other, deeper discomfort. After a beat in which he seemed to be rallying himself, he crossed the space personally and plucked the bead out of Chikakuni's hand. He contemplated it for only a few moments, though in that time the hairs on the back of Kazuchiyo's neck rose in a peculiar chill. Then Naoya replaced the bead and curled Chikakuni's fingers over it.

"Do you know how to use this?" he asked with quiet gravity.

Chikakuni stared back at him with only confusion. "No. Lady Dada said that if you saw it, you would understand, but... I don't know why that would be."

"Good." Naoya nudged Chikakuni's hand to his chest and then stood. "Return it to her if you have the chance, and in the meantime, rest. You've been through an ordeal." With that he turned, and ignoring the baffled looks of his guest and compatriots alike, he left the room.

Chikakuni left with the scout, and as soon as the panel closed behind him, Mahiro gave a quiet huff. "What's the problem with Oihata?"

"I don't know," said Kazuchiyo, glancing over his shoulder

at the exit he had gone through. "I'll be sure to ask him later."

"Better that you don't," said Beihou. "Anything we need to know, he'll tell us shortly, but he doesn't take well to prying."

"What was that thing Chikakuni showed him?" asked Yagi, and Kazuchiyo tucked his hand into his sleeve without thinking about it.

Beihou shook his head. "Be patient a moment, please."

Yagi and Mahiro exchanged less than patient looks, but each held their tongue. They did not have long to wait; as Beihou had said, only another minute passed before Naoya returned to retake his seat among them. Kazuchiyo watched him closely but could draw no explanation from his face.

"Excuse me for my absence," said Naoya with all his composure firmly reconstructed. "Shall we continue? Dengoro, if you please."

The scout nodded, seemingly unfazed despite the continued uncertainty of their Sakka guests. "As Sir Chikakuni described, some two thousand men from Tendo are laying siege to Etsugo. Those that survived the valley skirmish have joined with another fifteen hundred men in the foothills below, to prevent Jisu reinforcements. Etsugo is probably sturdy enough not to fall too easily, but they cannot afford to let a siege drag through to harvest season."

"All of that I can confirm," said Naoya. "Lady Dada is secure in the main keep, or at the very least she was two days ago. It seems she was able to root out a traitor among her council before they could cause further disarray, but there could be others. Tendo has certainly put some effort into this assault, and any aid would have to move very swiftly."

"Did that little bead tell you all that?" asked Mahiro, pointedly avoiding Beihou's disapproving look.

Naoya did not return her stare. "More or less."

Kazuchiyo frowned, and he was reminded of a visit Iomori had paid him once: she had gripped his wrist that bore the similar bead he, too, wore, and from it wrestled free the truth of Kazuchiyo having killed the eldest General Waseba.

He ached to know what more than raw magic the beads were capable of housing.

"Does Jisu not have other reinforcements it can call on?" he asked instead. "Chikakuni said they were preparing to attack Kibaku, so they must have greater numbers somewhere."

"We have other scouts trying to determine that," answered Dengoro.

"I will assist them," added Naoya. "We will need as much information as possible if we're to decide on a course."

Kazuchiyo weighed his own courses carefully before speaking. "Sirs, I think you already know my mind. If this is an opportunity for Sakka to carve a path toward the capital, I would be betraying my father not to seize it."

"The wiser course would be to side with Tendo," mused Beihou. "Overwhelm Etsugo together and then give them Izuho, like they wanted. That would smooth over having sided against them at Chouwa."

Kazuchiyo much disliked the idea of handing off someone else's land no matter the circumstances, and he shook his head. "I promised Izuho that we would not ask servitude of them, and I don't trust Tendo to honor that. I will not break my word."

Beihou gave a quiet chuckle. "If you can sit yourself in the shogun's hall with all your vows intact, that would be a miracle fit for the Dragon God indeed."

"If any men of Shuyun are up to the task, Kazumune is among them," Naoya swiftly came to his defense, but he then sobered. "Though be reminded that you've sworn no vows to Jisu yet. Their plight is their own doing, and it does not shame you to leave them to it."

Kazuchiyo took a moment to contemplate this, and in that time, he found his gaze turning to Yagi. There he found only stoic support as always; he had no doubt that Yagi would storm a mountaintop were it asked of him. He was also, however, reminded of Yagi's prodding words their first day at Rongi: to strike into the inner territories would solidify Aritaka's aims as his own, at a time when he remained uncertain of them.

Whatever Naoya's confidence in him, it seemed shameful to commit the lives of thousands of soldiers to a campaign he'd joined only to buy himself time—selfishly defending his own interests, as he had the year before.

Then he thought of poor Chikakuni, face pressed to the mats in front of his enemies, and his mind settled into its proper order. "I appreciate your advice, but as I said, my path is clear to me. I won't ask Kibaku soldiers to fight for Jisu, but if the lady Dada has asked for my aid, she'll have it."

"We have reinforcements on the way," Mahiro added. "We'll be over five thousand strong by then. Plenty to take on anything Tendo has."

"And more than that," agreed Naoya, and Kazuchiyo was a bit surprised by how relieved he felt. "I'll not let anyone say Kibaku lacked the dignity to aid its neighbors, even if those neighbors be unworthy of it." He turned to Beihou. "I'll send word to Lord Koedzuka immediately to appraise him of the situation."

Beihou sighed, but he was smiling, as if he had suspected all along that this would be Naoya's decision. "I can spare you two of my captains and their men. They've warred in Jisu many times and know the terrain well."

Kazuchiyo bowed his head to them. "Thank you, good sirs. We are honored by your support, and Sakka will not forget it."

Yagi and Mahiro followed his example, though as they raised their heads Yagi said, "You'll still be asking Jisu for something in return, right? What will it be?"

"That will be for Lord Koedzuka to decide," replied Naoya, and he pushed to his feet. "I'll return to my chamber to prepare the message. With luck, we'll have his reply this evening."

"Then in the meantime I'll start rounding up the troops," Mahiro volunteered enthusiastically. "You said we'd have to move quickly; I can have everyone strapped and saddled by dawn."

"The reinforcements might not be here by then," Yagi

reminded her as the rest of them stood.

"Then they'd better hurry up! I'm ready to meet all these ferocious Jisu women!"

Kazuchiyo cleared his throat. "Please do alert Commander Rakuteru and the other captains," he told the pair. "By sundown we'll have orders for them, and it won't hurt to be prepared whether we march immediately or wait for the reinforcements." Yagi and Mahiro nodded, so he turned his attention to his Kibaku hosts. "I'd like to speak with those captains about the terrain, but first, I hope you won't mind if I accompany you to your chamber, Sir Naoya?"

Naoya's brow furrowed with apprehension, but still he answered, "Your company is always welcome."

"Thank you."

The group divided to their tasks, and Kazuchiyo followed along behind Naoya, careful to wait until they were in the privacy of his handsome chamber in the upper keep before speaking his mind. "I wanted to thank you for offering your support for this campaign," he said as he seated himself. "I know there's a great deal of history between your provinces that makes it difficult for you, and I appreciate it."

"And I thank you for acknowledging that," Naoya replied as he gathered paper and ink. "I must confess, I don't believe you'll find a worthy ally in Jisu, but I'll honor our alliance." He sat down across from Kazuchiyo and prepared his supplies for the message. "Assuming Lord Koedzuka gives his blessing, of course."

Kazuchiyo smiled. "Of course," he said, and he watched with keen interest as Naoya spread out his paper and began to write. His script was as broad and fanciful as ever, and his language very formal in spelling out the current predicament. It was somewhat captivating to watch, and Kazuchiyo had to remind himself that he had come with a purpose.

"May I ask you something, Sir Naoya?"

"You may."

His manner was not very inviting, but Kazuchiyo carried

on anyway. "How were you able to confirm Chikakuni's story from that bead?"

Naoya frowned, but his writing did not falter; certainly he had anticipated such a question. "You've spent some time alongside Iomori no Jun," he said. "Has she described the use of magic to you?"

"No," said Kazuchiyo, and again he felt mysteriously compelled to hide the bead tied around his wrist within his sleeve. "I've seen her use magic many times, but she refuses to reveal its methods to me. I do know that she uses a string of prayer beads as a… a cup, she called it. A cup full of magic that can be tipped."

"I suppose that's an apt enough metaphor, though it doesn't match my view."

Naoya continued to write without explaining further. Kazuchiyo gave him a moment to be sure and then tried again, asking, "Will you teach me to use magic?"

"No," said Naoya without looking up.

Kazuchiyo blinked, taken aback by such a bluntly delivered refusal. "Why not?"

Naoya signed his letter and then set it aside to dry. With a deep breath he at last faced Kazuchiyo seriously. "I don't wish to explain it to you," he declared, startling Kazuchiyo further, "but you know my honor won't allow me to lie to you either. Will you please rescind your question?"

Kazuchiyo returned his determined stare with a baffled one, but there was only one way he could answer. "Of course. I'm sorry if I offended you. I won't ask again."

Naoya nodded gratefully and then busied himself with cleaning his brush. "Please understand, it's my concern for your safety that keeps me silent. Iomori was right to refuse you; if she ever does consent to teach you magic, you should be wary, for it means she cannot be trusted. That Lady Dada knew well enough to give Chikakuni that bead already ruins any trust I might have had in *her*."

Kazuchiyo leaned back, helplessly confused. "And yet…

you want her to have it back?"

"Yes. Well." Naoya glared uncomfortably down at his work. "It's not my place to interfere. I'm sorry, Kazumune. It's very complicated."

"You don't need to explain," Kazuchiyo hurried to reassure him. "I understand."

He did not, of course. Dear Naoya should have known better: Who could hear such declarations and not have their curiosity tempted? He did, at least, have the good sense to face Kazuchiyo again and level a sincere warning.

"If nothing else, remember this," he said. "Magic is dangerous, Kazumune, to the wielder as much as anyone—to a lord or a shogun, even more so. If magic is needed, you can leave it to me. Otherwise, try to put it out of your mind."

"All right." Kazuchiyo smiled, determined to ease any remaining tension between them. "Thank you for looking out for me. In any case, I trust *you*, Naoya, magic and all."

Naoya, sentimental as ever, was nearly moved to tears, and he nodded with great conviction. "And I, you. Thank you."

Once the ink was dry, Naoya folded his message into wings. The paper leaped from his hand and sailed out from the slats in his window swift as a bird, soon gone from sight. Kazuchiyo watched closely but gleaned nothing of the method employed, and the two of them descended from Naoya's chamber with no more words shared about magic.

But Kazuchiyo did not put it out of his mind. Far from it.

The next several hours were spent in study and discussion. Beihou introduced Kazuchiyo to his elder captains, and together with Naoya they pored over the available maps of Jisu Province. Using the knowledge from the scouts combined with Naoya's mysteriously gained intel, they prodded tiles into the formations they could confirm and speculated on the wisest modes of attack.

"If we attack from the south, all of Tendo will be at our backs," surmised Kazuchiyo. "Is there no path from the north?"

The elder of the two captains shook his head. "That terrain is too mountainous for an army of our size. We would have to circle Mount Etsuzan entirely and attack from the west."

"That would take too long," said Naoya, "and to travel that far north places us in range of Nomino's borders. If they took notice of us and chose to intervene, we would be delayed even further."

"Nomino Province," Kazuchiyo repeated, shifting his gaze farther north. It, too, shared a border with Kibaku in the northwest and, as far as he was aware, boasted warriors as beastly as Sakka was known for. A year ago, while facing Naoya from atop a doomed hill, when Kazuchiyo had begged his father that he be allowed to seek aid from Kibaku's neighbors, that aid would have had to come from Nomino. He knew too little of its governance now to anticipate if they would help a hated neighbor liberate another just as hated.

Kazuchiyo shook himself, already made weary from too many concerns. "Then we have little choice but to carve a path straight through to Etsugo."

The others nodded, and Beihou said, "Then it's probably time to include Chikakuni in this council. He ought to know where Jisu's remaining soldiers are."

"With permission, I'll fetch him myself," offered Kazuchiyo, and though the others must have recognized an ulterior motive, they agreed.

Chikakuni was seated in the center of the small room he had been offered, dressed in plain, borrowed clothes. With his legs crossed and fingers twined in his lap, he seemed to be in a state of deep meditation, and he did not stir until Kazuchiyo loudly cleared his throat. Dread and hope struggled in his expression before he lowered his head in a bow.

"Lord Aritaka, excuse me. I didn't hear you approach."

Kazuchiyo pursed his lips against the impulse to ask Chikakuni that he not call him that. "Not at all. You've a lot on your mind." Kazuchiyo stepped into the room and closed the panel shut behind him. "I'm here to collect you for the others, but I'd hoped we could have a short conversation first."

Chikakuni raised his head, betraying a grim smirk. "If it's to gently chastise me for my manners earlier, I welcome it. You were looking out for me, and I'm grateful."

Kazuchiyo smiled himself as he took a seat facing the man. "I could tell you'd practiced," he said, "and I'm impressed you kept your composure as well as you did, considering the circumstances."

"The circumstances," Chikakuni repeated, and he let out a quiet huff of incredulity. "Those being my father's greed plunging our homeland into the worst crisis it's faced in generations while he's too dead to see it." He scraped his sleeve across his mouth. "Excuse me, I shouldn't—"

"It's all right," Kazuchiyo assured him. "I didn't come here to berate you *or* him." He held Chikakuni's gaze seriously. "We're going to help Jisu. I'm bringing you to the generals so you can help us come up with a plan."

Chikakuni straightened, though he had difficulty putting the rush of emotions in his face into words. In time he settled with a simple, "Thank you."

"I'm willing to accept the conditions Lady Dada laid out, blunt as they were," Kazuchiyo said while Chikakuni forcibly composed himself. "I suspect Kibaku will ask for some greater payment for their help, but I can't march into an unknown province without them. I need you to be prepared for that, and your lady as well. Now is not the time for pride."

"I know," Chikakuni replied quickly. "I do know. Whatever Oihata asks, I'll pay it." Seeing Kazuchiyo's reply ahead of time, he added, "And so will Lady Dada, within reason."

Kazuchiyo nodded, relieved. "I know General Oihata is… in possession of an overwhelming personality," he said tactfully, "but he is a man of honor. If he says he'll fight for Clan Dada, he won't rest until Etsugo is safe. Be respectful and you'll have a strong ally in him."

"Yes, you're right." Chikakuni again managed a smirk. "Hell, though, it's embarrassing. I'm sure I've been doing this a lot longer than you have, but you're much better at it."

"If I am, I credit necessity," replied Kazuchiyo in kind, though he then returned to his seriousness. "Before we join them, there's one other thing I wanted to ask you: about that bead."

"Hm?" Chikakuni reached into his collection of shed belongings and produced the bead. "You mean this?"

He offered it up at Kazuchiyo's prodding. It was black in color, a hair larger than the one Kazuchiyo wore on his wrist, but in all ways unremarkable. Kazuchiyo rolled it between his fingers but detected nothing from it.

"Were you telling the truth when you told Oihata that you don't know how to use it?" he asked.

Chikakuni frowned at him in confusion. "It's... a bead. Is it magic?"

"Apparently." Though reluctant, Kazuchiyo handed it back. "Is the lady Dada trained as an onmyouji?"

"Not that I know of. They say her grandmother has some skill with it, but I've never seen the lady herself... cast a spell." Chikakuni eyed Kazuchiyo curiously. "Is that important somehow?"

"It may be." Kazuchiyo pushed to his feet, and Chikakuni followed suit. "General Oihata is a practitioner himself, but he seems very wary of others who use magic. Try not to bring it up around him if you can help it, and if you get the chance, ask Lady Dada to refrain as well."

"All right. Thanks for the warning." Chikakuni took in a deep breath. "If that's it, I'm ready for them."

The pair of them returned to the chamber, and Kazuchiyo braced himself for further tensions. To his relief, the Kibaku generals appeared to have worn through their personal displeasure and welcomed Chikakuni around the maps with even-tempered gravity.

"Sir Chikakuni," said Naoya, "please have a look and

correct us where necessary."

Chikakuni took a seat and bowed his head to the assembly. "Before that, please allow me to apologize for my embarrassing display earlier. That you would agree to assist us after such shameful behavior is more than I deserve, and I am deep in your debt."

Though again there was a strict, rehearsed tone to Chikakuni's words, they did as much good as intended: Naoya offered him a solemn nod and said, "Your apology is accepted. Let us move forward as allies to defeat these invaders."

"Yes, sir," said Chikakuni, relieved, and each turned their attention to the map. After confirming the location of the troops set out by Dengoro the scout, Chikakuni then laid out two more groups of tiles.

"Our thousand men were sent out with those from Tendo to take the Kibaku village," he explained, "but we had other, larger forces to the north and south: one reinforced by more Tendo soldiers in the south, who had planned to circle Rongi and prevent reinforcements sent by Lord Koedzuka; the other force in the north would cut off any assistance from Tettsu Castle, or from Sakka." He briefly made a face. "That had been the plan for weeks. We didn't know that Sakka had already sent Lord Aritaka here."

Kazuchiyo frowned at the arrangement. Though his army had come from the south, they had not detected any formations that close to the border, and he worried over those men. "If your southern forces were mixed with Tendo, I think we can assume they've been routed by the enemy already." He glanced to Naoya, reminded of the few words he'd spoken about Lady Dada's bead. "Or else that they've turned their allegiance."

"No," Chikakuni said quickly, though he was just as quick to rein himself in. "The lady Dada's own uncle is in command of those troops. He would never betray Jisu."

"Then we send scouts to confirm, based on their last known location," suggested Naoya. "To the south and the north."

Seeing Chikakuni swallow, Kazuchiyo took it upon

himself to voice what he suspected the man was restraining himself from saying. "We may not be able to wait for their report. If the castle is under siege now, a delay of several days could cost us everything." He reached forward to reposition the tiles. "If we cut straight west through Jisu, our approaching reinforcements could follow at a slower pace and halt any attempts to attack our rear."

Naoya hummed thoughtfully. "That sounds like a mighty gamble, but I don't dislike it. I can equip our scouts with the means to alert us quickly once they have determined the locations of the reinforcements, and General Rakuteru as well."

Beihou did not appear as convinced, and he looked over the pieces on the map again and again. At last, he eased into a wary smile. "Well, old friend, you know that all of Rongi stands in your defense. Go with our blessing, and we'll have a feast upon your return."

"We'll have more Tendo heads for you by then," Naoya replied with confidence.

They spent another hour discussing the terrain with Chikakuni's insights to guide them, and afterward, they summoned the rest of their commanders for supper in the castle's main hall. Kazuchiyo outlined their aims to the assembly, and though there seemed some reluctance from the Kibaku soldiers, Naoya's stern countenance prevented any from voicing complaints. Only Commander Ginta had the nerve to speak even slight misgivings.

"Are we not waiting for my father and his troops to reinforce us?" he asked, to which Kazuchiyo shook his head.

"They should be no more than a day behind us," he said. "It will place them well to guard our retreat, if necessary, and prevent a Tendo ambush."

Mahiro faced Ginta and chuckled. "Don't look so glum. Wouldn't you rather have a saddle full of heads by the time he catches up with us? This is the perfect opportunity to bring him some glory!"

Ginta and the others were encouraged by her words, and

Kazuchiyo smiled.

Toward the end of the meal, Purnima arrived. She was dressed in a simple gi and hakama for once, her full face and thick, pitch-black hair on display. Mahiro pretended to drink her saké while watching her every movement in rapt attention; Purnima spared her only a brief, cool glance on her way to Naoya's side. Kazuchiyo hid a smile in his own wine cup.

"My lord," said Purnima, and she offered up a piece of folded parchment. "A reply from Lord Koedzuka."

"Ahh, excellent." Naoya pushed his tray aside so that he could accept the message with his full attention. He gleamed with approval as he read over the contents and then folded the paper again.

"Lord Koedzuka blesses our march," he declared to the room, and all around his soldiers nodded with relief. "He has every hope that we can forge a strong alliance with Jisu, who has stood in opposition to us for so long." His eyes fell soundly on Chikakuni. "To that end, he has a request to make of Lady Dada."

Chikakuni, who had passed the meal avoiding as much attention as possible, straightened his back and took in a deep breath. "Of course. I'm eager to hear it."

"He requests a meeting in person," Naoya continued, and an excited murmur spread along the hall. "Once Etsugo is secure and the lady's safety guaranteed, he will travel here to Rongi, and hopes she will do the same so they can meet as equals in this fine hall."

"Oh my," said Beihou as the soldiers exchanged looks of amazement and eagerness. "We'll have to turn some of the tatami over."

Kazuchiyo kept his attention on Chikakuni, who remained very still. Clearly he did not know whether his master would consent to such an agreement in what was, likely by her estimation, enemy territory. Even so, he had no choice but to bow his head in thanks. "My lady would be honored, sir."

"Yes, indeed," said Naoya with great satisfaction. "To my

mind that is more honor than reparation, but if that is my lord's wish, we will see it done." He drew his supper tray back so he could reclaim his cup and raise it to the room. "Brave warriors of Kibaku and Sakka, let us liberate Jisu from the cowardly fish of the south!"

The commanders cheered and toasted; even Chikakuni downed his remainder of saké. Mahiro and Purnima locked eyes across the hall, and Naoya gushed to the men of what a great honor it would be to host Lord Koedzuka so far from home. Kazuchiyo took in their enthusiasm and relished it.

It would be a very interesting march into the west.

CHAPTER FIVE

That night, despite the ever-oppressive summer heat, Kazuchiyo and Yagi made the most of their last chance for privacy.

Privacy, as always, being a relative thing in a crowded fortress made of wood and paper; more than once one had to shush the other as their passions grew too fervent. Even after so many similar nights, Kazuchiyo would never tire of the strength of Yagi's body focused so intimately on his, fulfilling and overwhelming him. He buried his face happily in his futon and spared not one thought for war.

By morning, however, there was no choice but to face the full reality of the march. Mahiro was prowling the halls before dawn, rousing the commanders with eager bellows, and up and down the keep soldiers bustled with preparation. Kazuchiyo and Yagi had only enough time to scrub the worst of the night's sweat from their bodies before Beihou's attendants were upon them, eager to help them into their armor for the journey.

It was during this flurry of activity that Amai appeared, his sandals already worn with road dust. "There you are," Kazuchiyo scolded him as he secured his helmet. "I barely saw you at all yesterday. Where have you been?"

"We were worried you would miss the war," Yagi added gruffly.

Amai smirked at them, though Kazuchiyo had trained upon the man's expressions long enough to recognize weariness. "I'll have you know I was doing you a great favor," he said, and he began shooing the attendants out of the room. "Off with you. We'll handle the rest."

Kazuchiyo tingled with curiosity as each of them bowed and showed themselves out. Though Amai often played up the suspense far more so than necessary, instinct told him this was not one of those times. "What have you learned?" he asked. "Did you scout to the west?"

Amai stepped closer so he could take over the duty of tying the cords on Kazuchiyo's helmet. "The opposite, in fact," he said, and Kazuchiyo's heart skipped. "I rode east just enough to get a glimpse of our reinforcements. They'll be here by midday."

They were already so close that Kazuchiyo had no hope of hiding his breathless anticipation. "And?" he asked.

"And I saw black banners among their numbers," said Amai, watching for his reaction, "each bearing a crest made of three red rings."

Kazuchiyo swallowed. "Three red rings," he echoed, his mind aflame with a hundred more questions. "You're sure?"

"It would be an embarrassing mistake if I wasn't." Amai finished with the helmet but stayed close; though he was still smiling, his humor had sobered. "I didn't get close enough to make out their commander, as they were camped for the night."

"Do you know who it is now?" asked Yagi, his attention also fixed with some concern on Kazuchiyo.

The Dragon's three crimson rings—Kazuchiyo would never forget. "That is the crest of Clan Zaiga," he said. He urged Amai back so that he could retrieve his swords for his belt. "General Zaiga Tonehiro was one of my father's closest friends; his sister is married to my mother's brother."

Yagi pulled a face. "So... a distant uncle?"

"Something like that." Kazuchiyo checked and then

rechecked his armor, suddenly uncertain of the many lengths of cord and leather meant to be holding him together. "I didn't think anyone from Clan Zaiga still lived," he admitted. "Aritaka told me that all Father's loyalists pledged to him or cut their bellies open, but General Zaiga would *never* bow to Sakka, so he must have followed my father in—"

"Kazu, take a breath," Amai said gently, and it wasn't until then that he realized how much he needed it. "Whoever leads the Zaiga army now, you can ask them yourself when they arrive."

Kazuchiyo followed his advice and found that he had already begun to calm. There was no cause for such consternation before even laying eyes on whatever general had come, was there? "How far away did you say they are?"

"Assuming they rouse early, a few hours at most."

"Then we'll be gone before they arrive." Feeling thus reassured, Kazuchiyo finished the last of his preparations and led the three of them out of the chamber.

"I know you're not looking forward to meeting him," Amai said, "but I hope you're not rushing this march to avoid it."

Kazuchiyo tensed self-consciously, but Yagi rose to his defense before he could reply. "A castle is under siege right now. It was always the plan to leave as soon as possible."

"I was only teasing." Amai trailed along for a moment before offering, "Would you like me to ride back out? Find out for certain who it is?"

"No," Kazuchiyo replied, though he then regretted speaking so quickly, as if Amai would tease him for that too. "No, I want you to stay with me. We're marching into new territory, and we'll need your keen senses."

"I'm glad to hear it," said Amai, and he said no more as they made their way out of the keep.

Rongi's baileys were abuzz with activity as the army completed its preparations: generals instructing commanders, commanders instructing captains, captains instructing foot soldiers. Ginta and his riders had formed ranks just within the main gate, those on foot filtering in behind. Beihou surveyed their efforts without interfering while Naoya prowled the lines. Kazuchiyo spotted Mahiro among the vanguard, in her full decorative armor and already proudly seated atop Suzumekage.

"Sister," Kazuchiyo greeted her, "will you not be marching with us in the command block?"

"We're going into enemy territory," Mahiro replied with a mighty grin. "If there's an ambush waiting, I'll flush it out for you."

Yagi gave a snort. "You just want to be where *she* is," he said, jutting his chin to where Purnima was just taking to her horse among Kibaku's cavalry.

"And why shouldn't I?" Mahiro retorted with a toss of her mane. "I need to keep a close eye on her to know for sure that I'm showing her up. Besides"—she gestured toward another figure mounted close by—"I'm sure you'll want my eyes on *that one* too."

Kazuchiyo looked for himself and was not surprised to see Chikakuni waiting anxiously for the procession to get underway. "I would prefer if he rode with us at the center," he admitted, "though I suppose it can't be helped. His knowledge of the land will be of better use at the front as well."

"Are you not worried about him?" asked Amai. "This could all be a very elaborate trick."

"It would have to be, but no, I'm not worried." Kazuchiyo offered Amai his sterner version of a teasing look. "I have a skilled shinobi to scout ahead for us."

Amai huffed with amusement. "You're not as handsome as you think you are," he said, and with a half smirk he stepped back, quickly losing Kazuchiyo's gaze among the throng of soldiers.

"As slippery a fox as ever," muttered Yagi, and the pair of them bid Mahiro a temporary farewell.

Beihou joined them at the center where the command unit troops were assembled. He was dressed in full armor, as were his children, and when met with Kazuchiyo's curious look, he offered a wide smile. "It's a local custom," he explained, "for good luck. The might of Rongi is with you in spirit."

"Thank you," replied Kazuchiyo, and he and Yagi bowed at the waist. "For the gesture, and for your faultless hospitality. I hope you'll be kind enough to host us again upon our return."

"Nothing would please me more." Beihou bowed in reply.

Thus, on the twelfth day of the ninth month, the combined three thousand soldiers of Sakka and Suyama left Rongi Castle to march into the west. Once they were free of the castle, Kazuchiyo turned in his saddle to look behind, but their path had already taken them down the western hillside, and he had no hope of seeing banners on the eastern horizon, whatever crest they may have displayed.

"It may take us three days to reach Etsugo with an army this size," said Naoya as he rode alongside Kazuchiyo. "Our road takes us into the mountains, which are thickly forested, and we're likely to find opposition along the way."

"Well," said Kazuchiyo, "at least we might escape the heat."

The road was well traveled, and it stretched out in a near straight line for the first several hours of their march. Kazuchiyo and Naoya passed the time as they had before with poetry, taking turns bidding farewell to Kibaku's ocean-like plains of blissful green. As the morning passed into late afternoon, however, Kazuchiyo began to make out the hazy silhouettes of mountains in the distance. Having spent most of his childhood at lofty heights, he could not help but feel the rocky sentinels were calling to him in welcome.

Before they could hope to greet those ancient monuments, they first had to pass through the border gate that separated Kibaku from Jisu. It flanked the road with a pair of tower posts, each bearing slats for archers to shoot through. Though Kazuchiyo was relatively safe far behind the front line, he could see figures moving within the structure, doubtlessly armed.

Only a few tense moments passed, wherein Kazuchiyo

could hear Chikakuni's voice calling up to the guard captain. Then the gates parted, and the army was underway once more, crossing the boundary into Jisu.

"It must vex them, to have to open their borders to us," said Naoya as he and Kazuchiyo took their turn marching over the threshold. "I'm not without sympathy for them."

Kazuchiyo turned to see the guard captain at his post overlooking the gate. His face was haggard with age and exhaustion, the once-gold emblem on his helm darkly tarnished. Above him, the guardhouse ornaments stared down on the intruders in grimacing malice: the twisting body of a whiskered dragon on one side, a snarling tiger on the other.

Kazuchiyo turned forward in his saddle again. "Have you ever been into Jisu?" he asked.

"Yes, a few times," said Naoya, "but usually farther north than this. When my elder brother was given lordship of Tettsu Castle, he bid me to fortify the nearby borders. The Dada were attempting to construct a small garrison there, but General Sasahara and I put a swift end to it."

Kazuchiyo frowned thoughtfully; there were things he could say of the righteous generals of Kibaku crossing into enemy territory over their *perceived* threats, but he wisely chose to keep them to himself. "I understand you have several older brothers?"

Naoya beamed with pride. "Indeed! I am the youngest of my father's four sons and six daughters, all of them extremely accomplished in their stations." He looked to Kazuchiyo and was given pause, doubtlessly coming to remember that family ought to have been a delicate topic for his companion. "I've heard tell you also had several brothers."

"Yes; I was one of five." Kazuchiyo's mind was flung instantly back to that terrible day at the rainy camp, his dear Tomonaga's face split open from Nanpa's arrow. He shook his head. "Of us only I and my younger brother, Yoshimaru, are left, but he lives in seclusion now, with my mother. Lord Aritaka has not seen fit to tell me where."

Naoya nodded with heartfelt sympathy. "I pray that wherever he may be, he is at peace."

"Yes," Kazuchiyo replied distractedly, "so do I."

Once firmly within Jisu's borders, the landscape began to change: the sweeping fields rolled into tufted hillsides, some steep enough to curve the road around them; tall grass gave way to smatterings of trees that grew larger and closer together with every mile; even the air grew dryer, to the relief of man and beast alike. They passed forks in the path that led to villages and settlements, each displaying very little activity despite the time of day. Every traveler they passed moved an uncommon distance from the road to bow their head and wait for the procession to pass. Kazuchiyo found it difficult to enjoy the hilly countryside when it was so apparent how unwelcome they were.

This contrast was never so apparent as when they reached their destination for the evening. The road sloped downward into a valley, which in turn embraced a broad, swiftly-moving river. A large town had set its roots on either side of the riverbank, bordered in stone walls with rigid towers for guard posts, and sturdy bridges connecting east and west. The three-story roof of a pagoda lorded over a temple complex on the opposite bank.

But the most impressive sight of the town stood within the river itself: a dozen meters or so north of the center bridge stood an immense red torii gate, its thick pillars sunk deep beneath the water, its eaves stretching mightily as if to bear the weight of the darkened mountains towering beyond. Though weathered from the ages, its stoic majesty impressed on Kazuchiyo a profound sense of security and peace.

The town's inhabitants, on the other hand, were far less inviting. Though Chikakuni successfully convinced the guard captain to open the gates, such as they were, the man and his subordinates stared with blatant mistrust as his new allies entered the settlement. Up and down the streets, residents fled to their homes and shuttered every door and window.

As Kazuchiyo and Naoya entered, they were met swiftly by Chikakuni, who had stilled his horse to wait for them along with Mahiro. "My lords, please forgive this cold reception," he said, bowing as best he could in his saddle. "I'm afraid not everyone in Jisu fully grasps the urgency of the situation."

"No one can blame them for being wary," Kazuchiyo reassured him, "though I hope they have tolerance enough for us to make camp."

Chikakuni gave a quiet snort. "The elder and I are well acquainted; I can promise you her tolerance. I'm more concerned about safety." He pointed down the town's main thoroughfare. "It wasn't far from here that my soldiers were first ambushed on our return from Chouwa Valley. They're camped just within the wall now. I don't know how Tendo will respond, seeing we've amassed reinforcements."

"They'll be shitting themselves, that's how they'll respond," declared Mahiro. "Let Sakka set up camp outside the west wall. We're not afraid."

For once, Naoya could only agree with her. "The town is too small to comfortably house an army this size, and it's probably best not to mix the Jisu soldiers with mine. I'll have Purnima arrange our camp on the opposite bank."

"I'll tell her," Mahiro volunteered with smug glee. "I need to boast that I'll be closer to the fighting than her."

She spurred Suzumekage on before anyone could instruct her otherwise. Kazuchiyo could not help but smile fondly before returning to matters at hand. "Shall we visit the town elder before we retire?"

Each of their horses were taken by attendants, but when it came time for Yagi to dismount, he shook his head. "I'll go with Mahiro to the wall," he said. "To be sure of our defenses."

Kazuchiyo frowned up at him. "I don't know that that's necessary. I'm sure there'll be room for you within the town."

"Well." Yagi straightened his back, and still atop his horse the difference in their heights was intimidating. "I'm more or less a commander now. It's 'proper' that I be with the soldiers, isn't it?"

Though Kazuchiyo was reluctant, they had stalled long enough, and he knew how it would look for him to insist Yagi stay with him. "Yes, you're right," he said. "Keep us safe."

Yagi nodded, and he urged his horse on to rejoin the column heading through town. Kazuchiyo had trouble tearing his attention away. "Excuse me," he told Naoya and Chikakuni. "Let's continue to the elder." The pair of them regarded him with mixed sympathy and amusement as they agreed.

The elder did not receive them warmly, but dutifully. They were served a modest supper and offered a room in her estate, a handsome building set close to the town's venerated Kanrei Temple. Kazuchiyo took the opportunity to tour the grounds after supper, citing a curiosity for the local deities. In truth, he merely sought to occupy his mind in the absence of familiar company.

He was far from alone within the grounds: many townspeople had come to offer prayers at the shrine that stood at the center of the complex. Even without his full armor, the quality of his indigo hitatare and the crest embroidered into its chest and back impressed upon them that he was a guest of some high station, and all bowed their heads and made way for him. He caught a few curious glances among the wary, as Aritaka's coin-shaped crest was likely unknown to them. He resolved to put their minds at ease if he could, and to that end sought the temple's leading monk and administrator, a portly man with a gentle, round face.

"The kami enshrined here is that of Nari-Yamatsumi," the monk explained. "Every spring she descends from the mountain along the river to bless our fields with crop, and after the harvest, we celebrate her perilous journey home." His bushy eyebrows drew in with concern as he stared into the north, where the majestic silhouette of the torii gate cast its shadow across the eastern bank. "It is a difficult time now to offer celebrations, though."

"I would like to pay my respects, with your permission,"

said Kazuchiyo. "It's my hope that we can aid your people swiftly and have peace in time for her journey."

The monk bowed his head. "Your prayers are very welcome, young lord, and we are honored."

After purifying his hands and mouth at the temple fountain, Kazuchiyo approached the shrine proper, and, after watching the other worshipers to gauge the particular custom, bowed his head and clapped his hands in their same order to offer his prayer. As a child of the mountains, he had grown up honoring similar spirits, and even if he did not expect much contentment from a foreign patron so far from his home, it gave him peace.

As Kazuchiyo descended the few short steps from the shrine, the object of several appreciative looks from the local townsfolk, he at last took notice of the pair of stone guardians standing in the temple gatehouse; instead of a pair of lions or snarling kings, the grounds were protected by a handsome tiger and a spiraling dragon. Each was worn with age, their muzzles eroded from many years of petting hands. Some time in history, it had become deemed lucky to rub the snout, or so he assumed. Their blurred faces gave him pause.

"I saw this combination decorating the border gate into Jisu," Kazuchiyo remarked to the monk. "Is it popular in this province?"

The monk smiled knowingly and pointed to the west, where in the distance the barest hint of a tall peak jutted up above the others. "The mountain is their home," he explained. "Two children of Nari-Yamatsumi, who are bitter siblings. When the autumn storms roll in, you can hear them bicker all the way here."

Kazuchiyo smiled with nostalgia. "We said something similar back at Tengakubou. My mother told me that if only I could write down the lightning flashes as brushstrokes, I'd understand what the Dragon God had to tell us."

"Tengakubou?" the monk repeated, and his gaze went to Aritaka's crest on Kazuchiyo's robe. Kazuchiyo glanced away, uncertain how to explain the contradiction, only to spot a figure at the gate more deserving of his attention: Amai. Though his presence was a welcome distraction, his breathless appearance was plenty of cause for concern.

Kazuchiyo bowed his head to the monk, who responded in kind, and the pair of them bid their good nights. He moved outside the temple grounds to meet Amai and was relieved to see that tousled hair and a flush seemed to be the worst of his ailments. "Are you all right?" he asked anyway. "You look like you've been running."

"Faster than walking," Amai replied smartly. "Come on. We need you back in your armor."

He turned to leave immediately; Kazuchiyo hurried to keep up, asking, "Has something happened? An attack from Tendo?"

"Not yet, but it's coming," said Amai as they made their way back to the elder's estate. "I spotted their camp farther up the road, and they were already moving out. Five hundred archers at least, and nearly that many foot soldiers. More than what we let live at Chouwa, that's for sure." Amai cast him a sideways glance. "How come Yagi isn't with you?"

Kazuchiyo swallowed. "He's with Mahiro, looking after the soldiers."

"All right, but why?" Amai pressed. "He's always camped with you before."

"Does it matter?" Kazuchiyo retorted, but seeing Amai's eyebrows shoot up tempered him, and he tried again in a calmer manner. "It was his suggestion. I think he's becoming more aware of appearances and etiquette."

He expected more teasing, but Amai only nodded thoughtfully. "Fair enough," he said, and they quickened their pace to the estate.

CHAPTER SIX

At the elder's estate, Kazuchiyo changed swiftly back into his armor, and he and Amai set out again for the western edge of town. Word had already spread of the possibility of an incoming attack, and men walked the streets, encouraging the townspeople back to their homes and for the able-bodied to take up arms. By the time they reached their goal at the western gates, Mahiro had organized their soldiers—and most of Jisu's weary samurai—into ranks. Still atop Suzumekage, she prowled back and forth along the line and grinned with wicked anticipation.

"One day in Jisu, and already the little fish are throwing themselves into our boat! We've got spears enough for every one of them, don't we, men? Let me hear it!"

The soldiers gave a great roar of approval, and despite the promise of incoming conflict, Kazuchiyo had to smile. As he approached, the soldiers took notice of his helm and made way, allowing him to the front. There, waiting along the first line, stood Yagi; unlike Mahiro he had left his horse and instead faced the gate on foot, the butt of his spear planted in the dirt road. A dozen of their strongest soldiers had taken up positions behind and around him like an honor guard, including a few with purple Jisu cords on their armor.

"Kazu," Yagi said as soon as he'd spotted him. "You shouldn't—" He stopped himself abruptly; his frown, as characteristically stern as ever, was tinted with apprehension. "Should you be this close to the front?"

"I wanted to know the situation," said Kazuchiyo. "I was told we're expecting visitors."

"We are!" Mahiro crowed from atop Suzumekage. "We're ready for them too. These Jisu boys were a sorry lot when I first saw them, but they can't wait to prove their mettle now!"

The Jisu soldiers shifted eagerly, a few banging the ends of their spears against the ground. Kazuchiyo scanned their line and spotted the elderly commander from Chouwa among their number, but not their commander. "Where is Sir Chikakuni?" he asked.

Mahiro aimed her naginata at one of the guard towers that dotted the wall. The wall itself was no more than a single story high, making for not much of a vantage point, but Kazuchiyo was eager for some glimpse of the geography that would soon be a battlefield. "I'll confer with him and come back," he told Mahiro. "I know you're eager for a charge, but we'll wait to see what Tendo has planned before committing to any offense."

Mahiro gave a great snort. "I didn't earn the name Oeyo's Unyielding Gate for nothing. Not one fish will step foot past this wall."

Kazuchiyo thanked her, but before he could take more than two steps, Yagi shifted in his armor. "Should you be so close to the front?" he asked again.

Kazuchiyo hesitated, uncertain whether to meet Yagi's concern with sincerity when under so many watchful eyes. He settled with an easy smile. "A general's work is watching from hilltops," he said. "I'll have to satisfy myself with the tower." He started down the line toward it. "Tell your captains to hold their positions until my command!" Yagi did not look pleased, but he held his post.

Amai followed along behind, and when Kazuchiyo glanced

back, he was irritated to see a hint of a smirk twisting his lips. "What's so amusing?"

"Nothing, really," replied Amai. "It's cute."

Kazuchiyo's frown deepened, but now was no time for the flirtations of a presumptuous weasel, and he resolved to focus only on the battle ahead.

Up in the tower, such as it was, Chikakuni kept watch with a pair of young Jisu soldiers. He looked up with relief as Kazuchiyo joined them. "Lord Aritaka. You needn't have come yourself, but I'm glad you're here."

"When I promised my aid, I wasn't volunteering only my men," Kazuchiyo said. He moved to the edge of the guard post to get a view of the land. "Can you see them from here?"

"Just barely, straight ahead."

Kazuchiyo peered out into the falling dusk. Though the wall marked the edge of the town proper, there were still many buildings and dwellings that dotted the roadside leading into the west, with intermittent gaps made by old and weary maples. The occupants of the homes had been evacuated behind the gates already, but there were still hints of movement between the buildings and trees.

"I can't make much out," Kazuchiyo confessed, and he looked to Amai. "You're certain they're Tendo soldiers?"

"Carp crest on an aqua banner," Amai replied confidently. "Archers marching first, when I saw them earlier. They can't really expect to take the city against our numbers, can they?"

"Stalling for the sake of the siege at Etsugo," said Chikakuni. "They've laid a trap and want us to know it, so that we'll think twice about charging down their gullet."

Kazuchiyo nodded. "It's what I would do if I needed to stall an army larger than mine."

"If they want to stall, then we answer with speed," said Amai, casting Kazuchiyo a sly look. "Isn't that your usual play?"

"Defy him, always," Kazuchiyo quoted. "Though I wonder..."

Kazuchiyo's wonder was soon crudely interrupted, as each

of them atop the tower took note of a flurry of movement in the distance. They strained their ears toward what might have been a man's voice as a line of figures dashed out onto the road, and with a single command, a jagged shadow arched across the red-orange sky toward the town.

Kazuchiyo was no stranger to arrows. Even being too far to hear the twang of a hundred bowstrings, he felt the reverberations ripple across his skin in a chill, and his heart skipped in anticipation of the dreadful impact. What he did not expect nor even comprehend at first was when the narrow, dark projectiles burst into streams of fiery light mere moments before crossing the wall. A hundred shafts of burning wood hailed into the crowd of soldiers and bore into rooftops.

Kazuchiyo and the rest lurched back, stunned but unharmed as only two arrows had climbed high enough to bury themselves in the tower's wooden beams. Amai regained his senses first; he drew a tanto and leaned out of the tower to hack the burning arrows off its flank. Kazuchiyo instinctively grabbed his belt to steady him, and the movement jarred his reason back into place. As soon as Amai was safely retrieved, he turned to see what had become of their soldiers.

The attack seemed to have shocked more than it wounded; at such distance it did not seem any arrowheads had managed to pierce armor. Captains shouted to maintain order as the flames were cast down and stomped out. The far greater danger was to the village buildings. Here at the outskirts, several bore wooden and even thatched roofs, quick to take on the fire.

Chikakuni ordered his two soldiers down the tower to assist with the effort to douse the buildings, and then faced the enemy again. "A fire attack, at this distance? How?"

After reassuring himself that Yagi was unharmed from the barrage, Kazuchiyo, too, returned his focus to the road. The archers had already cleared, likely to string their bows safe from counterfire. "They weren't on fire when they were loosed," he said, and he put a hand to his wrist, where the small, red bead tucked into his bracer tingled with heat. "That was magic."

"We've never seen that from Tendo before," said Chikakuni.

Kazuchiyo believed him. It was difficult for him to imagine that the precise archers harrying them were the same unruly lot from the valley. "Where's Oihata?" he asked Amai. "If there's an onmyouji among them we'll need his insight."

"If he's not on his way, I'll drag him out for you," Amai promised, though then he gave a tug to Kazuchiyo's armor. "In a moment, that is."

"Incoming!" Chikakuni shouted, and the three of them ducked beneath the guard wall as another hail of arrows flared into a burning downpour. Several more found their mark in vulnerable buildings than before, and a few voices cried out—townspeople come to help fight the fires without the benefit of armor. As soon as the volley was complete, Amai disappeared down the tower ladder, leaving Kazuchiyo and Chikakuni to regather themselves.

"Fucking gutless trout!" Mahiro bellowed from below. "A spear to the belly is too good for them!" When Kazuchiyo leaned out of the tower to see her, she waved the blade of her naginata at him. "Brother! Tell me I can open the gate and ride down their throats!"

"No! It's what they're after!" With an onmyouji potentially among their opponents, he dared no reckless charge, though he did not wish to unsettle the soldiers by telling her as much. "Send some of our men to reinforce the other tower and fire back!"

Mahiro complied, though begrudgingly so. As Jisu and Sakka archers fired from the second tower, the Tendo men retreated again, disappearing among the buildings and trees.

"There's another way out of the town, south of here," said Chikakuni. "A peasant road that connects the village to the riverbank. A troupe could circle around behind the archers and catch them unaware, if we can keep them focused here."

"I was hoping you'd say something like that," replied Kazuchiyo. "What about from the north?"

"Mostly forest, but still passable." Chikakuni began to

climb down from the tower. "I have men from here that can lead the way."

Down below, the soldiers had, with Mahiro's prodding, retreated from the walls. They stood in their ranks wherever the street offered the room, and when a third volley sent more flames crashing into stores and homes, they quickly went to work to prevent further spread. Had the enemy a greater number of archers, they might have caused a great deal of damage, but given the relative size of both forces, Kazuchiyo could think of it as nothing other than bait. Whether that bait included attacks from the side as well as the fore, Kazuchiyo had no way of knowing, but he was determined to act.

Naoya arrived then, in his full armor and coat, a dozen soldiers and Purnima at his back. "Kazumune! Should we prepare horses? We have cavalry enough to run them down."

"Yes, but not yet," said Kazuchiyo as they gathered together. "We'll send two groups out from north and south to pincer them. Once their archers are distracted from the road, it will be safer for your charge."

"Excellent! Then the lady Purnima and I—"

"You're needed here," Kazuchiyo interrupted before he could set his own course too firmly. "I think there's an onmyouji behind this fire attack. If he knows we're armed with magic as well, it may distract him from the pincer."

Kazuchiyo watched closely for his reaction; as he suspected, a hard edge came into Naoya's eyes that spoke of immediate distrust. "I'll see for myself," he said with conviction, "and if it be so, trust that I'll make short work of them." He waved Purnima forward. "Take Lady Purnima and our soldiers, and I'll direct Commander Rakuteru to prepare to charge when the opportunity arrives."

"Thank you, friend," said Kazuchiyo, and each bowed his head before Naoya moved toward the gates. Kazuchiyo would have liked to stay and witness whatever the man was about to do to counteract the enchanted barrage of arrows, but watching the frantic efforts of the surrounding townspeople reminded him of his duty.

"Lady Purnima," he said, "please accompany Sir Chikakuni to the north. I'll lead an attack from the south with our Sakka troops."

Purnima regarded Chikakuni distastefully for an uncomfortable moment, but at last she nodded and looked back to Kazuchiyo. "Tell your sister I'll bring her back the enemy's head, as consolation."

Chikakuni gave a crooked half smile safely behind Purnima's back as she rallied her men. "Maybe we could trade."

"You can trust her," Kazuchiyo reassured him. "But be careful; there could be a trap for us."

"Same to you," Chikakuni replied, and he turned to call for his captains.

"Kazu," said Yagi, and Kazuchiyo startled to find him so close. His armor was singed from the fire, but his grip on his spear had not loosened. "You shouldn't—should you still be here?"

As touching as his concern was, Kazuchiyo had been seized by the momentum of the siege, and he no longer had much patience for it. "Don't worry about me," he said. "I need soldiers to come with me out the south exit. We're going to circle behind the archers and try to break their lines."

"Incoming!" came a shout from the towers; Yagi snatched Kazuchiyo by his armor and tugged him about, shielding him with his larger body even though they were already out of range. Kazuchiyo tensed in anticipation of fire crossing the wall, but he was instead buffeted from behind by an immense gust of cold wind. The arrows extinguished immediately after their ignition, and many spiraled off course to clatter uselessly along the rooftops.

Kazuchiyo pushed Yagi's hand off so he could look past him, disappointed not to have seen Naoya performing the magic as it was cast. The soldiers gave a cheer, but Naoya himself in the tower remained forward-facing, stoically awaiting the next volley.

"Now that they've seen the arrows can be repelled, they might change their strategy," Kazuchiyo mused aloud. "We should hurry before they think to retreat." He patted the oni face decorating Yagi's armor for good luck. "Those men who were with you earlier all looked hearty and eager. Will you…"

Kazuchiyo lifted his attention back to Yagi's face and trailed off, taken aback by the clouded look his lover was fixing him with. He gulped. "Will you gather them for me? We leave at once."

"All right," Yagi grumbled, but before he could turn to his task, Kazuchiyo halted him.

"Thank you for protecting me," he said.

Yagi nodded, and Kazuchiyo was relieved to see some of his ill temper abating. At last, he turned to the soldiers and pointed toward one of the captains who had stood close to him when Kazuchiyo first arrived. "You there! Collect your men and come with us. Your lord needs you."

"Sir!"

The burly captain snapped into a bow and then hurried to comply. As the group of them split off from the rest of the Sakka forces, Kazuchiyo turned to Amai. Even just a faint glimpse of a smirk set his teeth on edge. "Stop that."

"I'm silent," said Amai. "Not a word."

They gathered thirty men, and with another dozen volunteers from the knowledgeable Jisu soldiers, they set out from the town's southern gate. The Jisu soldiers took the lead, weaving a swift but cautious trail down the peasant road and into the surrounding dwellings. Through the trees they could hear the occasional thrum of bowstrings, followed by gusts of wind and shouts from soldiers. Kazuchiyo stayed close behind Yagi, at last appreciating that they were marching directly into battle. It had been over a year since he last drew his sword in earnest against an enemy, and the memory hitched his pulse into his throat.

They moved past meager row houses shut tight, all lanterns doused, leaving only the barest of moonlight to illuminate their path. Eventually the sound of passing arrows ceased, and the darkness of the unfamiliar land grew disorienting. Kazuchiyo gripped the handle of his katana. Then ahead he saw a flicker of movement among a stand of thick tree trunks, and the Jisu captain at the head drew them deeper off the road.

"They're there," the man whispered. "They're focused on the road."

"There's a lot more than you can see," Amai warned. "Even if they're spread out, they outnumber us several times over."

Kazuchiyo leaned out from around the tree that sheltered him, though he could catch only glimpses of the soldiers ahead. They did not appear to be carrying bows. "We only need to draw their archers from the road," he said. "That will open the path for our soldiers. We should try to surprise them as much as possible."

Yagi nodded, already brandishing his spear, ready for battle. "Then I'll take the lead. They'll be surprised."

Kazuchiyo had been envisioning more of a stealthy approach than he expected Yagi to be capable of, but seeing how eager the Sakka soldiers were to follow his example, he nodded along. "All right. Be careful."

Yagi set off at once. His was not a frame made for stealth, but his height lent itself to long, determined strides that carried him swiftly across the distance. By the time the enemy took notice and turned, he was already only a few more steps away, and their shouts for him to identify himself quickly turned to outcries of alarm. With a mighty bellow Yagi swung his spear, decapitating a man where he stood and severing the shoulder of another. A surprise to each, indeed.

The other soldiers followed his example; they rushed forward in a tight line of attack, slashing and hacking at the startled men. Their war cries echoed among the trees, though none so fiercely as Yagi himself as he charged from one man to the next. His beastly howls sent more than one soldier turning heel in retreat; Amai darted after as many as he could, slashing at their knees to prevent their escape. The Jisu men were more than happy to finish them off. As one arrowhead unit they plunged into the Tendo line and sent what had been an already loose formation scattering.

Kazuchiyo stood mostly removed from the fighting, four Sakka soldiers as his guards. Yagi's familiar voice rising in fury spread goose bumps rippling up his arms, and he found it difficult to look away from his violent spectacle. As they pressed forward, he heard similar shouts from the opposite end of the road, which he assumed meant the arrival of Purnima and Chikakuni on the northern side. Kazuchiyo diverted his small escort toward the road in hopes of a better glimpse of the current state of affairs, only for them to encounter another small pocket of troops—and among them, their commanders.

Two men on horseback watched over the attack: one a high-ranking samurai in black armor, with a tall, sloped rectangular helmet and a hard face; the other much older, a wild mane of silver hair spilling out from under his black cap and down the front and back of his kariginu. Despite their obviously high station, Kazuchiyo noticed no bannermen among their guard, and their attire was conspicuously devoid of family or provincial markings. In fact, when Kazuchiyo looked closely, it appeared that the samurai's helmet was meant to house an ornament that had been removed.

The pair's guards noticed them swiftly, and Kazuchiyo pulled back with his small entourage. As fortuitous as it would be to claim an enemy commander's head at the outset of their campaign, one glimpse at the samurai's heavy half-cross spear convinced him they were not up to the task alone. "Yagi!" he shouted; if he was farther down the road, there was a chance of him cutting off the commanders' retreat. "Amai!"

The two strangers turned in their saddles, their stern faces illuminated in the light of a soldier's torch. "That might be him," said the silver-haired man.

"Then he dies," replied the samurai, hefting his kamayari. Its two-pronged blade gleamed in the torchlight.

"Yagi!" Kazuchiyo shouted again, drawing his sword, but

by then the samurai had charged. His men cleared a path, and his horse leaped forward with greater agility than any would have expected from such a broad-chested beast. He swung his weapon with the full strength of his arm, and one of the Sakka soldiers jumped forward to intercept; the spear's trunk cracked his elbow with a sickening crunch, and the jutting prong stabbed into his armpit where armor did no good. With one firm, raking motion, the samurai tore him open.

Kazuchiyo lashed out with his katana, but the samurai was quick to withdraw, and he managed only to scrape at the spear shaft without damaging it. As soldiers from both sides clashed, Kazuchiyo and his hopelessly outnumbered, a great howl bore down on them. With huge strides Yagi charged toward the enemy soldiers and skewered the throat of the man closest to him almost before he could fully turn. The choking gurgles sent the men around him reeling back, and as the rest of the Sakka men barreled forward, Kazuchiyo could see the mounted samurai reconsider his odds.

"That's enough!" called the silver-haired man. "We've done our work!"

His hand emerged from his sleeve, and with a flick of his wrist a flurry of white, fluttering shapes whipped about in all directions. One stuck itself to the wall of a nearby row house and immediately burst into flames. Within moments the unnatural blaze spread up to the roof, and thick, dark smoke plumed into the trees.

The samurai turned his horse to retreat. In desperation Kazuchiyo again tried to strike, only to be drawn back by someone gripping the back of his armor—luckily too. The samurai's great, black horse kicked as it spun, nearly catching him with its hoof. Beast and rider burst out of the line of trees, back onto the road, and then into the west with the silver-haired man just behind. The soldiers, too, attempted to flee, though most were cut down by Yagi's spear and Sakka blades.

Kazuchiyo glanced behind him, startled but relieved to find it was Amai gripping his armor. "You're all right?" asked

Amai.

"Fine," Kazuchiyo replied breathlessly, and he tugged free so he could hurry to the road. All the enemy was in retreat by then, with figures on both sides of the path running deeper into the mountain's shadow. Moments later a fresh shout alerted him back to the town, where the gates now stood open, and Mahiro burst forth atop Suzumekage.

"Run them down!" she roared as she charged down the road, Ginta and his riders close behind. "Don't let any escape!"

They rode past in a thunder of hoofs and eager shouts. Kazuchiyo watched them, trying to catch his breath. Though it had been a brief encounter, his hands trembled, and he forced himself to sheathe his katana. "Yagi?"

"Kazu." Yagi took hold of the front collar of his armor to steady him. "Are you all right?"

"Yes." With one more deep breath Kazuchiyo had his bearings. "Tell the men to spread out and look for stragglers. We need—" He coughed on the growing smoke, realizing then that the fleeing onmyouji had set fire to a number of buildings all along the roadside. "We need one alive if you find one. I'll help organize the rest to fight the fires."

"But I should—" Yagi stopped himself, scowling, and then looked about. "Amai," he snapped, gesturing. "Stay with him."

"I'm right here," said Amai, shaking his left arm. "I'm not going anywhere."

"Stay with him," Yagi repeated anyway, and finally he turned to pass Kazuchiyo's orders on to the men.

Kazuchiyo and Amai exchanged a frazzled look. "Are you all right?" Kazuchiyo asked, eyeing the arm Amai was favoring.

"It's nothing," said Amai. He gave his elbow one last rub and then forced himself to stop fussing with it. "Seems like it's over."

Kazuchiyo took in his surroundings, and at last he remembered the soldier who had jumped in front of him to halt the path of the raging spear. That man lay on the ground a short distance away now, curled over on himself and soaked through with blood. Even as Kazuchiyo crouched down in front of him, he knew the man had very little time left. He was old and whiskered, a sturdy foot soldier who had likely seen many battles. Kazuchiyo even briefly wondered if the man had survived Shimegahara.

"You saved your lord's life," he said, and the man grimaced up at him. "Tell me your family name and I'll see they're taken care of."

"Mi…" the old man wheezed, but there was already blood in his mouth, and he couldn't get any more out than that. Despite Kazuchiyo's attempts to steady him, he crumpled, his last few breaths wet and gasping until he finally went still.

Kazuchiyo eased him to the ground, his skin prickly with anxious heat. He felt small and humbled, and he barely noticed at first that Amai was drawing him to his feet—was talking to him. "Kazu, keep your head high," he was saying. "You're the general and a lord's son."

"I know that, but…" Kazuchiyo shook his head; Amai was right. He could not to afford to falter any more than he already had. "The fires," he said. "We need to help the villagers."

Amai nodded toward the gates of the town; though dozens of men stood at the ready with weapons drawn, still more were flooding down the road to aid in dousing the fires. Eventually even Naoya himself emerged, and with so many put toward the effort, the flames were contained before they could spread too far. Once the bulk of the work was completed, Kazuchiyo at last allowed his Sakka captains to usher him back safely behind the walls. True to his orders, Amai did not leave his side.

"Did you see Chikakuni or Purnima?" Kazuchiyo asked. "They must have been successful, but I didn't see either."

"I did," said Amai, and his lip quirked. "Mahiro is going to be jealous."

Gradually the commotion subsided. The fires were

brought under control and the soldiers carried their wounded and dead into the town to be tended. Purnima returned with the head of a Tendo commander while Mahiro returned with several enemies slain but none of note. Though Mahiro's stare lingered on Purnima with intensity, it was not, to Kazuchiyo's experienced eye, a look of jealousy.

Several enemy soldiers were taken captive, and though Kazuchiyo was glad to relinquish their interrogation to his captains, he did take note of the Tendo emblems on their armor. None matched the honor guard of the two commanders, and after some investigation, it became clear that none of those men had survived. Those who had escaped Yagi's spear but not Mahiro's charge had cut out their own throats to avoid capture.

"It concerns me," Kazuchiyo confessed to Chikakuni as they regrouped. "Those men took some effort to hide their identity. Why, when the bulk of their soldiers are obviously from Tendo's clan Umafusa?"

"I didn't see them," said Chikakuni. "But like I said, we've never known Tendo to employ onmyouji."

"Not even a guess from Jisu's finest?" taunted Amai. "There are only so many places someone like that could have come from, who might also want to conceal their identity."

Chikakuni regarded Amai in silence for a moment. "You sound as if you have a guess of your own," he said, and he gave a quiet snort. "I'm far from our finest, but I am still a samurai, you know. Should a foot soldier be talking to me like that?"

Amai pursed his lips and rolled his eyes to Kazuchiyo, where he found no support; Kazuchiyo stared back, expectantly silent, suddenly curious to know how Amai would respond. Thus, begrudgingly, Amai bowed his head. "Excuse me."

Chikakuni betrayed his good humor with a subtle smirk and then returned his more serious attention to Kazuchiyo. "I don't think there's much good in speculating. They could be from Nomino in the north, Hagimine to the west." His expression momentarily darkened. "They could have been some family of Jisu turned traitor. There are a lot of clans that live up in the mountains and might have an onmyouji tucked away."

"Perhaps Sir Oihata will have some insight into that," said Kazuchiyo. He spotted the man atop the watchtower again, passing orders to his soldiers while keeping an eye on the western road. "I'll ask him at a better time. For now, you should return to your troops; there's still much to do before anyone can rest."

"You're right," replied Chikakuni, but then he hesitated to leave. "I never would have expected you to lead the assault personally."

Kazuchiyo winced as Amai cast him a look. "Believe me, I prefer the command ranks. Everything just happened so fast— I'm afraid I got swept up in it."

"Well, you defended these people, and I appreciate it," said Chikakuni with deeper sincerity. "Thank you." He offered Kazuchiyo a bow and at last strode off to rejoin his soldiers.

Amai clicked his tongue once Chikakuni was out of range. "Foot soldier, huh?"

"He's right, you know," Kazuchiyo teased. "It's one thing when it's me or Yagi, but not everyone knows you here. You'll have to watch your tongue."

Amai scoffed as if about to reply with something lewd, but instead he fixed Kazuchiyo with a more serious look. "He's smarter than he lets on, that Chikakuni. Did you notice the possibility he decidedly left out?"

"...I did." It was one Kazuchiyo was hesitant to voice, as if that would increase the possibility of it being correct. "The onmyouji looked straight at me and said, 'That might be him.' They expected me to be here, and they wanted me dead."

"Shogun's men," said Amai quietly, giving Kazuchiyo a chill. "Maybe even actual members of the Oomiyari clan itself."

"We don't have any evidence of that," Kazuchiyo cautioned him. "There are still those in Sakka who would pay to see me dead. Let's not jump to conclusions."

Amai hummed noncommittally. "Either way it won't

be the last time we see Master Onmyouji and his General Kamayari, I'm sure."

"I'm sure," Kazuchiyo reluctantly agreed.

With the skirmish decidedly ended, the soldiers turned their attention toward finally setting up camp for the night. Naoya descended from the guard tower but had very little to offer as to the identity of their magically inclined attacker.

"As you've no doubt gleaned, those of us trained in the arts do not share our secrets lightly," he told Kazuchiyo. "I did not get a good look at the man, though even if I had I daresay I would not have recognized him."

"In any case, he seemed very skilled," said Kazuchiyo. "We're all impressed with you for having bested him."

"It doesn't work that way." At first Naoya seemed content to leave his explanation to only that, but then he frowned uncomfortably and offered a bit more. "The magic of an onmyouji isn't like the stories you may have heard of courtly fortune tellers and magicians," he said. "There is no contest of powers or wills. He cast a spell to set the arrows aflame; I used wind to douse those flames. If our positions were reversed the outcome would be the same." He paused. "Though I thank you for the compliment. Whoever our adversary is, he is arrogant and wasteful, and I'll be sure to counter him thoroughly next time as well."

"I have every confidence," said Kazuchiyo. They bowed to each other and separated for the evening.

Before making his own return to the magistrate's estate for the night, Kazuchiyo weaved again through his soldiers. Yagi was still among the throngs, overseeing the setting of the tents. "Mahiro says that when I tell them what to do, they do it faster," he explained, his manners gruff with embarrassment. "So I guess I'm doing some good."

Kazuchiyo smiled, though his heart was conflicted. "I was going to offer again that you come back to the chamber the elder offered us, but it sounds like you're doing fine here."

"Well. Yes." Yagi shifted back and forth; it was morbidly

charming to see him so sentimental when the enemy's blood was still drying on his armor. "I'm sorry," he said in a quieter tone so as not to be overheard. "I didn't mean to be rough with you earlier. I'm..." He shook his head. "I wasn't as ready as I thought I was, to see you in harm's way again."

Kazuchiyo's chest swelled with emotion, for the moment drowning out his disappointment at them not being able to spend the night together. "Neither was I, I think," he confessed. "If this is going to be a long campaign, I'll do my best to stay behind the lines from now on. I promise."

Yagi nodded with relief. "Good. Then I'll see you in the morning."

"Yes, of course." Though any action of affection would have drawn a great many eyes, Kazuchiyo could not restrain himself entirely; he reached out to press his fingertips to the mouth of the oni on Yagi's armor, as if relaying a kiss. Yagi was not one for metaphor, but he caught on that time, judging by the extra color that tinted his cheeks.

"Good night," Kazuchiyo said, and they, too, separated for the evening.

"*I'm* very happy to spend the night with you," Amai volunteered as they moved away, and though Kazuchiyo hushed him, he was very glad.

Back in the elder's offered chamber, Kazuchiyo and Amai helped each other out of their armor. With guards stationed directly outside and a long day of marching and battle behind—and ahead—of them, Kazuchiyo was in no mood to rise to any of Amai's intimate invitations. He did, however, welcome him into his futon, and despite the yet-unyielding summer heat, they curled close together.

"Is your elbow all right?" Kazuchiyo asked, watching Amai's face in the candlelight.

"Hm? Oh, it's fine." Amai shrugged carelessly. "I was pushed into the side of a building, that's all."

Kazuchiyo reached out beneath the covers. He found Amai's wrist and followed it under his sleeve, up to the offending elbow. "It feels a little swollen," he said. "You should take care."

"Swollen," Amai teased. "Not as much as—"

Kazuchiyo scoffed with frustration. "Be serious, Amai. It's not your dominant arm, but there's a long road ahead of us, and any injury could cost you."

"I *am* serious," said Amai, though sounding no more serious at all. When Kazuchiyo started to pull his hand back, he caught it at the wrist. "I know what's at stake, believe me. It's nothing." He turned his hand so he could thread their fingers together. "I'll never be as strong or as *loud* as our full-oni Yagi, but I love you just as much, you know, and I'll fight just as hard."

Kazuchiyo blinked at him in surprise, completely taken aback by the casually delivered declaration. Though too flustered to reply, all it took was a subtle tilt of Amai's head for him to finally accept the invitation; he leaned forward and kissed Amai, firmly, conveying his reply as straightforwardly as he knew how. Amai returned the kiss in kind, his lips deftly reassuring where his manners had been flippant. There might have been true sincerity in the little rascal after all, but when Kazuchiyo broke the kiss and tried to speak, Amai quietly shushed him.

"It's really late," Amai whispered, his smile once again a teasing enigma. "We should both get as much sleep as we can."

Kazuchiyo tried to read his expression; did Amai not require a more explicit response? "All right," he agreed, sensing that any other reply would earn him another shush. Still, he wanted his heart known, and to that end he drew Amai to his chest. He wrapped him up protectively, and with a deep sigh Amai sank into him. There were times, Kazuchiyo pondered, when Amai felt very small in his arms.

CHAPTER SEVEN

In the morning, the army got off to a slow start. There were injuries to be treated from the night before, and scouts were dispatched down the road and through the woods to determine if what remained of the Tendo ambush had reformed farther ahead. Despite Chikakuni's eagerness to be underway, even his own soldiers were exhausted, and it soon became clear they could not avoid another night in the town.

The day was spent in tense but necessary preparation. By the time the scouts returned in the evening, they brought with them reports that the Tendo soldiers had fled deep up the mountain trail, and seemed to be retreating even farther. After much discussion with Jisu's knowledgeable captains, all came to the same conclusion: they were returning to the bulk of their forces surrounding Etsugo, to make up a rear guard for the siege.

"Now that they know just how long it will take for us to arrive, they will no doubt redouble their efforts to take the castle before then," supposed Naoya, as he, Chikakuni, and Kazuchiyo kneeled together over a rough map in the elder's home. "Even so, we mustn't be hasty. They've had plenty of time to plan for us and may have laid traps."

"I know," said Chikakuni, and he chewed his lip anxiously. "We have to trust that the castle can hold, but still…"

"It will hold," Kazuchiyo said. "Last night's ambush was fairly weak; if they're so desperate as to seek just one more day with such a small force, their position can't be that firmly in place." Chikakuni nodded, grateful to him.

Just as they were finishing their council, the panel slid open a small fraction. "Sir Oihata," said Purnima, head bowed. "If I may?"

She held up her hand, and a small paper figure leaped from it and fluttered across the room. "Ahh," said Naoya, holding up his hand in welcome, "it must be a reply from our earlier scouts."

However, the paper did not go to him; instead, it beat its small, tapered wings over to Kazuchiyo, where it landed in his lap. With looks of confusion shared all around, Kazuchiyo unfolded the message. There was only one person he could think of who would or could send him a shiki, and he was careful to keep the writing visible to only himself.

Lord Aritaka has departed southward from Gyoe. Any updates you have for him or me as to the campaign will have to be sent by way of General Oihata, assuming he'll oblige you.

Master Iomori no Jun's strict handwriting was unmistakable. Kazuchiyo read the short message over more than once before folding it back up. "It's from Master Iomori," he explained. "Lord Aritaka ought to be made aware of our situation, but he's traveling and may be unreachable by a conventional messenger. Can I trouble you to send a reply, Sir Naoya?"

Naoya's expression darkened at the mention of Iomori, but he nodded. "Yes, he ought to know as much of what goes on in as timely a manner as possible." He gave a thoughtful hum. "I don't know how he could have heard so soon, but maybe he thinks he can gain an audience with the lady Dada once we liberate her at Etsugo."

"Somehow I can't imagine they'd get on well," Kazuchiyo replied with a tempered smile.

Chikakuni glanced to Purnima as she shut the panel again, seemingly disappointed that the message she'd conveyed wasn't for her master after all. "What *about* the scouts you sent to north and south?" he asked. "Shouldn't we have heard from them by now?"

"I haven't had any reply," Naoya admitted. "If your forces are well hidden, they could be difficult to locate among the hills."

"Let's hope there's some word before we leave tomorrow," said Kazuchiyo. "I would feel better leaving the town behind us knowing we had directions to pass along to our reinforcements."

That evening, Kazuchiyo took his supper with his commanders Yagi, Mahiro, and Ginta. Amai did not join them, though he was certain to be creeping nearby.

"Lord Aritaka left south from Gyoe," he paraphrased Iomori's message for them. "Though we've dispatched regular messengers, he could not have heard before now that we've crossed into Jisu Province. I hope nothing is amiss at Gyoe."

Mahiro gulped down her mouthful of rice and then gave a snort. "'Left south from Gyoe.' As if there's any other way to leave Gyoe than southward."

Kazuchiyo bit his tongue; as always, she was not quite suspicious enough to read in subterfuge as her brother, but too clever to ignore it completely. He looked to Ginta, wondering if the young man had any clearer insight, but like his stony-faced father, he gave away very little.

"It's almost harvest time," Ginta said. "Perhaps Lord Aritaka is visiting the valley country, to pray for good yield."

"That would make sense," agreed Kazuchiyo, though he suspected Ginta knew better, even if he was keen enough to keep it out of his face.

Yagi offered no opinion until after Mahiro and Ginta had departed. "Is Iomori trying to warn you?" he asked once they were in private. "What's south of Gyoe?"

"Plenty of things," said Kazuchiyo as he pulled on his sandals. "Towns, villages. Hibayashi Fortress, Chijimatsu Temple." He straightened up with a frown. "Suyama Province."

"Do you have an idea of what he could want? Assuming it's something bad."

"No," Kazuchiyo admitted, which worried him greatly. "Unless something has happened that I don't know about, I have no idea..." He shook himself. "I still don't even know which of Suyama's generals he's sent, or what that means, or if—"

Yagi took his shoulders, and once Kazuchiyo had quieted, he slid his hands higher to cup his face. "It's not your job to worry about everything all the time," he said. "Whatever it is, when we know, you'll handle it. You always do."

Kazuchiyo relaxed in his hands with a grateful sigh. "Yes, you're right. Thank you." He tilted his head in welcome, and Yagi granted him a kiss before they separated for the night.

The next morning, the armies got underway. Joined by half of Chikakuni's remaining forces, Mahiro led their combined soldiers out the western gate up and up the long trail into the mountains.

In better circumstances, it would have been a very pleasant journey. The road twisted upward through the hills, thick forests on either side lush and green. They passed small settlements along the way, which were nestled into whatever flat spaces of land were available, and weathered stone guardians dotted the path to protect and encourage travelers. With every hour the heat peeled away, and the blessed release from stifling humidity helped everyone to forget the extra burden of hiking uphill.

But for a lordling responsible for over several thousand souls, the march was an anxious one. Kazuchiyo stayed at the center of the column as was his duty, flanked by tall, indigo banners that obscured much of the idyllic scenery. Those glimpses he did manage of Jisu's dense forestry were attempts to pierce the veil of secrecy it may have provided to an awaiting ambush. Could the nameless general be lying in wait for him, kamayari in hand ready to cleave through his ribs? His mind spun with all manner of concerns, made all the more dizzying as elevation thinned the air, and from all directions buzzed a constant drone of cicadas. He was very grateful when they rested at midday to water the horses, and Naoya indulged him with some poetry to pass the time and help him refocus.

They camped that night outside a small valley village, hilltops like sentinels guarding them, and bathed in silver moonlight. Kazuchiyo lingered outside his tent longer than usual, taking his fill of cooler air. The gnarled roots of ancient trees clinging to the mountainsides reminded him very much of the slopes of his dragon homeland, and his heart could not decide on solace or turmoil.

As he pondered this, he spotted a small shadow as it darted from one far-off tent to the next. With a hand on his sword hilt, he investigated and found nothing, only to spot the fleeting silhouette farther off. He started after it again but was drawn back by a hand on his sleeve.

"Chasing foxes at this hour?" Amai teased, and Kazuchiyo could have slapped him for coming upon him unawares like that. "Why, I'm right here."

"A fox?" Kazuchiyo looked again, and sure enough, he caught a glimpse of a bushy tail in the camp's torchlight. His hand relaxed from his sword. "A bold fellow, isn't he?"

"All foxes are," Amai assured him, and together they headed back to the tent. "These mountain foxes especially. I spotted a few circling the camp as it was being set up. Someone must have let them know we're going to war."

Kazuchiyo turned back one more time, but the creature

was long gone. "You think they mean to feed on our dead? Is that normal?"

"It is here, so say the Jisu soldiers. Servants of their Nari-Yamatsumi goddess, returning the spirits of dead warriors to the mountain or something." Amai urged him inside and shut the tent flap behind them. "But it's the Tendo fish they'll be feeding on after we arrive tomorrow. Don't forget."

"No, you're right," Kazuchiyo agreed, and they turned in for the evening.

Another full day of marching ensued. The forests remained eerily empty of any ambush forces, and the deeper and higher they went, all animals hushed except for the endless blaring of insects. The upward slope of the road and the mountains it carved through disguised much of the surrounding geography. It wasn't until early evening that they reached the trail's highest point, and Kazuchiyo was at last given a full view of the landscape that would be his battleground.

The castle Etsugo sat throned atop a lofty plateau, a proud and unshakable monument. Its silver eaves gleamed in the waning light, and its violet banners were raised high in defiance. The stone walls that snaked along the compound's perimeter, supported by archer towers and a mighty gate, did not appear to have been breached despite the siege of several days. In that, at least, Kazuchiyo could take great comfort.

The rest of the landscape, though profoundly picturesque, spoke of great challenges ahead. Roads from the castle carved into the hill's eastern and southern flanks: on the eastern road Kazuchiyo could see aqua banners among the trees, and to the south, the town nestled at the plateau's base was doubtlessly ransacked and overrun with enemy troops. To the north and west towered even more impressive mountains, the rocky summit of Mount Etsuzan itself looming over Jisu's embattled lords. An approach from either would be highly ill-advised, even supposing a path existed there. To all appearances, the only viable approach to Etsugo was a straight assault from where they now stood.

A course that would convey them straight into the enemy's gauntlet. The road to Etsugo's eastern ascent was guarded by a wooded hilltop to the south, wherein he spotted a temple's pagoda eaves among the trees; and to the north by an even taller hill that curled beyond the castle's doorstep like a slumbering wolf. If Tendo had even one keen general among their numbers, there would be soldiers positioned on both sides of their only road, ready to rush down in an ambush.

"It is an easy thing to see now why Tendo had to resort to such deceit before launching their assault," remarked Naoya as he surveyed the land. "They never would have been able to approach the castle at all if Jisu had men enough to cover these two hills."

Kazuchiyo nodded. "It reminds me somewhat of last year, outside your honored father's estate," he replied. "All that time spent trying to coax you up the hill, and now here I stand, charged with coaxing the enemy down."

"Actually, it's far worse than that: *two* hills, and very little time. If Etsugo is breached before we can snag these fish, it will take every one of your father's reinforcements to gain it back. But don't despair, Kazumune." He faced Kazuchiyo with conviction, quoting, "Before me it sits, an insurmountable foe: the empty parchment."

Kazuchiyo straightened his back, continuing. "Ink and brush are not enough; only courage slays the page."

An army of thousands is no small thing to settle. Under guidance from their Jisu allies, Kazuchiyo and Naoya instructed their samurai to make camp back down the road, where they had the benefit of elevation and level earth. The soldiers buzzed with anxious energy as they raised tents and prepared supper. Certainly the Tendo soldiers knew of their arrival, and there were no guarantees that they would not force an engagement as soon as possible, while they were rested and their enemies weary from marching.

As preparations for the evening continued under Mahiro's deft leadership, Chikakuni brushed a rough map of the terrain for his peers. "When I was here last, most of the Tendo forces were focused on the town," he explained. "A smaller number had blocked off the roads to Etsugo herself. Knowing about our reinforcements, they must have repositioned by now. I saw banners on the north hill, but I'm sure they've claimed the temple on the south side too." He gave a quiet huff of bitter admiration. "It's what I would do."

"Agreed," said Kazuchiyo. "We knew from the start that a straight assault from the east was the only viable option. It's only natural that they thought the same." He glanced to Yagi, who was staring very intently at the map, and he couldn't help but wonder what was going through his mind. "Even supposing we outnumber them, it's too dangerous to split our numbers between the hills, and more dangerous still to march through that gully all at once. We must coax one side down somehow."

He looked to Naoya, who answered his unspoken question with a sigh. "I know very little of Tendo's commanders. If their general has a stouter heart than foolhardy Waseba, they may be difficult to sway, and they have plenty more reason to stall for time."

He reached into his sleeve and pulled out a small piece of parchment with crease lines showing it had once been folded into a shiki. "I received word from my scouts in the north. They say that they found remnants of a Jisu raiding party close to the border, who were afraid to turn their backs to Nomino Province even to retreat."

"Remnants?" Chikakuni echoed, and at Naoya's grim expression he sank deeper into his shoulders. "How many are left?"

"Barely five hundred men," said Naoya with greater sympathy. "Kazumune, I suggest some of your Sakka reinforcements be sent to assist them."

"Yes, of course." Kazuchiyo stared down at the map, its

inelegant brushstrokes giving him the eerie sensation of hazy darkness at its edges. He could not afford to let paranoia get the better of him, and yet, more and more, the business stank of conspiracy. "General Rakuteru would be well suited to that task. But what of the scouts in the south?" He swallowed and cast a look at the crestfallen Chikakuni. "Any sign of the lady Dada's uncle and those men?"

"I've had no word from them either way," Naoya admitted.

"Then... then I'll instruct General Hosoda to find a camp just south of Kanrei Temple. If there's another Tendo army lying in wait somewhere, at the very least we have to prevent them from blocking our retreat." Kazuchiyo began to move his wooden tiles across the map. "Once Etsugo is safely back in Jisu hands, Tendo will have no choice but to withdraw and—"

Chikakuni climbed abruptly to his feet, and without one word to anyone he stormed from the tent. Though momentarily startled, Kazuchiyo rallied himself. "Excuse me," he said quickly. "I'll be right back." With a deep breath he followed Chikakuni out into the camp.

Chikakuni cut a path straight up the road back to the crest of the hill, where he paused. Whether he was seeking a moment of solitude or not, Kazuchiyo approached without hesitation, convinced they could ill afford any reckless actions. "Sir Chikakuni? Please tell me what's on your mind."

"I have to go to Etsugo," he said, just as Kazuchiyo feared he might. "I have to know what the situation is there."

"The castle is held," Kazuchiyo said gently, even knowing it was likely futile. "That means there are soldiers inside that can still fight, but unless we can draw one side from the hill, that won't help us."

"But even if the castle isn't breached, that doesn't mean that Tangiku—" Chikakuni caught himself, and he scraped his glove across his mouth. "The lady Dada herself may still be in danger. I have to know she's all right." He looked to Kazuchiyo plaintively. "Please understand. I *have* to."

Kazuchiyo's heart ached with sympathy. "I do understand,"

he reassured Chikakuni. "Truly I do, but you won't learn what you want to know if you're captured by the enemy. The roads are heavily guarded, and they know we're here."

"There's another road." Chikakuni pointed to the northern slope of the larger hill that guarded the approach to the castle. "A secret path used by Lady Dada's elite guard that weaves along the mountainside. It's how I got into Etsugo before, when she gave me the letter and the bead. A single-file line can get to the castle from here undetected."

Kazuchiyo followed his arm, but he could not make out any such path in the evening light. "That was days ago. There's no guarantee Tendo hasn't discovered that path by now."

"Even so, I have to go." Chikakuni began tightening the cords on his armor. "I'll go myself. Captain Yamamori will lead my men; I'll instruct him to follow any orders you give him."

"Wait," Kazuchiyo insisted, and he went so far as to take Chikakuni by the arm. "Don't be so hasty. There's no need for you to go alone."

"I'll go with him," said Amai, and Kazuchiyo startled to find him so close behind them. "Taking a secret path past the enemy into a castle is exactly the kind of job for a shinobi."

"Wait," Kazuchiyo said again, his anxiety burrowing deeper. "We've been marching all day. It will take hours to reach the castle by foot, let alone up an unfamiliar path in the dark. At least wait a day."

Chikakuni shook his head. "I can't, but I won't ask anyone to go with me."

"And I'm not going let anyone outdo me in sneakery, even if it is their own backyard," Amai retorted, though he then bowed his head. "If you'll excuse me for speaking so far out of turn, Sir Samurai."

Chikakuni scoffed, and as Amai lifted his head, an understanding seemed to pass between them. Though distraught, Kazuchiyo could see that there would be no swaying either of them. "Then at least come back to the tent first," he said. "We need to tell Sir Oihata what you're up to. If you insist on going, I won't let you go without us having some kind of plan. Who knows if we'll be able to pass messages even by shiki if the enemy has an onmyouji in their ranks."

At last, Chikakuni's shoulders relaxed. "Yes, you're right. I should have at least something to tell Lady Dada when I arrive."

"I'll go fetch the lady Purnima," Amai offered. "She might have an interest as well, and maybe we can convince Oihata to lend us a spell if she joins us."

"We'll meet you in the tent," said Kazuchiyo, and as he watched Amai scurry off, he let out a long, anxious sigh.

"I'm sorry," Chikakuni said quietly. "You've done too much for me and my homeland already. I shouldn't be asking you to risk someone so dear to you."

As dire as the circumstances were, Kazuchiyo could not help a flush of embarrassment in knowing that Chikakuni had caught the thread between him and Amai so easily. "It's war," he said. "We are all always at risk." He managed to offer Chikakuni a smile. "And it's for someone dear to you."

Chikakuni did not fluster quite so easily, though the pain in his smile convinced Kazuchiyo that he had not misjudged the nature of his loyalty to his ladyship either. He took in a deep breath. "Still, I am sorry. I am a better man than this normally, Lord Aritaka. I hope your second impression of me will be better than it has been so far."

"You seem a fine man to me already, but I look forward to knowing you better, too." As they turned to head back toward the tent, he chewed on the decision a moment longer and then added, "If you don't mind, you can start by not calling me 'Lord Aritaka.'"

He expected a curious look; given their relative status and short acquaintance, anything less formal in address could be considered disrespectful. Chikakuni, however, nodded immediately as if understanding at once the complex meaning of one's own name. "Whatever you want me to call you, I will. You'll never need to correct me again."

Kazuchiyo found that deeply reassuring. "Lord Sakka

might be most appropriate," he said, "though I think I'd prefer Lord Kazumune, as Sir Oihata calls me."

"I'm not as high in rank as Sir Oihata, but I already promised to do what you ask, so Lord Kazumune it is." His manners tempered to sincerity once more. "Thank you."

"I have the feeling your lady will have promoted you to general by the end of this," said Kazuchiyo, and he passed back into the tent first.

Naoya nodded along as he listened to Chikakuni outline his intentions. "I'm not sure it's wise, but I must admit, if it were my lord in peril, I would act no differently. If Lady Purnima consents, I'll have her accompany you. She is as skilled at stealth as she is in war and will hold you to a swift pace."

"I'm very grateful," said Chikakuni, bowing. "Should I send up a signal once we've arrived? I'll want to let you know what condition the castle is in, though I'm not sure how."

"I can send you with a prepared shiki that will return to me," offered Naoya, "but as you've seen, it's no more than paper. A keen onmyouji can easily intercept it."

Yagi, who had even then been keeping vigil over the map, finally raised his head. "So write poetry," he suggested, and when he was met with curious looks, he clarified: "You know, samurai code. In case the enemy gets it."

Kazuchiyo's mind began to whirl as he took up Yagi's scrutiny of the map. "A coded message that says the opposite of the truth could be useful. Whether it makes it back or is caught by the enemy, it aids us." He grumbled quietly and shook his head. "But what could even be said that would convince them off those hills?"

A moment of thoughtful silence passed, and then Yagi cleared his throat. "Sir Chikakuni," he said, "did you know who I was when you first saw me?"

Chikakuni raised an eyebrow. "I did. I imagine by now everyone from the coast to the capital has heard of Yagi-douji, the Howling Oni of the Bridge."

"Tendo too?"

"I'd wager, yes."

Yagi nodded, for the first time looking satisfied with his infamy. "Then maybe I can get some of them down."

He pushed one of their tiles farther up the road toward the castle. Given his strength, we can easily forgive him for forgetting that each tile was meant to represent several scores of men. "If I ask them to send the strongest they have to duel me, they will send someone, right?"

Kazuchiyo sat captivated by that singular tile and found he could not draw enough breath to speak. In his stead, Naoya offered a confident nod. "I can't imagine there's an army in Shuyun that *wouldn't* have a champion willing to meet that challenge. Though I don't know the full temperament of this Tendo lot."

"Oh, they'll send someone all right," Chikakuni assured them. "They'd line up around the hill for that."

"But that—" Kazuchiyo began, only to realize he still didn't have enough composure to finish. He took in a deep breath and tried again. "We may be able to flush out Tendo's best, but that won't move their whole army down the hill."

"No, but it will give us a much better idea of what we're up against," Naoya said, clearly enamored of the idea. "If Commander Ebara performs admirably, it would be a good excuse to invite their general down for a formal conversation. I'd feel much better about this engagement with a name and a temperament assigned to the man."

"They'd say the same about you," Chikakuni cautioned him, "but with Lord Kazumune at the helm I can't be too worried about that."

Kazuchiyo shook his head, though he had no means to refute their logic. "That's—yes, you're right. We can formulate a stronger plan once we judge our opponent. Have you no guess already, Sir Chikakuni?"

"I saw Umafusa banners when I came through before," he replied, "but old Lord Umafusa had a lot of sons. Some of them more foul-tempered than others, all of them stubborn."

"Lord Oihata?" Purnima called from outside the tent, and Naoya quickly bade her come in. She did so with Amai close behind and kneeled beside her master. "The fox here told me about a secret path to the castle," she said. "He's going to need my assistance to travel it."

Behind her, Amai smirked. His confidence was of little comfort to Kazuchiyo, who could feel the reins of the battle slipping through his fingers. "If there are enough soldiers in the castle left to fight," Purnima continued, "and if the enemy camp is weak enough, we'll claim the head of whoever leads the siege."

"Not tonight," Naoya cautioned her. He turned behind him to draw forward his inkstone and parchments. "It's already almost nightfall; getting there before dawn will be challenge enough. But I'll give you two shiki: one to send back if Etsugo is still strong, another if not. With brave Ebara's efforts come morning, that will put us in the most advantageous position to determine our next course."

Once the ink was prepared, he looked to Kazuchiyo. "Would you prefer the honor, Kazumune? You have a talent for it."

Kazuchiyo took in a deep breath and accepted the supplies. "Yes, if you insist."

He composed two short messages, each to be sent opposite to their true intentions. If Etsugo Castle was found to be weak, Purnima would send the letter claiming they were in fact strong, and that they intended to take the southern road to liberate the town below in hopes of swaying the enemy off their hills to support their men in the town. If Etsugo instead boasted warriors still full of fight, she would send the letter claiming they were weak, with no choice but to wait and hope for Sakka's several thousand reinforcements already on the way—urging the Tendo siege to rush its efforts and underestimate their foes. Whatever the case, Chikakuni was convinced that Lady Dada would hold her ground. In two nights' time, the counter-siege would begin.

As Chikakuni took the time to instruct his captain and Purnima accepted talismans prepared by her master, Kazuchiyo pulled Yagi and Amai aside for his final counsel. "You'll be careful, won't you?" he said, tightening the cords on Amai's too-thin armor. "Keep your eyes open and your wits about you."

"Oh, is that how it's done?" Amai replied, smiling with amusement at Kazuchiyo's fussing. "And here I was, about to stumble through blind and dull." When Kazuchiyo gave his belt a sharp tug, he couldn't help but grunt. "Don't worry so much; they'll definitely aim at Chikakuni before me."

"Amai," Kazuchiyo said crossly, but before he could say more, Amai darted in to steal a kiss from his cheek.

"I'll be careful," Amai promised. "And to save you another speech, so will Yagi-douji. We're both in our element here, you know."

Kazuchiyo looked to Yagi; he found the calm both of them were fixing him with even more vexing. "I don't like this," he insisted. "We don't know enough about who we're fighting. It's too dangerous."

"Fighting one man at a time is a lot safer than fighting at the vanguard," Yagi told him.

"And sneaking is what I'm best at," Amai added. He captured Kazuchiyo's hands and gave them a firm squeeze. "Don't worry so much, Kazu. You can't lose your head any time we're in harm's way, or you're going to end up just like Yagi here."

"What does that mean?" Yagi grumbled self-consciously.

Kazuchiyo sighed. "I can't *not* worry either. But... you're right." He urged Amai's hands down and then reached around behind him to tighten his hair tie. At last satisfied, he leaned back. "I have every confidence in you."

"That's more like it." Amai flashed each of them a smirk and then backed away to offer a crisp bow. "When you hear the fish crying that their general's lost his head, you'll know who it was," he boasted, and he turned to head down the path and regroup with Chikakuni.

"What did he mean?" Yagi insisted.

He sounded so earnest that Kazuchiyo couldn't stop from smiling. "Nothing," Kazuchiyo assured him. "He's right." He fixed his gaze to the west, where tiny pinpoints of torchlight glimmered to life along Etsugo's walls. "I brought both of you into this war, and several thousand more beyond you, all so that Aritaka continues to believe I'm loyal to him. It's selfish and unfair of me to let my confidence waver so easily."

"Not just for Aritaka," Yagi reminded him, frowning. "There really is a castle over there that needs our help."

Kazuchiyo felt his cheeks flush. "Yes, of course."

"Because if you're that worried about what Aritaka thinks of you, I've already promised to kill him," Yagi persisted.

"Of course—in time." The thought seethed and squirmed through Kazuchiyo's mind—that years of biding his time could end so swiftly and so easily, without any need for campaigns into the west or anywhere else. Then he looked again to Etsugo and shook himself. "You're right: we're here to rescue Etsugo. That's what matters now." He took and squeezed Yagi's hands as Amai had done for him. "I know you'll best any soldier the Tendo dare to send against you tomorrow."

"Good," said Yagi, "because I will."

Kazuchiyo would have liked to ask one more time that Yagi spend that night with him, but he wanted to prove his confidence in the man and so let him return to the soldiers. Even so, his heart was not easy to sway, so burdened it was by worries over the future. He slept very little that night.

CHAPTER EIGHT

By morning, there was no indication of how the sneaking party had fared. The castle stood tall and defiant as ever in the morning light, its banners proudly flapping, and the men on watch reported no movement from the Tendo troops that were visible. Kazuchiyo stood with Naoya atop the ridge to judge for themselves, but the landscape betrayed no hints.

"If Tendo intercepted the message saying that Etsugo intended to take the town back, we would see movement by now," Naoya reasoned. "That they show no movement proves that they think Etsugo remains weak, meaning that we still have warriors in the castle ready to fight."

"Or that no message was sent at all," replied Kazuchiyo. "We can't be certain that they even reached the castle." He shook himself free from his cynicism. "In either case, it does not change what we do now. Let us prepare."

As they had planned the night before, the camp took its time in rousing. The soldiers were given plenty of time to eat and fortify their positions, giving every indication that, though they were a liberating force, the Sakka-Kibaku army was confident enough not to rush. It was almost midday by the time they gathered on the road; fifty of Sakka's finest formed into ranks, Yagi at the head flanked by the squad that had been so eager to fight beside him at Kanrei Temple. Kazuchiyo kept to the rear, surrounded by his Sakka bannermen, with Mahiro at his side.

"I know your reputation is just as fierce as anyone's," Kazuchiyo reassured her as they began a slow march down the slope. "You could fill this role, too, but I'd rather save you and Suzumekage for the *real* battle."

Mahiro gave a great snort that was echoed by her mighty steed. "You don't have to flatter me," she said. "It's fine because I don't care for dueling anyway. Suzumekage and I prefer the front lines."

They marched down the road into the valley, bearing the weight of thousands of eyes: the rest of their army watched from the camp under Naoya's leadership; the castle Etsugo loomed ahead, both desperate for and resentful of their offered help; though most intimidating was the pair of hills, rising up like prongs on a spear on either side of the path. As they drew closer Kazuchiyo could at last make out banners through the trees on the north side. Based on their number he estimated at least a thousand men. A denser collection of aqua banners higher up the hillside hinted at the command unit, as well fortified as Kazuchiyo had feared. Even a half-wit general would be loath to give up such an advantage.

Their small unit stopped in the gully just before the two hills—close enough to be tempting, but in easy reach of their own camp should retreat prove necessary. There the pageantry began: Yagi stepped forward, clad in full armor cleaned and buffed to gleaming perfection, horned helm sharpened and spear flashing. He planted the blunt end of his weapon in the road and let loose his bellow across the hillsides.

"My name is Ebara Motonobu!" he shouted, and his voice echoed mightily. Etsugo's ramparts seemed to shudder with recognition, and I can even say with certainty that ears on the slopes of Mount Etsuzan herself turned to hear. "The Howling Oni of the Bloodstained Bridge! Any man who hopes to die on my spear, come down here!"

Kazuchiyo tightly gripped Hashikiri's reins. His admiration and his apprehension were already bloody from their own duel deep within his chest, and his heart thudded and stung like blades clashing against armor. As unlikely as it was, he feared that General Kamayari himself might answer the call, and he could not banish the image of the old, dead foot soldier from his mind. An eerie tension fell over the valley, where barely a breath stirred and only the cicadas droned on in seething anticipation. At length, the banners within the trees shifted, and the sound of footfalls announced a response.

A squad of Umafusa soldiers emerged at the base of the slope, equal in number to Kazuchiyo's and led by a commander of high rank, judging by the handsome, aqua jinbaori draped over his armor. Unlike their enemies at Kanrei Temple, these soldiers had no qualms in displaying their clan affiliation openly: Umafusa's twin carp sigil was embroidered in the lead soldier's lapels, and his helmet stood in the tallest cone Kazuchiyo had ever seen.

"Surprised he didn't catch that on a branch on his way down," Mahiro muttered, and Kazuchiyo managed a smile.

The troop stopped a dozen meters away, and from their number strode a tall, broad-shouldered man bearing a spear. His long beard bore a small charm tied to its end. "My name is Sorimine Zenjiro Matsunosuke," he introduced himself at his full volume, "and I accept the demon's challenge!"

The pair bowed stiffly to each other, and with no more preamble than that, the bout started. With spears forward they advanced, Sorimine with the confidence of a man who had faced many such duels. Yagi's demeanor was difficult to judge, his back to Kazuchiyo as it was, but his gait betrayed no hesitation. He held his spear before him in a relaxed and brazen posture, and before Kazuchiyo had even enough time to truly fear for him, Sorimine struck.

Yagi batted the elder samurai's blade aside with such force that the smack of lacquered wood echoed across the valley like a thunderbolt. With one step and one lunge he thrust his spear straight into Sorimine's face: the initial strike rid him of every tooth; the cross blades carved across his bearded cheeks a bloody smile. Sorimine had life in him enough to grasp the spear as he dropped to his knees. Then Yagi tore free, and Sorimine collapsed to the road with a gurgle, where he fell still.

The Sakka soldiers pounded their spear shafts against the road as Yagi flicked the blood from his spear and then stepped back to await his next challenger.

Mahiro whistled as Kazuchiyo let out a much more reserved exhale. "I have to admit, he's more beast than man," she said. "Shit, I wish I had seen him on the bridge."

Kazuchiyo's memory of Chibatake Bridge was only the aftermath, that of his lover standing bloody within a sea of corpses, breathless and weary, collapsing into his shaking arms. What Mahiro imagined was likely closer to how Kazuchiyo had first met his beloved oni on the fields of Shimegahara: a wailing demon, his strength as monstrous as his reason was lacking. Yagi as he stood on the road was as much Kazuchiyo's champion as he had ever been, but he looked nothing like either of those memories. He looked powerful and in control, and Kazuchiyo wasn't sure if it made him fear for him less or more.

The Tendo soldiers shifted on their feet, though they were not swayed. Their commander remained stoic upon his horse. Only moments later a second man stepped forward, younger than the first but still Yagi's elder. He brandished a cross-bladed spear like Yagi's, and he beat his fist against his chest as he faced his enemy down.

"My name is Aobatake Goroemon!" he declared, though he then had to pause to resettle his voice. The assembly's silent pity riled him up. "Son of Aobatake Goroshibe! I'll take this demon's head for my lord Umafusa!"

"Come take it then," Yagi retorted, and the young man charged.

He lasted a bit longer than poor Sorimine. The General

Aobatake Sr. Goroemon fought in the name of, dead many years, can boast that of his son's fortitude, at least. At Yagi's parry he managed to twist his spear free long enough to repel the counterstrike. He even lashed out and caught the shoulder of Yagi's armor, his cross-blade tearing a few of the cords and sending Kazuchiyo's heart into his throat. It was far from enough, however, and Yagi retaliated by driving the dull end of his spear into Goroemon's elbow. The man cried out in fear as much as pain, as the blow no doubt shattered bone, and there was no stopping Yagi from taking his head.

In the aftermath, Kazuchiyo risked a glance to either hill. Though his shoulders ached with the weight of their eyes, he detected sound and movement only from the northern slope. The red eaves of the temple to the south watched the gory spectacle without the faintest glimpse of a human presence, though it was still unfathomable to Kazuchiyo that even the most brazen fish would pass up a perfect gauntlet. And where was the onmyouji hiding with his formidable general?

The third challenger came without hesitation. He was a man of years judging by the wisps of gray in his mustache, and instead of a spear he wore a pair of swords. "My name is Furusada no Saiikimaru," he said, as if it were a name of some refinement where he came from. "Wielder of Itogiri, master of the school of—"

"I don't care that your sword has a name," Yagi interrupted, already hefting his spear. "Get on with it."

Furusada bristled indignantly, as did the Tendo soldiers behind him. Their commander remained stoic. However, the man's irritation did not goad him into action as it had his peers. He drew his "famous" sword and approached Yagi cautiously, with the patience of age. When Yagi jabbed with his spear, Furusada retreated back and to the side quite nimbly. Three more times he avoided the attacks, waiting for his opponent's patience to wear, and when it did, he made his move: Yagi aimed a jab at his throat and he pivoted, two quick steps sneaking him through Yagi's guard. His katana scraped across

Yagi's armor, aiming for the opening at his armpit. But Yagi was swift, too, and though the swing of his elbow did not hit Furusada, it did drive him back.

"That didn't hit him," said Mahiro. "He's fine." Kazuchiyo nodded but was holding his breath and couldn't reply.

They danced back and forth in that same manner for several agonizing minutes; Yagi tried to hold his ground, but his impatience got the better of him, and whenever he made too great an effort to attack, Furusada countered with incredible speed. Their audience drew tight as a bowstring as they watched the contest play out at an agonizing pace, long waits punctuated by unsuccessful strikes.

Then Furusada ducked low beneath Yagi's attack to slash at his knees. Kazuchiyo heard the scrape of metal against armor, and from his vantage could see no obvious damage done, but Yagi reared back with curses. A wild swing of his spear sent Furusada retreating out of range.

"You think you are fast," Furusada scolded him, and he flicked his sword. "You are, but only for one your size. You—"

"Shut up!" Yagi hollered, and gripping his spear at its furthest end, he swung at Furusada.

Furusada hopped backward, already out of range but startled enough by the sudden attack that instinct demanded he put more distance between him and his foe. But Yagi's aim was not to sweep his feet out from under him; he let go, heaving the mighty shaft of wood with such furious strength that it crashed into and tangled Furusada's legs before his weight was settled. He stumbled, and in that brief moment of confusion Yagi's long stride closed the distance.

The last of the Furusadas did not die well. When he lashed out, both hands gripping his katana, Yagi needed only one of his to catch his wrists and divert the hopeless attack. The other he smashed into Furusada's jaw in a fist of iron. Furusada crumpled and let out a piteous cry as Yagi's heel came down on and shattered his right knee. Soldiers on both sides grimaced as their ears rang.

"Wait," Furusada begged, but by then Yagi had retrieved his spear. "Wait, I'm—" The cross blades severed his head from his neck.

The Tendo soldiers gazed on in astonishment. Each seethed with frustration and even shame as Yagi wrenched the scabbard from Furusada's belt and sheathed the famous sword, only to then tuck it in his own belt. He left Furusada's body in the road and returned to the head of the Sakka ranks, who greeted him with a pounding of spears.

Though Kazuchiyo was far enough that his eyes could not be trusted, a glimpse of blood following Yagi back to his position was enough to spur him to action. He raised his hand, and Mahiro barked a wordless shout that stilled the men and their gloating. "Commander Umafusa!" Kazuchiyo called out to the stone-faced man who had watched three of his best fall in rapid succession. He turned his head deliberately back and forth to take in the two hills, hoping to summon whatever general stood watching over the affair. "*My* name is Aritaka Kazumune, son of Lord Aritaka of the North and of the East, and I have come to liberate Etsugo Castle. If your master would prevent me, I invite him first to come sit and drink with me so that I might know him and he might know me. There may be no need to lose any more of Tendo's skilled champions."

The Tendo soldiers looked to their commander, who remained so still atop his horse that he was beginning to appear statuesque. At last, he dismounted, and he held out his hand for a spear. Kazuchiyo's hope sank and twisted into frustration as the broad-shouldered samurai took up his position opposite Yagi.

"The beasts of Sakka are not welcome here," the commander said. "My honored general has no reason to know a toothless cub, no matter what demon he has leashed!" He straightened his back and puffed his chest. "My name is Umafu—"

Commander Umafusa was cut short by the blade of Yagi's spear piercing his shoulder. Perhaps the sight of Yagi's reckless throw against Furusada had deluded him into thinking the man had no skill to aim; if only he had witnessed his prowess at Izuho, and at Chouwa Valley, he might have feared a projectile. To his credit, it did not undo him entirely. As Yagi stormed forward, the commander ripped the spear from his shoulder and readied his own. His blood stained the carp sigil on his lovely coat red.

"You shut up!" Yagi bellowed as he advanced. The commander lunged, and driven by rage Yagi twisted too late to avoid it; the blade caught the left side of his helmet and tore it free to land a few meters away. It hindered him not at all. Fearlessly Yagi took hold of and wrenched the spear, then threw his weight forward to drive the dull end into his enemy's face.

"My lord is not a beast!" Yagi continued to holler, and as Commander Umafusa stumbled back, nose and mouth bloody, he ripped the spear out of his hands completely. "Don't you fucking say another word!" And with that he struck the commander hard in the side of the head.

Kazuchiyo watched the rest of the duel play out in an anxious haze. When Commander Umafusa leaned with the blow, his tall helmet dragged his head even lower, leaving him entirely exposed. Yagi once again attacked with the blunt wood, driving it down with such force that the man's jaw came loose with a sickening *crack*. Even when he collapsed into the road, Yagi struck again and again. Kazuchiyo flinched with each wet thud, until all that remained of Commander Umafusa's impudent mouth was a bright red smear stirred by choking gasps.

Yagi cast the spear down and stood over the body for a moment as his audience looked on. His shoulders trembled and Kazuchiyo ached, feeling as if his own chest were expanding with every haggard breath from his battle-drunk lover. Then Yagi retrieved his spear and his helmet. As he turned his back to the Tendo soldiers, Kazuchiyo was shocked to see blood matting his hair and slicking his face from the blow that had taken his helm. Even so, Yagi replaced his helmet and stalked back up the road.

The Tendo soldiers quaked, and one had courage enough to take a step forward. "Won't you at least kill him?" he cried as the commander continued to twitch and gurgle in the dirt.

Yagi faced the man and planted the end of his spear in the road. "He's a fish," he replied coldly. "Let him drown."

The remaining minnows glared back, some teary-eyed with the disgrace, each of them looking to the next as if one might be bold enough to avenge their master. Kazuchiyo gripped Hashikiri's reins to aching and did not know how to act. It was Mahiro who broke the tension; she gave a great laugh that spooked the assembly and then urged her horse forward. The Sakka soldiers quickly made way for her as Suzumekage strode to the fore, the beast's nostrils flared wide with the stink of blood, her great hooves clomping eagerly.

"Let him drown!" Mahiro repeated with vicious humor. "You poor fish are too far from your shore. Do you understand now who you challenge?" She reached Yagi and pointed to him with her naginata. "At Chibatake Bridge, the invincible Yagi-douji stood at the gates of hell and killed four thousand men single-handedly! If you have four thousand men to spare, line them up here on the road, and he'll have chewed them up by supper!"

Mahiro laughed again cruelly as she spurred Suzumekage on to circle in front of Yagi. "And once those men are spent, whoever's left can face the hell-gate itself: me!" Mahiro pounded her fist against the chest plate of her armor. "Mahiro, the Unyielding Iron! Only after that will any one of you have the privilege of facing our lord and his *ten thousand* troops. And if you think these two molehills will stop us, ha!"

Mahiro stopped in front of the soldier that had spoken in defense of his commander and leveled her naginata at him. "Carry your dead back up that hill and convince your general to bargain, or else you might as well throw yourself on my blade right now."

The soldier shrank back, furious but shaken. Mahiro let his own silence humiliate him a while longer and then with a satisfied "Ha!" she turned Suzumekage back and returned to Yagi's side. The pair of them watched, frightening sentinels, as the soldiers gathered their dead and nearly dead and retreated back into the forested hill.

Kazuchiyo unwound his stiff fingers and looked again to the southern hill. Only the temple's eaves returned his seeking gaze. Minutes later, a new commander appeared from the north and stepped onto the road. Though at first Kazuchiyo eyed him warily, he relaxed once more as the man offered a deep bow.

"My master, the general Umafusa, requests an audience with Lord Aritaka," he reported. "In three hours' time, at Agarigumo Temple just south of here."

At last, the grip on Kazuchiyo's ribs eased enough that he could answer. "In three hours' time, I will meet him here, and nowhere else."

The commander hemmed. "Forgive me if northern custom differs, but a meeting here? On the road?"

"Nowhere else," Kazuchiyo repeated. "We will hoist a tent, and he may bring some men if he likes. Tell him so."

"I will," the man said, and he bobbed once before righting himself to return up the slope.

Kazuchiyo led his own soldiers back up the road to their camp. At the summit Naoya and his commanders were waiting, all eager to congratulate the victorious Yagi-douji upon his return. Some of them failed in their courage to do so: Yagi was a fearsome sight, blood-splattered and eyes cold, every inch of him fit for his name. Even Kazuchiyo gulped as he lowered himself from his saddle. It was both so similar to and so different from his first memory of meeting Yagi on the battlefield, his heart did not know whether to turn toward anxiety or awe. He stopped in front of Yagi and was at a loss for what to say.

Yagi took in a deep breath and pulled the sheathed sword from his belt. He handed off his spear to one of the surrounding soldiers so that he could present the blade with both hands. "He said this sword is named... Itogiri. I don't know if it is famous, but it's yours."

Kazuchiyo accepted the weapon, though it felt heavier than he thought it should. "You performed exceptionally and did your lord proud," he said. "Have the physicians tend your wounds. You'll have a seat of honor at today's meeting."

Yagi bowed, and as he righted himself Kazuchiyo at last saw in him a momentary lapse: his eyelids fluttered dizzily, though his posture remained resolute. "I was only doing my duty," he said, and the surrounding men bowed their heads, inspired.

Yagi moved on toward the recovery tents, a flock of eager admirers in his wake. As he left, Kazuchiyo clicked Itogiri out of its sheath. Sure enough, the sword's name and the name of the smith who had forged it were engraved on the blade, though it was not one Kazuchiyo had ever heard of.

"Well?" goaded Mahiro. "Is it as fine as he boasted?"

"Hard to say." Kazuchiyo sheathed the blade once more and looked to Mahiro, standing so tall and sure of herself. "Thank you for what you did down there," he told her. "You were incredible."

Mahiro laughed and then leaned in closer. "What's *most* incredible is that you've fucked that," she said, gesturing after Yagi's retreating back. "Tell me it's as good as I'm imagining."

Kazuchiyo flushed and sputtered, and with another laugh Mahiro slapped his back. "I'm going to pull out all our finest for the meeting," she said. "We'll set up the tent and a perimeter. Get your stomach back by then, all right?"

Kazuchiyo took a deep breath and nodded. "I will. Thank you."

Naoya came to him next, eager to gush over Yagi's valiant performance. Kazuchiyo indulged him as much as his wits allowed and then related their plan for the meeting in three hours. With Naoya's assurance that he would help oversee the preparations, Kazuchiyo found the time to steal away for a while and headed for the physicians' tent.

He entered to the tension of a stalemate: Yagi sat at the

center, still half clad in his armor and drinking from a saké gourd, while those meant to be assisting him sat back in nervous indecision. Though Kazuchiyo himself had been struck with similar paralysis not long before, he had no patience or sympathy for the pair when Yagi so clearly required their care. He shed his gloves and swords, and marched to Yagi's side.

"Loosen those cords on his shins," Kazuchiyo instructed them as he kneeled beside his lover. "He may have been wounded near the knee."

"It's just a scratch," Yagi grumbled. He hissed and leaned back as Kazuchiyo slicked his bloody hair back, searching for the wound on his head. "Don't fuss over me—I'm fine."

"You're still bleeding," Kazuchiyo protested, and he sent a sharp look at the still anxious physicians. "Come and loosen these cords. I'm ordering you."

Both men bowed their heads to the floor and then scuttled closer. Just as Kazuchiyo had expected, removing the armor revealed a laceration just above Yagi's left knee where Furusada had struck. It did not look deep, but the blood had soaked through his pant leg.

Yagi snorted. "Just a scratch."

"There's no such thing," Kazuchiyo scolded him. "It will be difficult to care for it properly in a camp like this, and it may take us days to retake the castle. Promise me you'll let the physicians keep it clean and well-tended."

Yagi pulled a face, but seeing that Kazuchiyo would accept no other answer, he nodded. "Fine."

Kazuchiyo accepted a length of cloth from one of the physicians and used it to begin mopping the blood from Yagi's face. "Good. Now hold still."

Yagi begrudgingly did so, at last allowing Kazuchiyo to part his hair away from the shallow gash just above his temple. He betrayed very few outward signs of pain as the wound was cleaned, but when Kazuchiyo accepted a jar of bright red healer's resin to help close it, he began to squirm anew.

"The lord's son shouldn't be tending soldiers' wounds,"

Yagi mumbled.

"Soldiers shouldn't frighten off their physicians before they can be tended," Kazuchiyo replied, and he smiled with a bittersweet memory. "It's not the first time, in any case. If I can't fight with you at the vanguard, I can at least do this much."

Yagi fell still again while the physicians finished cleaning and wrapping his knee. He even allowed one to apply a length of clean linen around his head, though he grumbled all the while. "I'll take that off before the meeting," he promised gruffly. He pushed the saké gourd at them. "Bring more wine."

"Bring ginseng," Kazuchiyo corrected him, and he quickly dismissed the pair so he could face Yagi with some degree of privacy. Their time was short, and so many words had piled up behind his tongue. "You fought magnificently," he said. "I wish I had your bravery; I held my breath for so long, I'm surprised I didn't fall out of Hashikiri's saddle!"

Yagi frowned and glanced away. Realizing how he might have sounded, Kazuchiyo quickly corrected himself, adding, "Not that I doubted your strength. I always believed that you would win."

"So did I," said Yagi, and from any other mouth the words might have been boastful, but he spoke them bitterly. "They knew it, too, so I don't know why they bothered."

Kazuchiyo glanced to the exit of the tent to be sure they still had privacy and then scooted closer. "You *do* know—we've talked about this before. They were serving their lord's and their families' interests."

"Volunteering to be killed by a monster doesn't help *anyone*," Yagi insisted, gesturing in frustration. "I don't understand why—"

Kazuchiyo snatched his hand and gave it a firm squeeze. "Don't say that. You're not a monster, and that's not what happened down there."

Yagi's shoulders crept up. "That's not—that isn't how I meant it. That's not the point."

"I still don't want to hear you say that about yourself," said Kazuchiyo. When Yagi tried to pull his hand free, he did not allow it. "Whatever the enemy thinks, that's not what you are."

"But you're the one who—" Yagi started to say, though he then stopped himself with a guilty wince. Even not knowing how he meant to finish, Kazuchiyo's chest tightened. "It doesn't matter," Yagi tried again. "I offered to do this and it worked, so there's nothing to complain about."

"Yagi…" Kazuchiyo squirmed and did not know what to say, feeling just as he had on the road, watching his champion brandish his spear against strangers. He licked his lips. "You've been working very hard lately," he said. "I know you're trying to… do things, and be things, for my sake as the leader of this army. But I don't want you to push yourself this much if it's vexing you. You don't have to try so hard to be a samurai."

Yagi looked away again, and Kazuchiyo could see already that he would get nothing more from him. When he gave his hand a gentler tug, Kazuchiyo let it go. "Will you help me loosen this armor?" he asked. "I want to lie down for a while."

"Of course," said Kazuchiyo, and he did so.

By the time the physicians returned with brewed ginseng, Yagi was free from his armor and had fallen asleep. Kazuchiyo took some of the tea for himself and remained for a while. As he had anticipated, Yagi's sleep was not restful, and several times he passed his fingers through Yagi's hair to calm his unconscious grumblings. With his words having failed the task of consoling the man, he hoped a gesture of peace would suffice.

He wished very much that Amai was with him then.

CHAPTER NINE

hree hours after the end of the bloody duels on the road, the meeting among the four armies commenced. Kazuchiyo's soldiers had constructed a square perimeter of tall, fabric walls overlapping the packed earth, which required some monitoring from extra soldiers to keep them upright, or so it was made to seem. So, too, was it supposedly mere coincidence that the Sakka-Kibaku seat was placed at a slightly higher elevation than that of their guests, given the terrain. Even the easterly wall had been heightened with banners ostensibly to block the climbing sun, though it just so happened to also hide any movements from Kazuchiyo's camp.

Whatever the uncertainties in his personal affairs, Kazuchiyo performed the role of daimyo heir to a level of perfection Lord Aritaka would have envied. He descended from his hillside camp with his bannermen in full, flanking display, Naoya beside him in his tall, winged helm, Yagi and Mahiro flaunting their beastly armor and flashing weapons on either side. Spectacle fit for a future shogun, one might say. As they stepped down from their horses and took their seats within the enclosure, Kazuchiyo cast a glance to Yagi on his right. They had spoken only a few casual words since the tent, and though

130

Yagi looked to be in slightly better spirits, Kazuchiyo could not help that the tension between them weighed on him.

The panels ahead of them parted, and in stepped the general and his commanders. Kazuchiyo was somewhat disappointed to see at once that General Umafusa did not share the most obvious of his relation's faults: though his aqua jinbaori with carp brocade was just as fine, his helmet was squat and practical, and his demeanor was that of steeled patience. He strode to the mat that had been left out for him and took his place with the even pace of a man well used to the formalities of war; he was joined by a pair of equally sturdy commanders.

However, it was the second pair that followed that was of particular interest to Kazuchiyo: the two mysterious men from the fire attack on Kanrei. With General Umafusa so intent on holding his gaze, he did not think it wise to glance or signal to his companions, though he hoped that Yagi, if no one else, would recognize them, the elder onmyouji with his thick mane of silver hair, and his younger, nameless samurai—General Kamayari, Amai had called him. Both were still conspicuously devoid of family decorations, considering the flamboyance of their company.

"Welcome, gentlemen," Kazuchiyo greeted the assembly once everyone was seated. "I am Aritaka Kazumune, joined by General Oihata Naoya of Kibaku, and I thank you for accepting my invitation."

He bowed over his crossed legs, as did his companions. General Umafusa then returned the courtesy. "I am General Umafusa Kusagao, and I am honored to have accepted. It is good that we are able to meet."

"Will you not also do us the courtesy of introducing your companions?" asked Naoya, and the edge to his voice made it very clear to Kazuchiyo that he had picked the onmyouji out after all.

General Umafusa glanced to him, betraying in that moment what Kazuchiyo had begun to suspect: this was some ruse, and despite appearances the general was not the highest ranking of his group. Even so, the old man lowered his head with the deference of a common commander.

"My name is Mutsuyama," he said humbly. "I am only here as an advisor. Please do not bear me any mind."

The younger general bowed his head, though not far enough to break his malicious gaze toward Kazuchiyo. "Myself, likewise," he said, making no effort to introduce himself.

Naoya huffed quietly, but he held his tongue. Seeing that they could expect no more than that, Kazuchiyo sat up straighter. "Then we had best begin. I assume there is much for us to discuss."

"Not so much," replied General Umafusa. "Your interference here is unwelcome, and I would ask you to leave."

"I bet you would," goaded Mahiro. "Who wouldn't after seeing what our oni can do?"

Yagi sat up straighter. As promised, he had shed the bandage around his head and covered the one wrapping his knee to erase any evidence of weakness. The enemy's blood, however, he had declined to have cleaned from his armor. General Umafusa regarded him stoically, and though his face betrayed very little, he was not fool enough to be completely unintimidated. "The Yagi-douji fought exceptionally," he congratulated his foe grimly. "Four fine men to his credit, who would thank him for the opportunity."

Yagi frowned, and he struggled a moment as if hedging over a response. Kazuchiyo spoke up in his stead. "Four, General? Did your commander not survive his injuries?"

"No. He did not." Grief tightened his expression but was soon gone again. "But that has little to do with our reason for being here, or yours. Again, I ask you to leave."

"Not until you and your forces leave the castle Etsugo in peace," said Naoya, with such righteous passion that one might forget how callously he had regarded the Jisu plight upon first learning of it. "Has the Umafusa clan not shamed itself enough by throwing its squabbles onto our doorstep? There can be no glory in an unprovoked assault such as this."

"Unprovoked?" repeated Umafusa. "If your new Jisu allies haven't enlightened you as to our business here, perhaps the general Oihata should hold his tongue."

Naoya puffed his chest indignantly. "You have attacked temples and occupied a civilian settlement," he retorted. "You hold its people captive at the onset of the harvest season. Spin whatever poor excuses you will, but your behavior speaks for itself and is abominable."

"Our means are justified by—"

"My lords," interrupted Mutsuyama, and watching Umafusa silence himself so immediately solidified Kazuchiyo's assumptions of their true hierarchy. "I don't believe that anything can be gained by arguing over who started this conflict."

"Agreed," said Mahiro, smirking. "And no use wondering who will end it either. That's been long decided now."

Umafusa's attention slid to her with a wary disdain that had Kazuchiyo bristling on her behalf. He took a deep breath to settle his tone before he spoke. "As my sister has said, we here may decide the end of this conflict—right now if we choose. None of us wants to keep our soldiers away from their homes and families into autumn. If you insist on holding the siege, that could become a reality, but it doesn't have to be."

"Are you really here to bargain for Etsugo with not one member of Clan Dada beside you?" challenged Umafusa. "What do you have to offer?"

"To offer?" Naoya repeated incredulously. "As if it is Tendo that deserves to be appeased?"

"My father, lord of Tendo, has commanded me to extend his governance," said Umafusa, and he looked to Kazuchiyo. "Just as your father has doubtlessly commanded you. I will not return to him empty-handed any more than you will."

Kazuchiyo regarded the man silently for a moment. Whether his loyalty really lived in Tendo with his father, or in the silver-haired onmyouji that watched the pair of them so closely, Kazuchiyo had to admit that the general had so far outdone all his relations in terms of wit. It made him hopeful, and he felt the return of his confidence. This was an arena he could excel in unquestionably.

"You're not mistaken," Kazuchiyo said, "and I understand your aim. You would have me promise you Castle Shihomi in Izuho in exchange for Etsugo. Controlling the mouth of the river would be a great boon to a coastal province like yours. A wise man suggested that I do just that to end this war." Kazuchiyo sharpened his attention to Umafusa alone. "But let me make you a greater offer."

It seemed to take some effort on Umafusa's part to not again look to Mutsuyama for guidance. "I'm listening."

"In the time of legends, all of Eastern Shuyun was unified as a single kingdom," Kazuchiyo obliged him, summoning forth the grandiosity of his late father. "The unconquerable nation of Touyun, rooted in the heart of the Dragonlands. After a thousand years those bonds are being reforged through Lord Aritaka's strength of leadership." Though it put a thorn in his heart, he swallowed and continued. "Sakka and Suyama were once enemies, but now we are joined together as one. The merchants of Yaefu, the priests of Namugi, and the Jewel of Izuho have also pledged to our cause. We are even blessed to have earned the camaraderie of Clan Koedzuka and their mighty samurai of the plains." Beside him, Naoya tilted his chin. "By the time this conflict has ended, Mount Etsuzan herself will bow to Aritaka, Lord of the East."

He paused, allowing the gravity of those accomplishments to weigh on the general, and they appeared to do so quite heavily. Mutsuyama and his warrior, on the other hand, stared on without any change of expression. Kazuchiyo continued, saying, "And yet, with all this strength, we cannot boast that our naval prowess matches that of the fleet of Tendo. Even as far away as Sakka, Lord Aritaka speaks enviously of your fine ships. I would have that strength for my army."

"I'm sure you would," replied General Umafusa, "but a bear can never hope to tame the sea."

"I do not seek to tame the sea at all. I seek to unleash it."

General Umafusa leaned back, and for the first time since the meeting began, Kazuchiyo saw a shift in the kamayari general behind Mutsuyama: the man's gaze grew sharp and hard, not unlike the polished blade of his spear. In his dark eyes Kazuchiyo saw a strength of hatred he did not expect, challenging him to speak the rest of his design. Daring him to speak aloud a conviction not yet firmly settled in his heart.

Had I been at his side then, perhaps I would have cautioned Kazuchiyo against it. Perhaps I would have been wrong to do so; even hindsight is not always clear. But history will remember that Kazuchiyo looked the shogun's general in the eye when he said, "I would ask the navy of Tendo to help me take the capital when the time comes."

General Umafusa swallowed. "You would make an enemy of the Oomiyari and defy the emperor himself?"

"My father has charged me with the task of making him shogun," Kazuchiyo continued. "For that, yes, I would remove Lord Oomiyari. Hopefully with the emperor's blessing. We are all very aware that His Excellency did not appoint Clan Oomiyari for the love of them, and they have vastly underperformed in their duties. When was the last time a shogun's magistrate showed his face in the east?" Kazuchiyo allowed some of his true frustration to show through as he added, "If the lord of the emperor's armies can only stand idly by while us country lords reap slaughter on each other for generations, what purpose does he serve? Whose justice prevails?"

At last, Umafusa turned to look at Mutsuyama, but the old man betrayed nothing, leaving him to fend for himself. He cleared his throat. "The shogun's mantle is heavier than you know, young lord."

"My father has the strength to bear it," Kazuchiyo replied, feeling all the more bolstered. "As do I. Does the strength of my allies not attest so?" Kazuchiyo gestured to his companions, who all sat straight and tall and boastful. "Last year, I crossed the Fukugawa and claimed Lord Koedzuka as my ally. He has already pledged to come down from Ugarasu Castle to meet with me and the lady Dada once she is liberated, to seal our alliance."

He fixed Umafusa with a hopeful look. "I would like to invite the lord of Tendo to that same hall, so that when we march down from these hills into the emperor's hallowed lands, it will be with vibrant aqua banners alongside ours."

"I…" Umafusa stared back at him, at a loss. "I cannot speak for my father, not on a matter that important," he said haltingly.

"Of course not." Kazuchiyo relaxed his shoulders and gentled his tone. "Send a messenger to Lord Tendo and tell him I offer partnership, not servitude. We needn't be hasty when so much is at stake."

"And while we wait for his reply, your reinforcements will arrive," said Umafusa. "You are still demanding a choice from me."

Naoya cleared his throat, though he took Kazuchiyo's example by not employing his usual grandiosity when he spoke. "You and I are generals, sir, but our choices made on the field carry just as much weight as a lord's decree. You cannot escape the responsibility of that choice." He smiled. "But you needn't fear, for Lord Kazumune has come in trust and friendship, and if you meet him in kind, every ally of his is also yours."

Still Umafusa hedged, sweat on his brow. He looked to Mutsuyama, who still looked utterly unconcerned. The old man viewed Umafusa's strain stoically and told him, "You heard the man. Make a choice, General."

Umafusa grimaced, and his gaze went to Yagi. Kazuchiyo understood at once what his trepidation meant, but he kept his composure as Umafusa bowed his head and said, "Then I will return to my camp to prepare."

"Prepare your parchment," Mahiro goaded, "or prepare your soldiers?"

Umafusa pushed to his feet, and Yagi was the first to follow suit; Umafusa's attention to him had not gone unnoticed, and he also tensed in preparation. Kazuchiyo's heart began to pound as he and the others also stood. "General Umafusa, please," he tried one more time. "Think of your men."

"I am," Umafusa replied. "May you do the same." And with that he turned to exit the enclosure.

The Tendo commanders left with him immediately, but the nameless general hesitated, his face still full of hatred. Instead of returning his anger, Kazuchiyo calmly asked, "Are you hoping to make good on your threat from the other night?"

"Yes," the man replied instantly, fists clenching as if aching for his weapon. "Keep your neck clean so that it does not sully my spear when the time comes." Even after Yagi put himself between the pair, hackles raised, it took Mutsuyama patting the general's shoulder guard to convince him to withdraw. He saved his glare for Kazuchiyo as long as he was able.

"We need to go right now," said Yagi, just as someone beyond the tent gave a sharp whistle.

The four remaining in the tent threw themselves into the shadow of the enclosure's walls just as a hail of arrows arched from the hill. Several of the projectiles bore fire, which seared the fabric and the posts it was attached to; however, such a relatively small number had little hope of causing a significant blaze. Kazuchiyo had barely enough time to wonder at the strategy before Naoya was lifting his arm.

"Let go of the posts!" Naoya shouted, and as their soldiers followed the command, a great burst of wind erupted from his raised hand. The gust extinguished every flame, flattened the square enclosure with great flaps and clatters, and sent the second volley of arrows spinning off harmlessly to either side of the road.

The collapse of the structure revealed General Umafusa and his men having not withdrawn far; they were still clustered at the base of the hill, forming into ranks with more soldiers emerging from the woods. His sudden exposure seemed to catch him off guard, and he looked quickly between the fallen tent and the retreating Mutsuyama. "Master Mutsuyama?" he called in confusion.

Mutsuyama and his general had already mounted their horses. Though Kazuchiyo braced himself, expecting the old onmyouji to unleash his magic on them, Mutsuyama did not spare Umafusa even a glance as he spurred his mount. The pair of them and their unmarked entourage beat a hasty retreat to the south, toward the eaves of the distant Agarigumo Temple.

Umafusa stood bewildered. As he struggled to reclaim his wits and his command, Mahiro's whistle brought Suzumekage quickly to her. "Gutless minnows!" she bellowed as she hoisted herself into the saddle. "I'll carve out your eyes!" Naginata brandished, she charged down the hillside.

Half of Kazuchiyo's bannermen drew their swords and followed her with righteous shouts; the other half encircled their lord, Sakka banners raised high to guard against another volley of arrows. Though Yagi's mouth was twisted in a snarl of rage, he stayed at Kazuchiyo's side, one hand gripping his chest plate protectively. Kazuchiyo allowed his guards to urge him back up the road and saved his attention for the skirmish. As Naoya continued to deflect arrows with great swirls of wind, Mahiro and Suzumekage cut a path through the dozen hastily assembled Tendo soldiers. Umafusa's long spear stood poised, but he was no match for the peerless coordination of woman and beast that was the Iron Gate; Suzumekage dodged left and allowed Mahiro to slip past his defenses, and the flash of her naginata cut Umafusa's shoulder guard from his arm.

Hooves thundered down the road above, and Kazuchiyo turned to see Commander Ginta and his cavalry charging to their rescue. Seeing this as well, General Umafusa, awash with blood, shouted for the retreat. He and his men fled for the wooded hillside. Though the Sakka soldiers attempted to give chase, the Tendo archers adjusted their arched shots to more level, and more lethal, trajectories. Naoya called for retreat, and with haste both sides fled up their respective hills and into safety.

"Cowards and traitors!" Mahiro ranted as she and

Suzumekage paced back and forth at the road's summit. She twisted free an arrow that had lodged itself in Suzumekage's saddle and cast it down to be crushed by angry hooves. "I can't believe you offered to make them our allies, brother. They don't deserve to... to breathe your same air! Slimy, brainless eels, every one of them!"

"Mahiro, calm down," said Kazuchiyo, not that he expected to her to obey. He held still as Yagi checked him over for arrow wounds. "We knew there was a chance they would try to ambush us."

"Not enough pecker on all'a them combined for a full cock, the ungrateful cretins," Mahiro continued to ramble. "I'm going to take his head and steam it to garnish my supper!"

"Are you all right?" Yagi asked of Kazuchiyo, even having just surveyed him himself. "You weren't hit?"

"No, not even a scratch." Kazuchiyo took in a deep breath and let it out slowly to settle his nerves. "Damn it all, though. I really thought I had convinced him."

Naoya shook his head as the three of them turned to survey the two hills, which now stood as quiet and seemingly empty as they ever had. "You mustn't blame yourself, Kazumune," he said. "You spoke extremely well. Had Lord Koedzuka not promised us to your cause already, I would have sworn my loyalty on the spot!" He gave a huff of disdain. "If the generals of Tendo are too proud and foolish to sail the waters of history, let them be drowned by them."

"It was Mutsuyama," said Kazuchiyo. Already he had begun to replay the encounter in his mind, trying hard to remember every slight reaction of the men's faces and which words of his had caused them. "General Umafusa was too afraid to betray the shogun in front of him."

"He must have thought that being judged disloyal was more dangerous than Ebara's spear," supposed Naoya.

"Yes." Kazuchiyo sighed and extended his gaze to Etsugo. "Amai was right. Those men must have been sent by Shogun Oomiyari." He frowned. "If they're so intent on killing me, I

139

wonder why they retreated with so little effort."

Naoya nodded, his expression deeply contemplative. "A handful of fire arrows wasn't enough to set the tent stakes alight, but they might have been if only Mutsuyama had employed his magic. They must have intended to start an inferno. If so, why didn't they? Flattering though it would be, I can't imagine Mutsuyama is that wary of *me*."

"Even General Umafusa seemed surprised that Mutsuyama and his samurai didn't participate in the counterattack," said Kazuchiyo. "They had to have planned in advance. So, why the change?"

They stood silent and contemplative for a moment, but when neither was able to provide even speculation, Naoya shook his head again. "No matter. It tells us enough: that the Oomiyari know your aim now and are wisely apprehensive. We should end this siege as quickly as possible before they're able to draw more troops."

"I agree." Kazuchiyo allowed his manners to soften. "Thank you for your support and your confidence."

Naoya offered him a grin in return. "It is my pleasure, as always. You don't know what good it does my heart to hear your convictions stated so clearly. No man could ever doubt you lack the strength to bear the shogun's mantle."

"You honor me," said Kazuchiyo, though the praise in fact weighed heavily on him.

Once Naoya had moved on to tend his troops, Yagi stepped forward to take his place. "You're really all right?" he asked of Kazuchiyo.

"Yes, entirely." Kazuchiyo patted himself down one more time to prove it and then offered Yagi a smile. "I'm sorry—I really am doing my best to stay off the front lines, as I promised."

Yagi nodded, though his concern seemed to already be changing course. Once he had worked up the courage, he asked, "So you really *do* want to be shogun?"

Kazuchiyo was taken aback, and for the briefest of moments he even resented Yagi somewhat for asking such an obvious question he was nevertheless unprepared to answer. It had been so easy when swept up in the pageantry of the negotiation, but set before the stern eyes of his lover, there was no role for him to play and nowhere to hide. He swallowed and said, "That's why we're here."

Yagi frowned, seemingly frustrated by Kazuchiyo's obvious non-answer. Even so, he bowed his head in acknowledgement. "Then I'm with you."

"Then *be* with me," Kazuchiyo said, hushed and urgent so only Yagi would hear. "Say you'll spend the night with me tonight."

"All right," Yagi replied, to Kazuchiyo's great relief. He shifted within his armor. "For now I'll go talk to Captain Nishigame and find out how many were wounded in the ambush just now."

Kazuchiyo blinked curiously toward the soldiers still gathered on the road, who were tending to those struck by the Tendo arrows. Among them was an elderly captain, broad and sturdy, with scars on his face. Kazuchiyo recognized the man as having stood behind Yagi at Kanrei Temple and during the duels earlier, though he had never thought to ask his name, and was a bit surprised that Yagi had.

"Yes, please do," said Kazuchiyo. "Thank you. Now that we know Umafusa won't bargain, we need to shift all our focus to the battle."

"I'll return to you later," Yagi promised, and he moved away to complete his duty while Kazuchiyo continued on toward his.

CHAPTER TEN

As promised, Yagi spent the night in Kazuchiyo's tent. There was not much romance to be had, but the simple intimacy of having Yagi asleep in his arms was a much-needed comfort to Kazuchiyo. By morning, however, he was just as eager for Amai's company, and he resolved that the time had come to advance their goals.

Kazuchiyo gathered his peers and commanders in the war tent just after breakfast and there outlined his strategy. "General Umafusa was wounded in the ambush yesterday," he said, offering a nod of thanks to Mahiro. She puffed her chest proudly. "We'll have to act swiftly to take advantage of that, and also of the fact that there was confusion between him and his allies. The strength of their gauntlet depends on coordination between their two forces spread between the hills. Disrupting that cooperation is a must."

"Then we choose one hill and swarm them," suggested Mahiro. "All at once, full force."

"I thought we were going to try to draw them down," said Yagi, frowning.

"And what you did yesterday was a great success for us," Kazuchiyo was quick to reassure him. "Now that we've met the man face to face, we understand better who we're dealing with: a clever man split across two masters."

Naoya nodded along. "He's probably been ordered to keep that hill no matter the cost, and he fears the shogun's wrath more than ours."

"Yes, which makes our path clear." Kazuchiyo reached across the map spread before them to tap the southern hill. "We attack Mutsuyama's forces at the temple, swinging wide and attacking from the southeast. If we can take that hill, we'll have cut Umafusa off from Mutsuyama's influence. We'll also have prevented him from retreating and from receiving any Tendo reinforcements. He will be forced to act."

Captain Yamamori, a middle-aged man whom Chikakuni had left in charge of the Jisu troops, bowed his head shortly. "Lord Sakka, even an attack from that angle would invite Umafusa down the hill to pincer us. We would have to take the hill very quickly to avoid that."

"We will," said Kazuchiyo. "And we will have a deterrent to keep Umafusa at bay." He began positioning tiles across the map. "We attack just after dusk. Commander Rakuteru and his riders will light torches and stand ready at the crest of the road, ready to cut off any attempt of Umafusa's to descend the hill. Our plan with Commander Chikakuni was to attack on the second night after they arrived, so hopefully we can count on some support from the castle itself."

"My men will be ready," Ginta promised. "But have we even confirmed that Commander Chikakuni reached the castle at all?"

"No," Kazuchiyo admitted, "but I have faith in him, and in the strength of Lady Dada and her samurai."

Captain Yamamori nodded his wholehearted support. "Etsugo has stood for a hundred years. It stands ready now."

"Then we have our strategy," said Naoya confidently. "All we need now is to carry it out."

The council disbanded, and each of them separated to prepare each portion of their army for the coming attack.

They made no attempt to hide their efforts; emboldened by his measure of Umafusa and the support of his peers, Kazuchiyo felt confident enough that he hoped to draw the enemy's attention, as well as its dread.

He stood at the crest of the hill to survey the landscape that would soon be their battleground. The remnants of their collapsed tent remained at the bottom of the hill, bloodstains pounded into the dirt beneath it. Though he could see no movement from either hill nor the castle, he sensed each of the gathered armies, like cords of armor drawing tight.

As Kazuchiyo watched, painting images of the battle to come across the hills and roads, Yagi came to stand beside him. "Looks like he sent you a message after all," Yagi said, but it took him pointing toward the edge of the camp for Kazuchiyo to understand his meaning.

A small fox sat just beyond the brush surrounding their camp. Its fur was mottled rusty red, but its face was pure white, with startling blue eyes fixed straight ahead. Kazuchiyo met its gaze and could have sworn he sensed intelligence from the calmly staring creature.

"That's an unusual coat for a fox," said Kazuchiyo. "Perhaps it's a good omen." The longer the fox stared at him, however, the less he felt confident in that assessment. He would have expected it to skitter off after being discovered, yet it remained, with calm and unhurried judgment.

Kazuchiyo shook his head and turned away, determined not to be swayed by even such a handsome specter. "How are your injuries?" he asked Yagi. "I wish we could delay a little longer, for your sake."

"I'm fine," Yagi assured him, and he stomped his foot twice to prove it. "I'm not worried. As long as Oihata can handle their onmyouji, I'll take care of the samurai."

Kazuchiyo felt a chill as he recalled the hateful glare of Mutsuyama's nameless warrior. "That man was likely sent by the shogun," he cautioned. "He may be from the Oomiyari clan itself. I trust in your skill, but please don't underestimate him."

"No samurai can kill me," Yagi boasted, though he then fixed Kazuchiyo with a serious look. "You'll stay with the command unit, won't you?"

"I'll stay safe," Kazuchiyo promised. "I don't want you to worry about me while you're out there."

"Same to you." Yagi glanced past him and frowned. "Let's get back to work."

He turned to head back into the camp, watching Kazuchiyo expectantly. Kazuchiyo's curiosity got the better of him, and instead of joining him right away he looked back to the underbrush. The fox with the white face was still there, still watching him. He tried hard to put it out of his mind.

The eastern army formed their ranks as the sun drifted below Mount Etsuzan to the west. As the valley was draped in shadow, Commander Rakuteru and his fifty riders lit torches at the crest of the hill, illuminating their banners in a proud display. Their horses pawed the earth and they drummed the ends of their spears against the road. It would take a braver man than General Umafusa Kusagao to step brazenly upon the road, seeing what death waited above.

Meanwhile, Captain Yamamori led the bulk of their soldiers through the brush to the south. The terrain was rough and difficult to navigate in the waning light, but his Jisu troops were sure-footed and marked the path. Down the slope they marched, vigilant and eager for battle, Yagi and Mahiro steadfast at the fore. With Naoya among the leading troops as well, to counter Mutsuyama's magic, Kazuchiyo alone held the command unit, surrounded by his bannermen. He followed at a conservative pace and distance, one eye ever to the north.

The vanguard reached the base of the temple hill while Kazuchiyo was still descending. Though frustrated by the distance, it afforded him as clear a view as could be expected of the battle that was to come. He halted his march and looked on, determined to bear witness with impartial logic. Whatever a shogun's onmyouji and his soldiers could level at them, he would not be prepared to counter if his mind was full of personal concerns.

Then came movement from the north. Though the distance was too great for making out detail, a commotion of raised voices echoed from Castle Etsugo atop its plateau. The sputtering lights of torches outside Etsugo's main gate pitched and swayed, and in some places flared as if catching on tents or banners. Kazuchiyo strained his eyes to no avail.

"Signal the attack," he ordered, and the head of his bannermen put an oxen horn to his lips. Two hard blows spurred the vanguard up the southern hill, into the line of trees.

Kazuchiyo stared hard into the ever-growing darkness. He could barely make out the flash of Mahiro's white mane as she and Suzumekage plunged into the enemy's held territory, and then nothing. Each breath came, slow and measured, as he waited for the sounds of conflict to echo forth. As time passed, however, and more and more of his army disappeared into the trees, there were no clashes of steel or shouting men. The army's pace did not slow as it would if confronted with opposition. Their silence as fragments of commotion continued to echo down from the castle filled Kazuchiyo with anxiety, and when he could bear it no longer, he motioned one of his bannermen forward.

"Send a messenger to the front," he ordered. "Find out what's happening up there." The man nodded and passed the order on.

Within half an hour, the bulk of the army had progressed up the hill, and the Sakka messenger returned with curious news. "My lord, there aren't any troops on this hill. The temple is empty."

"Empty?" Kazuchiyo repeated, dumbstruck. "Is it certain there's no trap? Some ploy by the onmyouji?"

"Sir Oihata is examining the grounds," said the messenger,

"but he says there's no sign of curses or spells."

Kazuchiyo glanced again to the north, where the battle outside Etsugo's gate continued in unintelligible shadow. Though instinct told him to be wary, he could not bear the thought of that resistance going to waste, should he react with cowardice. "Then we advance," he said, and he motioned for his men to pass the order to the rest of the command unit. "We take the temple as planned. Onward!"

The remainder of the army marched ahead. As Kazuchiyo and the command unit entered the forested slope, they were greeted by Yagi and his growing number of admirers. "It looks like they've abandoned their camp here," Yagi reported, "but we wanted to accompany you, in case they've been waiting for you to show up personally."

"Thank you for your foresight," replied Kazuchiyo, and he accepted their escort the rest of the way.

The Agarigumo Temple was a tall, handsome building, its pagoda several stories tall, with sloped eaves that gave it a similar appearance to the evergreen trees surrounding it. It was also quite empty. Though imprints in the courtyard earth and piles of charred wood indicated the presence of a military camp only recently, no scrap of armor or provisions remained. After inquiring about the temple's administrators, Kazuchiyo was led by reluctant soldiers to the rear of the compound, where he was greeted by a gruesome discovery: a dozen corpses piled and burned, little more than blackened bone.

"Monstrous," said Oihata tremulously, tears in his eyes as he beheld with Kazuchiyo the cruel spectacle. "If these *are* the shogun's men, his rule cannot end soon enough."

"Agreed," said Kazuchiyo, and though his heart ached for the unfortunate victims, he was just as anxious as to learn of his own army's fate. "Did you find no trace of them?"

Oihata shook his head in frustration. "There are several narrow paths down the hill, all heavily forested. Any one of them could have shielded their retreat. I've sent scouts out to try and determine their whereabouts."

"We don't have time." Kazuchiyo grimaced at the piled bodies and then turned to march into the temple.

While Mahiro kept order and vigilance among the ranks, Kazuchiyo scaled the pagoda as high as the weathered stairs would allow. A young captain with the same thought was already at a window on the top floor, peering out through the nighttime haze. He snapped into a bow as Kazuchiyo approached. "My lord! It's very difficult to make out, but I believe Etsugo's gates are open."

Kazuchiyo leaned forward to see for himself. The castle was lit up with torches, the distant battle cries of its soldiers a seething murmur. "You're right," he said, and his impatience grew sharp in his chest. He crossed the chamber to a south-facing window. Though Jisu's dense woods and the hill itself prevented a clear view, he was sure of his eyes: torches were burning in a gully to the south.

"They knew we'd come," Kazuchiyo said, unable to keep from speaking the revelation aloud as soon as it reached his mind. Mutsuyama and his shogun's dog, who had given up their chance to assassinate him just a day before, had been biding their time for the chance to ensnare Kazuchiyo's entire army.

Kazuchiyo hurried back down the pagoda and gathered his peers in the courtyard. "Mutsuyama and his men are south of us," he reported. "I'd ask our scouts to confirm, but we've very little time; Etsugo has opened its gates and is pressing the attack. If we don't persuade Umafusa to engage us now, he'll have an opening to take the castle."

"If that old fart is to the south, he'll march right up our ass the moment we try anything against Umafusa," Mahiro warned him.

"That is true even if we remain on this hill," replied Oihata. "If they've camped on this hill for days, they will know the best avenues of attack. We are already caught in their pincer."

"Then we take a note from the fish and wiggle free!" Mahiro pounded the butt of her naginata against the packed earth. "Let's make a line directly for the castle! Mutsuyama won't be able to catch us before we reach it, and that dickless eel will still have our cavalry riding down him."

In his haste, Kazuchiyo was tempted; his sense caught up quickly enough that he shook his head before he could agree with his brazen sister. "We would be too vulnerable from their archers on the hill."

Captain Yamamori struggled to contain his urgency, looking very much like his commander, Chikakuni, as his jaw worked. "We must defend the castle," he said. "They're fighting now because they expect our aid. If Etsugo falls, all of this will have been for nothing."

"I know," Kazuchiyo reassured him. "And we will." As much as his mind was full of different paths and strategies, it was seeing the man's desperation that convinced him of their course. "But not at the main gate. We'll head for the town just below the castle. We have to get off this hill as soon as possible without leaving ourselves vulnerable on the road. If we reclaim the town, we'll at last have a direct line of communication with Etsugo."

Captain Yamamori nodded vigorously. "I'll rally the men," he offered, and he hurried away to do just that.

Yagi watched him go, frowning. "If we take the village, and Mutsuyama comes back to this temple, won't we be right where we started?" he asked. "Pinned down and under siege?"

"Maybe," Kazuchiyo admitted, "but it's the only way we can keep Etsugo standing." He watched Captain Yamamori passing eager orders to his men. "There are probably Jisu soldiers here who live in that town. They'll fight hard to reclaim it. If we're swift, we can then send them up the hill to Etsugo and reinforce the main gate."

"I agree," said Naoya. "There's no greater advantage than a soldier fighting for his homeland." He clasped his fist to his chest. "We Kibaku soldiers will hold the rear, should Mutsuyama and his magic attempt to attack from behind."

"We're counting on you," said Kazuchiyo, and with

Mahiro and Yagi promising again to hold the vanguard, they hurried into their new formation.

The air was tense as the army made its way down the other side of the hill. Kazuchiyo felt as if his skull was mounted on a pike, swiveling back and forth, north to south. There was noise and movement from the northern hill where Umafusa was camped, but he had no means of determining who was engaging whom; to the south, torchlight gleamed through the dense trees. Every time he looked he was convinced their glow was drawing closer, only to rub his eyes and judge differently. When he looked to the east and their own camp at the road's summit, he was startled to find their lights had been extinguished. Had something become of Commander Ginta and his men? Had they heard of Mutsuyama's departure and abandoned their post for some inspired scheme? Though Kazuchiyo knew General Rakuteru to be a wise soldier, he realized then that he knew his son Ginta's demeanor very little outside his ability to follow orders. With their chain of command muddied, how would Ginta act?

There was no way to know, and so Kazuchiyo could do nothing but take a deep breath and trust the young man to his judgment.

Captain Yamamori and his Jisu soldiers reached the base of the hill first, accompanied by small squads of Sakka men led by Mahiro and Yagi. Without hesitation they marched down the last bit of road that led to the town at the base of Etsugo's broad plateau. The town itself boasted very little protection: a perimeter wall that stood barely above a tall man's head, and one gate manned on either side by small towers bearing archers. It was immediately clear that Tendo's army had allocated very few of their soldiers to holding the town, and the flight of their arrows barely rose to the level of a spring shower, let alone a hail. The determined Jisu soldiers were harried not at all as they charged fearlessly to the wall and began climbing over top of each other to breach the interior.

"Open the gate!" Mahiro roared, pacing back and forth in

the road atop Suzumekage. If only the walls were a hair shorter, she and her fearsome mount might have flown clear over them. "Get that gate open and point me toward the commander's head!"

The soldiers roared in answer and redoubled their efforts. Yagi himself put his back against the wall just beside the gatehouse and motioned soldiers forward. Captain Nishigame was the first with courage to approach, and with very little effort Yagi boosted him up onto the wall. One after another, Sakka's finest were lifted handily over the barrier by Yagi's great strength. Though Kazuchiyo's knee ached with sympathy for Yagi's wounded leg, seeing the men rely on him with such trust warmed his heart.

The sounds of clashing steel echoed from behind the walls. Atop the guardhouse towers, the Tendo soldiers began shouting and gesturing to each other, and two abandoned their posts. When they returned, Kazuchiyo could at last see clearly in the torchlight that the pair was pushing toward the edge of the wall a wooden cart bearing a large, iron pot.

"Shoot them!" Kazuchiyo hollered, and though his archers nocked arrows to comply, with Yagi just below the unknown contents of that heated iron, his desperation overpowered his faith in them. He ached for a weapon, or anything within his grasp that could act in those precious few moments. Without thinking, his hand went to his sword. A ring of heat burned into his wrist. His chest swelled with a sensation like roiling steam, and though it was familiar, he had no time to contemplate its source; instinctively he drew his sword, and from the swinging blade erupted a burst of wind not unlike one of Naoya's spells. A blade of curving air swept across the battlefield, diverting arrows from both sides and bowling grown men off their feet. It crashed into the guardhouse as a mighty bellow, rattling the wooden beams and sending both pot-bearers tumbling to the ground.

For a moment so critical to the fate of a nation, it disturbed the battle very little. The soldiers picked themselves back up and pressed the attack, perhaps thinking it Naoya's work. Captain Nishigame and his men killed the Tendo guards and laid open the gate. Suzumekage thundered down the path and into the village, with Mahiro cutting a bloody streak through those wriggling fish still resisting. Yagi followed soon after with his own monstrous roar, having never realized he had been saved from a painful fate.

Kazuchiyo relaxed back in his saddle and sheathed his sword. A few of his bannermen cast him looks of amazement, having correctly judged him the cause of the gale. He avoided meeting their eyes, for he had no explanation to offer, and only amazement himself. The small, red bead tied to his wrist grew cold and heavy.

"My lord!" A man of Sakka approached and dropped to one knee. "My lord, General Umafusa's troops appear to be descending the hill!"

Kazuchiyo turned Hashikiri about to look for himself, and sure enough, he could see movement among the lowest trees on the hill. Though harried by so many threats in so many directions, Kazuchiyo took a deep breath to compose himself before relaying his orders. "Form a line on the side of the road to greet them. And you there!" He indicated one of his bannermen. "Go to the village. Tell Captain Yamamori to stall the Tendo there if they can't overwhelm them, and summon Lady Mahiro and Commander Ebara to the new front!"

Both men hurried to obey, and in the meantime Kazuchiyo continued to guide his command unit into the new position. He spared a moment to check on the Kibaku soldiers guarding their rear, and was relieved and perplexed to see them unmoved; it seemed that old Mutsuyama had not yet moved to close his pincer after all. Though it made Kazuchiyo wary, he trusted Naoya to hold their line, allowing him to focus entirely on Umafusa's troops.

The Tendo army burst from their hilltop refuge at great speed. With furious shouts and spears raised they flooded out onto the road like men possessed. Though their ranks were not well formed, the sheer number of wailing, charging soldiers seemed to bear down on the Sakka line like a tsunami. Kazuchiyo's skin rippled with goose bumps as the Tendo warriors drew closer, crossing the long distance between their armies with no sign of slowing.

"Form ranks!" Kazuchiyo ordered, and he drew his sword again to single out and direct his captains as they raced to comply. "Crescent-moon formation! Wider! Brace your spears!"

The Sakka warriors fanned out, creating across the road a broad, half-circle formation with spears pointed inward. Tendo's charge was fierce, hoping to swarm over their enemies with sheer determination and wrath; a fitting strategy for coastal pirates, perhaps, but no match for men of discipline and wit. The two armies collided not unlike water sloshing into a cup; stern spear walls pierced the first wave of Tendo's reckless advance and then closed in from the flanks, surrounding and containing them.

General Umafusa's command unit emerged from the woods. Kazuchiyo could barely make out his figure among raised banners, and before he could pass any orders to take advantage, an oxen horn sounded from farther up the road. Though still cloaked in shadow, there was no mistaking the hammer of calvary hooves that cascaded down toward the bloody gully. General Umafusa realized his error too late, and though his command unit attempted to retreat back into the woods, they were cut off by Ginta's riders. Their shimmering aqua banners whipped back and forth and were trampled into the earth.

"Forward!" Kazuchiyo shouted, quivering with relief as he watched the Tendo army crumble. One more anxious look over his shoulder proved again that Mutsuyama was not coming to anyone's rescue, but he was still anxious to have the battle done with as quickly as possible. "Aim for all captains and commanders!"

Mahiro and Yagi at last rejoined the fray, twin oni whose war cries seemed to dwarf even the thousands of wailing fish.

With each taking up one of the flanks and Ginta's riders forming a barrier against the woods, the Tendo army was surrounded. Within the hour, they had surrendered completely.

Once the fighting had soundly ended, Kazuchiyo had his bannermen form into a modest enclosure and ordered General Umafusa to be brought to him. Mahiro did the honors, and to her credit she performed her duties with greater restraint than was expected of her. Still mounted proudly atop Suzumekage, she urged General Umafusa into Kazuchiyo's makeshift assembly with her naginata at his back, no cruel words necessary. The general and two of his commanders offered no resistance as they knelt before their enemy for judgment.

Kazuchiyo stood before them, willing the chaotic energy of the battle out of his blood. A new choice lay before him, one just as important and potentially just as lethal as any carried out on the field. General Umafusa's fine coat was stained with blood and dust, and his right arm was bound tightly to his chest in a way that suggested he had no use of it after tasting Mahiro's blade the day before. Resignation carved into his features like deep scars, and one of his commanders had tears on his face. They each knew what fate they had earned.

"Lord Aritaka," said General Umafusa, and he bowed his head. "I have surrendered to you myself and my army. With my death, in whatever manner you choose, I hope to make amends for the dishonor of my actions yesterday."

"General, you have more to answer for than the foolish attempt at assassinating me," replied Kazuchiyo. He felt as if a scale had been thrust into his chest, its bows leaning to and fro with the weight of different options offered to him. "I am only here on behalf of Clan Dada, as it is they you have wronged most grievously."

Umafusa lifted his head. "I will not offer amends for, nor can I regret following, the orders given to me by my father," he said. "I submit myself to your judgment, not theirs."

Kazuchiyo frowned, but he refused to let his expression or posture betray his frustration. Mahiro rolling her eyes and Yagi moving to his side both gave him strength in their own way. "Your devotion to your lord is commendable, but that makes no difference," Kazuchiyo told Umafusa firmly. "Who judges you is not your choice to make."

A horn sounded from behind the assembly, higher in pitch than a Sakka battle horn, and one that General Umafusa seemed to recognize. His manners grew impatient, and he locked eyes with Kazuchiyo. "I would have preferred you," he said, and Kazuchiyo felt a chill as if the words were imparted with a deeper meaning.

The bannermen at the rear made way for the approach of a dozen soldiers; though two at the front bore lit torches, the rest were warriors, bloodstained from the fighting. With a jolt of surprise Kazuchiyo realized that almost all of them were women. Each wielded a nagamaki, which Kazuchiyo had heard of but had very little experience with: blades as long and fierce as a katana, but with corded handles three times the normal length for powerful and precise manipulation. The women's manners were tempered with discipline but still ready and eager for more war, and Kazuchiyo could *feel* Mahiro's eyes popped wide at the spectacle they made.

They were led by the very welcome Commander Chikakuni, and just ahead of him, a tall woman in ornate, gold and violet armor, with crane feathers adoring her helmet. The long oval of her face sat upon a wide jaw, and her eyes were dark and deeply set. She surveyed the assembly with a cold and discerning glare, saving particular venom for the kneeling Umafusa. Then she looked to Kazuchiyo, and the authority of her countenance made it very clear exactly who she was.

Even so, Chikakuni bowed his head as he made the introduction. "Lord Sakka, allow me the honor of fulfilling my oath to you," he said. "I introduce to you Lady Dada, head of Clan Dada and daimyo of Jisu Province."

Kazuchiyo bowed in return, as did his surrounding men. "Lady Dada, the honor is mine," he greeted her. "I am relieved to see you unharmed."

Lady Dada regarded him in silent and seemingly judgmental contemplation for a long moment before her reply came. "Lord Sakka," she acknowledged him, and her voice was much deeper than Kazuchiyo expected. "You are very welcome in Jisu, but our usual hospitality will have to wait. I'm here to collect General Umafusa's head."

The assembly parted again at Kazuchiyo's back, and he spared a glance to take note of Naoya joining the gathering as well. The lady Purnima was at his side, and her presence excited a hope in Kazuchiyo; he made a quick scan of the surrounding faces for Amai. Failing to locate him, and recognizing the tight, disapproving expression Naoya was fixing him with, sobered him once more. There were too many eyes on him, and too much at stake, for him to divert his attention from the assembly before him.

"The general's fate is in your hands," Kazuchiyo told Lady Dada, "but if you don't mind, I have questions for him first."

"Anything he tells you will be a lie," she cautioned him. "You shouldn't waste everyone's time."

Umafusa stared fixedly at Kazuchiyo, though not, it appeared, with any intent to convince him that the lady was mischaracterizing him. He was only waiting for his last opportunity to speak, and Kazuchiyo was determined to hear him. Despite the many vengeance-hungry soldiers looking on, Kazuchiyo gathered himself up and said, "Even so, I will ask my questions."

Lady Dada frowned at him crossly, but a slight shift of posture from Chikakuni drew her attention. They shared a meaningful look, and she nodded. "Go ahead then, but don't bother believing his answers."

"I'll take your counsel to heart. Now." Kazuchiyo at last devoted himself to the study of Umafusa's stoic face. "Who sent you to lay siege to Etsugo?"

"You already know," said Umafusa without hesitation. "My lord father, the daimyo Umafusa." His gaze flickered to Lady Dada and back again. "To expand his governance."

"You intimated before that you were provoked," said Kazuchiyo, trying to watch both samurai at once for their reaction.

Neither gave anything away in their faces. "Provoked only by my father's desire to expand his governance," Umafusa replied. "I have no apologies to offer and no more answers to give you. Take my head."

"Master Mutsuyama," Kazuchiyo pressed him. "Who sent him? And who was the samurai general that accompanied him yesterday?"

"My advisor and his bodyguard only—take my head and let us be done!"

Lady Dada gave a great huff. "Give him what he asks for; there's nothing more to be gained from prolonging this coward's life."

Though Kazuchiyo was wary of antagonizing the woman at her own doorstep, with so many of her armed subjects at her back and watching closely, he could afford even less to let show any weakness before such a powerful daimyo. "With all due respect, Lady Dada, I'm not finished," he said firmly, and beside him, Yagi thumped the butt of his spear against the earth. Though frowning intensely, the lady Dada leaned back.

"I have nothing more to say," Umafusa insisted. "Will you grant me a sword to cut my belly with?"

"No. You've done nothing to earn any favors here." Kazuchiyo stared him straight in the face one more time, determined to glean at least some small bit of information from the stubborn fish. "You're about to be put to death. Any samurai of yours who wishes to follow you will be allowed to do so. The rest will be driven south back to Tendo, bearing your swords to your father with news of what his greed has earned him."

At last, a twist of strain was visible around Umafusa's set jaw. "Very well," he said, and he removed his helmet to hand to the commander on his left. The man accepted it with shaking hands. "Then I have only one request to make." He took a deep breath. "Please let my men make their own way home."

The surrounding assembly frowned at him in confusion, but Kazuchiyo understood his meaning at once, and he nodded. Not wanting to draw any further attention to that agreement, he turned to Lady Dada. "I'm finished with the general."

Lady Dada looked to Chikakuni, and without a word shared he stepped forward, drawing his sword. Umafusa pressed his palm to the ground and leaned forward to expose his neck, and with one fine, clean stroke, the katana cleaved his head from his shoulders. The commander holding Umafusa's helmet clutched it to his chest; the second did not flinch. Both men bowed their heads as Chikakuni flicked the blood from his sword and then sheathed it again.

"You and I should have a very long conversation," Lady Dada said to Kazuchiyo as Chikakuni returned to her side. "It can wait a while longer, though. Once your army is settled, come to Etsugo. Our hospitality is stretched thin, but you are welcome."

"I look forward to it," said Kazuchiyo, trying not to look at the body as he and the lady bowed to each other.

Lady Dada and her entourage turned to go, though Chikakuni stalled long enough to flash Kazuchiyo a pleased, relieved look before joining them. Mahiro's eyes were still quite wide as she watched them depart. Just as Kazuchiyo was preparing orders for his own bannermen, Naoya moved to his side, with such stern, fiery intent that it startled him.

"You and I also need to have a very long conversation," Naoya said, emotion hard in his face. He then stormed off just as quickly as he'd approached. Even Purnima glanced between the two of them in confusion before following her lord back into their ranks.

Kazuchiyo's heart sank as he watched Naoya's long coat disappear among the soldiers. He looked to his wrist, where the magic bead Iomori had given him long before still nestled unseen. It weighed very heavily against his skin then, with the realization that Naoya had doubtlessly seen his display during the fight.

"What's got his loincloth so twisted?" asked Amai.

Kazuchiyo startled and his head snapped up; there in front of him stood Amai, soiled from the battle and with a smear of blood across his smirking mouth, a hand on his hip as if he'd been lazily posed at Kazuchiyo's side all along.

"There you are," Yagi scolded him. "You should have shown your face sooner."

Amai shrugged. "I was worried that if Kazu saw me he'd be so overcome with joy he'd break character in front of—"

Kazuchiyo's body acted on its own; his gloved fingers were twisting hard in Amai's collar even before he realized he'd moved. Relief quaked painfully through his every joint as he held Amai at arm's length, fearful that if he drew him any closer, he truly would further embarrass them both in front of all his bannermen. Amai blinked at him in surprise as he untangled his breath well enough to speak.

"You're all right?" he asked.

Amai needed a moment himself to react; he even managed to look somewhat moved before his insufferable grin returned. "Didn't I tell you not to worry?" he said. He covered Kazuchiyo's hands with his and began to ease them off. "Sorry I kept you waiting."

With a deep breath Kazuchiyo let him go, and he shook himself, self-conscious over his lapse in composure. "I want to hear everything," he said firmly. "The path, the castle, the battle—every moment of it." He paused again to regain his senses and his footing. "Soon. There's much to do first."

"Of course," replied Amai. "Whatever you need from me."

"Clean that blood off your face for now. And then…" Kazuchiyo at last allowed himself to take in the results of their victory assembly: General Umafusa's body leaking blood across the road, his two commanders still prostrated on either side. "Wait here for a moment."

Kazuchiyo moved toward the higher ranking of the commanders, and despite the breach of propriety it was, he crouched down in front of the man. "Commander. What is your name?"

The commander, still holding his general's helmet, dared not lift his head. "Umafusa Soujirou, sir."

Kazuchiyo was beginning to wonder if every man in Tendo wasn't an Umafusa somehow. "You and your men are going to be held outside the town at the base of the plateau for the time being," he said. "Tend to your wounded. When the time comes, be careful which road you take back to Tendo. Master Mutsuyama and his soldiers guard the valley just south of the temple."

The commander's shoulders drew in tightly, and his head bobbed as if he were tempted to raise it and look Kazuchiyo in the face. "Thank you, sir."

Kazuchiyo straightened up, and at his gesture a Sakka captain came forward to escort the two commanders. He then returned to Yagi and Amai to explain in low tones, "For whatever reason, Mutsuyama didn't even try to aid Tendo in the battle. If the shogun goaded Umafusa into this war and then betrayed them, there's a chance they won't let the Tendo soldiers go home safely either."

"Why?" asked Yagi. "If they wanted you dead, they should have come at us from both sides when they had the chance."

"I don't know," said Kazuchiyo, and he sighed. "There's still so much I don't know." He turned in place. "For now, though, I just want to get off this road once and for all."

CHAPTER ELEVEN

I t was nearing sunrise by the time Kazuchiyo and his armies were able to settle. Though he had been assured a chamber at Etsugo, he chose instead to remain among his troops for the time being, as did Naoya. The latter suggested, and Kazuchiyo agreed, that the threat from Mutsuyama could not be considered fully past, and so the Kibaku troops took their rest within the village, ideally placed to counter any attack from the south. Kazuchiyo and his Sakka troops, in the meantime, returned to their camp at the peak of the road. Come daylight, they would have an easier time assessing if Umafusa's camp on the northern hill was worth reclaiming for themselves.

"Did you see Lady Dada?" Mahiro asked consistently throughout their efforts. "Her guard? Those *women*?"

"We saw," Yagi grunted the third time she raised the subject, as they were leading their horses to their makeshift stalls. "You'll get to see plenty of them when we visit the castle."

"Damn right I will! And I'll make sure they see *plenty* of me too. They won't be able to keep their hands off me!"

Kazuchiyo allowed one of his bannermen to take his Hashikiri to be tended, and in the meantime, he met with Commander Ginta just outside his own tent. "Commander, you gave me a bit of a fright when you put out your torches," he admitted. "Wise that you did, though. Umafusa might not have come out onto the road otherwise, and we'd still be fighting uphill even now."

"I'm sorry I wasn't able to communicate my intentions to you sooner," replied Ginta, bowing deeply. "It seemed like you took the temple with too little effort, and I was concerned that something had gone wrong. I was hoping to confuse the enemy, not my lord."

Kazuchiyo quickly shook his head. "There's no need to apologize. Your instincts were sound." He smiled. "A fine gift from your father. You've done him proud, and I'll make sure he knows that."

Ginta's face beamed with pride. "Thank you, my lord."

After he had been dismissed, and orders for a continued watch to be upheld while the army were settled, Kazuchiyo at last entered his tent. He was pleasantly unsurprised to find Amai already inside, helping himself to a sip from the wine gourd.

"I've earned it," Amai quipped, and rather than argue Kazuchiyo took a long gulp for himself. With the taste still on their lips, he drew Amai in for a long-awaited kiss. Amai's body swaying into his, perfectly receptive, was just what he needed.

"Were you really that worried about me?" Amai teased. His nimble fingers began loosening the cords on Kazuchiyo's armor. "I'm not sure if I should be deeply moved or insulted."

"I always worry," said Kazuchiyo, remaining still as Amai worked. All he cared about in that moment was keeping Amai close beneath his hands. "And I missed you."

"Missed me?" Amai hummed as if skeptical, but even he could not hide how pleased he was with the news. He lowered Kazuchiyo's shoulder guards to the floor of the tent. "When you have your great, big oni here to comfort you?"

"He's..." Kazuchiyo sighed, uncertain how to put his feelings into words. A portion of his heart was still shaken after seeing his bold champion in peril, the rest of it tender from insecurity. "He's been difficult to handle lately," he confessed, and Amai paused in his work. "I feel like there's something he's trying to say that I'm missing." He frowned at Amai's raising eyebrows. "*Yes*, I have tried speaking to him."

"Well, at least the battle is over for now," said Amai as he went back to removing Kazuchiyo's chest plate. "Generous Lady Dada has offered you a chamber at Etsugo." His lip quirked. "Maybe you can try speaking to him another way."

Kazuchiyo rolled his eyes, though he couldn't say the thought hadn't occurred to him. Before he could reply, they were interrupted by the unmistakable sound of a soldier in armor snapping to attention just beyond the tent entrance.

"Lord Aritaka!" the soldier called. "Forgive my intrusion, but General Oihata is approaching the camp!"

Kazuchiyo's brow furrowed with concern, and when Amai looked confused, he waved him quiet. "I'll be ready to receive him!" he called back, and he joined Amai in removing his armor. "Damn. I was hoping he'd give me a little more time."

Amai kneeled down to untie Kazuchiyo's shin guards. "I'm too tired to be dealing with Oihata, too, but did I miss something?"

"He must have seen me on the field. I accidentally…" Kazuchiyo frowned, uncertain how to explain just what had happened. He struggled over the words, knowing how important they would be once he had to repeat them to Naoya. "I used magic. A gust of wind, like we've seen him do before."

Amai shot him a look. "You *accidentally* magicked?"

"I don't know how," Kazuchiyo insisted, and with the last of his armor shed, he straightened his robes as best he could. "It was like at the river; I felt that I needed to, and then… I did." As exhilarating and frightening as that prospect was, he couldn't afford to dwell on it. "But Naoya was extremely firm about not wanting me to know anything about magic. He doesn't know I have that bead from Iomori; he'll think I lied to him."

"You kind of did, though, right?" asked Amai as he moved

around behind Kazuchiyo. When Kazuchiyo tried to turn and follow, he took his shoulders to prevent him. "You could have told him."

"He would have tried to take it from me," Kazuchiyo said irritably, though he held still as Amai tidied and retied his hair. "You know very well how he can be."

"I know. That's why I'm telling you." Amai straightened the line of his collar and then moved in front of him to do the same for the lapels. "He's very stubborn, and you can be very defensive. That's not a good combination."

If he was trying to convey some manner of advice, Kazuchiyo was not in the greatest state to hear it, and in frustration he urged Amai's hands off him. "I know you enjoy pointing my flaws out to me, but now isn't the time," he said. "It's not helping."

Amai was given pause, though the impish humor leaving his face gave Kazuchiyo no pleasure either. "Sorry," he said. "I didn't mean it like that." He took Kazuchiyo's hands gently in his. "Just take a breath and calm down. He *is* going to call you a liar, so you might as well brace yourself. Have an answer ready for him and you'll be fine."

"Amai..." Kazuchiyo nodded, and he did take a deep breath. "I'm sorry, I'm just—"

"Exhausted?" Amai darted in to kiss his cheek, and he gave his hands a squeeze before letting go. "My face isn't about to help his temper any, so I'll be eavesdropping just outside the tent. Good luck."

"Thank you," said Kazuchiyo, and as Amai crawled beneath the back wall of the tent, he took the time he had left to compose himself.

When Naoya arrived, he was in just as much of a foul temper as Kazuchiyo had anticipated. Though missing his helmet, he was still wearing the rest of his armor, and he marched into Kazuchiyo's tent with stern purpose. Kazuchiyo was already seated awaiting him, so he lowered himself to his knees in a formal posture before him.

"Lord Kazumune," Naoya greeted him; his tone was hard with displeasure that Kazuchiyo had not been fixed with in a long time. "You must know my reason for being here right now."

"I do." Kazuchiyo took in a deep breath, and with Amai's advice close at hand, he bowed his head. "I owe you an apology. There's something in my possession that I've concealed from you."

Naoya's temper did not visibly abate with the admission, though when Kazuchiyo lifted his head again, he could more clearly see the threads of hurt tightening around his eyes and jaw. Naoya did not respond, and so Kazuchiyo elaborated. "Before last year's campaign, Master Iomori gave me a small bead. At the time, I didn't know what it was or what purpose it had." He frowned. "Even now I don't really know."

"I saw you cast that spell on the field," Naoya declared.

"It wasn't intentional," Kazuchiyo said quickly. "That was only the second time I've ever used it—I don't even know how I was able to. It was instinctual."

His words had the opposite effect to his intentions; Naoya leaned back with alarm. "You mustn't," he said, and he held out his hand. "If that's the case, it's too dangerous for you to have."

Kazuchiyo did not move; he tried to channel as much of his focus away from that small weight against his wrist, as if he might give away its location to Naoya subconsciously. "I'm not going to give it up without some explanation as to why I should."

"Wielding magic is as dangerous to you as anything you use it against; I've explained this to you before." Naoya motioned insistently. "Please, give the stone to me."

"No," Kazuchiyo replied swiftly. "This bead saved my life at Nodo Bridge, and was a gift from Master Iomori. I don't wish to part with it."

Naoya withdrew his hand. "Iomori no Jun cannot be trusted. That she would burden you with the stone and not caution you against its use is at best negligence, at worst malicious cruelty!" His expression twisted with pain and distrust. "Or perhaps she did, and you conceal that from me as well."

Kazuchiyo wound his fingers tight in his pant legs. "I'm not lying to you."

"I want to believe that," said Naoya, the emotion in his voice threatening to infect Kazuchiyo as well. "But you knew very well how I felt on the matter and concealed your engagement with it regardless. Would I not be a fool to take you at your word now?"

The words stung Kazuchiyo more deeply than he had expected, and he was careful to bite his tongue before answering too impulsively. "Sir Naoya, we have enjoyed each other's trust for some time now. I don't want to see that trust tarnished over this."

"Then you will give the stone to me and everything will be settled," Naoya persisted, once again offering his hand.

Kazuchiyo did not move, and once Naoya saw his resolve so clearly, his open palm became a fist. "Very well then."

The tent flap behind him opened, and Yagi stepped through despite the anxious advice of the bannerman on guard. He, too, was still in his bloodied armor, and he instantly caught upon the uncommonly tense mood of their meeting. "What's going on?" he asked bluntly.

"We're just finishing," said Naoya as he pushed to his feet; Kazuchiyo did the same. Naoya faced his host with an air of tragedy as only he could convey. "As Lord Koedzuka commands, our alliance will continue. However, I am deeply disappointed in you."

Kazuchiyo's chest constricted painfully, and this time he could not contain his true feelings. "I say the same," he replied. "I hope that once your hypocrisy becomes apparent to you, we can have a more productive conversation."

Naoya gathered himself up. "I beg your pardon?"

Yagi glanced between the two of them in confusion as Kazuchiyo, too, straightened to his full height, even if he was no match for Naoya's. "All you can say is that you don't wish me to have it, without any explanation, while you frequently wield magic yourself. You're concealing just as much I as ever have."

Naoya flushed as he glared back at Kazuchiyo. "My restraint is for your benefit," he said with forced confidence.

"Then explain it to me," Kazuchiyo pleaded. "If it's dangerous for me to use it inadvertently, teach me how it works."

"You don't understand." Naoya shook his head. "And if you did, then—then you would understand!" Yet again he offered his outstretched palm. "Kazumune, please."

Even so Kazuchiyo remained unmoved. "If I hadn't used the magic when I did, Yagi might be dead," he said. Yagi looking to him in bafflement only hardened his resolve, and he faced Naoya unflinchingly. "I have no intention of giving it up."

Naoya leaned back, conflicted. "Then you'll have to excuse me, for I have nothing further to say," he replied, and with gritted teeth he turned and marched from the tent.

Kazuchiyo let his breath out. "Of all the selfish, sanctimonious—" He stopped himself, scrubbing his face with both hands. Anger bit into his ribs, a more tolerable sensation compared to the sincere hurt buried beneath it. Naoya had never been an easy friend, and it surprised him how deeply the rejection pierced when it was exactly what he'd expected.

"Kazu?" Yagi shed one of his gloves and took Kazuchiyo by the shoulder. "Are you all right?"

"Yes, I'm fine." Kazuchiyo gave his face one last rub and then reached for Yagi's cords. "Let's get you out of your armor."

Yagi prevented him, still watching Kazuchiyo with concern. "What was Oihata so mad about?" he asked. "And what did you mean, I 'might be dead'?"

"It's... hard to explain," said Kazuchiyo. Amai slid up alongside Yagi; the two of them watching him so expectantly prevented him from dodging the question a second time. "I never told him that I have that magic bead from Iomori," he confessed. "He saw me use magic on the field and is upset about it. Now let me help you out of your armor."

"I'd rather keep it," Yagi admitted. "It's full daylight now, and the soldiers might need me. But what about this magic?"

He and Amai continued to stare at Kazuchiyo expectantly, so he at last surrendered the rest. "When you were helping to boost the soldiers over the wall, I saw the men in the tower pushing an iron pot toward you. I thought it might have been boiling oil…" He clenched his fists against the oni decorating Yagi's chest plate. "I couldn't do nothing."

Yagi was quiet at first, his heavy brows drawn in. Then he took Kazuchiyo's face in his hands, his broad, warm palms oddly hesitant. "Then I'm sorry he's mad at you because of me."

Kazuchiyo gripped Yagi's wrists. "No—don't apologize," he said, and he sighed. "It's my own fault for hiding it from him in the first place."

"He saved your life, you know," Amai piped up, and he poked Yagi in the arm. "Just say thanks already."

Yagi glowered at him, but in his own time he worked the words out. "Thank you."

"I'd do it again." Kazuchiyo kissed the meat of Yagi's thumb through his glove and then reluctantly let him go. "We'll be expected to at least have supper at Etsugo tonight. I think we could all use some rest before then." He fixed Amai with an expectant look. "And I still want to hear what happened on your side."

"Oh, there's not much to tell." Amai retrieved the wine gourd as the three of them moved deeper into the tent. "Chikakuni's secret path was exactly that. We didn't run into any trouble on our way to Etsugo."

Kazuchiyo took a seat and was disappointed when Yagi did not settle close enough for his liking. He would have preferred having his strong body to lean into after the fury and uncertainty of the recent battle. "What about the castle?" he asked of Amai to stay focused. "And Lady Dada, what did you think of her?"

"I think she's exactly how I *thought* she'd be." Amai paused for a drink of wine and then passed the gourd to Yagi, who was especially eager for it. "Proud and stubborn and an absolute mare. Can't blame her, though, given what she's up against." He leaned back against his hands. "She really seems to have a soft spot for Chikakuni, though, and he couldn't be more grateful to you, so once you do your thing she'll come around."

Kazuchiyo motioned for a drink of his own. He didn't want to admit just then that his confidence in his political negotiations had been somewhat hampered by his recent failures with Naoya and General Umafusa. After a gulp of wine he motioned for Amai to continue. "What about Etsugo itself?"

"Tired, but not broken. They're hardy mountain folk." He idly traced a map of the perimeter against the floor with his finger. "They were just about out of food when we arrived. Lost a lot of their soldiers, but those left were each worth a few." He raised an eyebrow. "Did you not get the shiki we sent back?"

"No," Kazuchiyo said, remembering it for the first time. "No, we never did get a reply."

"The old man must have intercepted it after all," said Yagi. "So why didn't he fight?"

Kazuchiyo shook his head. "I don't know, and that bothers me. The two of them still out there even now." He frowned down at the subtle shapes in the tent's rug floor where Amai had pinched a crease, picturing Mutsuyama's army waiting below the southern hill. "And the battle last night? I was worried about you when we saw the main gates opening."

Amai waved a hand dismissively. "Their commander was already dead by then," he boasted. "Purnima and I snuck into the camp just beyond the gate and cut his throat while he slept." He smirked and drew his finger across his neck to demonstrate. "Tendo may have a few smart fish leading their swarm, but without them they're helpless. Lady Dada herself led the attack, and they scattered like minnows."

"*You* took the commander's head?" repeated Yagi. "Or was it Purnima?"

"It was a collaborative effort: she exposed his neck; I stabbed it." Amai shrugged as if it was barely worth mentioning. "I don't need any credit for it, unless she tries to take it for herself, in which case I outperformed her splendidly."

"Whatever the case, I'm very grateful," said Kazuchiyo. "Every effort that pushed Umafusa off that hillside was a boon to us."

"Oh?" Amai corked the gourd and squirmed closer, nearly putting himself in Kazuchiyo's lap. "*How* grateful are you?"

Kazuchiyo held still despite the rush of heat that raced through him at Amai's tempting stare. "Very grateful," he replied. "So much so, in fact, that I think I'll save showing it until after we've rested so that I can convey it properly."

Amai licked his lips, tempting Kazuchiyo's self-control. "Then we'd better get some sleep right away," he said, and he stretched out across the tent's mattress.

Kazuchiyo was tempted to follow straight away, only to be reminded that Yagi was still in his full armor, and in fact was pushing back to his feet. "I'll go back to my tent then," he said. "Just in case."

Though disappointed, Kazuchiyo nodded. "I'll summon you for supper tonight."

Yagi nodded stiffly and then withdrew from the tent. Making every effort to avoid Amai's seeking looks, he joined him in the futon, determined to sleep. There would be better opportunities for a full conversation another time.

CHAPTER TWELVE

C ome evening, Kazuchiyo donned his handsome hitatare, and along with Yagi, Amai, Mahiro, and a small retinue of soldiers, he rode to Etsugo Castle.

In the hours since the end of the battle, the road had been mostly cleared of bodies, and the blood had dried to rusty red. Kazuchiyo could not stop his eyes from wandering to the stage of Yagi's duels and, further on, to the spot where Umafusa's head had fallen. As they continued on, his focus shifted more curiously toward the edge of the road, where the forest sloped down to greet it, toward the small, dark shapes darting to and fro in the underbrush. He recalled Amai's words from days before: that in Jisu it was said that foxes conveyed the souls of dead soldiers to the mountain. He supposed they must have been quite satisfied with their yield that day. And though it may be inappropriate of me to admit, I know very well that they were.

The path up the plateau was steep and treacherous. Despite their many failings, the Tendo soldiers were bold indeed to have ever set their sights on a fortress like Etsugo. The remnants of their ruined camp lay just beyond the massive front gate, with a pyre burning their colorful, carp-sigil banners. The Jisu soldiers on guard bowed as Kazuchiyo and his companions rode past, through the open gate and into the castle proper.

Even in the aftermath of bloody war, Etsugo was a handsome sight. The tall outer walls surrounded a broad compound decorated with many broad-leafed trees, with stone carvings on either side of the path leading between the different buildings. A small shrine lay just within the entrance, adorned with many offerings for soldiers who had passed recently and long ago. The rooftops were capped with gold figures of tigers and dragons much like Kanrei Temple, and large, round lanterns hung from the eaves, proclaiming Jisu's victory over the invasion. Lady Dada's female guards were waiting to receive their guests, and they were strict in their composure as they escorted the procession into the main keep.

Chikakuni awaited them in the central courtyard. He was in the finest shape Kazuchiyo had ever seen him by far: bathed and rested, his hair combed back into his topknot, a handsome, lavender robe draping his slight frame. He bowed deeply at the waist as Kazuchiyo dismounted. "Lord Kazumune, you are very welcome here in Etsugo."

"Sir Chikakuni." Kazuchiyo bowed his head in return. "There wasn't time to say so earlier, but I'm very glad to see you well. I heard you took very good care of one of my associates, and I'm grateful."

Chikakuni scoffed, and he and Amai shared a smirk. "I'm the one that's grateful," he replied. "And I hope you're prepared to put up with me saying so all night long." His manners softened with sincerity. "I owe you and your companions more than can ever be repaid."

"You can start with dinner," said Mahiro. Though she had shed her armor plates, she had insisted on wearing her tiger furs and mane, and she grinned wickedly in anticipation. "And by introducing us to your lady."

Chikakuni's little smirk returned. "Of course," he said, and he turned to lead them inside.

The main hall in the central keep had been prepared for

them, with two long rows of trays set out, bearing cups of wine. Several of Jisu's samurai were already in place, and they bowed in respectful greeting even though Kazuchiyo sensed hesitation and even bitterness from a few. Kazuchiyo was not surprised by nor could he take offense to the reaction; it could not be an easy thing for proud samurai to welcome foreign aid even in their neediest moments. In particular, an elder samurai was eyeing Naoya and Purnima, who had also already been seated.

Kazuchiyo attempted to catch Naoya's eye, but the man deliberately lowered his gaze, looking uncomfortable and perhaps even embarrassed. It was a hair's width more encouraging than raw anger, and Kazuchiyo contented himself with that short interaction as he seated himself near the head of the assembly.

"This is quite a room," Mahiro remarked, her eyes hungrily scanning the interior. Though the panels closing them in were beautifully painted with mountainous panoramas, blooming chrysanthemums, and birds at flight, one can only assume she was most captivated by Lady Dada's soldiers standing guard at each corner. They were all tall, sturdy women, though none were as tall or as sturdy as Mahiro herself, and they seemed to be paying her as much attention as she was them. "A good thing Jisu's samurai are as tough as they are, to keep this place untouched. I hope their lady is showering them with the praise they deserve."

Though each was clearly determined to keep up their duty of stoic indifference, Kazuchiyo could see their eyes gleam with the praise. Among the Jisu officers gathered for the supper was a middle-aged woman in partial armor, bruises on her jaw indicating she had been on the field. She bowed her head slightly to Mahiro in thanks. "Our lady does indeed take good care of us," she assured her. "And we are just as thankful to you, Mahiro the Unyielding Iron, for your assistance."

Mahiro puffed her chest, practically aglow. "It was my pleasure," she said, so fixated on the woman that she missed when Kazuchiyo did not that Purnima deliberately looked away.

The sliding panel at the far end of the chamber opened, and in came Lady Dada herself. She was dressed in an old-fashioned kimono draped in a flowing over-robe of lavender brocade, the chrysanthemums that made up her house sigil embroidered in brilliant silvers and golds. Though in pale makeup with her long hair bound in elaborate pins and combs, the stern nature of her features came through, and it was then that Kazuchiyo remembered Chikakuni's description of her intense beauty the first day they met. As she took her seat at the front of the assembly, however, a closer look revealed to him at last that, lady though she was, her bust was quite flat, and the white painting her throat could not conceal the subtle protrusion there.

Lady Dada was joined also by a very elderly woman, whose robes were just as fine, though her hair was brittle and white, and not very well combed at all. Her wrinkled lips were curled in a crooked, foxlike smile as she peered at each of their guests in turn.

Kazuchiyo and the rest of the assembly bowed their heads, as one of the ministers made the introduction. "Here sits the lady Dada Tangiku, head of Clan Dada and daimyo of Jisu Province." He then bowed to Kazuchiyo. "Lady Dada, tonight we welcome the son of the lord of Sakka, Aritaka Kazumune, along with his sister, the lady Mahiro, and generals Ebara and Oihata."

"And then some," Lady Dada noted, glancing between Amai and Purnima with familiarity. "You are all welcome here, though we don't have much hospitality to offer you. Even tonight's supper was generously donated from your own rations, I understand. Now that the siege has been lifted, we will call upon our remaining lands to replenish what was spent and stolen, and you will be repaid in full for what you've offered."

"Some rice and vegetables are all well and good," said Mahiro, leaning forward to put herself more firmly in Lady Dada's line of sight. "What about our great effort on your behalf? You'll be repaying us for that as well?"

The Jisu half of the gathering shifted uncomfortably, though Lady Dada herself did not stir an inch. "I made the young lord Sakka an offer, and he accepted," she replied. "Jisu will fulfill its promise."

"A promise to stand idly by while we conquer the capital?" Mahiro gave a great huff of laughter that again had the ministers squirming.

"That is what Jisu offered," said Kazuchiyo, keeping his tone calm and level as he watched Lady Dada's face. Even then he was still working to develop his strategy. "Sakka accepted. I won't demand any more from Jisu than that."

Mahiro continued to chortle as servants came forward with supper. "Fine by me. It just seems a shame to waste Jisu's fine soldiers. I was looking forward to outdoing them all on the field."

The middle-aged woman who had spoken earlier returned Mahiro's smirk with her own. One wonders what her reply might have been, if not for her mistress looking on. Lady Dada herself remained unmoved, replying, "The samurai of Jisu have nothing to prove."

"Do they not?" spoke up Naoya, and Kazuchiyo flinched. Even when they were on the best of terms he had harbored concern for this eventual confrontation, and he braced himself.

"Jisu has made no offers or promises to Kibaku," Lady Dada said immediately, as if she, too, had prepared for this inevitable conversation. "You and your soldiers came of your own volition."

"We're very grateful for Kibaku's assistance," Chikakuni rushed to reassure Naoya before he could speak. "We might not have been able to overcome the garrison outside our gate if not for the efforts of Lady Purnima." He nodded to her, a gesture she returned. "And Lady Dada is prepared to meet with Lord Koedzuka as promised."

The minister closest to Lady Dada cleared his throat. "Only after the threat to our lands has fully passed," he added hastily. "He cannot expect us to expose our lord to danger so soon after a siege."

Naoya returned the man's stare with tenfold intensity. "Commander Chikakuni assured me of his lady's compliance, and I will see it done," he insisted. "I have no intention of leaving Etsugo if not to escort her directly to my lord Koedzuka in Rongi. Though that is not even the greatest of my concerns."

"He's right," Kazuchiyo cut in. Tempers in the hall were too great already, and he feared the momentum of this conversation racing too far ahead of his control. "I have no intention of leaving Jisu until Lady Dada has fulfilled her promise to Lord Koedzuka either." He offered her a brief smile. "I'm looking forward to having a seat at the meeting after all. However, before then, we must be certain that Jisu is now reasonably safe from Tendo. Master Mutsuyama still holds the valley to the south, and we have no measure of his intentions."

"Whoever he is, he is now outnumbered and outflanked," said Lady Dada. "The harvest time is close, and he cannot keep his samurai from their homesteads any longer than we can. He will withdraw." She paused for a moment, meeting Kazuchiyo's searching look. "But of course, we're not opposed to you and your armies remaining until that time when he does."

"Whoever he is," Naoya echoed. "Can you really claim not to know whose wrath you've summoned?"

"Mind your manners," said Lady Dada's lead minister. "Know who you're addressing."

"I will not hold my tongue." Naoya fixed the Lady Dada with an unflinching stare. "My men and I heeded the lady Dada's call for aid, even after she had sent her armies to invade my lord's sacred lands. I have the right to know how this conflict began, and by whose hand."

Lady Dada leaned back, returning his glare with her own, strong-willed defiance. It reminded Kazuchiyo of Amai's warnings in the tent about clashing personalities, and before the lady could speak, he again interjected. "We know Master Mutsuyama was sent by Shogun Oomiyari," he said, and the name drew the entire chamber in more tightly. "There's no use trying to conceal that now, and General Umafusa indicated to us that this siege was not unprovoked."

The lady Dada at last glanced away, her eyes seeking Chikakuni's for council while the ministers and samurai ground their teeth. Beside Kazuchiyo, Yagi took a long drink from his wine cup, seemingly unaffected by the gravity of their discussion. He clapped his cup down on the tray before him and said, "What are you all so worried about? You already know we're planning to war with the shogunate. If you've pissed them off, you're better off just telling us."

"He has a point," said Chikakuni with half a smile aimed at his mistress.

"I suppose he does." Lady Dada took in a deep breath, resettling herself in her robes as she faced Kazuchiyo and his peers. "Very well. The truth is as you suspect." She paused for a sip of her wine and then continued. "Until late last year, one of the shogun's magistrates lived here at Etsugo. He was a lazy and arrogant man, a distant relation of the royal family. After the death of my father, he opposed me taking leadership of the clan."

She locked gazes with Kazuchiyo, conveying much meaning with the confidence, and yet the subtle frustration, within her voice. "He insisted that each provincial daimyo be subjected to the shogun's approval, and that I in particular would never be offered that approval. So I evicted him."

"Evicted?" Mahiro repeated with eyebrows raised, though her manner was ripe with approval.

"Evicted, not killed," Lady Dada reassured her. "A replacement was sent at the new year, but I refused him at the gate and have not heard one word on the matter since."

"It has been many years since the shogun even attempted to assign one of his magistrates to the east," mused Kazuchiyo. "Not since before I was born." He looked to Naoya. "What about Kibaku?"

"Magistrate Yushiro has held his position for over fifty

years, though it amounts to very little," replied Naoya. "He has a comfortable residence and performs no duties that I know of."

Mahiro snorted mightily. "See how the shogun lacks teeth? All the more reason to combine forces against him."

Kazuchiyo sipped his wine, thinking back to Umafusa at their negotiation and his strained demeanor. "Not entirely without teeth," he corrected Mahiro. "He still managed to convince Tendo to war for him."

"And then abandoned them the first chance he got," Mahiro retorted. "A cowardly windbag full of empty promises." She flashed her toothy grin to the assembly. "Between me, our oni, and Jisu's women, by this time next year we'll all be dining in the royal gardens, with princesses serving us tea and sweets!"

She lifted her cup in a toast, though only Yagi and the woman across from her responded in kind. Naoya was still frowning deeply in disapproval while Lady Dada remained stoic and her ministers exchanged furtive looks. Beside Lady Dada, the old woman who had not spoken a word to anyone began to eat, looking for all the world as if she had not heard a word from anyone either. She smiled to herself, and when Kazuchiyo happened to catch her eye, she winked at him.

Kazuchiyo cleared his throat. "My sister isn't wrong," he said, "but our intentions to take the capital can be explored another time. All that matters now is that we make sure the danger for Jisu has passed, and that its people have the means to recover before the winter. To that end our armies will remain at least until Mutsuyama and his forces have withdrawn, and perhaps a while after that to be certain. With Lady Dada's permission, I hope."

"You have my permission," Lady Dada replied.

She reached for her supper, and the meal continued at a more comfortable pace. Mahiro and Chikakuni dominated much of the conversation with their recounting of the battle, from the hilltop to the village to the road. After supper, a brief ceremony was held for the viewings of the heads that had been claimed, including that of General Umafusa. His emotionless expression in death gave Kazuchiyo a chill, and he pitied him.

At the conclusion of the evening, Lady Dada gave each of them a chamber in the castle for the night. "We don't have much to offer, but they're comfortable chambers," she said. "At the very least, you can bathe."

"My place is with my men," Naoya replied immediately. "If Master Mutsuyama does plan to use his sorcery, better that I am at the front to prevent him." His brow knit into a guilty expression. "Excuse me, but I must take my leave."

He and Purnima left the chamber, deliberately avoiding Kazuchiyo's attempts to catch his eye. Though Kazuchiyo managed not to let his disappointment show at their behavior, Mahiro made no such effort. "That's a shame," she declared, "but it's their loss. *I*, on the other hand, would love to stay." She downed the rest of her wine and smacked her lips. "And I hope by morning I will have seen many of Etsugo's comfortable chambers."

"Then the rest of us might as well, too," said Amai while Kazuchiyo felt his cheeks flush. "If only so that we're here to apologize for her behavior come tomorrow."

Lady Dada scoffed quietly with amusement. "Then I'll have you all shown to the rooms so we may all retire for the evening." She nodded to Kazuchiyo. "And yes, speak again come morning." Kazuchiyo bowed his head in acknowledgement, and the group disbanded for the evening.

Kazuchiyo, Yagi, and Amai made their way immediately to the bathhouse. Though not as hot as Kazuchiyo would have liked, the clean water was a great comfort to his weary body. He scrubbed the road dirt from his thirsty skin and helped Yagi unwind the bandages from his wounds.

"You've definitely overworked your knee," Kazuchiyo scolded him gently as he cleaned the healing gash, "but it doesn't look infected. Come morning I'll ask Chikakuni if their physicians can spare some ointment for it."

Yagi pulled a face that drew a chuckle from Amai. "You can tell them the ointment's for me," Amai teased as he ladled water over his hair. "I overworked myself too." He flashed Kazuchiyo a wink. "And I plan to again later."

"He can tell them whatever he wants," Yagi muttered back, clearly missing his innuendo. "It's not that bad." Kazuchiyo tried not to look at Amai again as he finished rebandaging Yagi's knee; he didn't want to encourage him until they were in a less public place.

The room offered to them was larger and finer than the quarters at Rongi. Kazuchiyo opened one of the slatted windows and was granted a sweeping view of surrounding mountains and valleys, tipped in silver from a moon narrow and curved like a katana blade. So high up the air was cool and thin, and even the stars seemed to glow a little brighter. It was not difficult to imagine why the lord of Tendo had been so eager to claim the gorgeous landscape for his own with only frail incentive from the shogun, and why Jisu's people were willing to go to such lengths to defend it.

But panoramic scenery was not at the forefront of Kazuchiyo's mind that evening. As he turned away from the window, the sight of Yagi and Amai stretching out the futons impressed on him the full realization that the three of them had not had this measure of congregation and privacy for many days. Though Amai's receptiveness to the opportunity was clear, Yagi's furrowed brow was a more difficult read. Letting his sleeping robe hang loose around him, Kazuchiyo joined the pair just as they sat down. He kneeled in front of Yagi, took his face in both hands, and kissed him.

It felt as if it were a longer time coming than it had been. Kazuchiyo leaned into Yagi's wide mouth, delighting in the warmth of clean skin beneath his hands. With their battles temporarily over he wanted nothing more than to shed the weights of duty and uncertainty that had bound them.

Yagi's quiet rumble, a sound by now as familiar to him as his own heartbeat, convinced him in the moment that he had succeeded. Yagi met and returned his kiss, wrapped his arms around Kazuchiyo's back, and drew him in. Even Amai making some kind of sarcastic remark Kazuchiyo only half heard was a welcome familiarity.

Kazuchiyo turned to the side, gripping the collar of Yagi's robe to draw him down after him. He was eager for Yagi's broad form to shield and smother him after too many nights feeling adrift. Yagi followed at first, meeting him for another kiss as Kazuchiyo rolled onto his back. But when Kazuchiyo spread his knees in welcome, Yagi hesitated. He kissed Kazuchiyo again, harder even, but the rest of his body was still frustratingly out of reach, and no tugging from Kazuchiyo could convince him to bridge the gap.

"Are you all right?" Kazuchiyo asked, stroking Yagi's face. Though he was no stranger to patience, he found it difficult to call upon when his body was so eager for friction and release. "I'm sorry—is this hard on your knee?"

"No, it's nothing," Yagi insisted. He leaned down for another kiss, but it ended faster than those before. Frustration hardened the lines of his face, which Kazuchiyo tried to smooth away with encouraging lips and a tender caress. Seeing no other option, Kazuchiyo slid one hand down between them. Though Yagi hissed against his mouth at the long fingers and their intimate strokes, Kazuchiyo was surprised and dismayed to find no real trace of arousal in his lover.

With a hard sigh Yagi rolled back, onto his side. "I'm sorry," he grumbled, and he raked his fingers through his hair. "Sorry, I'm… too tired for this right now."

Kazuchiyo wilted against the mattress. What heat had still clung to him from the bathhouse swiftly evaporated, and he even felt a lump of emotion harden in his throat. After a few deep breaths to loosen it, he said, "It's all right. It's been… a difficult few days."

Then he looked to his left, where he found Amai watching

them with raised eyebrows. Whether his expression was one of smugness or sympathy, Kazuchiyo was in no mood to interpret. "Amai."

Amai, stretched out on his side, propped his head up on his palm. "Yes?"

Kazuchiyo twisted toward him and all but pounced. Though he was concerned for Yagi's feelings as well, his own frustration got the better of him, and Amai was too tempting of a target to pass up. He pushed Amai onto his back and crawled on top of him, determined to make the little weasel pay for being so inviting.

Amai hummed happily as Kazuchiyo leaned in for a kiss. As always, his lips were teasing, and he squirmed beneath Kazuchiyo playfully. "Oh, be gentle," he purred, but there was a challenge in his smirk that only proved to excite Kazuchiyo's temper.

Yagi watched them. Kazuchiyo could feel his eyes, but he didn't want to look for fear that it would sour this opportunity too. Instead, he focused his full appetite on Amai; he pinned Amai's narrow wrists to the mattress, demanded long, passionate kisses. When Amai played at resistance by drawing his thighs together, Kazuchiyo greedily parted them with his knees. He scraped their sweat-moistened bodies together, thrilling in the contrast of the soft, cotton sleep robes pooling against warm skin. In the lust-addled mind of an anxious youth, *this* was the reward for all they had suffered. Amai wilted in complete surrender at the perfect moment, and Kazuchiyo felt powerful as he sucked murmurs of pleasure from his lips.

The moment Kazuchiyo pulled back, seeking some means of easing their love-making, Amai rolled onto his stomach; his silvery eyes flashed in the dimly lit room, their usual mischief shed in favor of earnest desire. Kazuchiyo hurried back with balm in hand, and once Amai was prepared Kazuchiyo slid deftly into him. He made love to Amai in firm strokes fueled by tension that had reached its peak with Yagi's rejection, by too many worrisome nights staring at a darkened castle in the distance, by too much politics and not enough romance. He dug his fingers into Amai's slender hips as if his aching knuckles could convey how he had longed for his clever-tongued lover during his trials. Amai could not have been more receptive. He panted and purred, meeting Kazuchiyo stroke for stroke but no more, allowing him to set the ferocity and pace. He arched and stretched and rocked like art being drawn into form beneath Kazuchiyo's hands. When both came to release it was with shudders and gasps, as if neither had expected to inflict upon the other such raw, sorely needed intimacy.

Kazuchiyo leaned back on his heels, mopping his brow with the collar of his robe as he caught his breath. He felt exhausted and new, and when he at last looked to Yagi again, he was surprised by what he found: Yagi was gaping openly, eyes round as saké cups, his cheeks deeply flushed. But where Kazuchiyo might have expected jealousy or disappointment, there was only blatant intrigue, evidenced even more clearly by his robe tented over his lap.

Kazuchiyo slicked his bangs out of his face. His body was still reeling from stimulation and his emotions slow to work—he had no idea how to react just yet. "Not so tired after all?" he said.

Yagi flushed more deeply and looked away, only to be interrupted by Amai chuckling.

"Don't tease him too much," said Amai as he sat up, stretching his back. "We've always known he likes to watch."

"That's not—" Yagi started to protest, but then Amai crawled over and slipped his hand beneath Yagi's robe. He couldn't gather himself fast enough to prevent a startled, aroused groan from squeezing through his teeth.

"Seems a shame to let it go to waste," Amai teased, all bratty mischief again as he licked his lips and lowered his head. "I know you're not too tired for *this*."

"But—" Yagi protested, but Amai's mouth was as clever and enticing as ever, and once enveloped, the poor man had no defense. He dropped back onto his palms with a helpless murmur.

Kazuchiyo was not, however, one who could only watch. He crawled around Amai, leaving him to his talented work so he could sit instead at Yagi's shoulder. Dear Yagi fidgeted beneath his scrutiny, trapped between pleasure and embarrassment. Though Kazuchiyo could not entirely suppress the sharp pit of confusion and hurt their strained relationship had lodged in his stomach, he hated to see his brave lover so uncertain. So he kissed him.

Yagi tensed, and his breath hitched between their mouths, thrown askew by Amai's suckling talents below. Soon enough his carnal instincts overpowered all else, and he took a fistful of Kazuchiyo's hair to keep him close. Kazuchiyo shook with relief and happily obliged. Kiss after kiss dragged them down to the mattress, where Kazuchiyo stroked his chest and preyed on his lips until Amai's ministrations overwhelmed him.

They lay there for a while, breath on each other's faces, as they sought the proper words. "Sorry," Yagi mumbled at long last. "It's... not you."

"Shh, it's all right." Kazuchiyo smoothed Yagi's hair back, taking special care toward his healing wound. "Even if it is, you can tell me." Seeing Yagi's brow beginning to furrow again, he rubbed his thumb against his lover's forehead and quickly added, "In the morning. Can we talk then?"

Yagi gulped. "All right," he said, and he returned one more kiss.

The three of them tidied themselves and the bedding up as best they could to last the night. Before they could each stretch out, however, Kazuchiyo tugged Amai close to whisper in his ear. "Thank you."

"Mm, you wouldn't believe how welcome you are," Amai whispered back, and he gave Kazuchiyo's ear a little nibble. "Come get some sleep."

Kazuchiyo smiled, and was even more relieved when Yagi welcomed him under his arm. With his head pillowed on Yagi's chest and Amai snug against his back, he slept deeply all through the night.

CHAPTER THIRTEEN

The next morning, Kazuchiyo awoke before his companions. It was rare that he bested Amai in this regard, and he took the opportunity to watch him sleep, idly speculating on what imagery painted a shinobi's dreams. Something pleasant, judging by the little smile quirking Amai's lips. Kazuchiyo pressed to them a delicate kiss as if he might share a taste.

He then turned to Yagi. Even when at his most serene Yagi's face never reached an expression of unquestionable peace, but at least he seemed calm. Kazuchiyo stroked his hair and prayed that when the conversation they'd each agreed to came about, he would find the words his lover needed.

The floorboards just outside the chamber creaked, and a woman's voice softly called, "Lord Sakka?"

Kazuchiyo crawled out from between from his two lovers as carefully as possible and moved to the panel. "Yes?"

"Please excuse me, lordship," said the maid. "My lady bid me ask you if you'll take breakfast with her this morning before you depart. We'll have something brought for your companions as well."

Kazuchiyo glanced to the chamber's open window,

realizing from the bright sun pouring in just how late the hour had grown. "Yes, of course," he said through the panel. "Please offer her my apologies for keeping her waiting. I'll be ready shortly." He started to turn away and then stopped himself. "I know supplies are scarce, but if your physician could spare some rosewood and ginseng?"

"Yes, of course," said the maid. "Straight away."

"Thank you."

When Kazuchiyo returned to the futon, Amai was awake and yawning. "Go ahead," Amai urged him. "I'll keep an eye on this silly brute."

Kazuchiyo shook his head. "I don't want him to wake up and find me gone," he said, and he gave Yagi's shoulder a gentle shake. "Yagi?"

"Mnn?" Yagi grumbled wordlessly as he scrubbed his face. "Kazu?"

"I'm going to meet with Lady Dada," Kazuchiyo told him, once again combing his fingers through Yagi's hair. "They'll bring you some breakfast here, and after that we'll all head back to the camp."

Yagi swallowed as he awakened fully. "I'll be ready," he said, and hoping to reassure him, Kazuchiyo kissed him on the forehead before moving away to get dressed.

The castle had a weary but relieved air to it, Kazuchiyo thought as he was led to a chamber in the greater keep. Soldiers and servants who had for days stood in anxious vigil carried out their business slowly, as if they, too, had only just been roused from a long sleep. It made Kazuchiyo feel a bit better about his manners. Inside the chamber waited Lady Dada, dressed in a simpler kimono than the night before, though her face was still elegantly made up. She invited Kazuchiyo in, and they each drank fresh tea and thickened broth garnished with ginkgo nuts.

"Now that it's just the two of us, I hope we can converse with less politics in the way," said Lady Dada.

Yet they were *not* the only two in the chamber; Kazuchiyo

glanced to the wall behind Lady Dada, where one panel lay open to reveal a dew-covered garden in the courtyard beyond. Seated in the open doorway, staring out into the manicured greenery, was the old woman from supper. She paid them no particular notice, but Kazuchiyo still tilted his head and asked, "The two of us?"

"My grandmother," Lady Dada introduced the woman without turning to look. "Lady O-bou. Please don't pay her any mind."

"Very well." Kazuchiyo took another long sip of his breakfast. "I'm grateful for this opportunity. Your generals and ministers all seemed very capable, but it's difficult to speak openly in such a large assembly of differing viewpoints."

"To say nothing of Oihata," replied Lady Dada, and she scoffed. "Arrogant dramatics, from the eldest to the youngest."

Kazuchiyo pursed his lips and chose his next words carefully. "I beg your pardon, Lady Dada, but General Oihata is a good friend of mine."

"Oh? You didn't seem so last night."

Kazuchiyo counseled himself then to never underestimate Lady Dada's perceptiveness. "I have to admit, our friendship is strained of late," he said. "Actually, I hope you might be able to help me on that front."

"I have doubts," she replied, refilling her teacup, "but you might as well explain what you mean."

Whatever her claims, her bluntness reminded Kazuchiyo of Naoya a great deal, and it gave him the confidence to continue. "He and I quarreled over the use of magic. He says it's too dangerous for me to use."

Lady Dada raised a painted eyebrow while behind her, Grandmother O-bou tilted her ear toward them. "It probably is. A man determined to become shogun could find many uses for it, and just as many reasons why he shouldn't."

"But you do hold a bead," Kazuchiyo pressed. He had not expected to receive the same warning from Lady Dada as he had Naoya, and it put him disproportionately ill at ease. "The one you gave to Sir Chikakuni. You must know how it works, then?"

"I knew well enough that it would convince an onmyouji of what went on here," said Lady Dada, and she drew Kazuchiyo's attention to the band of fabric cinching her kimono: the bead was tucked into the knot there. "But my grandmother warned me years ago that dabbling in magic would be a mistake for me, even more so than…" She paused, frowning as she reassembled her words. She met Kazuchiyo's gaze with clear effort to caution him. "Using magic will change someone if their will isn't strong enough. Men with ambition most of all. If you want to be shogun, give up on magic."

Kazuchiyo leaned back, and though her cryptic words frustrated him, he was even more concerned that Lady Dada would intuit the frailty of his convictions. "I wish one of you would simply explain it to me," he admitted. "The more you warn, the more curious it makes me."

"I don't trust you with the truth," Lady Dada declared. "I said I won't stop you from becoming shogun, but I won't fight for you either. Not until you've proven your character to me."

"Proven myself?" Kazuchiyo stared back at her, struggling to repress his exasperation. "Risking my life and my men for the freedom of strangers wasn't enough?"

"No, it wasn't." Lady Dada drew her cup closer. "Not when you have that oni fighting for you."

She drank, and Kazuchiyo bristled at the unexpected mention of Yagi. Before he could demand a greater explanation, his attention was drawn to O-bou; she was giggling into her sleeve, and she turned just enough to cast him a playful wink. It baffled him enough that his irritation stumbled, and he was able to reply with greater composure. "I don't understand what Yagi-douji has to do with it, but very well. I accept your challenge."

Lady Dada smirked, and she tipped her cup in a salute that Kazuchiyo mirrored.

"I hope this isn't too impertinent of me to ask," Kazuchiyo

said after some time, "but you said just now that magic would be especially dangerous for you. Because of the way it 'changes' people?"

"Yes, exactly so." Lady Dada took in a deep breath before continuing. "When I was born, my father was overjoyed thinking he finally had a male heir to succeed him. Unfortunately for him, he was mistaken." She swept a lock of hair behind her ear. "It's taken a long time to convince my clan of the woman I am, and I will not jeopardize my identity for anyone or anything."

"I understand," Kazuchiyo said, making an effort toward delicacy. "I don't wish to insult or patronize you with too much sympathy, but I can imagine you must have faced many challenges. I respect your courage."

Lady Dada watched his face, measuring. "By that do you mean that once you are shogun, you'll acknowledge me as the daimyo of Jisu, so I had better accept your magistrate when he comes calling?"

"I meant what I said, just as I said it," Kazuchiyo replied, but then he offered a smile. "But yes, that too."

Lady Dada returned it with one of her own—a more genuine smile that Kazuchiyo had yet seen on her, which softened her stern face considerably. "I appreciate it. I take it you haven't met a woman like me before?"

"Not in so high a station," Kazuchiyo admitted. "Lord Aritaka has an unfortunately narrow view of the qualities of women. A province like Jisu, ruled by a woman and employing so many female warriors on the battlefield, would be very foreign to him." He grimaced. "His own daughter has had to fight very hard for his recognition. I'm afraid you won't receive much hospitality from him."

"Then it's a good thing I made a pledge to you and not to him," said Lady Dada, and Kazuchiyo felt a rush of heat. Before he could dwell on that implication, she continued. "What about Lord Koedzuka, since he's the one I'm now honor bound to meet with?"

Lucky for them that Naoya wasn't present for such

a question; certainly he would have filled the better part of an hour with praise, and might have resented Kazuchiyo even more for not doing the same. "Lord Koedzuka is a true gentleman," Kazuchiyo said. "Wise and generous, and hopeful for peace. You have nothing to fear from him, and I would have something to say if you did." He allowed a bit more gravity into his tone. "However, neither of us have forgotten how this conflict first started."

Lady Dada finished her remaining soup and pushed the tray aside. "Neither have I," she said, but then she seemed to reconsider her manners, and she let out a quiet sigh. "I'm not a simpleton. I sent my army to invade his lands, and he sent his army to save us. Jisu will make its amends. Though I also hope *he* has not forgotten that we are not the only ones to have crossed borders unprovoked."

Kazuchiyo was reminded then of Naoya unashamedly declaring campaigns he and General Sasahara had embarked on in Jisu lands, and he nodded. "If he has forgotten, I'll be there to remind him," he promised. "Though ultimately I hope we can put all of that behind us." Encouraged by the honesty Lady Dada had offered him thus far, Kazuchiyo braced his heart and continued. "The east has been at war with itself for too long. The back and forth you've shared with Kibaku is very similar to how Sakka and Suyama used to be, and that, those battles escalating, is what cost me my birth father and brothers. I don't want to see the same happen to either of your homelands."

Rather than be moved by his well-meant counsel, Lady Dada watched him only more closely. "You have a new father now, don't you?" she asked. "Okiaki told me that you prefer not to be called by his name."

Kazuchiyo swallowed; tempted as he was to speak as bluntly as she did, he couldn't yet bring himself to trust her any more than she did him. "I did," he admitted. "And I noticed that you're not the only one he told. I appreciate it."

Lady Dada waited for him to elaborate, and when he did not, she nodded. "A samurai's name is sacred to them. Though

I'm not certain that 'Lord Sakka' tells your full story either."
She offered him a vulpine smile. "Maybe I should be calling
you Touyun no Kami, Lord of the East."

It was a grand title, both exhilarating and intimidating,
and Kazuchiyo could not help a huff of nervous amusement.
"Lady Dada, you flatter me, but for now 'Lord Kazumune'
suits me fine."

Though Lady Dada seemed disappointed to have been
denied the drama, she relented gracefully. It was then that
Chikakuni called gently out to them from behind the closed
panel. Lady Dada invited him in, and he bowed his head to the
floor before Kazuchiyo.

"When I heard you had roused, I hurried over," he
explained. "I want to again express my deep gratitude for the
aid you've offered us in our time of need."

Kazuchiyo smiled, bowing his head. "You've thanked
me more than enough already," he replied, "and as much as I
appreciate the formality, I like your honesty better."

"This is my honesty," Chikakuni insisted as he sat upright,
though with more relaxed humor. "You always speak so well; I
can't help but try to match you."

"There's little chance of that," scolded Lady Dada. "He has
a cloud's tongue."

Chikakuni chuckled at Kazuchiyo's confused expression.
"A local saying," he explained. He flashed Lady Dada a look of
mock reproach. "Not the kindest one either."

Lady Dada remained unconcerned. "Words are never kind
or unkind, only true or false."

That had Kazuchiyo smiling to himself, reminded of
General Rakuteru and his fondness for the saying. "Well then,
trust I'm being truthful when I say I don't need any more
expressions of gratitude from either of you. I'm only happy to
have reunited a pair so well matched."

Lady O-bou giggled from the engawa. A blush darkened
Chikakuni's cheeks; though Lady Dada's makeup prevented
the same from being visible on her, Kazuchiyo could sense

it all the same. The two exchanged a look of much meaning, and it wasn't until that moment, with Chikakuni dressed in a simple robe and his full face and figure evident, that Kazuchiyo realized just how much the pair had in common after all.

"Yes, well," said Lady Dada in embarrassment, "in that case my gratitude has run out." She made a shooing motion.

Kazuchiyo continued to smile as he again bowed his head. "Then I take my leave, though I trust we'll remain in close contact until the threat from Mutsuyama has passed."

"Yes, indeed." She bowed in return, humble despite her remarks, and Kazuchiyo showed himself out of the chamber with Chikakuni alongside him. He took notice that Lady O-bou watched them the entire way out.

"There was another reason I thought I should come fetch you," Chikakuni said once they were out in the hall. "Your sister."

"Oh." Kazuchiyo winced with his own embarrassment and allowed Chikakuni to lead the way. "Maybe I shouldn't have used up so much of Lady Dada's gratitude with Mahiro still on the grounds. I hope she didn't cause too much trouble?"

"That depends on one's definition," Chikakuni replied smartly. "But no, I don't think anyone who crossed her path last night regrets it."

"That's encouraging, I suppose."

Chikakuni took them to another, smaller garden courtyard, where a young maid was gathering empty saké gourds and cups onto a tray. Her hair was only loosely held in a messy bun, and she was smothering a yawn against her sleeve, though she snapped into a bow upon seeing the two men approach. Chikakuni excused her, and she scuttled off to her chores.

The garden itself was in a similar, lazy disarray, more cups nestled among the flowers and stones. Mahiro was sprawled among the shrubbery, draped in her robes and snoring quietly. Two muscular women were similarly stretched out on either side of her. Kazuchiyo sighed with amusement. It was not the first time he had discovered his sister in a like state, and given her success on the battlefield the night before, he could not blame her for making the most of so many willing companions.

"Thank you," he told Chikakuni. "I'll take her to my room. She'll be out of everyone's way there."

"Won't you need some help?" Chikakuni suggested, eyebrows raised.

"Could be." Kazuchiyo crept forward and, trying not to disturb the other two women, he crouched down to rock Mahiro's shoulder. "Sister?"

Mahiro grumbled and swatted at him, and at last at his insistence grumbled herself awake. She glared blearily up at him. "What?"

"Let me take you to bed," Kazuchiyo offered. Though she wasn't much help at first, he tugged her upright so he could better fit her into her robe sleeves. "Come on now. You'll catch cold out here."

"I'm plenty warm," Mahiro protested drunkenly, and it took Chikakuni's help after all to get her on her feet. By then the other pair was rousing, and in hopes of sparing their modesty, Kazuchiyo hurried to lead Mahiro out of the courtyard.

She stumbled along with her arm around his shoulders. "I could use a bath."

"You could," Kazuchiyo agreed, grateful that she could not see his expression. "Sleep a bit longer first, or you're likely to pass out in the tub."

"Where's Purnima?" Mahiro craned her neck to look about, even though she was having a mighty hard time keeping her eyes open. "Is she here?"

"No, she's down in the village with General Oihata."

"Oh." Mahiro hummed in disappointment, but she stumbled along with them down the hall.

They arrived at Kazuchiyo's guest chamber and found Yagi and Amai fully dressed and conversing quietly over breakfast. The anxious look Yagi cast at the doorway as it was opened made Kazuchiyo extremely curious as to what their topic had been, though within seconds Yagi's face had again relaxed. He even lent his strength to easing Mahiro onto a futon, and then the four of them left the chamber to give her privacy.

"She's welcome here for as long as she wishes," Chikakuni assured Kazuchiyo. "You all are."

"I'm anxious to get back to the camp," said Kazuchiyo. "I want to hear from our guards and scouts if there's been any movement from Mutsuyama, and send word to our reinforcements."

He glanced to the closed panel of the chamber, and Chikakuni smirked, urging, "Go ahead then. We'll look after your sister until she's in a mood to travel. I'll feel better about that onmyouji still skulking about as long as the Unyielding Iron is here protecting us."

"I appreciate it. And I apologize on her behalf in advance, if she gives you trouble."

Chikakuni walked with them out of the keep, and they parted ways. The small troop of Sakka soldiers that had accompanied them from the camp were out in the courtyard, awaiting their lord. Kazuchiyo tried not to frown at them, disappointed by the reminder that it would be yet longer until he and Yagi were afforded some measure of privacy. Dressed again in his armor, Yagi looked as stoic as ever, but Kazuchiyo was convinced much still lay on his mind, and he was anxious to address it. As they made their way through Etsugo's terraced baileys toward the main gate, he managed to catch Yagi's eye and asked, "How do you feel this morning?"

"Fine," said Yagi. His gaze darted to the collection of soldiers leading their way. "In private?"

"Of course." Kazuchiyo in turn looked to Amai, who followed behind as was only correct for his lower station. He selfishly hoped he would have the chance to confer with his more intuitive partner before fulfilling the conversation he himself was instigating. "When you're ready."

Yagi nodded and left it at that.

When their small procession reached the main gate, they encountered an unexpected well-wisher in the form of Lady

O-bou. Though she had to have traveled at a much quicker pace than she seemed capable of to have beaten Kazuchiyo to the gate, there was nothing harried in her face or manner. Her white hair fanned out about her in happy dishevelment, and her eyes twinkled as she beckoned Kazuchiyo to approach. Though the soldiers eyed her with confusion, Kazuchiyo showed no hesitation in heeding her.

"Lady O-bou?" Kazuchiyo bowed respectfully. "Thank you for coming to see us off."

The old woman smirked and lifted both her hands to him. "Give me your wrist," she said in a quiet, birdlike voice.

Though Kazuchiyo was startled, his curiosity spoke over his concern, and his heart quickened its pace as he extended his right hand to her. Lady O-bou took it with one hand while her other clasped the inside of his wrist. She squeezed, her palm pushing deliberately against the small, red bead that sat ever tucked beneath its ribbon. It felt especially warm in her grip.

"Oh, be careful," she whispered, so that Kazuchiyo had to lean close to hear her. "Your well is almost dry."

"What?" Kazuchiyo watched her very closely, realizing at last that the Lady O-bou was not as senile as she chose to appear. "Is… is the cup empty?" He fidgeted. "How can I fill it?"

"The fox," said O-bou, nodding a few times. "Follow the fox to the mountain." She let go of his hand and pointed one short, knobby finger toward the looming figure of Mount Etsuzan to the northwest. "And be polite." With a secretive little giggle O-bou released his wrist as well, and she stepped back. "Good luck."

Though mystified, Kazuchiyo bowed his thanks, and he motioned for his entourage to continue. It was not until they had been reunited with their horses and were heading down the plateau's slope that any of them spoke another word.

"What did the old woman say?" Yagi asked. "What was she pointing at?"

"She said I should 'follow the fox to the mountain,'"

Kazuchiyo related, and he thought immediately of the handsome, piebald fox that he had glimpsed watching him from the roadside. Could it have been that same fox he spied sneaking through their camp before ever arriving at Etsugo? The memory of its piercing, blue eyes gave him a strange chill.

"I'm happy to take you myself," boasted Amai, "though it would be nice to know what I'm looking for. Is there anything up there?"

"I don't know. If it's the home of their harvest goddess, I imagine there's at least a shrine of some sort." Kazuchiyo turned in his saddle as best he could to see the mountain's lofty peak. "Chikakuni said Lady O-bou had some skill as an onmyouji. Maybe she knows something."

Amai harrumphed. "Or she's a sneaky old fox herself playing tricks on you. You're so gullible, Kazu."

Kazuchiyo turned forward again. "That's hardly true."

"Oh, I beg to differ. You had better tell us what Lady Dada had to say, too, so we can be your judgment for you."

Kazuchiyo scoffed, though it did feel remarkably normal and relaxing to trade barbs with Amai again. As they continued down the path toward the main road, he recounted for them the essentials of his conversation with Lady Dada, and his intentions once they had returned to their camp. "We can't let our guard down too completely until Mutsuyama has retreated from the valley," he finished. "Only then will Jisu breathe easily, and we'll have to keep the remaining Tendo soldiers as prisoners until they have a safer route home."

"Does that really matter?" asked Yagi. "Their general rejected your offer. It doesn't sound like whoever's in charge of Tendo will help us, so why not let Mutsuyama kill them if you really think that's what he'd do?"

"I'm convinced he would," said Kazuchiyo. "General Umafusa was loyal to him, but Mutsuyama betrayed him to his death. If word of that betrayal reaches *Lord* Umafusa, that will weaken the shogun's power over him." He hummed to himself as he tried to recall all the maps he had studied in his youth of the geography and topography. "Tendo's navy really is strong. Even if we take the capital, we'll never hold it without Tendo on our side. Maybe there's still a chance for us to coerce them away from the shogun before then."

Yagi frowned and fell silent. It made Kazuchiyo's skin crawl, and again he looked to Amai, who was only smiling blankly ahead, giving away nothing.

They returned to their camp at the crest of the road, where Ginta met them to deliver news: happily, a lack of news. Naoya's Kibaku forces had instilled a small group of scouts at Agarigumo Temple, and that morning had reported a total lack of movement from Master Mutsuyama's troops. Ginta had also prepared a pair of their own scouts to send back eastward with news of the successful retaking of Etsugo, who waited only for Kazuchiyo's blessing to disembark. Kazuchiyo thanked him for his foresight, and he prepared a letter for the scouts to convey to General Rakuteru. Afterward he toured the camp to be certain their men were well-tended and alert, and once all his duties were completed, he returned to his tent with his companions.

By then Kazuchiyo's nerves were strained nearly as tight as they had been on the battlefield, and seeing Yagi just as uncomfortable only made it worse. "Can I help you out of your armor?" he suggested, hoping that keeping his hands busy with a familiar task would help to settle him.

"I'll keep it on," said Yagi, and he sat on one of the tent's stools. He unfastened his helmet and set it down, but removed no more than that. "There's still a lot of the day left, and we don't know what will happen."

"No, you're right." Kazuchiyo sat cross-legged in front of him, though he had no idea how to begin. He could not help but look to Amai, who was already halfway through shedding his own light armor. "What were you two talking about this morning when I came in?"

"You," Amai said breezily. He cast his chest plate aside and then stretched out. "But that's all I'm going to say. If he wants to tell you, he can tell you."

Yagi glared at him. "Little weasel."

"Yagi, please," said Kazuchiyo. "If something is weighing on you, I wish you would tell me." He offered a hopeful smile. "I'm not as strong as you, but I want to bear your burdens with you."

"I've tried," Yagi replied, which immediately sent Kazuchiyo's memory spinning backward, trying to claw out his meaning. "But I'm not smart like you. I don't know how to explain it properly."

Kazuchiyo took a deep breath to keep frustration from getting the better of him. "It doesn't have to be smart, or proper. I just want to know what you're feeling." He swallowed. "Have I hurt you somehow?"

Yagi's brow drew in. His failure to correct Kazuchiyo immediately had the poor boy in knots, but he waited, determined to give the man his time. "It's not that," Yagi said at last, and he leaned forward to brace his elbows on his knees. "It's just, I won't ever be a good samurai for you."

"I told you not to worry about that," Kazuchiyo protested. "You've done plenty for us already, and you've worked—"

"Hold on," Amai interrupted. "Let him talk."

"I am!" Kazuchiyo shot him a look, but seeing Amai's expression devoid of its usual teasing reminded him of their conversation before confronting Naoya, and he forced himself to rein in his defensive impulse. "I'm sorry," he tried again as he faced Yagi. "Please; I'm listening."

Yagi had looked away again, and it took him another moment to gather his words. "You said before that I was trying too hard to be a samurai, but that's not what I'm doing, or what I want." Having finally found his momentum, he spoke more quickly, and with greater insistence. "All I want is for you to be safe. I don't care about samurai names and honor and who is whose father or the names of their fucking swords.

I don't understand poetry and scheming, and I'm not going to throw myself at a monster just to die and leave you alone! That's stupid!"

Yagi shook his head and then grimaced, scratching the healing wound at his temple. "But you're a samurai, and you're good at it. You're smart and you always know what to say—but sometimes you don't mean it, and I can't tell the difference. I don't like feeling that you're so far away from me." Yagi grumbled wordlessly as his shoulders fell. "Makes my stomach hurt."

"Mine too," Kazuchiyo confessed softly, but then he stopped himself, waiting to see if Yagi would continue. When he couldn't bear the silence any longer, he crawled closer and took his lover's hand. "I don't always know what to say." He sighed, trying to expel the lump in his throat. "I have no idea now."

"Sorry," Yagi mumbled. "I'm still not saying it right."

"No, I un—I *think* I understand." Kazuchiyo glanced again to Amai, hoping for guidance. Though Amai's patient expression was encouraging, it didn't provide much help. "It's true that we're very different, and I'm sorry I haven't done more to... to bridge that gap somehow." He tightened his grip on Yagi's hand, willing it to give him the strength it always had—strength enough to ask the question he dreaded. "Those duels seemed very hard on you. Do you not want to fight?"

"No, I do," Yagi replied immediately that time, gripping Kazuchiyo back. "It's what I can do, and I want to." He scoffed roughly. "I want to fight for you like you need me to, but I don't want to *be* like them, so eager to die for no reason at all, thanking each other for the chance. But... it's because they're samurai, and you're samurai, so if I can't be like that, it'll cause trouble for you." He gestured helplessly with his free hand. "How can I want two totally different things at the same time? It's stupid!"

"It's not stupid," said Amai, smirking at him. "It's very normal; you've just never had a lover before."

"He's right," added Kazuchiyo. "I'm not any different." He touched Yagi's knee, where the linen bandage was only barely visible through the open spaces of his armor. "You're magnificent on the field, and I need you there, but I don't want to see you hurt." He met Yagi's gaze and held it, determined that, this time, they would connect properly. "I was really impressed with how well you worked with Captain Nishigame and his men. I wanted to encourage you more, but..." He grimaced. "I miss you when you're not in my bed. Everything I want conflicts with something else; I don't really know what to do either."

Yagi blinked down at him, as if he had never truly considered Kazuchiyo was that fallible. "You don't?"

"No, not at all!" Kazuchiyo chuckled, but he was then startled to find his eyes wet with emotion. He scraped the collar of his hitatare across his face. "I wish I was as wise as you think I am, I really do. But I'm pretty helpless, aren't I?"

"Oh." Yagi frowned as he took that in. "Really?"

"Yes." Kazuchiyo smiled, raising his eyebrows. "Does that make you feel any better?"

Yagi shook his head doggedly. "No! I was hoping you'd just tell me what to do."

Kazuchiyo couldn't help but chuckle again, but it hurt. His chest ached. He took Yagi's face in both hands so that neither of them would be able to look away again. "I can't," he said. "I'm sorry. But I love you, and I want us to figure it out together. All right?"

"All right," Yagi replied, and he tugged on Kazuchiyo's robe. Kazuchiyo stood and welcomed Yagi's head against his stomach, drawing them close together despite the points of Yagi's armor that dug into his body. When he lightly scratched Yagi's scalp, he even hummed like a contented beast. It was the closest Kazuchiyo had felt to his lover in days, and he kept his eyes and mouth tightly closed to keep the sensation from overwhelming him.

Amai's hand touched his back, and though he wasn't ready

yet to look, he took great comfort from Amai leaning into his shoulder.

After a few minutes, Yagi urged them both back. "I'm going to find some soldiers who want to train," he declared, and he rubbed his nose in embarrassment. "*That* will make me feel better."

"Go easy on them," Kazuchiyo teased, and though he wasn't much help given their difference in size, he took Yagi's hands to draw him to his feet. "I need every one of my soldiers."

"I know—I will." His face screwed up briefly. "We'll talk more over supper?"

"Yes, of course. If you like." He rose up for a quick kiss while Amai bent down to retrieve Yagi's helmet. "I'll see you then, if not before."

Yagi nodded, though he still looked a little awkward as he replaced his helmet and showed himself out. As soon as he was gone, Amai took his place, wrapping his arms sturdily around Kazuchiyo's midsection. It wasn't until he was granted that stability that Kazuchiyo realized how weak his knees suddenly were.

"That couldn't have been easy, but you did well," Amai said close to his ear.

Kazuchiyo hugged him tightly around the shoulders. "Amai, thank you. I thought all this time I was encouraging him, but…"

"You didn't do anything wrong. He's more complicated than even he knows." Amai tried to lean back, but Kazuchiyo prevented him, needing the support a while longer. Amai hummed, understanding, and rubbed his back. "I promised I wasn't going to say anything more, but I'm also a liar," he continued. "Yagi told me this morning he's confused about where you stand on being shogun. Apparently you give a lot of pretty speeches while telling us your heart isn't in it."

"It isn't," Kazuchiyo replied, but then he had to reconsider. He sighed into Amai's hair. "I honestly don't know. It does make for a pretty speech."

"You would be good at it," Amai said. "And we've come this far. You already plan on killing Aritaka eventually. Why not wait until the capital is under your belt? Have you really not considered it?"

Kazuchiyo frowned and could only admit the truth. "I haven't really. It seems so impossible; I've never even seen the capital. How could I rule the country?" He thought of Yagi, Mahiro, and Naoya alongside him then, their support and their strength. "But then again... it was only in uniting against the shogun that we were able to make peace with Kibaku in the first place. Aritaka's ambition is selfish and cruel, but if not for that, we might not have been able to avoid a siege at Izuho, and we wouldn't be here now at all. A better shogun than Oomiyari could make use of fair magistrates, maybe even calm all this war..." He licked his lips. "Do you really think that I...?"

Amai waited for him to complete the thought, and when he didn't, he hummed thoughtfully. "Yeah, I kinda do. You don't have to make up your mind yet, but you will soon. You won't be able to bluff your way through Koedzuka and Dada both, especially if Aritaka is thinking of butting into that meeting."

"No, you're right." Kazuchiyo gave Amai one more squeeze to regain the last of his strength and at last leaned back so they could see each other face to face. "I'll think on it more before then, and in the meantime, I'll try to explain to Yagi why it's so difficult. I don't want him to think I've been lying to you both."

Amai smirked. "That's not what he thinks, believe me. You're his entire *world*, Kazu. I'm not sure he could think ill of you if he tried."

"That's what worries me," murmured Kazuchiyo, but then he frowned, watching Amai very closely. He slid his hands down to cup Amai's face as he had Yagi's only minutes before. "Is there anything *you* need to tell me, Amai?"

Amai stared back at him, his eyes a little wider, his smile a little hesitant. "Like what?"

"You've been looking after both of us this whole time,"

Kazuchiyo said, desperate to believe that he was not completely oblivious to both his lovers' needs. "I appreciate it dearly, but I don't want you to think that's the *only* reason I turn to you. Please don't be jealous."

"Oh my," Amai sang, nuzzling Kazuchiyo's palm, "you've cured me."

Kazuchiyo's first instinct was to scold—how often had Amai deployed humor against his seriousness?—but as Amai himself had counseled him, he kept his patience. "Good," he said softly, unyielding. "Because I need you, and I want you to need me too."

Amai's face didn't change much, but he swallowed. "I do."

Kazuchiyo drew him close again, and feeling Amai wilt into his chest gave him a selfish reassurance; Amai may have been the better liar, but his insecurities were not always so difficult to suss out. He hugged Amai tight, stroked his hair, and kissed his temple, and Amai's cheeks were very hot as he hid them against Kazuchiyo's collar.

"I'm looking after you, too," Kazuchiyo said. "I'm sorry if I've neglected you."

"Oh, I'd forgive you if you had," Amai teased him, winding his fingers into the back of Kazuchiyo's robe. His voice lowered to a purr. "You more than made up for any slight last night."

Kazuchiyo's own face grew hotter with the mention of the previous evening. As always, Amai was warm and inviting beneath his hands, and in better spirits he would have strongly considered a few minutes more of privacy. He eased Amai back before he could let those thoughts dig their claws into him. "And I will again," he promised. "The next time we have thicker walls than these."

Amai licked his lips, though beneath his playful exterior Kazuchiyo could sense hints of sincerity. "I'm looking forward to it," he replied, and he retreated from Kazuchiyo's arms. "In the meantime, I'll get back to work. I'd like to sneak down the village and see how the crows are faring."

"Please do," said Kazuchiyo, and after Amai had left he

took one more deep breath before returning to duties of his own.

The rest of the day was blissfully uneventful. Though most of Sakka's soldiers were eager for recuperation, Yagi found several eager to test their might against him, which Kazuchiyo observed for a time. Though Yagi's manner remained sour, the exercise did seem to do him good. Toward the end he even offered a few gruff words of admonishment to his opponents that to Kazuchiyo's ear sounded like attempts at critique. Captain Nishigame watched the training with a stern but unmistakably pleased eye.

As the sun grew heavy Kazuchiyo moved to the edge of the camp overlooking the road, laying before him the full, panoramic view of the Etsugo castle, the valley, and the majestic shadow of the mountain beyond. It was a view that would have stirred almost any heart, and Kazuchiyo was moved again by the similarity the forested slopes bore to his dragon homeland. He had hoped it would thus provide him with inspiration and clarity, but it only clouded him further. He couldn't help but wonder how much of his memory of Suyama remained true. Were its peaks not rockier, and steeper, than the emerald valley before him? He both longed to know and dreaded being confronted with the truth, that his attachment to the home of his youth was frailer than he'd been imagining.

So instead Kazuchiyo turned his gaze to the town. Though there were still conversations for him to have with his lovers, he was already eager to reconcile another fractured relationship. He had brought with him a small wooden flute fit for travel, and he brought it to his lips to play "Enmei's Willow Garden," which he knew to be Naoya's particular favorite. He hoped its pure tone would echo down to the ears it was meant for, and though I can assure you that it did, it also attracted another, equally refined audience.

Kazuchiyo finished the song just as the sun dipped behind Mount Etsugo, and in the failing dusk he spotted a pair of vibrant eyes watching from the edge of the road. It was the piebald fox. Its blue eyes caught the camp's torchlight and twinkled back at Kazuchiyo, impressing on him that it had been watching and listening to him play for some time. When he took a step toward it, the fox remained still, watching him expectantly. When he played a few more notes, the fox's tail swayed happily back and forth.

"Lady O-bou said to follow you," Kazuchiyo mused, daring to take a few steps closer. The fox stood up on but showed no alarm. "Where would you lead me, little fox? Are you an onmyouji too?"

The fox tilted its head, and for the first time Kazuchiyo saw a piece of dark twine nestled in the mottled fur around its neck. He followed it down to the animal's throat, where a small, blue bead hung.

Kazuchiyo blinked in amazement. "Maybe you are," he said, and his heart pounded as the fox turned away and then looked back, clearly intending for him to accompany it. Tempted as he was to venture into the darkened forests of a foreign land, with only nature's cleverest beast to guide him, he was interrupted by the clop of horse hooves approaching from the slope. By the time he had confirmed it was the mighty Suzumekage and looked back, the fox had slipped away.

"Kazumune!" Mahiro called from atop her steed. She brandished a woven basket at him. "I brought you a gift from the village, and a fox with it!"

Kazuchiyo startled, only to realize that Amai was in the saddle behind her. He flashed Kazuchiyo a smirk as he hopped down. "Sorry I don't have any gifts for you too. No more than usual, anyway."

Kazuchiyo glanced one more time to the roadside, but the piebald fox was long gone. He struggled to push it from his mind. "What news from the village?"

Mahiro swung down from the saddle to instead lead

Suzumekage by the reins. "I'll tell you over supper," she said, her manner uncommonly irritated. "Come, I want wine!"

She led the way back to the camp, and Kazuchiyo and Amai fell in step behind her.

"Any insight on this one?" Kazuchiyo whispered.

"You won't need my help with her," Amai replied, shaking his head.

The three of them took supper in Kazuchiyo's tent, where it took very little wine to loosen Mahiro's tongue. "I went to the village to tease Purnima, and she wouldn't have anything to do with me," she lamented. "If she's mad at herself for not sticking around after supper last night, that's understandable, but she shouldn't take that out on *me*."

"I'm certain she felt she had to leave with her lord," said Kazuchiyo. "I'm very sorry if Sir Naoya's frustration with me is affecting the two of you."

"Then she should be mad at him, not me!" Mahiro insisted, waving her empty cup for Kazuchiyo to fill. "Next time we're on the field, I'm going to kill twice as many men as her and take three times as many heads. Then she won't be able to take her eyes off me!"

"I'm sure she won't." Kazuchiyo waited for her cup to settle before filling it for her, though not with as much as she probably wanted. "Though you should consider that maybe her disposition isn't a good match for last night's amount of spectacle."

Mahiro rolled her eyes at him. "Don't talk about spectacle to me, little brother, I know you made just as much of it as I did."

Kazuchiyo coughed in embarrassment while Amai continued to smirk to himself. He reached for his own cup. "That's hardly the point."

"Next time, I'm going to *woo* her," Mahiro promised. "Just you wait."

"We can't wait to see it," Amai assured her.

The gift Mahiro had brought turned out to be Jisu pears,

somewhat overripe as they had been picked just before the beginning of Tendo's occupation and hidden away. She took one for herself and stalked off, claiming that Suzumekage needed her tending before the night was through. In her place came Yagi, sweaty and exhausted after his afternoon of sparring, but seemingly in better spirits. He allowed Kazuchiyo and Amai to help him out of his armor and joined them in sharing the juicy dessert.

"I'm sorry about earlier," he said, accepting a pear slice from Kazuchiyo. "I didn't mean to be... that."

"You don't have to apologize," Kazuchiyo hurried to reassure him. He handed another slice to Amai. "I *want* you to share your feelings with me always. Both of you." He smiled hopefully. "Do you at least feel a little better now?"

"Yeah. I think so."

Yagi sucked thoughtfully on his pear, and seeing that he didn't seem ready to share more than that just yet, Kazuchiyo cleared his throat. "I have an idea," he said. Part of him wished he'd had the chance to put his thought to Amai first; the other was determined not to rely on him *too* much. "I think it might put your mind at ease a little." He faced Yagi with his full but compassionate seriousness. "I'm going to demote you."

"Demote?" Though Kazuchiyo had his breath held and Amai raised his eyebrows, Yagi frowned with confusion more than concern. "What rank am I now?"

Amai scoffed. "You're Commander Ebara Motonobu, son of General Ebara Toranobu. Equal to General Rakuteru's son Ginta."

"I'd like to demote you to captain and promote Captain Nishigame to commander in your place," Kazuchiyo explained. "It's the lowest I'm able to demote you without stripping you of your status entirely, which might suit you better, but I could never explain such a dishonor to your father or to Aritaka. It means you'd be closer to the foot soldiers in status and take orders from Nishigame."

"Oh." Yagi continued to munch on his pear, and Kazuchiyo

gave him the time and space needed for him to process. "I wouldn't mind that."

Kazuchiyo's shoulders relaxed. "It also means you wouldn't always be welcome at councils and ceremonies," he carried on gently. "Not that I don't appreciate your input—the road duels were your idea, and they worked—and you're still the most famous warrior in our army. But it's generals and commanders that make up the war council, and samurai who lead negotiations. You'd be spending more time with the troops."

Though Kazuchiyo expected some resistance to the notion, Yagi nodded along, surprising him. "That's fine. I don't really like being there anyway." Abruptly he frowned. "Will that cause trouble for you, though? Sleeping with someone that low in rank?"

Amai sucked pear juice from his fingers and laughed. "It's a little late to worry about that. He's been fucking me almost as long as you."

"Why, what rank are you?"

Amai sputtered in exasperation. "I'm not a samurai; his sandal-bearer is higher in rank than I am."

"Neither of you needs to worry about that," Kazuchiyo said. "I don't care if it's proper or not. Only Aritaka himself can scold me, and he won't."

"Because he's afraid of you," Amai quipped to Yagi.

Yagi snorted. "Good."

Kazuchiyo smiled, relieved that the three of them had lightened the mood. Though he hated to risk disturbing that, there was still more to say. "I know this is going to be different for us, and I don't expect it to be easy at first. But I hope it will ease some of your uncertainty, Yagi. I want you to be able to worry less about what's expected of you."

Yagi scratched the back of his neck. "No, I'm… thank you. I don't want you to worry about me, but I'm glad. I think I'll like that more." He even blushed a little. "Nishigame thanked me for beating up his soldiers."

"You looked like you were enjoying yourself," Kazuchiyo said, prodding.

"I was. The other soldiers are afraid of me, but his aren't so skittish. It's a relief." Though hearing him say so hurt Kazuchiyo's heart to hear, Yagi only hummed and continued on. "Maybe if we're stuck here for a while, he'll let me do it some more."

"Might as well," said Amai, nudging him with his foot. "You'll have our whole army whipped into shape in no time."

Kazuchiyo took a deep breath; there was still one final subject for him to fully address. "We will have a little time, for certain. At least until Mutsuyama is long gone and we return to Rongi to meet with Lord Koedzuka."

Yagi's gaze sharpened on him, but he did not reply, so Kazuchiyo continued. "My plan there is to negotiate a peace between him and Lady Dada, and to earn both their support in furthering Aritaka's campaign. Both of them assume that I'm fighting for Aritaka to become shogun."

"I know you're not doing it for him," said Yagi. "I meant it when I said I'd kill him *and* the shogun for you, if that's what you want."

"I believed you. But I..." Kazuchiyo swallowed and at last surrendered the truth. "I don't know what I want yet. That much power might be beyond my reach." He pressed his thumb against the bead still tied to his wrist. "What I do know is that Aritaka will suspect me of being disloyal if I don't at least act like it's what I want. I don't know if I'm ready yet, to oppose him outright. And..."

While he hesitated, Amai smiled and leaned closer. "And it does make for a pretty speech. There's nothing wrong with enjoying something you're good at."

"You are good at it," Yagi admitted. "When you talk like that, it sounds to me like you mean it. But what if someone else can tell that you don't?"

Kazuchiyo leaned back and took his time in answering. "So far, I don't think anyone can. I'm here with an *army* after all." When Yagi continued to frown at him, he relented. "You're right, though. I need to make a decision, one way or the other. And I will. Soon." He licked his lips. "Until then I want you to know that whenever it's just the three of us, I'm telling the truth. I haven't and will never lie to you."

"I know," Yagi said quickly. "I never thought you did." He shrugged. "But I can't always keep up with you. If you're demoting me just so I won't have to listen to you lie to them, that's probably for the best. I'm fine with just following orders when they come to me."

"Oh, Yagi." Kazuchiyo sighed and crawled forward. To his great relief, Yagi showed no hesitation in welcoming him into his lap and embrace. "You're so straightforward," he murmured, wrapping his arms around Yagi's strong shoulders. "I wish we could all be more like you."

"Not sure I agree, but thanks," Yagi grumbled. He eased Kazuchiyo back and kissed him. Surely it had not been as long as it seemed since Yagi was the one to initiate their affection? Kazuchiyo kissed him back eagerly, emotion heavy in his throat. If only they could race back to Etsugo and a private room once more.

"Don't worry," said Amai as he swiped the last section of pear. "I'm not jealous."

"Why would you be?" Yagi retorted without missing a beat. He motioned for Amai to join them. "You're one of us."

Amai blinked back at him. He could not quite hide how pleased the affirmation made him as he crawled closer, despite his attempts to remain flippant. "You're damn right I am," he said, and Kazuchiyo gladly leaned back so the pair of them could share a kiss.

They spent a well-deserved night of rest together, the most peaceful they had seen in many days.

CHAPTER FOURTEEN

In the morning, the Kibaku scouts reported that Mutsuyama's soldiers were breaking down their camp.

Kazuchiyo sent one of his captains down toward the valley bearing the flag of a messenger, but he returned saying no provocation from him had prompted a response other than bows drawn warning him and his men back. For caution's sake, Kazuchiyo lined their ranks on the road, and Naoya his outside the town, prepared for deception. As the day wore on, however, it became clear that Mutsuyama had no intention of engaging with them whatsoever. Once their preparations were complete, they marched from the valley into the southwest. Back toward the capital.

Celebrations were held, though they were muted. Kazuchiyo promoted Nishigame to commander, as he had planned, in a quiet ceremony that was followed by an evening of drinking. Though Yagi's demotion, which came with it, was a surprise to many, none of them questioned the decision, and Nishigame's men took it as an honor. One brave soul even challenged Yagi to a drinking contest, and though soundly defeated, to see such jovial behavior surrounding Sakka's insurmountable champion did wonders for the general morale.

Even Yagi himself seemed to enjoy the attention for once, which put Kazuchiyo's heart deeply at ease.

And thus, Castle Etsugo and its surrounding lands finally breathed easier. The remaining Tendo captives were sent home the following day, after Kazuchiyo had received many sincere thanks and apologies from young Commander Umafusa Soujirou. Kazuchiyo returned to the castle proper for another meeting with Lady Dada and her ministers, who in turn had good news of reinforcements and supplies at last being able to approach from Jisu's western border. A bargain was struck: in three days' time, if they had received no troubling news from Tendo or the shogun, Lady Dada would honor her commitment and travel to Rongi.

"I'll be accompanying the party, of course," Chikakuni bragged as he again saw Kazuchiyo and his entourage out at the gate. "It will be my first official duty in the capacity of *general*."

"I knew you would have that title before long," Kazuchiyo said, grinning. "Congratulations. I'll be glad to have your company a while longer."

"Same to you." Chikakuni cast a sly glance behind them. "That little fox of yours will have to be doubly cautious of his mouth now."

"Caution is my entire business," Amai retorted. "You have nothing to fear from my mouth."

They chuckled, though as Kazuchiyo glanced behind him, he was reminded of the rest of their party: Naoya and Purnima followed at a distance, each uncomfortable as Mahiro chatted ceaselessly alongside. As they approached Yagi waiting for them with the horses, he struggled to think of something to say in what time they had.

Naoya took notice of his attention, and with a deep breath he quickened his pace. Kazuchiyo in turn slowed his, hoping his nerves did not show in his face. Though he had not yet devised a strategy for navigating the current state of their friendship, he was eager for Naoya to know it weighed heavily on his mind and heart.

Of course, Naoya made no such effort to hide his struggle. As the pair of them halted a few steps from the rest of their group, he faced Kazuchiyo with sorrowful eyes. "I was certain I heard a flute playing from your camp the other night."

"I'm glad," Kazuchiyo replied. "I was hoping you would."

Naoya grimaced. "You play extremely well," he said, and then he moved on to reclaim his horse. Though Kazuchiyo frowned in frustration, he let him go.

"I'm leading a party down to the valley camp to see what's left of it," Mahiro carried on telling Purnima. "If you're interested in the spoils, you should come with us."

"Only if my lord commands it," Purnima said distractedly, and she, too, left Mahiro behind.

Mahiro set her hands on her hips, and Kazuchiyo watched her, expecting that she might press too hard. But Mahiro only looked on as the Kibaku pair mounted their horses and departed, and Kazuchiyo sighed, pained with empathy.

"Seems like Sir Oihata still isn't happy with our progress," Chikakuni noted as Kazuchiyo and Mahiro rejoined the remaining group. "What's got him so upset?"

"It's no slight against Jisu, nor her lady," Kazuchiyo reassured him. He pulled himself up into Hashikiri's saddle. "He and I are in disagreement on a personal matter, that's all."

"They're both stubborn old goats," Mahiro muttered as she took to Suzumekage. "Well, it won't ruin my fun. I'm going to take some men down to that camp."

"Be alert," Kazuchiyo warned her, but she was already spurring Suzumekage onward, and the pair quickly stormed out the gates.

Yagi and Amai took to their horses while exchanging a look. "Maybe you should try talking to him again," Yagi suggested. "It'll help."

Kazuchiyo smiled despite himself, hopeful that Yagi's optimism for such a conversation came from their own recent experiences. "I will, but first..." Kazuchiyo glanced up toward the mighty Mount Etsuzan, then back to Chikakuni. "Is there anything on Mount Etsuzan? A village, a shrine?"

"There are some old hermits that live up on the hillside. There was a shrine, but it was damaged generations ago, which is why Agarigumo was built to replace it." Chikakuni shrugged. "Lady O-bou makes a pilgrimage up the mountain once a year, but there's not much left up there to see. The trees are too thick for even a good view."

Kazuchiyo looked again and hummed thoughtfully. "I see. Thank you."

They bid each other goodbye for the time being, and Kazuchiyo led his two companions away from the castle. The day was peaceful, breezy, and it made for a pleasant journey down the slope of the plateau. Much too pleasant to be left alone.

"It's still fairly early," said Amai. "I bet we could get pretty high up that mountain and make it back here by nightfall."

Kazuchiyo smiled. "Am I so transparent?"

"To me, you are."

"What do you think is up there?" asked Yagi. "Some kind of magic?"

"I'm not certain, but I want to know." Kazuchiyo frowned at himself, surprised by how saying the words aloud made them so much heavier in his chest. "I want to reconcile with Sir Naoya," he admitted. "He's not always an easy friend, but I miss his company. Except I'm not certain that I can until I understand why he's so stubborn when it comes to magic."

"You could ask the old woman again," Amai suggested.

"No, I think I have a better idea."

Kazuchiyo stopped his horse, and his companions theirs. That morning he had tucked his flute into his sleeve, and he pulled it out then to press to his lips. His slow, heart-warming rendition of "Enmei's Willow Garden" flowed out over the valley—what sweet music, paired so expertly with the unparalleled view and cloudless sky. It took only a few minutes of playing before his intended audience came to pay its respects. The piebald fox had returned, its blue eyes twinkling

215

as it watched Kazuchiyo from the forest's edge.

"There you are," Kazuchiyo murmured as he lowered his flute. "Why do I get the feeling you've been following me for a long time?"

The fox stood, turned away, and then stopped, just as it had before. There was no mistaking its intentions.

"Foxes are smart, but not this smart," said Yagi. "Should we trust it?"

Kazuchiyo tucked the flute back into his sleeve, and in the process was reminded of the small bead nestled against his wrist. "Lady Dada said that if I wish to become shogun, I should give up all interest in magic. If the two are that well linked, I must know." He urged Hashikiri a few steps forward. "Please, little fox, lead the way."

With a swish of its tail, the fox started back up the trail toward the castle. Kazuchiyo and his lovers gave chase, but as they drew closer to the gates, the creature darted off in another direction. Though it was a challenge navigating the horses through the densely forested hillside, the fox never went too fast that they were in danger of losing it. Soon it had brought them to another narrower path of packed earth, which twisted back and forth behind the castle up toward Mount Etsuzan.

"Aha," said Amai. "This is part of the trail that Chikakuni took us on when we first got here. The secret road."

"It's certainly well hidden." The path was so narrow they had no choice but to go single file, and even then, low branches and shrubs brushed against Kazuchiyo's shins. It took some extra coaxing for Hashikiri to maintain a decent pace through the tunnel of trees. The charming breeze was replaced with the droning of spiders, and the farther they went, the more eyes Kazuchiyo sensed on them.

"More foxes," Yagi grunted. "On both sides."

Amai chuckled. "Don't worry, I'll put in a good word for you."

They passed a branching path that Amai said would take them to the rear of the castle, and continued on. Over the next hour the road grew steeper, the spiders louder, the air thinner. Ancient trees strangled the encroaching daylight with thick, gnarled branches. But the fox never wavered, pausing only once in a while to make sure he had not lost his companions before striking out again. Kazuchiyo kept a close eye on him while leaving scrutiny of the surrounding woods to Yagi and Amai. With very little idea of how much time was passing, they continued until the road deposited them upon their destination.

It was, as Chikakuni had said, the remains of a shrine. Just before them stood the mighty torii gate that marked its entrance, scrubbed clean of its once-red shine over years of rain and neglect. Kazuchiyo felt a chill as he passed beneath it and into the compound that was once a site of many youthful pilgrimages. Half a dozen small buildings were nestled into the mountainside, each on its own small terrace with tree roots creeping out from under their porches. Many of the walls had rotted through, the paper screens empty shells. Ropes tied around the eldest trees to signify their divinity were curiously intact, though covered in moss. And peering out from every available shelter and nook was a pair of fox eyes.

Their piebald friend who had guided them so faithfully sprinted ahead, toward the largest and least disheveled of the buildings. Kazuchiyo continued to follow but at a more casual pace, counting the dozens of tiny creatures that watched them from between the trees and beneath the engawa. Some were rusty red, some pure white, some stormy gray. Some tittered excitedly at the visitors, and some remained warily stoic. A particularly handsome fellow, coal black, sat like a guardian at the edge of the path to the main hall. Kazuchiyo looked closely and spotted another length of twine around its neck.

"Maybe they are all onmyouji," Kazuchiyo mused aloud. He dismounted and gave Hashikiri a reassuring nose rub. "But why did they bring us here?"

A scrape of wood drew Kazuchiyo's attention fully to the main hall, and the front panel that was being pushed open by a slender hand. A woman stepped out onto the drooping engawa, pale and petite and bundled in a long, autumn-colored kimono. She parted the veil draped over her head and face to reveal a curious smile and bright, amber-colored eyes.

"Oh my," she said, looking the trio over. "It's been a while since I had visitors."

And this is how I met Kazuchiyo.

CHAPTER FIFTEEN

N ow worry not—this story belongs very much to
Kazuchiyo. There is a great deal of my own perspective
I could share on the events leading up to our meeting: the
occupation of Jisu, my interest in the approaching armies, and
of course the many fascinating secrets whispered to me by my
treasured companions. How strongly I am tempted to share
just how many charming coincidences and machinations went
into this introduction! But I am rather proud of myself for the
restraint I've shown thus far in keeping these silly musings to
myself, and thus, I shall strive to continue as such.

I was not what Kazuchiyo had expected to find on the
mountain, naturally. When one hears of mountain hermits,
their first thought is not of fair maidens draped in silk, with
age-white hair still thick and soft. He bowed his head politely,
and his companions did the same. "Please forgive us for the
intrusion," he said. Here was the object of his search, and yet
he was so caught off guard by the form it had taken that he
could depend only on his manners to guide him. "We were
following one of your handsome foxes for curiosity's sake and
found ourselves here."

"It's no intrusion," I assured him. "In fact, I'm very pleased to have you." I took a step back and gestured for the three of them to join me inside. "Won't you come in?"

Yagi moved quickly to Kazuchiyo's side. "I don't like this," he muttered, casting a wary look around at the foxes. "Who is this woman?"

Amai led his and Yagi's horses toward one of the sheds, where tufts of long, succulent grasses had already attracted their attention. "We came all the way up here," he said, securing the reins only loosely on a low branch. "We might as well find out, hm?"

Kazuchiyo nodded, and he handed over Hashikiri's reins to Amai as well. "Thank you," he told me. "We're honored by your hospitality."

With the horses secure and peacefully resting, Kazuchiyo followed me into the shrine's once great hall, his companions close behind. It had been a sight to see in days past, the columns vibrantly painted, with brass lanterns hanging from the ceiling and watercolor paintings along the walls. Time had eroded almost all these decorations, leaving bare wood pillars, dewy moss on moldy paper, and fox dens in the cupboards. Only one of the great brass lanterns remained intact, though it sat on the floor to serve as a stove. At the center of the chamber, the other foxes and I had pulled up the boards to be replaced with tatami mats, which were worn and covered in paw prints.

The hall gave every appearance of having been abandoned for years, save two important features: a lacquered cabinet that sat against the far wall bearing handsome and well-polished engravings, and myself in my red-orange kimono. My life is very modest, and the bulk of my care for material things rests in these two items most acutely. This did not escape Kazuchiyo's notice, which pleased me.

"My name is Aritaka Kazumune," he introduced himself, and at the time I knew no better than to take him at his word. We sat down facing each other on the sagging tatami as his friends sat on either side. "These are my companions, Ebara Motonobu—better known as Yagi-douji—and Amai. We came from Sakka to help Jisu repel the invasion."

"It is a pleasure to make a lord's acquaintance," I replied, and I bowed my head, though only enough to designate us as equals. This did not escape his notice either. "You may call me Lady Enmei."

Kazuchiyo leaned back, struck with recognition. He had, after all, only hours before charmed a handsome fox with a song bearing that name. "The pleasure is mine," he said, wondering if he ought to comment on the coincidence. "I hear the lady O-bou makes a pilgrimage up this mountain every year, and it was she who suggested we visit. Do you happen to know her?"

"Oh yes, very well," I said, more and more interested in him with every word. The lady O-bou very rarely shares her secrets, let alone with a complete outsider. "Every spring she comes to drink tea with me. We should do so now."

I tapped my fingers against the mats, and my little foxes hurried to gather the necessary items. They're quite dexterous when called upon, and with so many it didn't take long at all for them to fetch cups, a tray, the kettle, and a gourd of fresh water.

"You have them trained very well," said Amai as I began the preparations. "It takes a lot to domesticate a fox."

I didn't care for this assumption of his, and I let that displeasure show in my expression as I set the kettle, now full, on the top of the brass lantern. "Why, they're far less domesticated than you are," I told him, and I cast a bit of magic to fill the lantern with fire, to heat the water.

Kazuchiyo watched the casting of this simple spell with great interest. "You used magic just now. Are you an onmyouji?"

Though I couldn't blame the boy for not knowing any better, it still made me laugh. "No, dear boy, and as far as I'm concerned, there is no such thing. There are only those who have used magic and those who haven't."

"But you do use magic," pressed Yagi. He eyed the dried tea leaves I was preparing with an intensely doubtful look. "How does it work?"

I hummed as I worked, playing on their suspense. It isn't often that I have the opportunity to entertain three handsome young gentlemen at once, after all; who could blame me for drawing their company out? "Is that why you've come up here? You're curious about magic?"

Kazuchiyo, to his credit, did not fidget or falter. "I am," he confessed, with exactly the unadulterated confidence needed to impress a careful fox like me. "I've heard it's dangerous, and if I don't have any skill in it, I'm prepared to give it up. But not until I understand it."

"It is dangerous," I replied, though merely as a statement of truth rather than any attempt at a warning. "An amateur can easily kill themselves if they're not careful."

Kazuchiyo remained steadfast. "I'd rather avoid that," he said, so matter-of-factly that I smiled. "But I can't avoid a danger I don't understand." He paused for a thoughtful moment. "Lady O-bou said my well is nearly dry."

This captured my attention; though I had known all along from the fox-whispers that the young lord carried a stone, I couldn't be sure of how much he understood until then. I encouraged my lantern fire to burn brighter and turned to Kazuchiyo with hands offered. "Let me see."

"Kazu, careful," said Yagi, and even Amai seemed to think better of it at first. Kazuchiyo himself hesitated when he saw the long, sharpened state of my fingernails, which I'm embarrassed to admit were not fit for company. However, he soon rallied himself and surrendered his left hand to me. I covered the stone he kept tied to his wrist and learned so much.

Kazuchiyo felt some of that too. Just like it had been when Iomori touched him after his first battles with Naoya, images from the recent battles flashed across his vision in a swarm of heat and blood, then silence. Armed with the knowledge gained from Naoya that the stones could convey unknowable truths, he was more eager than ever to understand the method, and what I had gleaned from it. Even then I understood that desire of his clearly, and I obliged him.

"A man died to save your life not very long ago," I said, and Kazuchiyo's hand flexed against my own, recalling that poor old soldier laid open by the samurai's kamayari back at Kanrei. "As he died, you promised to honor his family. His name was Mizutane."

"Mizutane," Kazuchiyo repeated. His heart pounded, and though he had every intention of carrying out the promise he'd made to the old soldier then, his more pressing interest was in how I had learned a name the man himself had not managed to speak. "So it is as Sir Naoya said—the bead contains knowledge somehow."

I let Kazuchiyo go, and with the kettle water now hot enough, I filled four cups to continue preparing the tea. "My darling O-Bou was right," I said. "Your well is very nearly dry. Why, if you cast too powerful a spell now, you'd absolutely be doomed."

Kazuchiyo gulped, taking the warning seriously despite my breezy tone. "How can I fill it? Will you teach me?" I raised an eyebrow, and he amended his request. "Or, at the very least, explain to me what makes it so dangerous so that I'm *not* doomed?"

Ah, so many eyes on me! Even my foxes watched closely, curious to see if I would spill the magic's great secret. Sir Naoya and Lady Dada were right to preach caution; to a restless heart, even the knowledge of magic is a dangerous burden to bear. Even to you, dear readers. But I can't very well relate the rest of Kazuchiyo's tale without this revelation, now can I?

"The use of magic requires a Soul Stone," I explained, and I drew back my sleeve to reveal to Kazuchiyo the many stones disguised as beads wrapped about my arm. Kazuchiyo's eyes grew wide at the sight, realizing at once that my collection far outdid that of Iomori. "Or, at least, it does if you value your life. Without another source, a mystic trying to cast a spell will have only their own soul to draw from." I pushed Kazuchiyo's cup toward him. "A heavy cost."

Kazuchiyo accepted the cup, though his mind was aflame

with the realization I had pointed him toward, and he was too distracted to drink. "A Soul Stone," he repeated as his allies' warnings took new shape in his mind. "Then the 'well' the beads hold, each is filled with…"

"Yes," I said, lifting my own cup to my lips. "The source of magic is life."

"You mean, the dead?" said Yagi, uncharacteristically astute, as I sipped my tea. "Instead of the heavens or hells, the dead go into your little beads?"

"Not always," I reassured him. I served him and Amai next, and though Yagi eyed his cup squeamishly, Amai was bold enough to drink from his straight away. "The stone must be nearby, after all. Some will require a mystic's guidance. But yes." Unable to resist the drama of it, I smiled his way. "To cast magic requires the help of the dead."

Amai laughed. Normally when delivering this secret, I am met with solemn understanding or sometimes even grim delight, but his dry humor caught me off guard and was very unwelcome. "The Jisu soldiers are convinced your foxes are *honoring* the dead," he said. "That they're conveying the souls of samurai up to the mountain. They're more right than they know, huh?"

"I don't see why that is so amusing to you," I replied, "but yes, I suppose that's true."

Yagi's accusatory glare was much more expected, and it did not bother me at all. "You're harvesting the dead so you can do magic tricks."

"I am, and so is your lord."

Kazuchiyo remained quiet for a bit longer. He understood the depth of this truth more acutely than his companions, and his mind raced with every memory he had of magic and its use: Naoya's concern for his well-being, set against his casual deployment of spells; Lady Dada's warning that a shogun should not seek magic, especially one whose fiercest warrior killed men by the hundreds single-handedly; most of all, the cryptic motives of Master Iomori, who had given him a Soul

Stone but no explanation along with it. He had too many questions and only a few I could answer.

Kazuchiyo took a sip from his tea, and I did the same as he collected his thoughts. The drink was relatively plain on his lordly tongue, as we of the forest take what we can find, but the earthiness wasn't unpleasant to him. As he replaced his cup, he remembered Naoya's warning that a mystic willing to share the secrets of magic was not to be trusted. He was probably correct, but thankfully Kazuchiyo was too clever to reveal that to me at the time. Instead, he faced me with a cultivated, unimpassioned curiosity.

"Are the spirits… aware?" he asked, making a great effort to hide the sick feeling in his stomach.

"Oh, no," I said. "Well, not in a form *you* would recognize as awareness. Your sense of self is more dependent on a sense of time than you realize, and there is no time inside the stone."

"And you would know?" challenged Amai. "You ever been inside?"

I grinned, though I was not yet prepared to spill *all* my secrets. "Allow me to explain."

I turned to Hakumen—my handsome, piebald friend—and mimed opening a book. Very gladly he rushed to my cupboard and pulled from it a bound tome, the most recent I had been working on. To my guests it did not appear as much, a roughly sewn bundle of paper, but it would serve as the most effective demonstration. I laid it before them and flipped to the last page that I had added just the day before.

"To some, a Soul Stone is like a well," I said, and Kazuchiyo learned forward, curious to see my writing. Despite the quality of my implements, my penmanship was and remains impeccable, and he was able to make out a few lines describing the life of a young Jisu samurai killed in the recent battles. "To me, it is a book. Each stone contains hundreds of pages upon which the departed write their life stories. Those skilled in its use can read those memories as easily as these pages—the pages cannot read themselves."

Kazuchiyo nodded; he had seen both Iomori and Naoya do exactly that. "But if that is the source of an onmyouji's magic, how is it that some can read signs of the future?"

I laughed. "They *can't*. And anyone who says otherwise is a liar." I paged through the book to show Kazuchiyo the many, many pages I had written, and this book only the latest of hundreds like it. "There is no one who knows magic as well as me, young lord; I can promise you that."

"What does it have to do with spells then?" asked Yagi. "Like wind and messages?"

"That is the second reason why the stone is like a book," I said. Flipping back to the last filled page, I tore it from its binding and fed it to the fire in my lantern. The flames crackled happily as they licked the paper black. "The lives of men are fuel, you see, and they can be manipulated to do any manner of things. Stir the wind, stoke a fire." I cast Kazuchiyo a sly look. "Slay a man. You are only limited by your imagination, and the size of your book."

Kazuchiyo watched the smoke coil through the gaps in the blazing lantern, remembering the shudder of heat as he unsheathed his sword, only to sheathe it again in the body of the snake Nanpa. He swallowed, in turmoil. "What happens to the souls that are spent?"

Would that I could say I answered that question gracefully, but as I have been true for Kazuchiyo, I shall be true for myself: I closed my book quite petulantly and turned my nose up. "Nothing. They carry on their way, as any soul that dies alone, unharvested."

"Are you only saying that because you don't know otherwise?" goaded Amai.

"As I said, no one understands magic better than I do." I fixed him with a sharp look. "If you are curious, I know just what spell I'd cast with you."

Yagi fisted his hakama in admirable defensiveness of the little weasel, but it was Kazuchiyo who spoke to dispel that moment of tension. "Lady Enmei," he said, "I'm very grateful that you're so willing to answer my questions. I understand now why others have been hesitant." He took in a deep breath, hesitant himself to voice the conclusion of the knowledge I had imparted. "You're saying that if I want to be able to use magic, I have to kill for it."

By then I could see clearly that Kazuchiyo was one of those rare men whose rank has not robbed them of perspective. It is easy to imagine what a man like Lord Aritaka might do with the knowledge that his mystic's power depended entirely on a willingness to slaughter, but here was a young lord humbled by it. Taking pity on him, I drew the string of beads from my arm and untied the final knot to slip one stone free.

"You've been very entertaining company for me," I said as I retied the string. "To thank you, let me offer you a gift." I held it up for him to see; like the others, the stone was lacquered black to give the appearance of a simple prayer bead. "This 'well' is nearly full, fed from recent battles here in Jisu. I've already made a record of those inside that interest me, so it's yours to take."

I motioned for Kazuchiyo to give me his hands, and with only minor misgivings, he did so. I pressed the stone into his left hand, closed his fingers over it, and held it tight; his right I also clasped. "Later tonight, when your heart is quiet, take one stone in each hand and close your eyes," I instructed. "Imagine that each of your hands is like my lantern, and that each of these stones is a burning coal." I lowered my voice and locked eyes with Kazuchiyo to impart all due seriousness. "Wielding magic is part skill, but part talent as well. If you cannot hold both stones and know instinctively which of them burns brighter, then you *must* return them both to me. Otherwise, you risk your life with every spell. Do you understand?"

"Yes," Kazuchiyo said immediately, sobered. "Thank you."

I let him go, and Kazuchiyo leaned back. He thought of his thoughtless action on the field days before that had saved Yagi's life, wondering just how close he might have come then to sacrificing everything for his lover without having realized it.

He tugged his sleeve up so he could add my bead to the red one already tied around his wrist. With his manners subdued, Amai took it upon himself to fill the silence.

"It seems like a waste," Amai said. "You have so many beads, but you're hiding up here on the mountain, using these poor foxes to hoard your riches. What are you using them for?"

"Nothing of consequence to you," I replied, and I chuckled. "My, you are so curious about me, aren't you? If you'd like to know more, I'm happy to have you stay the night."

Yagi cleared his throat loudly before Amai could answer. "We should go. It'll already be getting dark by the time we get down the mountain."

Kazuchiyo met my eyes again. Though he, too, was still full of curiosity for me and the magics I wield, his caution overpowered it. On close inspection he could see that the pupils in my amber eyes were less round than a human's should have been, that my thick, white hair was combed especially to disguise my pointed ears, and that I was draped in many layers of fabric that hid any clear definition of my figure. A close look at my teeth would have told him even more, but they were clues enough for a clever boy to know better than to stray after dark.

"I'm afraid my companion is right," said Kazuchiyo. "My commanders will already be upset with me for having wandered off without alerting them first. We should take our leave." He sipped politely from his tea one more time, and I did the same. "Thank you for your hospitality. Your advice may have saved my life."

"I have a great deal of advice that I could offer you, young lord," I replied, reminded of so many young men of promise I had known. "I hope you will visit me again, though if you do, it will be your turn to offer a gift."

Kazuchiyo nodded thoughtfully, his mind already sharpening itself on the challenge of what manner of gift would be suitable. He bowed deeply, and though his companions seemed reluctant, they did the same. "I'd be honored. Until then."

I saw them out, and as they retrieved their horses, I motioned Hakumen forward. "Little Hakumen will show you the way out. You won't find your way back here without him, so if you do return, play for him first."

Kazuchiyo pulled himself into Hashikiri's saddle, and there he could not stop himself from asking one more question. "Enmei's Willow Garden," he said. "I don't suppose it's a coincidence that it's a favorite not only of foxes, but of my onmyouji friend as well?"

"No, it is not," I replied, offering a smile and nothing more.

Again, Kazuchiyo was tempted to question me further, and again his caution won the day. "Thank you again, for your generosity," he said, and with a nod he turned his horse, and the three of them rode out of my temple with Hakumen leading the way.

CHAPTER SIXTEEN

Kazuchiyo remained quiet for the first leg of their trip back down the mountain. There was a great deal on his mind, and the droning of insects was so loud that to attempt conversation when they were already single file would be a waste of effort. He closely watched the bouncing gait of Hakumen as they descended through the trees. Despite his turmoil, it did not escape Kazuchiyo's notice that they were taking a slightly different route than they had on their way up, and he feared that losing sight of their guide could prove disastrous.

At last Hakumen returned them to the secret path behind the castle, and with a salute of his bushy tail, he disappeared into the underbrush. Kazuchiyo urged Hashikiri forward a few paces and then glanced back; already he could not make out which trees they had woven through only moments ago. That as much as anything convinced him of the truth behind my words at the temple. Only another fox knows how to find their den.

He knew then, as well as I did, that we would eventually meet again, though at the time he did not wish for it.

Even on a proper path, the packed earth was too narrow for two horses to ride alongside. Yagi pulled forward as far as he could and asked, "Kazu, are you all right?"

"Yes," Kazuchiyo replied quickly. "Yes, it's just a lot to think about." He turned as best he could to see his two companions. "What about the two of you?"

"I think it makes more sense now, why Oihata didn't want to tell you," said Amai. "Though it also makes him twice the hypocrite." He shrugged. "You're both samurai in war. Soldiers die. Making use of them after they're dead is what a samurai would want."

"You don't think it's… weird?" said Yagi, also turning to give Amai his attention. "Shoving a person's soul into a box just so you can spring it on someone else later? What if it was you?"

"Better in a box than poked at by oni for a millennium. Some of us have that to worry about." Amai leaned forward to look at Kazuchiyo. "If that bead she gave you is recent, do you think it has the victims of Yagi's duels in there? I didn't get the best view."

Yagi scoffed loudly. "That's disgusting."

Kazuchiyo glanced to his wrist and frowned; he had not yet considered Amai's question, and it turned his stomach to wonder what it might be like, seeing through the eyes of a man on the sharp end of Yagi's spear. He suppressed a shudder and urged Hashikiri to resume their journey back. "Let's hurry back to camp," he said. "By now we'll be missed." The three of them continued on as the light through the trees diminished, and conversation again ceased.

By the time they reached the road proper, the sun had set behind Mount Etsuzan, leaving the valley road in shadows deepening by the minute. Kazuchiyo rode up to Etsugo's front gate, hoping Lady Dada would grant them a chamber, as he had not thought far enough ahead to prepare for riding at night. At the gate, however, the captain at watch hurried to greet them and bowed low at the waist.

"Lord Sakka, good that you've come," she said. "Your honored sister was asking after you, as well as the captain of your bannermen."

"Thank you for letting me know," Kazuchiyo said with some embarrassment. "Can you spare a messenger to send to our camp, to let them know that I am well?"

"Yes, of course." She hesitated before adding, "Lady Mahiro made it sound as though you had guests at the camp awaiting you. Shall the messenger alert them that you mean to spend the night here?"

"Guests?" Kazuchiyo looked toward their hilltop camp, where torches were being lit for the first watch of the night. He could barely make out their own banners, let alone any indication of a change in the camp's fortunes or occupants. "Did Mahiro say who it was?"

The captain bowed again in apology. "No, sir, but we saw some fifty men come over the ridge."

"Reinforcements?" Yagi supposed. "They finally caught up?"

"They had orders not to join us," said Kazuchiyo, frowning. With little point in speculating, he returned his attention to the captain. "In that case, please ask your commander if they can spare some soldiers to escort us back to our camp, as we have no torches to light the way."

"Yes, sir!"

"Rakuteru probably got fed up with not being on the front lines," Yagi supposed while they waited, and Kazuchiyo nodded along. Amai offered no comment.

The Jisu soldiers arranged for an escort in short order, and surrounded by twenty armed samurai Kazuchiyo and his companions made their way back to the Sakka camp. They were met at the entrance by Commander Ginta and Kazuchiyo's bannermen, who were deeply relieved to see them. They bowed and offered the most delicately worded admonishments as they could given their relative statuses, and Kazuchiyo in turn offered sincere, though hurried, apologies. He was far more concerned about their supposed guests than the usual pleasantries.

"The general is waiting for you in the council tent," said Ginta at last. "He claims he was sent by my father to find out how we're faring."

"Did they not receive our messengers about the battle being won?" Kazuchiyo asked as the pair of them walked toward the tent, all others trailing behind.

"They did." Ginta smiled apologetically. "I'm certain my father was disappointed to hear his troops wouldn't be needed. It doesn't surprise me that he sent someone to confirm."

"And who—" Kazuchiyo began, but as they approached the tent, the small group of men stationed outside it halted him in step and in breath: ten soldiers in black armor with red cords. Their captain, an elderly man with white whiskers, bore a sash around his waist with an embroidered insignia: three red rings.

The men bowed respectfully. "My lord," said the old captain. "Our master awaits you inside."

Kazuchiyo gulped. It was cruel timing indeed that forced him into this meeting when he was at his least prepared. He took a deep breath, and as he let it out he forced from his mind all the sticky cobwebs made of magic and foxes and little beads. "Thank you," he said. "I'll speak with him."

Yagi took a step forward. "Kazu—um, my lord—"

"Captain, please report in with Commander Nishigame," Kazuchiyo told him. He tried to convey lightness and confidence in his voice, but Yagi's furrowed brow cast doubt on his success. "Thank you for accompanying me today."

Though clearly unhappy, Yagi bowed and stalked off. Amai by then had already slipped away, and Kazuchiyo hoped that he had already picked some spot around the tent to spy from. With one more moment to steel his nerves, Kazuchiyo stepped into the war tent.

The general was waiting for him, standing over the rough map of Jisu Province that still held tiles bearing their formations from battles won. He turned, and the frail defenses Kazuchiyo had tried to build before entering threatened to rattle apart as the man's coal-dark eyes fell on him. He remembered those warm, round eyes, that tall forehead, and the jutting nose and jaw that Kazuchiyo had in his youth likened to the mountain-dwelling macaques of their homeland. It was General Zaiga Tonehiro, his distant uncle and his late father's dearest friend.

He was dressed in his full armor, which Kazuchiyo recognized very well: black lacquer freshly polished and red cords tied in ringlets between the plates, though his helmet he set aside as they faced each other. Just as Kazuchiyo remembered, he was a quiet man, calm and measured, and he fixed Kazuchiyo with a long, searching look. Each tried in those brief moments to judge the other, tried to read six years of unknown history in their faces. Was the pain tightening Zaiga's mouth a rush of nostalgia? Or perhaps bitter disappointment?

Then Zaiga let his breath out slowly. "You look so much like your mother," he said.

Kazuchiyo shuddered. Most days, it was difficult for him to remember his mother's face. "General Zaiga." It took monstrous effort, but he gathered himself up and moved closer. "Why are you here? Is there trouble farther east?"

Remembering his manners, Zaiga bowed to show his respect. "General Rakuteru is growing anxious," he explained, watching Kazuchiyo's face very closely. "He had hoped we were marching west to support your conquest of Jisu, only to hear we're not needed. There's not much season left for campaigning, so he's anxious to hear where we march next."

"Yes, that sounds like him." Kazuchiyo stopped just beyond Zaiga's reach and did his best not to fidget. Though he was at last the man's equal in height, he felt very small in his presence. His ears rang with memories of wooden practice swords echoing through Tengakubou's halls, and he ached to know how much he could trust this monument from his past. "For that, he could have sent one of his captains. There was no need for a general to come personally."

"No, there wasn't," Zaiga admitted. "But like General Rakuteru, I was anxious." He lowered his voice. "Anxious to see you, when few others would be able to see us."

The pain twisting his features gave Kazuchiyo a chill;

certainly it was grief and not scorn that drew his features into a grimace. Kazuchiyo could not hold back any longer, and he, too, lowered his voice to a whisper. "I thought you were dead. Aritaka said that everyone who refused to bow to him took their own lives."

"I had intended to," said Zaiga, his hand brushing instinctively at the left side of his abdomen. "I thought at first that it was cruel fate that intervened, but now I wonder." His gaze darted to the war map and then back to Kazuchiyo's face. "Commander Ginta was telling me about your exploits. He said you offered Tendo a partnership like you did Izuho, and that even when they rejected it, you were lenient with them as captives."

From another man, these declarations may have easily been mistaken for admonishment. Now that Kazuchiyo had begun to overcome his shock at their unexpected reunion, he could see clearly that they were a test—one that vibrated with hope. The realization that he could confidently answer Zaiga's unspoken question by giving him the truth brought tears to his eyes.

"Of course I was," Kazuchiyo said, and he drew back his sleeve. "My father taught me well."

He showed Zaiga the two beads tied to his wrist. Though it was a coincidence that they were red and black, to Zaiga they would have appeared as a deliberate representation of the dragon banner's colors. The general smiled, and struggle as he might, he could not hold back his own tears. He urged Kazuchiyo's sleeve back down and clasped his shoulder in a tight grip of affirmation.

Kazuchiyo depended on that strength to remain steady as he wiped his face with his sleeve. "I've tried," he said, too many words eager to burst out of him that he couldn't get them in their proper order. "I have never—"

"Hush—I know." Zaiga nodded as relief and shame continued to twist his familiar features. "Neither have I." He sighed, momentarily overcome before a deep breath steadied him again. "I'm certain we each have many stories for the other, but we don't have much time before we'll begin to look suspicious."

"Yes," said Kazuchiyo, grateful that his previous avoidance of the meeting had led to a happy result; he shuddered to think of what Sakka's samurai would think to see him cry openly in the company of a Suyama loyalist. "How did you convince General Rakuteru to let you come? Aritaka would have never allowed us to meet alone like this."

"He barely needed convincing," said Zaiga, and he frowned as he leaned back. "I do wonder at his motives, but I couldn't pass up the opportunity." Once again he met Kazuchiyo's gaze seriously. "There is one other thing that can't wait, if you're ready."

"Ready?"

Zaiga moved around Kazuchiyo to put himself between him and the tent entrance; Kazuchiyo naturally turned in place. Seeming unconvinced by his nephew's preparedness, he said, "Cover your mouth."

Baffled, Kazuchiyo did so. He looked to the tent entrance, and at Zaiga's whistle one of the soldiers that had been standing guard outside stepped through the flap. It was a young man in black armor, wearing a simple helmet and a ghoulish face mask. As soon as he was safely inside, the young man removed this covering, and the first glimpse of his face had Kazuchiyo smothering a gasp against his palm.

Too much talk of ghosts played tricks on him; he thought at first that a specter confronted him then. The face gazing back at him was surely that of his closest brother, Tomonaga, killed years prior on the rainy outskirts of Shimegahara. His broad eyebrows, bright eyes, and coarse hair—Kazuchiyo stared and expected that at any moment he would again watch his dear kin pierced by an enemy's arrow. But the boy only stared back, hesitating at Kazuchiyo's reaction.

"I know I look pretty different than when you last saw me," he said, and even his voice bore a strong resemblance to Tomonaga's, though Kazuchiyo was starting to realize the truth. He took a step closer. "But I—"

Kazuchiyo rushed forward before he could finish. He clasped his younger brother's shoulders, marveling that the boy he'd last seen as a ten-year-old was now a soldier. He was, in fact, a hair taller than Kazuchiyo himself. They held each other, breathless and incredulous, until Kazuchiyo finally managed to sputter out, "Yoshimaru?"

His brother let out a weak chuckle. "I haven't been Yoshimaru for a long time," he said, voice thick with emotion. "Uncle Tonehiro gave me my samurai name: Shigeyuki."

"Shigeyuki," Kazuchiyo repeated, but he was too overwhelmed to say more, and he looked helplessly to Zaiga.

Zaiga moved closer, beaming. "He came to me almost a year ago. To the world he's my sister's bastard, Bii Fumihiko, whom I've formally adopted."

"My aunt," Kazuchiyo said. "Lady Bii, is she—" A subtle shake of Zaiga's head was enough to confirm her fate. Kazuchiyo swallowed and looked back to Shigeyuki.

"You look just like Tomonaga," he admitted aloud at last, though it put a thorn in his gut. "Which means you look just like Father." A swell of panic had his fingers digging into the plates of his brother's armor as he struggled to keep his voice down. "You can't be here—he can't be here," he said, torn between the two of them. "He's supposed to be in exile. If Aritaka finds out, then Mother—is Mother all right?"

"She's fine," Shigeyuki reassured him, smiling though his eyes were red. "No one knows. A boy from the village took my place at the temple; the monks will protect them." He took a deep breath, and Kazuchiyo felt a shudder pass through him. "I couldn't do nothing anymore. Not after I heard what you did at the river against Kibaku. I had to…" He hesitated once more, his face screwing up tight. "I had to make sure you're still my brother."

Kazuchiyo's heart clenched hard in his chest, and he drew Shigeyuki tighter into his arms. "Always," he said through tears. "I'm still a dragon." He wilted with relief as Shigeyuki embraced him back. "I thought… you might hate me," he confessed, "for bowing to Aritaka like I did."

"He did, once in a while," said Zaiga.

Shigeyuki stiffened. "General!"

"I hated myself, too," Zaiga continued, and both brothers turned toward him. Shame carved across his features like a jagged scar. "Someday, I will atone for failing your father so terribly. Until that day, I will do whatever it takes to restore your birthright to you both."

Shigeyuki leaned back, that same shame painted across his own face. "I didn't really hate you," he said. "I just didn't understand sometimes."

"It's all right." Kazuchiyo was quick to reassure him. He had bludgeoned himself in anticipation of his family's anger too many times already for him to dwell on this. "Just know that everything I've done was with the hope of reclaiming our home one day. All that matters is that you stay safe until then." He glanced around the interior of the tent before focusing back on Zaiga. "How many know?"

"Only us, the monks and your mother at Dendou Temple, my captain outside, and a few of the servants at my homestead in Yuukaoka. I've been training him in solitude ever since he appeared on my doorstep."

Zaiga flashed Shigeyuki a fond smile, which Shigeyuki returned with a grin. Kazuchiyo, however, was mortified. "You traveled from Sakka to Yuukaoka alone?"

"I had to," Shigeyuki said with a shrug.

He was interrupted from saying more by a shout from outside the tent, and a heavy clopping of hooves. Kazuchiyo recognized both very easily, and he rushed to return Shigeyuki's helm and mask to him. "I want to hear everything when there's time," he said as he and Zaiga made efforts to clean their faces. "Be careful here—not everyone can be trusted."

More voices rose outside the tent that sounded like a scuffle about to break out, Mahiro's shout above all others demanding to be allowed in. Rather than risk her seeing or questioning the three of them together, Kazuchiyo threw open the tent flap and stepped outside. He hoped very much that the tall torches casting shadows across his face would disguise the fact that he had been crying. "Sister? Is something the matter?"

"Kazumune!" Mahiro turned away from Zaiga's captain, who had puffed himself up to prevent her from passing. She was red in the face, and likewise, Suzumekage irritably pawed the earth a few meters away. "There you are! Where in the eight hells have you been all day?"

"I chased a handsome fox into the woods to see where it would lead me," Kazuchiyo answered honestly, and Mahiro gave a great scoff as if it were innuendo. "How did you fare at the enemy camp?"

"Picked clean!" Mahiro lamented, rolling her eyes. "Not a scrap left except for dead peasants. Mutsuyama's a heartless old snake, that's for sure." She jutted her chin past Kazuchiyo. "What are these little beetles doing here?"

The captain glowered at her. Behind him, Zaiga and Shigeyuki emerged from the tent and offered respectful bows. "General Zaiga was giving me an update from General Rakuteru," Kazuchiyo explained. "They're going to accompany us back to Kanrei when the time comes."

Mahiro regarded them suspiciously, but finding nothing more to take issue with or remark on, she shook her head. "All right, well, don't run off like that and make your sister worry," she scolded him as she turned back toward Suzumekage. "Go get some sleep."

"I will," said Kazuchiyo, and as she led Suzumekage away he turned back to Zaiga and his men. The wary look Shigeyuki cast at Mahiro's back gave him pause for a moment, and he cleared his throat. "General, we've already agreed with Jisu's Lady Dada that we will leave in three days' time. You and your men are welcome to remain with us until then. There's space on the far slope of the hill for you to camp."

Zaiga bowed his head. "We would be honored, sir."

Kazuchiyo nodded. There was still a great deal he had left to say, and he was certain his brother felt the same, but for the moment the safest course was to part. With a deep breath he turned to leave for his personal tent at the center of the camp.

His attendants were waiting for them. Having neglected them and his duties all afternoon, Kazuchiyo couldn't bring himself to turn them away. He bathed and changed, and he accepted a modest supper before finally dismissing them. It was only then, when he was alone, that Amai came to visit. Though he often prided himself on creeping under the wall of the tent, this time he was forced to seek permission from Kazuchiyo's bannermen to enter through the normal entrance.

"Guard is up all over the camp," Amai said, quite put out, as he sat down very close to Kazuchiyo at the center of the tent. "Your Sakka men don't appreciate these visitors, and your Suyama men certainly didn't appreciate me. Wouldn't let me anywhere near the war tent." His tone softened apologetically. "I didn't get to overhear anything. Are you all right? How did it go?"

Kazuchiyo stared back at him and felt his tears threatening to return. "My little brother is here."

Amai blinked in astonishment. "That's mighty bold," he said. "Didn't Aritaka demand he give up his lineage and live as a monk?"

Kazuchiyo nodded, but he couldn't manage to say more than that. He was exhausted from his long day of startling truths and new burdens. Seeing this, Amai scooted alongside him so he could wrap his arm around his shoulders. After giving Kazuchiyo a few minutes to compose himself, he said, "The general that brought him here, was that the man you told us about? Your... distant uncle? Zaiga?"

Kazuchiyo nodded again, so Amai resumed speaking. "I'm sure he didn't come all this way with your brother in tow, risking all your lives and the future of Suyama, just to scold you for not toppling Aritaka's rule when you were twelve. Did he?"

Kazuchiyo sighed and wiped his sleeve across his face. "I

was thirteen. But no." Remembering Zaiga's warm and relieved look strengthened him. "No, they were both glad to see me, and I them."

Amai leaned his chin against Kazuchiyo's shoulder. "And Zaiga. He's a smart man, yes?"

"He was my father's closest friend and advisor."

"Then I'm sure he's been very careful. He wouldn't let anything happen to you or your brother. Right?"

"Yes... you're right." Kazuchiyo took in a deep breath and reached up to touch Amai's arm. "Thank you, Amai. I'm all right. It's just... a lot today."

Amai gave a little snort as he rubbed Kazuchiyo's back. "I'll say," he muttered. "If they measured the title in noble burdens alone, you'd already be shogun. They might as well just hand you the seat."

Kazuchiyo scoffed, but Amai's teasing did the trick to lighten his mood. He turned his head to nuzzle Amai's cheek. "If this is what all my days will be like if I accept, then I forfeit," he replied. "This is plenty."

"But you handle it so gracefully!" Amai kissed the corner of his mouth and then leaned back. "Should I fetch Yagi? Or..." He frowned. "He's not great for keeping secrets, but..."

Kazuchiyo frowned into his lap. "I hate to make him lie for me," he said quietly, "but I couldn't bear to keep this from him either." He squeezed Amai's hand. "Will you go tell him for me? I don't know when I'll have the chance to see him alone again."

"If you want." Amai pushed to his feet. "Should I come back after?"

"No, I..." Kazuchiyo stood as well to move toward his futon. "Don't take this the wrong way, but I think I want to be alone tonight."

"You're sure?" Amai pressed, watching him closely. "You'd better not be embarrassed about crying on my shoulder all night if you need to."

Perhaps he was hoping good humor would spur Kazuchiyo

again with scorn, but instead Kazuchiyo smiled. "It's not that," he promised. "I just need a little time to myself, that's all." He held Amai's gaze firmly. "I appreciate everything you do for me."

Amai nodded, thus convinced, and he offered Kazuchiyo a little smile of his own before heading for the exit. "Then leave Yagi-douji to me, and we'll see you in the morning. Try to sleep well, Kazu."

"And you."

After he was gone, Kazuchiyo climbed into his futon. His head was weary, but he was convinced he would hardly find sleep. Uncle Zaiga, alive! Alive and without blame to offer him; instead, he was confident enough to have reunited Kazuchiyo with his long-lost brother. For years Kazuchiyo had counseled himself toward patience, knowing that as long as he outlived Aritaka Souyuu, eventually his homeland of Suyama would be under his rule. There had been little point in wondering what the remaining Suyama nobles would think of him and his indigo Sakka banners when that time came. Now he could know; now, with Zaiga and Shigeyuki at his side, he could reclaim their loyalty as well as the land itself. With two dragons behind their banner, maybe they didn't have to wait for Aritaka to pass on at all. He needn't war for Aritaka's interests in a distant land for a title he did not need or want; he could fight only *one* more war and be home, with what remained of his family beside him.

Kazuchiyo drew the tent lamp closer, and in doing so, he was reminded of the two beads tied to his wrist. There was another dilemma, one of equal weight in fate if not in his heart. He drew the beads closer to his face, the words of a mysterious and beautiful hermit ringing through his ears. But I had been particular in warning him only to judge his magical merit when his heart was quiet, and he could not hope to approach that then. He was even beginning to understand the strong merit to Naoya's suggestion that he leave magic well enough alone entirely.

No decisions were about to be made that night. Kazuchiyo blew out the lamp and burrowed deep into his bedding. Despite his concerns, exhausted ushered him quickly to sleep. He would need to regain his strength for the days ahead.

CHAPTER SEVENTEEN

Come morning, Yagi sought Kazuchiyo out almost immediately. His face was hard and anxious, and Kazuchiyo drew him quickly into his tent to avoid as many ears as possible. "Amai told me," Yagi whispered, with so much effort to measure every word that Kazuchiyo could not help but be charmed by it. "About your visitors. Are you all right?"

"Yes, I'm all right," Kazuchiyo assured him, though he was even more so once Yagi took him into his arms. He sighed, relaxing into his lover's stronger body. "I'm afraid for them, but I know they'll be careful."

"I'm a bad liar," said Yagi. "I don't want to know which one he is or what his real name is. I just know I'd give him away without meaning to." He sighed, frustrated with himself. "I'm sorry, but—"

"No, don't be sorry." Kazuchiyo leaned back so he could take Yagi's face in his hands. "I hate asking you to lie for me, and the truth is…" He grimaced at the difficult days ahead. "The truth is *I* have to avoid him now too; otherwise I'll give him away. General Zaiga is going to station them on the far side of the slope, so hopefully we won't cross paths for now." Kazuchiyo took in a deep breath to try to calm the sudden churning in his stomach. "When it's finally safe, I'll introduce you to him myself."

Yagi nodded, and they shared a kiss before separating for their daily duties.

Their remaining three days outside Etsugo passed in relative peace. Still there remained no sign that Tendo or Mutsuyama would make another attempt at taking the castle. On the second day, a small force of Jisu samurai arrived, having been called down from their mountain retreats in the northwest. The duty would be theirs to protect the castle and surrounding towns once Lady Dada made the trip to neighboring Kibaku Province.

No word ever reached them of Lady Dada's uncle and his thousand men who had prepared to storm Kibaku from the south, nor the shinobi Naoya had sent to discover them.

Kazuchiyo kept himself as busy as he could, given the circumstances. He encouraged Mahiro to take him on a tour of the abandoned enemy camps, met with his commanders and their captains to ascertain troop fitness and morale, and even held council with Jisu's remaining generals to offer plans for defense and assistance, should Tendo move again come spring. He visited the town beneath Etsugo's plateau to receive thanks from its elder, and made offerings at Agarigumo Temple in hopes of settling the spirits of the monks killed there. He saw almost nothing of the Suyama troops, who stayed in their camp and ate from their own rations.

Now was not the time for magical foxes or long-lost dragons. He told himself this many times.

The evening before they were to depart, Kazuchiyo sent Amai down to the Kibaku camp to invite Naoya to supper. Far too much time had progressed already with the two of them at odds, and knowing the challenges that lay ahead of him made him eager to have their friendship rekindled.

"I think you just want to win him over again before you meet with Lord Koedzuka," Amai teased as he accepted the message. "His heart already beats on the outside; Koedzuka will notice that he's gone from openly campaigning in your name to avoiding you and start to wonder."

"I'm more concerned about my sister's wrath than Lord Koedzuka's," Kazuchiyo joked back. "I need to heal this breach so that the lady Purnima will be permitted in her company again."

Laughing, Amai agreed, and he set off to his task.

Naoya arrived precisely at the appointed time. His manners were stiff and unwelcoming, and Kazuchiyo could not help but be intimidated. He was relieved, however, to see that Naoya had brought Purnima along with the rest of his attendants.

"Purnima!" Mahiro bellowed as soon as their horses had been taken away, thus preventing the other woman's escape. She was dressed in her armor despite there being no call for it, and she eagerly motioned for Purnima to join her at her tent. "It's about time you showed your face here—as much of it as you ever do, I guess. Come have a drink with me while the little lordlings talk."

Clad in her typical face mask, only Purnima's dark eyes were visible, and they narrowed on Mahiro with disdain. "I would rather eat with my soldiers."

Mahiro covered her momentary flash of hurt with a great scoff. "Well, fine! Then me and my soldiers will join you, and I'll outdrink them all!"

She began shouting instructions to have the meal and drinks she'd prepared brought to the soldiers' common tent, and with no further means of extricating herself, the lady Purnima was forced to follow along. Kazuchiyo winced with sympathy as he watched the women march off. He did not have much hope for his sister faring well.

"I hope your sister does not have improper intentions for this meal," said Naoya. "The lady Purnima has no tolerance for base manipulations."

"No, I can't imagine she does," Kazuchiyo replied. "Mahiro will behave herself. I believe she simply misses the company." He sought Naoya's gaze. "As have I."

Discomfort twisted Naoya's features as he headed for Kazuchiyo's tent. "I don't see what they would be, when you've both acclimated yourselves to Jisu so well." With a deep breath, Kazuchiyo followed him inside.

The meal had already been laid out for them, and both were served wine. Kazuchiyo then dismissed his attendants so that they could speak privately. Though he had spent the better part of the afternoon readying himself, it took him a few moments more to reach his full composure.

"Thank you for accepting my invitation," he began, with every effort toward warmth and sincerity. "It's weighed on me that we've been on such poor terms lately."

"On me as well," Naoya replied, though he did not look up from his meal. "It has kept me up some nights, though I must confess, I do not know the way forward."

Kazuchiyo smiled fleetingly. "I'm not certain I do either," he admitted, "though something has changed since we last spoke, and I wanted you to know that." He took a sip of wine for courage and then straightened his back. "I understand now where the magic comes from."

Naoya had just taken up his bowl of rice, only to replace it on its tray once more. At last, he met Kazuchiyo's eyes, his own full of grief and resignation. "I knew that you would," he said quietly. "I am deeply sorry that I failed to prevent you."

"You have nothing to apologize for," Kazuchiyo insisted gently. "Master Iomori gave me my stone before you and I had ever met. Nothing could have prevented me from learning the truth eventually." He lowered his voice. "You were right, though: I do understand now how great of a burden this magic is—how great of a burden you've taken on yourself by wielding it as you do."

Naoya's deep-set, brown eyes grew tearful. "I tried to prevent you," he said again, passionately. "*Your* burdens are great enough already for a heart as tender as yours. A nation before you, a father looming over each shoulder—your duty is lined with the dead, and having their souls clenched in your sword hand will make that duty heavier, not lighter."

Kazuchiyo leaned back, struck with an unexpected swell of emotion. He had known immediately that Lady Dada's refusal to teach him of magic had stemmed from mistrust and the belief that he would misuse such a terrible power and secret; on the other hand, here sat Naoya, whose refusal had been rooted not in doubt but in faith in his character. He swallowed, throat tight with shame. "You really were thinking only of my well-being when you asked me to give up the stone."

"I was!" Naoya declared, though he soon checked himself, calming his spirits with a gulp of his wine. "I was. But now you know, and I will despise Clan Dada forever for that."

"It wasn't the lady Dada who told me," Kazuchiyo hurried to interject. "In fact, I asked for the truth, and she rebuffed me."

Naoya bristled not unlike a hunting dog catching a fresh scent. "Who then? Who else knows?"

"It was…" Kazuchiyo hesitated, as well he ought to. He had no means to predict how Naoya would respond to fantastic tales of mountainous fox temples. However, facing Naoya in that moment, he could not bring himself to answer this man of honor with anything less than the full truth.

"It was a hermit living on Mount Etsuzan." He sighed. "My friend, I was so tempted to lie to you just now. I want us to make amends, and I'm afraid that if you don't believe me, we'll lose our chance at that. But it's because I lied to you in the first place that we're here, and I won't make that mistake again. So, however remarkable it sounds, please… believe that what I'm about to tell you is the truth. I swear it on both my fathers."

Naoya blinked at him, taken aback, but Kazuchiyo's sincerity appeared to move him deeply. "I will believe you," he promised. "Go on."

"I followed a unique-looking fox into the woods," Kazuchiyo obliged him. "It led me to an old temple on the slopes of the mountain, where I met a… a woman. She was accompanied by many foxes, and she explained the source of magic to me. She even gave me this."

Kazuchiyo pulled his sleeve up to show Naoya the bead I had given him. Though the sight of it seemed to cause Naoya pain, he did not interrupt as Kazuchiyo carried on. "She said that my previous stone was almost empty, and that I should test myself by comparing it to this new, full stone. If I cannot tell the difference between them by my sense of will alone, I'm supposed to give them both up."

"You know my mind on the subject," said Naoya.

"Yes, I do." Kazuchiyo's shoulders sloped as he lowered his eyes. "And it may be that I give them up regardless. There is too much on my mind now to even want to undertake the test, so I hope it will put *your* mind at ease to know that, if nothing else, I have no intention of pursuing magic at this time."

Naoya frowned, and he took another sip of wine as he collected his thoughts. "It does, a little. Though I wonder now why you thought so ill of my trust in you, Kazumune. Why would I not believe you about this hermit woman if you're wearing the proof on your arm?"

Here Kazuchiyo was certain to give Naoya his full attention. "The woman called herself Lady Enmei."

Naoya's eyes grew wide, full of shock and wonder at my name, which really *ought* to be familiar to anyone calling themselves by that silly title of onmyouji. I imagine even unshakable Naoya found it difficult to fill his oath of believing Kazuchiyo implicitly in that moment. "Lady Enmei," he echoed reverently. "You're certain?"

"I couldn't be more so," Kazuchiyo said, praying that this time Naoya would not resist telling him the full truth. "It was playing her 'Willow Garden' melody that coaxed her fox servants to me."

"But... Lady Enmei lived at the emperor's court nearly a thousand years ago," Naoya protested. "She must be an admirer using the name as a title."

Naoya's denial swayed Kazuchiyo not at all, and rightfully so. In my words and manners I had given him plenty of cause to believe that he had, for that brief afternoon, been the guest of a creature both ancient and supernatural. Forgetting at once that he had sworn not to lie, even by omission, to his friend any longer, he chose not to press the issue, and instead pursued a different line of inquiry. "I've only ever known 'Lady Enmei' to refer to a courtesan in times past, a writer of poetry and music, like the melody you're so fond of."

"Yes, indeed!" Naoya, now seemingly of good humor, began to eat heartily. "Consort to Emperor Seiun during his tiger years! Extremely talented woman, who cultivated magic in ways that none had before her. See here."

Naoya reached into the front collar of his robe and drew forth the string of beads kept hidden there. He pointed to a small, black stone that sat at one end of the collection. "This Soul Stone was given to me by my great-grandfather," he said with pride. "He told me that Lady Enmei herself owned it once. Alas, its magic was spent by the time I inherited it. What mysteries might it have held?"

Kazuchiyo lost Naoya to his repose for a long moment, but then a pall came over his face, and he hurriedly tucked the string of beads away. "I should not boast," he scolded himself. "Each is a burden, not a trinket to display. Please accept my apologies."

Kazuchiyo, meanwhile, smiled openly. "I do. I understand how it feels to have a powerful secret in your heart, and how badly you want to speak of it once you have the chance. Now that I know the truth, my ears are yours if you need them."

Naoya looked very tempted, and he continued to eat as he weighed Kazuchiyo's offer against his own caution. At last, he shook his head. "No. No, it won't do to tell you more. You may yet abandon magic entirely."

Ah, poor man. So hopeful he was. Kazuchiyo nodded vaguely as he took up his bowl, determined not to comment on the likelihood of his curiosity ever fading entirely. "What about my hermit?" he asked after they had both settled their temperaments. "Suppose she truly was that same Lady Enmei of Emperor Seiun. Could a mystic as talented as her live a thousand years, with the help of magic?"

"Even if she could have, she did not," replied Naoya with a fool's confidence. "She was killed during the war over the emperor's succession and entombed at her birthplace, near Mount Akinobi."

"Yes, you must be right," said Kazuchiyo, unconvinced. "You're quite the scholar, Naoya."

"Hers is a history worth knowing. I have accounts of her life at my estate in Tettsu, if you ever have the occasion to visit." Once again, he was given pause as a new thought occurred to him, and he fixed his eye very sternly on Kazuchiyo. "I am reconciled with you understanding the truth of magic, but now that it's come to your mind, please allow me to be quite firm on one subject: magic cannot and *should not* be used in the extension of a life."

Though startled by Naoya's abrupt declaration, Kazuchiyo took his warning seriously. "Please explain why," he said. "I'm sorry, but 'because it's for your own good' will not satisfy me, even if I know your intentions are pure."

Naoya shut his jaws against what was undoubtedly the same answer Kazuchiyo had just rebuffed. He took another moment to reconsider, and blessedly, he lowered his voice. "Magic can do many things, but there are many things it *cannot* do, and that truth is the hardest to bear. If you choose to wield it, you must never forget that you are commanding *the dead*, Kazumune. If you use that magic upon yourself, you are inviting the souls of the dead into you. Save your life, it might, but it wouldn't be only *your* life any longer. Do you understand?"

Kazuchiyo felt a chill, and he took a sip of wine for his nerves' sake. "Lady Dada said she had been warned not to dabble in magic, because it might 'change' her," he recalled aloud.

Naoya nodded, and it seemed that all his earlier resentment toward the woman swiftly reversed. "There are

251

tales of onmyouji who have employed their magic to terrifying ends," he continued. "Men who can change their form, heal their wounds, perhaps even cheat death. But the end always comes, and it *is* terrifying. It would pain me deeply to see you experience such a fate."

"I understand," Kazuchiyo reassured him. "Thank you for the warning."

Naoya picked up his bowl once more. "Whoever your hermit is who aspires to *call* herself Lady Enmei, she likely is not as powerful as she seems." He scoffed. "Why, if our plans were not so firmly set as to have us leave tomorrow, I would seek her out and tell her so in person. I can't help but wonder if you waited until now to tell me, in order to prevent that."

"You're right," Kazuchiyo replied openly. "Forgive me, but it was for *your* own well-being that I concealed her from you until now."

Though Naoya was momentarily taken aback, a searching look of Kazuchiyo's face must have confirmed for him that Kazuchiyo was being honest. He nodded, again moved to great emotion. "In that case, thank you for your interference. I trust your judgment."

The rest of their conversation passed in idle pleasantry as they discussed their upcoming march back to Rongi. Naoya said more than once how eager he was to introduce Lord Koedzuka to their new allies and how honored Lady Dada ought to be by the privilege. Happy to see him in his element, Kazuchiyo agreed and encouraged him all the while.

"The season has grown very late," Naoya remarked as they at last exited the tent together. "Once our celebrations at Rongi are complete, I imagine our lords will command us all home for the harvest. Lord Aritaka's campaign will have to wait until spring."

"Three more provinces are sworn to his banner," replied Kazuchiyo. "If we can convince Nomino through negotiation instead of battle, then, Tendo aside, he'll command the entire east of Shuyun." He raised his eyes to the sky, where a sliver of moonlight seeped out from behind rushing clouds. "Touyun no Kami, they'll call him."

"I won't be calling *him* that," Naoya replied immediately, and Kazuchiyo smiled, relieved that, if nothing else, Naoya no longer seemed to loathe the idea of continuing to march alongside him.

Naoya's retinue approached then with the horses, Purnima among them. She was not a woman whose manners were easily read, but to Kazuchiyo she seemed quieter than usual, and she fidgeted as she handed Naoya his reins. "Are we leaving?"

"What's the matter?" Naoya asked with concern, though he then cast Kazuchiyo a quick glance. "Does it need to be addressed here?"

"No," Purnima said quickly, and she wasted no more time in mounting her own horse. "I am ready to leave."

She urged her horse ahead of their party, and though Kazuchiyo was tempted to offer her an apology for whatever had transpired, he sensed it would only embarrass her further. Instead, he turned to Naoya. "I feel I might have to apologize for my sister's behavior, whatever it might have been, to offend your lady Purnima," he said quietly.

"Lady Mahiro's propriety is often lacking," Naoya replied, though with just as much effort to prevent Purnima from overhearing them. "However, I suspect that in this case apologies are not necessary." He sighed wistfully. "Such is the complexity of love!"

Kazuchiyo's brow rose, though he wisely did not probe further as Naoya took to his horse. "Then I'll see you tomorrow for the march."

"Indeed. The rear guard will suit us well." Naoya offered Kazuchiyo a nod. "Thank you for tonight's invitation."

Kazuchiyo bowed in reply, and he saw Naoya and the rest of his soldiers off. As soon as they were out of sight, he headed for the tent Mahiro had drawn her companions to.

Mahiro was still inside, their Sakka men surrounding her, each drinking their fill. Everyone seemed to be in good spirits without any immediate clue as to what might have put off Purnima. The soldiers bowed clumsily at Kazuchiyo's entrance, but Mahiro only continued to laugh in the wake of some mighty joke recently told.

"Sister," Kazuchiyo greeted her. "Did everything go all right?"

"Hm?" Mahiro shrugged carelessly. "Why wouldn't it have? We were having a fine time of it."

Kazuchiyo wasn't convinced, but he couldn't very well ask in front of her soldiers. "Make sure you retire before too long. It's going to be a long march tomorrow."

"Yes, lord!" the men said at once, and Mahiro bobbed her head in agreement. Determined that he would get the truth from her another time, Kazuchiyo left them to the remains of their meal.

The next day, the entire encampment set out from Etsugo to make the trek back to Rongi Castle.

At the head of the procession rode General Zaiga and his fifty men from Suyama. Untouched by recent battle, they were rested and well-suited at the front. Kazuchiyo had only a few moments in the early morning to exchange a greeting with Zaiga, who treated him with the calm deference of any general addressing his lord. Kazuchiyo was not able to spot his brother among the soldiers in the little time he gave himself to look. He vowed to find another opportunity someday soon.

The rear guard was solidified by General Naoya and his Kibaku troops. If Mutsuyama did have any very well guarded plans at ambushing them from behind, Naoya declared he would foil them. Just ahead of him came Lady Dada's soldiers and a hundred samurai under the newly promoted General Chikakuni's command. Among her bannermen were many of her female warriors, bearing their flashing nagamaki blades.

And at the center of the contingent rode Kazuchiyo

with his main army from Sakka, Commander Ginta at the head, with Nishigame and Yagi close behind. Kazuchiyo set out flanked by his bannermen, and because Mahiro had been denied the vanguard, she rode beside him. It proved the perfect opportunity for Kazuchiyo to ask her about the night before.

"I know you were hoping to spend a more pleasant evening in Lady Purnima's company," he prompted. "How was it?"

Mahiro heaved a dramatic sigh. "I don't understand that woman," she declared. "I was behaving myself *very* well, and everyone was having fun. And then she walks out!" She gave a great snort that was echoed by Suzumekage as if in agreement. "Humorless."

Kazuchiyo watched her face. "Could it have been something you said?" he asked as delicately as possible.

"I didn't say *anything* that could have offended her," Mahiro snapped, and she spurred Suzumekage forward enough to end their conversation.

Kazuchiyo sighed, hopeful that the two would have some other chance at reconciliation before the end of their time at Rongi.

CHAPTER EIGHTEEN

The three-day march back to Rongi Castle passed without incident. The armies spent their second night in and around the town surrounding Kanrei Temple, which could not have been happier to receive them, contrary to their first visit. Most of the damage they had suffered from Mutsuyama's night attack had been repaired, and the village elder welcomed them as returning heroes. There was a great deal of commotion over the arrival of Lady Dada herself, and she reacted to it with proud stoicism that nevertheless conveyed a lord's warmth for her people. A ceremony was held at the temple to celebrate Etsugo's freedom and the coming of the harvest: a quiet but meaningful affair that spoke to the diligence and sincerity of Jisu's citizens.

That evening, Kazuchiyo was again offered a small chamber in the elder's home. He accepted, and there was greeted by two unexpected visitors: Generals Rakuteru and Hosoda awaited him, eager for news of how the campaign had fared and what lay ahead. The three of them discussed their plans over dinner.

"My men are still camped to the north," Rakuteru explained in his typical, no-nonsense fashion. "There are some five hundred Jisu soldiers there, still licking their wounds.

Apparently, they had been trying to sneak their way into Kibaku at the start of this, but were turned back by an army from Nomino Province. They suffered heavy losses."

"Nomino," Kazuchiyo repeated, having nearly forgotten that possible threat. "We took the quickest route to Etsugo because we considered Nomino might be hostile, but I had no idea they'd acted already. Where is their army now?"

"Back behind their own borders for the time being. They won't be able to stay deployed for much longer." Rakuteru made no effort to hide his disappointment. "The weather is finally turning, and turning fast. We'll all need every man in the fields."

Kazuchiyo nodded. Unlike his trusted general, he would be quite content to put their battles to rest until spring. He even harbored a tiny hope that Lord Aritaka would allow him to winter somewhere in Kibaku rather than returning to Gyoe, on the pretense of resuming the campaign as early as possible. "I know you were hoping to test your mettle against these inner territories, but we've accomplished a great deal already. Lord Aritaka can have no reason to complain."

Rakuteru looked skeptical, and so General Hosoda took it upon himself to speak. "I am a little concerned about the south," he admitted. "It sounds like we were supposed to find another Jisu army that way, but we've seen no sign of them."

"Over a thousand men," Kazuchiyo confirmed. "Led by Lady Dada's uncle, so I was told." He frowned, wishing he had a map to spread between them. "They would have been joined by forces from Tendo. We can only assume they were betrayed and overrun. Possibly destroyed down to a man."

"You ought to tell Lord Koedzuka to be cautious," said Rakuteru. "Armies don't vanish. Tendo could have wiped them out and moved farther south, where they lie in wait."

"Yes, you're right. I'll send a messenger to Izuho as well— that was their original goal, after all." Kazuchiyo drew his supper closer, using a few mouthfuls to collect his thoughts. "For now, I'll have both of you keep your armies where they are, at least until this meeting with Lord Koedzuka is through. I think it unlikely that Nomino or Tendo will try anything just yet, but we want *everyone* to see that Sakka does not abandon its allies. Kibaku, Jisu, and Izuho are all under our protection now."

Both men agreed, and once the meal was through, they shared one more drink of wine to close the evening. Rakuteru drank his in one mighty gulp and then fixed Kazuchiyo with a curious look, as if only just then coming to the point of their assembly. "Were you put out that I ordered General Zaiga and his men to check in on you?" he asked. "If so, I'm prepared to make amends in a way you see fit."

Kazuchiyo tried not to betray how eager and how anxious the question made him. He had suspected from first laying eyes on Zaiga that Rakuteru had some special motive in allowing them to meet; now might prove the time to suss it out. "I was surprised but not offended. I hope the three of you got on well while you were campaigning in Namugi."

"He's a very capable man," said Rakuteru, which from him was a high compliment indeed.

"It couldn't have been easy for him to fight alongside us, considering the history between our homelands," added Hosoda. "But he was honorable and very cordial with us. I am glad to count him as an ally."

Kazuchiyo glanced between the two of them, careful not to let his hope get the better of him. "I'm very glad to hear it."

"I *would* have been glad to count him as an ally at Sabi and Fukugawa too," Hosoda added, rubbing the scar that ran across his cheek and jaw.

Kazuchiyo held his breath, and sure enough Rakuteru continued in Hosoda's stead. "There's no point in conquering a province if you don't intend to make use of it," he said. "Aritaka has resisted using Suyama soldiers for a long time out of paranoia. But it's because Suyama is strong that we took it. It was a waste not to use Zaiga before now." He met Kazuchiyo's gaze firmly. "All these lands are going to fall to you someday. It's only right that you use each of them to their fullest, whether that's us, your uncle, or your new allies. All of us are yours to command. Do you understand?"

"Yes," Kazuchiyo replied immediately, and he bowed his head only as far as a lord ought to, grateful to the two men for their declaration of loyalty to him. "I promise to make full use of your services, for the betterment and glory of all Shuyun."

It would have been more correct and proper then to pledge their strength to Sakka, or to the Aritaka clan, but both men bowed deeply in reply nonetheless. "Yes, lordship."

Kazuchiyo saw them out, and in doing so noticed young Tomoto among Hosoda's gathered attendants. Upon seeing Kazuchiyo, Tomoto bowed very low at the waist, and as he snapped upright again he was grinning.

"My lord, I'm very sorry we won't be taking the field together again," he said, "but I'm very gladdened and honored to see you well."

"And you," Kazuchiyo replied, smiling back. "Please continue to take good care of General Hosoda for me."

Tomoto nodded enthusiastically, and a close eye would have noticed Hosoda blushing as he took to his horse. Before moving to his own horse, however, Rakuteru turned to Kazuchiyo one more time.

"My son told me you received a message from Master Iomori before setting off into Jisu," he said, with an effort to hide his voice from the other soldiers. "Has Lord Aritaka really left Gyoe?"

Kazuchiyo lowered his voice as well. "That's what Master Iomori said, but I haven't had any word from my father himself. I have no idea what has called him away."

"We haven't heard anything either," Rakuteru admitted. "Will you send word, if you do?"

"Immediately," Kazuchiyo promised.

With the last formalities exchanged, the two generals and their entourages departed to camp with their men, before returning to the north and south lines as they had decided.

By the time Kazuchiyo returned to his chamber in the elder's home, Amai was there waiting, helping himself to the last of the saké.

"There, you see?" said Amai as he shook the last drops from the gourd into his cup. "Everyone loves you."

Kazuchiyo released a deep sigh as he dropped down beside Amai, as if the breath he had held earlier had remained captive in his lungs ever since. "Rakuteru is a brilliant general, and Hosoda has a lot of men. I'm lucky to have them."

"Luck? Pah." Amai downed the last gulp of saké and leaned into Kazuchiyo's side. "You've wooed them with your prowess. It's what you do."

Kazuchiyo chuckled as he relaxed against Amai. "Is it?"

"It is, I guarantee it." Amai let down Kazuchiyo's hair and began to comb it with his fingers. "And I'm not the only one. Yagi's hoping he'll be able to join you in your chambers at Rongi again when we get there."

"Yes," Kazuchiyo said immediately, only to blush at his own impatience. "Yes, of course. When we're on the march he belongs with his commander, but once we're at Rongi…" He closed his eyes as he enjoyed Amai's soothing attention. "I'm glad to hear he wants to."

"I think it's good you've spent some time apart. Lets you miss each other." Amai chuckled and kissed Kazuchiyo's cheek. "Let's go to bed. The sooner we sleep, the sooner we get there."

Kazuchiyo turned, capturing Amai's lips in a kiss. "Even if it's the same tiny room, you're welcome to join us this time," he said, though it did not come out as much of a request as an order. Amai chuckled some more.

"Gladly," he said, and they laid out the futons to sleep.

The next day their armies, wreathed in a glowing sunset halo, returned to Rongi Castle in Kibaku Province.

Beihou's grand generosity was on full display. With the gates laid open, dozens of samurai in their full, polished armor bowed in rows to welcome their returning kin and guests.

Delicious smells wafted out of the kitchens, promising a memorable feast. Beihou and his family waited in the central courtyard, each in their finest to receive their once enemy lord. Having taken up the rear for the march, Naoya hurried to the front to be the first to accept Beihou's welcome and congratulations. They slapped each other heartily on their shoulders and grinned openly.

"General Oihata returns, champion of those in need," Beihou teased, his youngest children giggling alongside him. "Well done, my friend." He then looked to Kazuchiyo. "And you, young lord." He bowed.

Kazuchiyo nodded as he and Lady Dada stepped forward together. "Thank you for again receiving us so warmly, General. May I introduce to you Lady Dada Tangiku of Jisu Province."

Lady Dada bowed her head. She had dressed in simple trousers for the long ride, but her kosode top was rather extravagant, brocaded in lavender chrysanthemums. She wore a wide-brimmed straw hat with a veil draped from its edges that obscured her made-up face from the surrounding men, an old-fashioned display of modesty for a woman of her station. "General Sasahara," she greeted him with her usual implacable poise. "Our two lands have been at odds for a long time, but now I am humbled and grateful to be accepted within your walls."

Beihou bowed deeply. There was a twinkle of humor in his eye that hinted he may have been tempted to tell some joke on the subject, but his wife was watching him very closely, and he seemed to take notice. "You are very welcome here," he said. "I must beg your forgiveness for the small rooms I have to offer you. Rongi isn't accustomed to housing three samurai lords at once! But there's space enough for you and a small number of attendants."

"Have you heard from our lord?" asked Naoya, his face practically aglow.

"We expect him the day after tomorrow." Beihou smiled dryly. "We'll do our best to amuse you all until then, starting tonight with a feast! I hope the travel has made you hungry."

"Famished," Mahiro spoke up. "You'd better have enough wine."

Luckily for all, there was plenty of wine to be had. Kazuchiyo had expected that Beihou would withhold at least some of his generosity, as he would be hosting many guests for several days to come, but if he had, there was no telling that based on the feast that was laid out before them. Mahiro claimed the center of attention, fueled by drink and the rapt attention of Rongi's soldiers as she recounted their battles in Jisu. The fire attack at Kanrei, Yagi's duels on the road, the retaking of Etsugo—already they seemed so long ago to Kazuchiyo. His mind was ever pointed forward, to the mysterious stones still wrapped against his wrist, to General Zaiga dining with the other generals, and to Lord Koedzuka heading toward them for a meeting he wasn't yet prepared to have.

That night, Kazuchiyo was escorted to the same interior chambers that had been his during his first visit to Rongi. Though the heat had broken considerably since then, the rooms remained rather stuffy, and with three warm bodies filling the space, it was necessary to leave a panel ajar. Those discomforts mattered very little to Kazuchiyo, tucked away with his two lovers, content in the belief that their wars had ended for the year.

The next day was spent in a flurry of preparation. Beihou's soldiers and servants put the finishing touches on their welcome arrangements, everyone excited to be receiving their honored lord himself. Kazuchiyo stayed mostly out of the way for the morning, volunteering to give Lady Dada and Chikakuni a tour of the grounds as had been done for him. With Chikakuni's help, they put to rest as many of Lady Dada's concerns for the incoming meeting as possible. But by the time afternoon came about, with most of the necessary tasks accomplished, the air became charged. The many waiting soldiers had too much energy and nothing left to do but wait.

By the time Kazuchiyo and his two companions reached

the lower bailey, a crowd had formed. He assumed at first that some impromptu competition had sprung up, much like their first visit to Rongi, and it was only noticing Yagi at the center that drew his full attention. With Lady Dada's agreement, they moved closer for a better look.

"That was too slow," Yagi was saying to a young soldier opposite him, who was shaking a sting from his hands. Both were dressed in simple gi and trousers for training and brandishing wooden practice spears. Though Yagi barely looked winded, his opponent was breathing hard from their exercise.

"Sorry, sir," said the soldier, bobbing his head. "Thank you."

Yagi waved him out of the ring while their crowd murmured and set forth its next eager challenger: a stout, older samurai with a green sigil embroidered on the lapel of his robe. Kazuchiyo assumed he was one of Beihou's, as he faced Yagi without the trepidation of a man who had seen the oni duel. He bowed his head. "Thank you for the opportunity, Commander."

"Captain," Yagi corrected him, brandishing his wooden spear. "Show me your strength."

The pair fought a brief but impressive spar. Beihou's man was as sturdy as his general, with the patience and experience of age on his side, but he was no match for Yagi's overwhelming power and greater height. A blow to his ribs left him wheezing, but once he had his breath again he bowed to Yagi, just as grateful as the younger man before him.

"If I was tired, you might have had me," Yagi told him. "Next time, wait for a while before volunteering." The surrounding men laughed at that, goading each other on to wear Yagi down for them.

Kazuchiyo smiled. Though an onlooker might have considered Yagi's manners short and even curt, he could see this was not the case; Yagi was confident and calm in his position as impromptu teacher, and the attention it fixed on him. It filled his lover with gladness.

"He's really not that much of an oni after all," remarked Chikakuni dryly. "Like this, he looks rather tame."

"He's one of the best men I've ever known," said Kazuchiyo, chest swelling with emotion. "Honest, loyal, and considerate, on top of being the strongest warrior in eastern Shuyun. I'm—"

A new challenger stepped into the ring to spar with Yagi, stealing Kazuchiyo's breath from his throat: it was his brother Shigeyuki, dressed as casually as the rest of the soldiers, his coarse hair tied back in a tuft. His face gleamed with enthusiasm, and the audience cheered especially loudly for his youthful courage. Yagi regarded him with the same stoic interest as his previous challengers, without any indication he might have suspected whom he was facing.

Kazuchiyo gulped, and realizing that Chikakuni was watching him with eyebrows raised, he cleared his throat. "I'm very lucky," he finished. "No other daimyo of Shuyun can boast my riches."

"You're not a daimyo yet," Lady Dada corrected him with stone-faced amusement, and the three of them watched as the bout started.

Shigeyuki was swifter than Kazuchiyo had expected and, by all appearances, swifter than Yagi had expected too. He twirled the staff around his body with the deft precision of a dancer and lunged like a cobra. Yagi defected the first attack, the smack of the wood echoing hard in Kazuchiyo's ears, but Shigeyuki used the momentum from that defense to spin his spear back the other way, landing a solid blow against Yagi's unguarded right hip.

The crowd gaped, Shigeyuki most of all. Before any could draw a breath to cheer, Yagi scowled and thrust the butt of his spear into Shigeyuki's face.

Kazuchiyo's hands went to his mouth as he watched Shigeyuki thrown to the ground. His brother laid low, blood on his face, reminded him so sharply of Tomonaga felled at Shimegahara that he was certain his heart ceased beating. The surrounding men barely knew how to react either to what was unmistakably a harsh retaliation. But when Shigeyuki rallied himself enough to sit up, his eyes were still bright with exuberance despite the blood pouring from his nose.

"That was an unfair hit!" he protested. "I had you."

Yagi planted the end of his wooden spear in the ground and stared back, unmoved. "I didn't yield."

Shigeyuki spat blood in the dirt as their audience continued to look on. "If I was using a real spear, you'd be dead."

Yagi regarded him silently for a moment, and then he drew his left arm into the sleeve of his gi. Pushing his robe off his shoulder revealed to Shigeyuki and to the assembly at large the many scars that covered most of his torso. He pointed to one in particular that ran over his hip—rather close, in fact, to where Shigeyuki had just struck. "See this scar?" he asked. "What made it?"

Shigeyuki's boyish petulance immediately sloughed off, and he sat up straighter. "A spear?"

"So? Am I dead?"

"No," said Shigeyuki, a flash of cooler eagerness in his face that further heightened the energy of their audience.

Seemingly satisfied that his point was clear, Yagi offered Shigeyuki the end of his practice spear. "Neither are you," he said, and Shigeyuki gladly accepted the help in climbing to his feet. "If you're going to fight, fight until you're dead."

Shigeyuki hurried to grab up his weapon, mopping his bloody face against his sleeve. "Yes, sir!"

The ring of soldiers encouraged them with renewed vigor and respect. As they resumed their sparring at a more casual pace, Kazuchiyo finally relaxed enough to let his hands fall. He released a long, anxious breath.

Chikakuni cast Kazuchiyo a curious look. "That boy isn't in Sakka colors. Do you know him?"

"He's…" Kazuchiyo quickly shook off the rest of his nerves; Yagi was definitely going easier on Shigeyuki then, with no further cause for concern. "I believe he's General Zaiga's adopted son." He glanced over the assembly but didn't see the man, which was just as well, as he would have been tempted to march over and scold him for neglecting Shigeyuki so spectacularly. "I hope he doesn't take offense."

"Two dozen witnesses will say he asked for it," said Chikakuni, and he chuckled. "I take back what I said. Your oni is plenty ferocious."

"'Considerate,' you called him," Lady Dada added.

Kazuchiyo took the opportunity to turn his full attention to her. "Yes, I did. Only Sakka's enemies have anything to fear from Captain Ebara." He lowered his voice. "He may be able to kill by the dozens, but he takes no pleasure in it, and he takes no trophies either. I know you were concerned about my interest in magic in part because of his prowess, but he is no shinigami sent to collect souls for me."

Lady Dada appeared taken aback by his bluntness, and she gathered herself up. "I was concerned," she confessed, "and I continue to be. But, for now, I am glad for the chance to see his strength in person." She looked a moment more to Yagi, who was waving for Shigeyuki to come closer again. "And his character."

Yagi grasped Shigeyuki's bloody nose, and with a stomach-churning crunch, he shoved the cartilage back into place. The audience cringed and Kazuchiyo felt faint, but Shigeyuki bore it admirably, and afterward he bowed and thanked Yagi for sparing him a trip to the physicians. Yagi then pointed to his own nose, likely relating an experience of his own, but Kazuchiyo didn't think his nerves could take much more if he stayed to watch.

"Let's head back to the keep," he suggested. "I think our presence here might be encouraging them too much."

His companions agreed, and the three of them made their way back to Rongi's main keep. As soon as was appropriate Kazuchiyo disengaged to seek out General Zaiga, whom he found in a small sitting room in the lesser keep with his elderly captain. Though fairly certain the man could be trusted, Kazuchiyo waited until the captain had been dismissed before facing Zaiga with his displeasure.

"Your 'son' is out with the troops in the lower bailey," said Kazuchiyo, and after the scene he'd witnessed he didn't have the means left to hide his anxiety. "He challenged Captain Ebara to a fight."

Zaiga perked up at the news. "Oh? How did he fare?"

"He—" Kazuchiyo let out a sigh as he took a seat across from Zaiga on the tatami. "He landed a hit and got his nose broken for it."

"Landed a hit on Yagi-douji?" Zaiga smiled proudly. "I wish I'd seen it."

"Did you not hear the second part? How can you let him be out there like that, unguarded?" Kazuchiyo shuddered at the memory of Chikakuni's curious look, burdened by the impossible thought that he suspected their fraternal connection somehow. "His face bare for all to see, even more so after what Yagi did to him. What if someone recognizes him?"

Seeing his distress, Zaiga gentled his tone. "I felt the same way when he first appeared at my door, but he is a soldier now. To hide his face in the general company would be even more suspicious. Try not to dwell on it; no soldier from Suyama would dare mention the resemblance, and no mere soldier of any other province would recognize your father himself if he were to ride through the camp." He smiled sympathetically. "And he doesn't hold all that much resemblance to you, if you'll forgive me for saying so. No one here would ever suspect who he is."

"I know," Kazuchiyo admitted, frustrated that he could not banish the concern still festering beneath his skin. "You're right; I'm just afraid for him. It's not safe for him outside Suyama."

"I'm not going to let anything happen to him," Zaiga said immediately. He edged closer so he could clasp Kazuchiyo's wrist. "To *either* of you. With two dragons united we have a real chance to retake Suyama now, in your names. I will do everything in my power to protect that."

As encouraging as his support was, Kazuchiyo hesitated to reply. "Suyama is already destined to be mine, once Aritaka is dead," he said, genuinely uncertain of Zaiga's reaction. "All I need be is patient."

"That's not enough," Zaiga replied immediately, releasing him once more. "That would still mean Suyama bows to Aritaka's indigo banners." He frowned, doubtlessly reassessing the insistence with which he had spoken just then. "Would you be satisfied with that, young lord?"

Kazuchiyo lowered his voice, paranoid of the very close walls of their small chamber. "My only other option would be to betray Lord Aritaka and declare war." Even speaking the words gave him a chill, as he remembered the promise Yagi had made to him long ago to one day take the old bear's head.

"The clans of Suyama will rise at the first opportunity," Zaiga assured him just as quietly. "I'm half convinced Generals Rakuteru and Hosoda would join the dragon banner if given the chance. We can drive Aritaka's brother off his seat at Tengakubou and claim Suyama for the dragon lords again. Then we can forget for good this nonsense of attacking the capital."

Kazuchiyo was taken aback. "Nonsense? You think our chances are that poor?"

"I think it's a waste of time and resources, even if you could," said Zaiga, as his tone took on that of the patient teacher Kazuchiyo had once known him to be. "You've done very well to secure the loyalties of so many provinces. That will help us against Aritaka, certainly. But the shogun's men and magistrates haven't stepped foot in Suyama for over a generation; there's no need for us to challenge them when we can exist very well on our own."

"I suppose that's true," Kazuchiyo replied carefully. "I only volunteered to lead this campaign toward Aritaka becoming shogun so that he would not suspect betrayal from me."

"And that seed now bears fruit. The time will soon come to harvest." Zaiga paused then, again reflecting on Kazuchiyo in a new light. "Unless you have your own designs on becoming shogun?"

"I..." Kazuchiyo returned his uncle's searching look, and though this time he was quite sure of his reaction, he could not stop himself from speaking the truth. "I've considered it. I think I would be a fool not to."

"Your father had no ambition to become shogun, and he was not a fool," Zaiga chided him, though patiently. "Don't let Aritaka's warmongering infest your spirit, young lord. It doesn't suit you."

How tempted Kazuchiyo was then to reveal to Zaiga a truth he may not have known then: that it was precisely that lack of warmongering ambition that had brought about the Red Dragon's downfall, betrayed by the bloodthirsty Waseba brothers. This time, however, he held his tongue. "I understand," he said instead. "However, until the time comes that I am able to denounce Aritaka entirely, I still think it necessary to play the part of dutiful son. It's what Lord Koedzuka and Lady Dada will expect of me."

Zaiga did not look happy at the prospect, but he bowed his head. "I can only imagine the trials you've had to endure thus far. It's inappropriate for me to lecture you; I trust your judgment."

"When I was a child, you lectured me; now I consider it council," replied Kazuchiyo, smiling. "I appreciate it."

That evening, Kazuchiyo took supper in his chamber with Yagi and Amai. Rongi's excitement had reached a fever pitch, and he was more than ever eager for a few hours of rest and calm.

"You looked like you were enjoying yourself today," Kazuchiyo told Yagi as they ate, testing the waters.

Yagi nodded and gulped down a huge mouthful of rice. "Everyone was shifting around with nothing to do, so I thought it would keep them busy and out of the way."

"And they'll be very busy tonight, nursing their bruises," teased Amai. "A job well done."

"I'm sure General Sasahara appreciates it," said Kazuchiyo. "Though I suspect you'll be asked to exhibit again once Lord Koedzuka is here. He'll be as eager as the rest of them to see your strength on display."

"I don't mind if it's just for show. It's good exercise and everyone seems to like it. They're less afraid of me for it, at least." Yagi took another bite and chewed thoughtfully for a moment before swallowing. "I like it."

Kazuchiyo smiled and passed over the wine gourd, which he gladly accepted. "I'm very glad to hear it."

Amai took over the conversation then, eager to share some of the gossip he had gained from around the castle. It wasn't until the meal was nearly over that Kazuchiyo decided to broach the subject. "I saw my brother today."

"Was he well?" asked Yagi.

Kazuchiyo wanted to scoff, but then he realized what the true answer would be, and he couldn't help but smile. "Well, yes. He seemed very happy."

"Good." Yagi shook his head. "That's all I want to know about it. If anyone's going to give him away, it won't be me."

"All right." Kazuchiyo relaxed. He knew it would be a mortifying conversation one day, but for the moment, he was relieved to have avoided it. "Someday I'll introduce you properly."

Amai glanced between the two of them, keen as ever. His sly eyes were too much to resist, and Kazuchiyo grimaced a little and tapped his nose when Yagi wasn't looking.

For once, Amai's composure did not hold; he snorted loudly, and when Yagi frowned at him in confusion, he laughed.

"Why is that funny?" Yagi demanded. "I know my limits, and I'm doing my best."

Amai shook his head, but he couldn't stop laughing. Confronted with the absurdity that his lover has broken his brother's nose without realizing, even Kazuchiyo found the humor in it. He laughed, feeling guilty to see Yagi so hopelessly affronted in his confusion, but it felt good to laugh.

CHAPTER NINETEEN

I t was late in the afternoon when green banners were spotted arriving from the eastern road. By then all of Rongi's anxious energy was sharpened to that of battle readiness, and every soldier, servant, and civilian within the fortress walls rushed into position. It was then the twenty-ninth day of the ninth month of 1488.

Kazuchiyo joined Lady Dada, Naoya, and Beihou in the central courtyard. Each was formally dressed for the occasion, though none could match Naoya for enthusiasm. His hair was elaborately braided and smoothed with fragrant oil, reaching up into a fine, black silk cap, and his face was aglow with anticipation. Even so he kept perfectly still upon the engawa, demonstrating the utmost devotion to his incoming lord.

The procession was indeed a handsome one. Lord Koedzuka Danzou entered on his speckled horse amid a host of tall, emerald banners, clad in gold-corded armor and embroidered jinbaori. As ever his face was pleasant and dignified, his mustache and beard immaculately trimmed. His was the bearing of one Kazuchiyo would have been pleased to call shogun.

Koedzuka dismounted with the assistance of his attendants.

All around, the soldiers bowed deeply in respect as he and his guard approached their hosts; Beihou and the rest stepped off the engawa to greet him as equals.

"My lord," Beihou said, bowing a second time. "You are very welcome to Rongi. I hope you do not find it in worse condition than your last visit."

"I'm certain I won't," Koedzuka replied. "General Sasahara's generosity is legendary." He then offered a deep nod to Kazuchiyo and Lady Dada, who responded in kind. "It's an honor to be here with you both. Thank you for agreeing to this meeting."

"It should be me thanking you," said Lady Dada. "There are very few daimyo, I think, who would welcome their enemy into their lands not some weeks after an attempted incursion."

Naoya, having reached the limit of his restraint, rose quickly to his lord's defense. "Lord Koedzuka is like no other daimyo of Shuyun. He is not resentful or petty; you have nothing to fear from him."

Koedzuka smiled, full of both embarrassment and fondness. "It's good to see you, General Oihata," he said, though as Naoya beamed, he turned back to Lady Dada. "Though I think there are even fewer daimyo that would accept an invitation like mine. So still, I thank you for your trust. I will work hard to prove it was not misplaced."

Lady Dada nodded, and though her face was still covered by her veil, Kazuchiyo felt her relief, which he shared. He had high hopes that their meeting would be amiable.

Lord Koedzuka's procession made way for the arrival of a palanquin borne by decorated attendants. One of Koedzuka's own guardsmen moved to help its occupants disembark: the lord's wife and young son, whom Kazuchiyo had not yet had an occasion to meet. The lady Koedzuka rose from her boxy transport with effortless nobility, draped in exquisite, cream-colored robes, one of which pulled up high over her head to shield her shiny, black hair. Her bronze complexion and downturned nose suggested a similar ancestry to Purnima's, which was also apparent in her son. The young heir to Kibaku was no more than five years old then: a tottery child with wide, curious eyes. He clung to his mother's hand as she led them toward the waiting assembly.

"My wife, Lady Anisha," Koedzuka introduced her proudly. "And our son, heir to Kibaku, Koedzuka Danmaru."

"Very pleased to meet you both," said Kazuchiyo, bowing his head.

Danmaru's wide eyes hopped from one figure to the next. When Anisha gave his hand a little tug, he straightened up as if remembering his lessons, and he bowed in return. "Pleased to meet you."

"There'll be time for more formalities later," said Beihou as his own wife and children cooed over the young Danmaru. "For now, you've come a long way and I'm sure you'll want to rest. Let me take you to your chambers."

"Yes, thank you," said Lord Koedzuka. "We'll need to recover before the feast you've doubtlessly constructed."

Beihou grinned happily as he led the trio into the keep. Once they had departed, Kazuchiyo turned to Lady Dada. He had hoped to offer a few words of reassurance, but he was cut off even before he'd begun by Naoya.

"As you see, Lord Koedzuka is a man of great nobility," Naoya told her. "Peerless in his civility. You could not hope for a stronger ally."

"He is," said Lady Dada, and though she was agreeing with him, her tone was as stoic as ever, which Naoya regarded disapprovingly. "I am looking forward to having a productive conversation with him, and with young Lord Kazumune. It is to *him* we owe this alliance."

This time, Kazuchiyo rushed to supersede Naoya. "If I have contributed to a peace between your two provinces, I am very happy for it. I, too, am looking forward to our meeting." He smiled. "That is, after we've recovered from the amount of wine General Sasahara has prepared for tonight."

"Ha! Indeed." Back in good humor, Naoya laughed.

"Brace your stomachs for Kibaku's finest! It will be a night to remember."

He left then to follow after his lord, and gradually the assembly dispersed. At last, Kazuchiyo was able to face Lady Dada to gauge her honest reaction. "How do you find Kibaku so far, Lady Dada? I hope you're not too anxious."

"Lord Koedzuka seems very much like you said," Lady Dada admitted, and he was glad to see her shoulders relaxing. "But our history is long and bloody. The ministers of Jisu will not be pleased if I am too meek with him."

"I'm sure he knows that. We're not gathered here to punish Jisu *or* Kibaku for past transgressions, only to navigate a mutually beneficial relationship going forward. I'll stand by that."

"Thank you." Lady Dada's voice softened then, just a bit. "I appreciate it."

The banquet was every bit the splendid affair that everyone expected. The lords, ladies, and generals attended in their finest robes, house sigils on prominent display, their hair smoothed with fragrant oils. Though his new rank ought to have excluded him from the meal, Yagi-douji's fame awarded him an invitation as well. The guests assembled in two facing rows with Lord Koedzuka and his family at the head, Kazuchiyo and Lady Dada on either side. They were served wine and soup, dried fruits and pickled vegetables, poultry and fish. A small but talented assembly of flutes and drums provided accompaniment, though mostly as a stage set for Mahiro to spin tales of their exploits.

She was certainly in rare form that evening, thrilled to regale yet another new audience with the battles in Jisu. Koedzuka's young son, Danmaru, listened with absolutely rapt attention. Her rendition raised Lady Dada's now uncovered eyebrows a time or two, but she did not intervene or contradict Mahiro.

Kazuchiyo provided context as requested, but otherwise was content to let his sister take the spotlight. He would have plenty of opportunity to perform for his neighboring lords.

"You've certainly accomplished a great deal," Lady Anisha complimented Mahiro as she reached the end of her epic. "I believe the people of Jisu owe you a great debt."

Lady Dada pursed her lips, but before she could offer a comment, Mahiro laughed. "Not really," she said breezily, motioning for one of the servants to refill her wine cup. "It was the strength of Jisu's samurai that pushed Tendo off Etsugo's gates! Their women are the most ferocious in the world—behind me, of course."

"Lady Mahiro is very kind," spoke up Chikakuni. "Though Jisu also owes a great debt to Kibaku's own talented warrior woman, Lady Purnima."

"Ha!" Mahiro made a show of scanning the room. "And where is Kibaku's Lady Purnima? I don't see her here."

Anisha smiled secretively. "Oh, I believe we'll see her soon."

As they continued to chat, Kazuchiyo glanced down the line of diners to where Yagi was helping himself to another serving of herring. Naoya was seated beside him, pantomiming along with some grand tale of his own. Kazuchiyo only caught enough words to guess that he was describing Yagi's duels to Zaiga and one of Koedzuka's recently arrived generals. Though Yagi looked as surly and embarrassed by the attention as ever, he did interject a few times to correct something Naoya had said.

"Yagi-douji does seem rather more sociable than I was led to believe," remarked Lord Koedzuka.

"He has made a dedicated effort," Kazuchiyo said, "though it may embarrass him to know I said so. Sakka is exceedingly proud of him."

"As it should be. I hope it won't be too much to ask that he display some of that prowess for us before this visit is done."

Kazuchiyo smiled. "Not at all. We assumed that would be

the case, and Captain Ebara is becoming ever more comfortable with exhibition."

"Ah, and speaking of," said Koedzuka, who motioned to Beihou with a wave of his hand. Beihou in turn whispered something to his youngest son, who scampered out of the chamber.

"Some entertainment?" Kazuchiyo supposed.

"And a rare performance at that," replied Koedzuka. His gaze drew Kazuchiyo's attention to Anisha, who had noticed the goings-on and was now beaming with excitement.

The musicians began to play more loudly, drawing the rest of the assembly's eyes and ears to them. As conversation hushed, the main panels at the far end of the chamber were drawn open by unseen servants, and in stepped the tardy Lady Purnima. She was dressed in green and gold, but not in the straight, narrow lines of a traditional woman's robe: the blouse, sleeves, and trousers fit close against her skin while a wide, round skirt flowed from her waist. Her hair had been bound up in a gold headdress, and similarly flashing jewelry adorned her wrists, neck, and ears. Around each ankle, strings of bells jingled with each step.

Kazuchiyo had never seen anything like it, and so seemed to be the case for every non-Kibaku native in the room. Though he was hesitant to look away, he snuck a glance at Mahiro and found her eyes as wide as he had ever seen them. It was rare already to see Purnima's full face on display; Kazuchiyo would never have expected to behold it with painted eyelids and rouged lips.

Purnima smiled, and it was as if a warm breeze passed through the chamber just as she began to dance.

The provinces of Sakka and Suyama in those days were not well known for being bastions of courtly culture; poor Kazuchiyo had witnessed religious ceremonies, and sometimes even a peasant gathering, but he was not at all familiar with the elegant and precise dance of aristocratic pleasure, let alone one from a foreign land. But even to the untrained eye

Purnima moved with graceful and exacting precision. The bells at her feet punctuated each form she took, elbows and knees set at practiced angles, each turn of her wrist and curl of her fingers hinting at deeper meanings in the dance. Though, to Kazuchiyo, her expression was as much of a marvel, reflecting warmth and emotion he had never been able to glean from her voice and demeanor before.

Though clearly more familiar with the dance than anyone, Lady Anisha watched with greater attention than anyone in the hall. When Kazuchiyo looked closer, he could see her hands twitch and sometimes sway with the music, as if she might leap to her feet and join Purnima at any moment. Her eyes were glossy with nostalgia and awe. He understood then just how far these two beautiful ladies were from their home, and that he and the rest of Koedzuka's guests were being treated to no mere entertainment; this was a celebration of a world beyond Shuyun's meager borders, ancient and untouched by the petty squabbles of war.

As soon as the dance had concluded, Mahiro whirled on Koedzuka and his wife. "What was that?" she demanded. "What's it called—where does it come from?"

"It's a kathak dance," said Anisha, seemingly charmed by Mahiro's almost violent curiosity. "It's a dance from our homeland."

"But where is *that*? Why are there bells? Purnima!" Unable to contain herself, Mahiro leaped to her feet and stormed down the chamber. "Purnima, you can dance!"

Purnima kept still as Mahiro approached; her grin had vanished with the end of the performance, but her eyes were still narrowed happily as she feigned indifference to Mahiro's flurry of questions. Relieved, Kazuchiyo turned to Anisha himself. "May I ask where that homeland is?"

"Purnima and I were born in Ghirrabi," Anisha obliged him. "A large country far to the west of Shuyun, with palaces carved from stone and white marble." Her wide, dark eyes gleamed with the memories. "Unfortunately, no less accustomed to war than Shuyun. We were forced to leave as children, but managed to escape here." She looked to her husband with great affection. "The former lord Koedzuka was kind enough to harbor us, and Kibaku has been our home ever since."

"Kibaku is blessed to have them," said Koedzuka, giving her hand a brief squeeze. "It is our great hope that once Shuyun is unified under one banner again, we can open better relations with the Ghirrabi empire so that my son will be able to learn even more of his heritage."

Kazuchiyo felt a pang in his chest. "Yes, I hope so too."

As he knew would be the case, Koedzuka took the opportunity to segue into the one topic Kazuchiyo had been hoping to postpone. "As it stands, you're currently the best hope Shuyun has of achieving that."

"I honestly still find that hard to believe," Kazuchiyo said with a self-deprecating smile. "It doesn't feel like so long ago that I was young Danmaru's size."

"You didn't seem so small when you had your sword to my throat last year," Koedzuka replied with a smirk of his own. "There'll be time for a more formal conversation tomorrow, but will you join me in my chamber after this?"

Kazuchiyo managed not to gulp. "I'd be happy to." He caught Lady Dada's eye on them and added, "If you'll permit I bring a guest."

Koedzuka smiled knowingly and turned to include her in the conversation. "Lady Dada is also welcome, if you're amenable."

"I am," Lady Dada said immediately. "Whenever you're ready."

The merriment continued around them, and with enough encouragement even Purnima was convinced to perform again. As she began a new dance, Lord Koedzuka led his family from the hall with Lady Dada and Kazuchiyo in tow. Yagi caught Kazuchiyo's eye on the way out, questioning, but Kazuchiyo reassured him with a smile and continued on.

He wondered, as they climbed to Koedzuka's chamber at

the top of the main keep, if Amai was somewhere close by in the walls.

The lord's chamber at the keep's summit was a great deal more impressive than Kazuchiyo's meager room, though it did fall somewhat short of the splendors of Gyoe. A wide alcove set against the eastern wall displayed a large hanging scroll, depicting Kibaku's abundant plains, accompanied by a vase of vibrant, red spider lilies. Nearby sat a handsome shogi table with pieces already laid out, which Danmaru scurried over to as soon as the group entered. Kazuchiyo smiled with nostalgia as he watched the boy's stubby fingers prod the pieces across the board.

"He loves nothing else as much as shogi," said Koedzuka, and he chuckled. "Though sooner or later, he will have to memorize the rules."

"There's nothing wrong with a little improvisation," replied Kazuchiyo. Though he very much wished young Danmaru was his opponent then, he took a seat with Koedzuka and Lady Dada at the center of the chamber.

"I imagine you excelled at shogi as a child as well," said Lady Dada, folding her robe delicately beneath her knees.

"I wish I could say so. My brothers always complained that I took too long."

Lady Anisha seated herself beside, though slightly behind, her husband. "In my home country we play a similar game, but with four players instead of two." She glanced about at the four of them, and her smile grew sheepish. "Forgive me if that sounded like innuendo. There is no competition here."

Lady Dada arched an eyebrow, though after meeting Kazuchiyo's gaze she seemed to change her mind on her reply. "Very true. There are only three armies on this board now, in any case."

"I'm sorry to pull you away from the banquet so soon," Koedzuka began, and Kazuchiyo tried both to steel his nerves and relax them at the same time, in preparation of whatever the conversation might rouse. "The truth is there are a lot of people in this castle, and all of them are going to want to share with me their version of what transpired in Jisu. I'd prefer to have your accounts before any further gossip reaches my ears."

Though Kazuchiyo could easily imagine that Koedzuka had come to this conclusion following his sister's many boasts, he wondered if Naoya wasn't also a source of possible concern. "We appreciate it," he said, though he then checked himself, making a note not to speak for Lady Dada in front of her, however trivial and obvious the remark may be. "My sister spun a fanciful tale down in the hall. I don't blame you for being cautious."

"The lady Mahiro's version is not all that far from the truth, at least for the parts for which I was present," said Lady Dada.

Koedzuka nodded. "I'm glad to hear it. It paints all of us in a favorable light, after all."

He glanced to Kazuchiyo, and though nothing in his expression changed, Kazuchiyo was certain he sensed a question beneath the look. It was just as possible that he had heard an account from Naoya already, and in light of that, now was a much-needed opportunity to make his intentions very clear.

"There was one event that Mahiro didn't touch on," said Kazuchiyo. "While attempting to free the village, I used magic against Tendo soldiers. It was a necessity of the moment, and not something I'm keen to make a habit of."

Though Kazuchiyo feared that Koedzuka would fix him with the same look of disapproval that Lady Dada was then, he was met only with great curiosity. He knew at once that Koedzuka himself had no knowledge of the origins of magic, and that he had better not breathe one word of it in order to avoid any wrath from Naoya.

"Magic?" Koedzuka repeated, and he chuckled as he shook his head. "I can't imagine General Oihata approved of that. He's extremely guarded on the subject."

"He is. In fact, we quarreled over it afterward." He glanced at Lady Dada, who was watching closely and stoically. "We have since come to an understanding. I'm certain he'll want to discuss the matter with you, and it is not my wish to interfere. I only thought it best that you heard it from me first."

Koedzuka nodded, very clearly aware of his most loyal subject's temperament. Even Anisha smiled with patient understanding and said, "General Oihata is honest to a fault, and Kibaku is blessed by his service. But he is also a man of great passion, and he holds others to a very high standard."

"He does, and I'm glad of it." Kazuchiyo hoped that in his faint smile he could convey his full sincerity. "Few men can boast such strength of character, and to have earned his friendship is a hard-fought honor that I cherish."

Koedzuka's eyes thinned, though they were still full of great fondness. Kazuchiyo sensed and was glad for the understanding that passed between them: that they shared a friendship as challenging as it was rewarding. As daimyo, Koedzuka bore the weight of a province on his shoulders, from the concerns of tens of thousands of subjects, to the personal judgment of his closest allies. How much greater would that weight be upon a shogun?

"Well," said Lady Dada, "it sounds as though I'd better make my amends with General Oihata straight away if I want to impress you all."

The others chuckled. "Your character is not in question here," Koedzuka reassured her. "Though there is one question I had hoped to put to you, before any further conversation between us."

Lady Dada lifted her chin. She seemed to already know what he would say. "Then please, ask."

Lord Koedzuka's pleasant expression hardened, but only slightly. "Why did you launch your attack on Kibaku?"

She did not answer immediately, still clearly weighing the question, though she had expected it. Kazuchiyo kept very still and reminded himself that it was not his place to interfere. Though he hoped always to smooth over these kinds of negotiations, no peace would last between them if she did not speak with honesty here. At last, she took in a deep breath.

"It was Tendo that came to us with the details of our partnership," she explained, frustration lacing her tone. "My ministers, my uncle, and several of my most trusted generals were in favor of the plan, and so was I. We assumed that your defeat at the hands of Aritaka last year had left you weak. We knew that if we waited too long, you would have the full weight of Sakka and Suyama behind you, and we would lose our chance at expansion forever. So I acted." She hesitated, swallowing, and then added, "I would have been a coward to let the opportunity pass, and I could not afford that."

Koedzuka nodded, for there was no fault in her logic, and history tells us that even a leader as magnanimous as he had been swayed by similar reasoning in the past. "In General Oihata's first message to me, he indicated that you had suffered some betrayal internally," he said.

A scowl flashed across Lady Dada's face. "Yorowata, our minister of trade. He had always opposed me taking leadership of my clan. I was lucky that my grandmother sussed his motives out before he could do more damage than he did."

"And your ministers now?" Kazuchiyo asked. "Has your council changed their mind about Kibaku, after Etsugo's ordeal?"

"If not, I will change their minds for them or have them replaced." With another deep breath for composure, Lady Dada bowed her head in deference to Lord Koedzuka. "Acting out of fear of being labeled a coward is cowardice itself. Kibaku has no need to fear that behavior from me again."

"I'm glad to hear it," said Koedzuka, and he and his wife bowed in equal measure. "Kibaku promises the same."

Kazuchiyo bowed his head as well, but he did not speak. He could not promise a lack of cowardice from Sakka, not while Aritaka Souyuu remained its lord.

"Shall we have one more drink?" Anisha suggested as everyone righted themselves. "I believe that's enough politics for the evening."

"Yes, I agree," said Koedzuka. "Something light to end the night with."

Anisha moved to the panel leading into the hall, but before she could open it, a voice called out from the other side: "My lord! Please excuse the interruption!"

Anisha startled, and with an embarrassed smile she pushed it open. A soldier stood in the hall, breathing hard from a run. "My lord, excuse me," he said again, bowing crisply at the waist. "The southern gate—" He stopped short when he noticed Kazuchiyo and Lady Dada in the room. "Your presence is requested."

Frowning, Koedzuka pushed to his feet and approached. As hard as Kazuchiyo strained his ears, he could not make out the very quiet words that passed between lord and servant. After a brief exchange, Koedzuka nodded and sent the man scurrying away. He turned to face the room. "Excuse me for a moment. I'd like you both to remain here and take that drink with my wife. I'll be back soon."

"Trouble?" asked Lady Dada.

"I should hope not." With a smile, Koedzuka left.

As soon as he had left, little Danmaru, who had spent the entire conversation absorbed in his shogi board, scampered across the room to the south-facing window. Kazuchiyo kept an eye on him while Anisha called for a servant to bring them beverages. "It's probably my sister," he joked. "After scandalizing all of Jisu, she set her sights next on Kibaku."

Lady Dada scoffed. "As impressive as the lady Mahiro is, it will take a great deal more than her exploits to make Jisu blush. If Kibaku finds her too much to bear, at least that's one victory to our name."

"Kibaku is not so frail-spirited either," Anisha retorted playfully. "I'm sure it's nothing at all. A mishap at the stables, or…" She glanced at her son, who was staring out the window so intently. "Danmaru, come away from the window."

"Someone's there," he said, pointing through the slats.

Kazuchiyo felt a chill and pushed to his feet. The two

ladies followed him to the southern wall of the keep, where each took to a window to see for themselves. By then the night was fully dark, a swelling half-moon mostly obscured by high clouds. Paper windows from the buildings below glowed with candlelight from Rongi's celebrating occupants, and past the castle walls a few small fires burned among the tents of the encamped armies. Kazuchiyo could hear raised voices echo up from the main bailey, but it took some time for him to spot the "someone" Danmaru must have been referring to: a man stood perched on the wall of the fortress, a few paces out from one of the guard towers.

"Is he drunk?" said Lady Dada.

Anisha tugged gently at her son. "Come away from the window, dear."

Danmaru latched onto the window slats. "What's he doing up there?"

Kazuchiyo scanned the window for some way to open it fully, hoping for a better look, but as Rongi was a fortress built for border war, there was no such option. He turned his focus back to the man just in time to see a puff of fire, the light from which illuminated his face in the dark—and even more so, his thick mane of silver hair.

CHAPTER TWENTY

"Get back," Kazuchiyo said, grabbing Danmaru by his robe. "Get back!"

What hit the keep was little more than the single thunk of an arrow piercing a window frame one floor below them. What followed was a roar of fire that surged up the side of the building, curving up and over the eaves as if it had the mind of a living thing. Though Kazuchiyo and his companions lurched away from the windows before it reached them, the rush of heat through the wooden slats flared against their skin. Only seconds later the tatami beneath their feet trembled with another hit farther down, and all throughout the keep and surrounding courtyards voices rose in shock.

Kazuchiyo relinquished Danmaru into his mother's arms. "We can't stay here," he said, urging them farther away from the windows and the smoke that was beginning to pour through. "This isn't normal fire—there's no telling how far it will spread."

"Who's attacking us?" Anisha asked, clutching her son to her chest as she and Lady Dada followed Kazuchiyo to the exit. "Did Tendo regroup?"

"Tendo has never used onmyouji against us before," said Lady Dada. "Even when Etsugo was under siege."

She looked to Kazuchiyo, but his mind was reeling, and he shook his head. "It doesn't matter right now," he said as he led the way out of the chamber and toward the staircase. "We have to get out of the keep and regroup."

A pair of soldiers were already on the stairs, only their helmets visible. "Lady Anisha!" one cried while motioning them forward. "Hurry, we'll—"

Kazuchiyo did not see the arrow—only the great plume of fire that followed, swallowing up the two men and engulfing the entire stairwell in a blaze. He had never seen fire so noxious and thick, moving with such blatant purpose. The screams of the two men clawed at his ears, and it took Lady Dada drawing him back for him to regain his wits.

"Is there another way down?" Lady Dada demanded of Anisha as they retreated back up the hallway. "Another stair?"

"I—I don't know." Anisha's face had grown very pale; she, it seemed, had memories of fire like this. She kept Danmaru pinned to her chest and tried to staunch his ears with her sleeve. "I think there's a shinobi entrance, but I don't know this castle well." She looked to Kazuchiyo. "Can't you use magic against it?"

"I don't know how," Kazuchiyo admitted. He could hear soldiers on the floor below shouting for them, but the inexplicable movements of the flames kept his courage at bay. "Come on—this way."

He led them to the northern wall of the keep's top floor. It took him and Dada together prying and shoving to break enough of the window slats that he was able to crawl out and onto the sloping roof. The clay tiles, as uneven and untrustworthy as they were, calmed him with their familiarity. "We'll drop to the roof below," he said as he waved for the others to join him. "Give me the boy."

Anisha tightened her arms reflexively around her son. "It's all right," Kazuchiyo insisted. "Nothing will happen to him, I promise."

Though still reluctant, Anisha unwound Danmaru from

her and urged him into Kazuchiyo's arms. The boy was silent, eyes wide with confusion and shock. Kazuchiyo drew the boy's short arms around his neck and tucked his legs into the sides of his robe.

"It's all right," he soothed as he reached back to help the two ladies out. "I did this all the time when I was little. Just hold on tight, okay?" The boy didn't answer, so Kazuchiyo gave his back a rub. "Okay, Danmaru? You're... you're a little crow taking his first flight, that's all. I won't let you go."

At last, Danmaru nodded against Kazuchiyo's neck. "Good boy," Kazuchiyo told him, and he straightened up.

There was no breeze that night, and the air was hot and thick with smoke. Kazuchiyo stared out over the northern edge of the compound and was relieved to see that Mutsuyama's attack continued to be one-sided, leaving their descent clear. As he moved to the edge of the roof, however, he noticed, glinting in the distance beyond the walls, pinpoints of orange light, stretched out in a row facing them.

"We're surrounded," Lady Dada said grimly.

Kazuchiyo gulped. Though instinct had his mind churning toward strategy, toward reason, there was no time for that with more of the keep catching fire every moment. "We have to go." After making sure Danmaru was secure against his chest, he turned around and lowered to his knees. "We all have people below who would brave this fire for us. We can't let that happen."

Danmaru whimpered close to Kazuchiyo's ear. It made him think of his brother. "Close your eyes," he said, and he climbed down from the edge.

It was not long to fall; directly below them rose another steepled roof that extended farther than the eaves above, and Kazuchiyo had no trouble landing on his feet. It was the angle that complicated their descent. His socks slid against the curved tiles, and with Danmaru's extra weight he had to lean hard to compensate as he kept his momentum even. Once he had reached the flatter portion of the roof, he turned back, and was relieved to see Lady Dada helping to lower Anisha onto the slope. He stood ready, and as soon as Anisha had slid down close enough, he grasped her arm to keep her from drifting too close to the edge.

"You're all right?" he asked, and she nodded, breathless. The pair of them then helped Lady Dada to keep her balance as she joined them.

"Should we keep going down this way?" Lady Dada asked, but after a look over the edge Kazuchiyo shook his head.

"We'd have to move to the other side of the building to find another safe drop. We need to keep the building between us and Mutsuyama." He headed up the roof toward the building proper again. "We should see if there's another stair we can use first."

The third floor of the keep boasted an observation deck around the outside of the building, with only a short wooden fence separating it from the roof. Several of the panels leading in had been thrown open, and Kazuchiyo was not much comforted by the smoke billowing out of the rightmost entry. Still, he was eager for safety as quickly as possible, for the sake of their companions as much as themselves. As they reached the deck, however, Lady Dada took his shoulder.

"There's someone there," she said, pointing into the smoke.

Kazuchiyo did not see it at first, with the smoke twisting and swirling. The blackness then parted, making away for a man clad head to toe in dark gray clothing. He lurched toward them, drawing a short sword from the sheath at his back.

Lady Dada intercepted him without hesitation. She drew one of the combs from her hair, and once the man was in range, she whipped her long sleeve about, diverting his slashing arm and leaving him open to attack. The comb stabbing into his neck left him howling and gurling, and he stumbled back toward the building, where he met his sudden death on the end of Amai's dagger.

Kazuchiyo stared; it had happened so fast he hardly had time to process. It wasn't until Amai—soot-stained, panting—

latched onto his sleeve that he fully appreciated his presence. "Kazu," Amai was saying urgently. "Are you all right?"

"Y-Yes." Kazuchiyo fisted Amai's sleeve, too, and he had to fight the tight relief out of his throat before he could properly speak. "We're all right."

"That old man mystic sent assassins," said Amai. He turned back toward the fallen man, though he was prevented from moving too far away thanks to Kazuchiyo still gripping his sleeve. "There's a few of them in the keep already."

Lady Dada crouched over the man. "You said Mutsuyama," she said as she wrenched her comb from where she had embedded it just below his jaw. She cleaned it against the assassin's robe and tucked it into her sleeve. "These are the shogun's shinobi?"

"They must be." Kazuchiyo shuddered at the thought, which he thrust to the back of his mind for the time being. "Amai, where did you come from? Is there a way out of the castle?"

Amai nodded and sheathed his short sword. "Follow me."

He led their small group into the building; each shielded their mouth and nose, and they kept low to the ground to guard as best they could against the smoke. They passed two bodies: one samurai, another shinobi. Kazuchiyo rubbed Danmaru's back as they went and prayed the boy had taken his advice to keep his eyes closed.

Their destination was one of the interior rooms. Though one of the far panels was already on fire, Amai didn't falter as he drew them to an open closet. A small section of the floor had been removed, revealing a ladder that led down, close along the sturdy, wooden beams of the castle's skeleton.

"I'll go first," Amai volunteered, already climbing into the opening. "There might be more of those assholes around."

"What about everyone in the hall?" Kazuchiyo asked.

"I don't know. I came straight here to find *you*." Amai lifted his head and offered Kazuchiyo a quick, reassuring smile. "I'm sure he's fine. Let's get out of here before he tears the whole place down to find you."

Kazuchiyo smiled grimly back, and he motioned for Anisha to continue ahead of him down the ladder.

The five of them descended as quickly as they were able within the narrow confines. The walls surrounding them were warm to the touch, and the smoke steaming through their cracks was choking. Kazuchiyo staunched his nose and mouth against Danmaru's shoulder for much of the way. Several times he felt Lady Dada's feet against his head and shoulders as she tried to climb faster than he was able.

They had to have been passing the second floor when Kazuchiyo heard a familiar, though muffled voice bellowing on the other side of the wall. He could not help but draw in a breath as if he might call out, only to have ash invade his lungs. A fit of coughing kept him still until he could expel it; his knuckles ached around the rungs of the ladder.

"Are you all right?" Lady Dada called down to him.

Kazuchiyo grimaced and continued downward before he had air enough to speak. At last he croaked, "Yes! Keep going."

At long last, they reached the bottom. Kazuchiyo felt Amai's hands on him, and then his feet touched the floor. He stumbled out of the passage with Danmaru still clinging to his chest, and though his first instinct was to gasp, he managed not to this time; there still was nothing clean to partake of. It wasn't until Amai had led them out through a sheltered exit on the north side of the keep that they were free from smoke and fire, and all could safely breathe.

As soon as Anisha was steadily upright, she turned to her son. "Is he all right?" she asked, smoothing his hair from his face. "He's—"

"He'll be fine," Kazuchiyo assured her quickly. He could feel the poor boy shaking against his chest, but also quiet breaths against his neck and tiny fingers twisting into his robe. "Is anyone injured?"

"We're all right," said Lady Dada, "but we can't stay here either."

Kazuchiyo looked for himself. They had come out close to the northern wall—fairly secluded, as it was farthest from the main gate, with only a few decorative trees and a path upward to the northern guard tower. A handful of soldiers were several yards away at the edge of the keep, and they started hurrying over at the sight of them. From the outside, the damage to the keep didn't seem quite so dire, though Kazuchiyo had to remind himself that Mutsuyama's attacks had all been aimed at the south wall, backed by skilled infiltrators. There was no way to tell yet how many enemy soldiers lay beyond the walls, if large-scale battle had begun, or how many had escaped the celebration in the hall.

"My lady!" the soldiers cried as they rushed to their mistress's aid. Many of them were singed from the fire, as if they had only just escaped the blaze themselves. "Lady Koedzuka, are you hurt?"

"N-No," replied Anisha, though she gripped Kazuchiyo's elbow. "My husband—where is your lord?"

"Safe, my lady," the lead samurai assured her as the others quickly scanned the area for threats. "We'll take you to him."

They turned to lead the way, though Kazuchiyo hesitated when he realized Amai was already turning back toward the secret passage they'd come out of. "Amai?"

"I'm going to find that fool oni of ours before he makes himself too at home in there," said Amai, though he had a harder time than usual rallying humor to his voice. "Pretty sure we'll be needing him."

"Be careful," said Kazuchiyo. He relied on Anisha to guide him straight the first few steps, as he could not pry his eyes away from Amai until he had long disappeared back into the smoking mouth of the fortress.

The rest of them made their way quickly around the outside of the main keep, the commotion growing as they went. Only once they reached the main courtyard did the extent of the attack become clear: the south-facing wall of the keep was ablaze, black smoke roiling up and over its eaves to melt into the night sky. Soldiers and servants hurried water and sand into the building while samurai formed ranks, some still tightening their armor. Already chaos was giving way to order and purpose, and at the head of that effort stood Koedzuka Danzou.

As much valor as the man displayed commanding his forces against the inferno, his courage faltered at the sight of his wife and child approaching. He stopped speaking mid-order and left the hands of the attendants who had been trying to tighten his armor around his shoulders. He met the lady Anisha in a desperate embrace, and each reassured the other that they were unharmed. Their attention then swiftly turned to Kazuchiyo, who still carried their son against his chest.

Kazuchiyo urged the boy's face away from his shoulder so that he could see, and upon spotting his father little Danmaru grew animated once more. "Papa!" he cried, throwing his arms out, and Koedzuka accepted him gladly. Kazuchiyo took a step back as the family celebrated their reunion. It wasn't until he felt Lady Dada's hand press stealthily against his back that he realized he was swaying on his feet just a bit, still light-headed from the choking smoke. He flashed her a grateful look just before Koedzuka returned his attention to him.

"Last year, you spared my life," Lord Koedzuka said, Danmaru braced in one arm and Anisha close at the other. His eyes gleamed with sincere emotion. "Tonight, you've saved my wife and son. I'll never be able to repay this debt to you."

Kazuchiyo swallowed. "If I aided them at all, it was my honor to do so," he replied. "It was Lady Dada who spared us from the assassin."

"I might have fallen to my death if not for her," Lady Anisha agreed.

"It's too soon to congratulate each other," Lady Dada said, her eyes darting to the surrounding crowd. "We're still under attack, and my soldiers—" She cut herself off, a look of elation overtaking her for a moment. With a deep breath she continued. "The soldiers I brought were camped outside the walls, as were many from Sakka. They're all in peril."

Kazuchiyo followed her gaze and spotted Chikakuni gathering Lady Dada's small entourage among Koedzuka's troops. He allowed himself his own moment of relief, though also an anxious glance at the keep. "What about the onmyouji? Was he apprehended?"

"Not yet." Koedzuka handed young Danmaru back to his mother as his attendants finally caught up to him, insistent on finishing with his armor. "Oihata managed to drive the old man back over the wall, and Lady Mahiro rode to the southern gate. Once the fire is more firmly under control, we'll be joining her."

"I'll go at once," said Lady Dada, already sweeping her hair back into a tight ponytail. "The gate will be held."

"We're grateful, and we'll be there soon."

Lady Dada moved away, and immediately Chikakuni fell into step alongside her with their small retinue. His relief at seeing his lady unharmed was palpable, and Kazuchiyo turned back toward the keep, hoping that for himself. There was still no sign of Yagi or Amai.

"There are soldiers beyond the north wall," he said. "How could they have rounded the fortress? Did your guards not see anything until they were upon us?"

"Nothing," Koedzuka admitted, though it clearly pained him. "Their onmyouji may have been preventing it somehow. I worry for the village south of here." His frown deepened. "Though soldiers from the north might mean that Nomino is cooperating with the shogun against us."

"Nomino?" Kazuchiyo repeated. Despite having known all along that Kibaku's northwestern neighbor was no friendlier to them than Tendo or Jisu had been, he had never expected such a bold move. He was speechless, but then shouts rose from the keep. He turned just in time to see Yagi burst through the half-mangled panels. His hair and robes were singed, and Kazuchiyo could have sworn he saw a portion of live flame on his sleeve only then extinguishing itself. He stormed down into the courtyard; Kazuchiyo had only a moment to brace himself before Yagi had him by both shoulders.

"Kazu!" He looked Kazuchiyo over, and even after finding no burns he tried to brush the ash off his robes and out of his hair. "Are you all right? You're not hurt?"

"I'm—" Kazuchiyo fought to suppress a cough and urged Yagi's hands off him. As much as he wished he could fall into Yagi's strong arms then, he felt the weight of responsibility keenly against his back. "I'm fine, but our men aren't. We need to hurry to the gate to know what's really happening."

"I killed two of their spies already," Yagi said, and only then did Kazuchiyo notice the blood staining his hands and speckling his robe. "Amai says he did, too, but there could be more. You should stay here in the lesser keep where the men can protect you."

Kazuchiyo glanced past him and was equally relieved to see Amai combing the ash out of his hair a few meters away. He drew his attention quickly back to Yagi. "No, I need to be there. We have men beyond that gate, and—"

The heat of the blazing keep turned then to icy cold against Kazuchiyo's skin as a terrifying revelation overtook him: he could not see General Zaiga or his Suyama men among those gathered around the courtyard. Rongi was a mighty fortress, though not accustomed to housing so many soldiers at one time, leaving many encamped around its walls—among them, Zaiga's one thousand troops, and one young foot soldier in particular, with rough hair and a broken nose.

Kazuchiyo shuddered, and Yagi took his shoulder again, understanding hardening in his face. He gestured at the nearby Sakka men meant to be Kazuchiyo's personal guard within the fortress. "Your lord needs armor," he told them fiercely. "We're going to the gate." Kazuchiyo gripped his sleeve, quaking with gratitude.

It was soon revealed that Kazuchiyo's indigo Aritaka armor was certainly lost within the burning keep, shuttered away in the small guest chamber. Insisting that none of his men should be made to give up their own for him, he instead accepted a rather plain chest plate, helmet, and thigh guards from among Rongi's spares, which pulled on over his hitatare. Yagi-douji's snarling oni armor, however, remained quite intact, having been stored for appearances' sake with Captain Nishigame in the lesser keep. Both dressed with all haste, and with Amai and their Sakka guardians in tow, they made their way through the compound's twisted baileys into the south.

Just as Kazuchiyo had feared, the southern gate was already embroiled in cacophonic battle. Kibaku archers crammed every guard tower and wall face, firing their arrows in constant volleys through narrow openings into the enemy beyond. Steel clashed, and distant voices bellowed and cried. Servants who had hours before been carting food and wine now ferried ammunition. As Kazuchiyo approached, he first spotted Mahiro up on the scaffolding with the archers. Having almost no talent for archery, she gripped her naginata and shook it at their enemies beyond the walls, shouting encouragement to their soldiers all the while. Farther out, Naoya—still dressed in his fine hitatare from the banquet—shouted orders from atop one of the guard towers while Lady Dada and her small Jisu troop reinforced the archers below him.

"Yagi, wait here," Kazuchiyo said. "Rally the troops that aren't armed with bows in case we're able to open the gate." He then turned to Amai. "Will you go to the eastern wall? If those soldiers in the north are heading this way to aid the siege, we need to know."

"On it," said Amai, and he rushed off while Yagi double-checked the cords on his armor.

"Tell them to open the gate," said Yagi. "I'll take that old man's head for you."

"Don't underestimate him," Kazuchiyo replied quickly. Though the blood Yagi had unintentionally smeared against his shoulders was not his own, feeling it cling to him gave Kazuchiyo a chill he couldn't shake. "Though you will have your chance." He then hurried on to mount the guard tower that Naoya had staked as his command post.

"Target their bannermen!" Naoya was ordering his men as Kazuchiyo reached the covered platform. "Flush out their command ranks!" Despite his ferocity he noticed Kazuchiyo's approach right away, and his face briefly crumbled with relief. "Kazumune! Thank the heavens you're safe. Did Lady Anisha and—"

"Yes," Kazuchiyo interrupted as he approached. "Yes, everyone with us made it out unharmed. What's the situation?"

"Come see," Naoya invited him, grimacing, and Kazuchiyo joined him to look out over the battle.

The orange light from the burning keep illuminated a field in strife: the Sakka, Suyama, and Jisu troops that had made camp outside the fortress had formed a hasty line of defense just beyond their tents, locked in combat against enemy foot soldiers. The numbers of these invaders were impossible to count, stretched out into the night's shadows as they were, but there was no mistaking the gold banners punctuating each battalion that made up their line. Each bore a black crest that any samurai in Shuyun would have recognized at once: the spear that pierces the mountain, symbol of the Oomiyari clan. The clan of the shogun.

Kazuchiyo leaned forward against the guardrail as he peered into their ranks. The sweat drenching his skin chilled in the night air, and his fingers whitened around the wood. At the center of the enemy line, bordered but not impeded by the tallest and broadest of the Oomiyari banners, sat the command unit. Their general was a tall man atop a sturdy, black horse, his two-pronged kamayari in hand, a sloped, rectangular helmet atop his head. This time, however, the helmet bore a gold emblem: the head of a spear. The hairs on the back of Kazuchiyo's neck stood on end.

"That's the samurai Mutsuyama brought with him to our meeting with General Umafusa," Kazuchiyo said.

"We all suspected he was Oomiyari," replied Naoya spitefully. "As cowardly as all his clan, apparently. How dare they claim to represent the emperor's will when they attack with fire and assassins in the dead of night."

"They didn't gather this army since Jisu." Kazuchiyo's gaze swept the line, trying to estimate how many now fought. Their own soldiers were outnumbered two to one at least, with no clear indication of how many more were hidden beyond the glow of the flamelight or on the other side of the fortress. "If they had this many waiting alongside Tendo's army, they could have overwhelmed us at Etsugo easily. So why didn't Mutsuyama—"

Kazuchiyo stopped. His heart gave a painful thud as he recalled that negotiation on the hillside, where he had looked the kamayari general in the face and declared his intention to unseat his entire clan from the shogun's duty. How the man had returned his confidence with hatred while Mutsuyama had gone quiet and still. But, most shamefully, how he had revealed to them so carelessly that Lord Koedzuka of Kibaku himself would leave his nest to be at Rongi now.

"We were cautious, but not cautious enough," Naoya lamented. "To take this many men away from their homesteads so close to the harvest will harm the capital more than it will us! I never would have expected the shogun himself to be so reckless." He looked to Kazuchiyo. "We must weather this storm and prove their folly to them."

"I—Yes." Kazuchiyo took a deep breath and shook himself. There would be much time later for guilt. "Yes, we have to act quickly. Our soldiers won't stand for long against those numbers. We must find a way to pull them within the gates. Rongi can survive a siege for longer than the Oomiyari can afford to maintain one."

"That is true, but we cannot open the gate. One swift charge and we'd be breached entirely." His brow contorted with conflict. "I mourn those men and their sacrifice, but I would rather bury a thousand before inviting any harm to my lord."

"I know, but..." Kazuchiyo leaned back to take note of the soldiers gathering in the bailey, as well as those already manning the walls. "General Zaiga," he said. "Have you seen him?"

Naoya huffed with exasperated admiration. "He went over the wall before you came—tied a rope and lowered himself from the guard tower. I've never seen his like before."

Kazuchiyo stared hard into the throngs of struggling, red-armored soldiers, but he could not make out General Zaiga among them, let alone his brother. He had no choice but to cling to the hope that Zaiga's devotion to their family would keep them far behind the line. "We cannot risk the castle being breached, but we cannot abandon these men either. Is there nothing your magic can do to drive them back?"

"Even magic cannot take the place of an army," Naoya replied, shaking his head. "A gust of wind would only deter them for a moment, and Mutsuyama would be able to see through or dispel an illusion. I do not know how much power he wields. If I spend my magic too carelessly, he may return again to strike the keep."

"I don't see him with his general," said Kazuchiyo, no matter how he stared into the crowd.

"I haven't been able to detect him either, not since he first retreated."

Kazuchiyo clenched his teeth in frustration. "We can't afford to wait. There must be some way—another way out of Rongi?"

Naoya looked hesitant, but he nodded. "There is a tunnel that leads out from the eastern wall. It's meant to be an escape route, in case the castle was ever breached."

Kazuchiyo's hopes leaped upon the opportunity. "Can a horse pass through?"

"Two abreast, yes." Still Naoya looked concerned, though he continued. "But even with all our numbers out on this field, the Oomiyari—"

An arrow streaked toward them, faster and at a straighter angle than should have been possible. It struck Kazuchiyo straight in his borrowed shoulder guard; the familiar, gut-turning impact left him reeling, and it was followed by a far more recently familiar flaring of heat against the side of his face. Before the arrow could combust entirely, Naoya was there, wrenching the shaft free with his bare hand. He cast it into the corner of the platform, where it swiftly ignited.

The surrounding archers momentarily abandoned their posts to douse the flame, smothering it beneath their deer-hide boots. Kazuchiyo and Naoya retreated deeper into the tower, eyes trained on the narrow opening ahead of them for any more projectiles, but none came.

"It's me they're after," Kazuchiyo realized. "That arrow was for me."

"Of course it was," Naoya replied contemptuously. "Who poses a greater threat to the current shogun than the future one?" He turned to Kazuchiyo and checked to be sure the ties on his shoulder guard were still tight. "Stay behind me, and Mutsuyama's sorcery won't be able to touch you."

He returned to the fore, waving for the archers to do the same. "Did anyone see where that arrow was fired from?" he demanded. "Where does the onmyouji hide?"

But Kazuchiyo could not bear to stay. Watching Naoya move ahead of him as a sentinel when he wasn't even clad in his armor reminded Kazuchiyo all too fiercely of the danger his carelessness had put them in. He pushed away from the wall of the tower and moved toward the ladder he'd come up. "I'm going to the eastern wall," he declared. "If they see me leaving, it may draw some of their forces away."

"What?" Naoya whipped back around. "Kazumune, no!"

By then Kazuchiyo was already climbing down. "Mahiro!" he shouted as he went, though she was still bellowing at the Oomiyari through the walls. "Mahiro, I need your blade!"

Kazuchiyo reached the floor of the bailey, and there Yagi had done good work in drawing together what numbers could be spared from saving the keep and manning the walls. He hurried over, mindful that Naoya was giving chase. "Yagi! There is another way out, through the eastern wall. We'll exit the fortress there."

"Is there room for horses?" Yagi asked, nodding along. "If so, we can charge their flank and drive them off the walls."

"No—I mean to *draw* them away. I'm the one Mutsuyama is here to kill."

"What?" A hard snarl streaked across Yagi's mouth. "Then no—you're not going out there."

By then Naoya had caught up to them, and he and Yagi faced Kazuchiyo down together. "He's right: you're a lord's son, Kazumune. You have no business being on the field in these circumstances."

"We don't have the numbers to drive them off the wall by force," Kazuchiyo insisted. "What other choice do we have to save our soldiers?"

"Every soldier of Sakka out there would die to keep you safe," Naoya retorted. "As every soldier of Kibaku fights for our lord, and of Jisu for theirs. If you put yourself in harm's way, you dishonor their sacrifice."

Yagi nodded emphatically. "Mahiro and I will lead the charge. If we can cut through to their general, that's all the force we need."

"There are at least four thousand troops out there," Kazuchiyo shot back. "And an onmyouji whose power we don't fully know. Charging into them will only get you killed, and it won't save—"

Kazuchiyo caught himself before he could speak the great fear in his heart. He met Yagi's eyes, willing him to hear the unspoken words. "We mustn't abandon those men," he said, his voice taut.

Yagi leaned back, seeming to fully take Kazuchiyo's meaning. "Then open the gate," he said without hesitation. "We'll bring them all in through the front."

"Out of the question," Naoya said immediately. "They would have every opportunity to breach the castle."

Yagi did not so much as blink. "I can hold the gate if Mahiro and a few others are with me. It's the fastest way to get everyone inside."

"Dear captain," said Naoya, "were it not my lord himself at stake, I would not doubt your prowess, but this I cannot leave to chance. Unless we can thin their numbers or drive them back, that gate will remain closed."

"Then what are we waiting for?" crowed Mahiro, startling everyone with her intrusion. "We're not going to accomplish anything on this side of the wall. Let me fetch Suzumekage and we'll swing about to rake their backsides."

"We're wasting too much time talking about it," Kazuchiyo agreed. He faced Naoya squarely. "Naoya, please return to the tower to keep watch for Mutsuyama. You're our only defense against his sorcery, and as you said, the gate must hold. I'll accompany our soldiers to the eastern passage and design a strategy from there."

Naoya frowned at him severely, but even he could wisely see they could not afford to wait any longer to act. "I shall," he said. "Please be cautious, for all our sakes." He motioned to one of the surrounding Kibaku samurai. "Captain, find a horse for any man who does not wield a bow and see Lord Kazumune to the eastern wall. Follow whatever commands he gives you."

The captain bowed, and he began passing the order to his men while Naoya returned to the guard tower. "I watched that little beetle from Suyama go over the wall," Mahiro said as the men gathered up. "I would have followed right over if these Kibaku pigeons hadn't cut the rope behind him; you know I would have."

"I know," Kazuchiyo replied, "though I'm glad you didn't. We'll need Suzumekage's strength to win this."

"It's yours, then!" With a boisterous laugh Mahiro stormed across the bailey to where Suzumekage was already tethered and waiting.

"Oihata's right about one thing," Yagi said once he and Kazuchiyo had a moment to themselves, fleeting though it was. "You shouldn't be the one to leave the castle."

"We'll see," Kazuchiyo replied as a pair of soldiers brought them their horses. Each mounted, and they rode swiftly off.

CHAPTER TWENTY-ONE

Along Rongi's eastern wall there stood a broad storehouse with a low roof, and a wide aisle between the racks of goods ostensibly for the drying of herbs strung from the ceiling. It was here that Kazuchiyo gathered ranks for the charge. By then the fires around Rongi's keep had been mostly extinguished, making it a grim and blackened overseer to their efforts. Barely thirty horses and their rides could be summoned, barely a hundred more soldiers on foot past that—all others stood in defense of their lords or of the walls. At the moment their devotion overrode their desperation, though Kazuchiyo could not help but wonder if their spirits would remain so once they were facing down the thousands from the capital.

The horses lined up in pairs with Mahiro and Purnima at the front. Purnima's green-gold armor had been strapped hastily over the fine blouse and trousers she had worn for the banquet. Just behind them, Yagi glowered with spear in hand. While others lined up anxiously behind them, Amai found Kazuchiyo among the crowd.

"An army from Nomino is closing in from the north," he reported. "They're damn hard to see in the dark—brown armor and flags. I think it's Clan Ba'nyuunuma."

"I don't know anything about them," Kazuchiyo admitted. "How did Mutsuyama convince them to come?"

Amai shrugged helplessly. "Beats me, but I'd bet twenty pieces of gold they're going to circle around and attack this exit the moment they know it's here."

"All the more reason to strike as quickly as possible." Kazuchiyo undid the tie on his hair to be retied more securely. "A handful of us will ride out to draw their attention. It's me they're here for—they should send some men, maybe even Mutsuyama himself. Then Yagi and Mahiro can cut through them and hopefully take the command unit by enough surprise that they'll fall back."

"You?" Amai scoffed. "You're not going out there."

"It's me they're after," Kazuchiyo repeated, though he kept his tone low so that the surrounding soldiers would not hear. "It's my fault Mutsuyama is here at all. I won't fight. I'll just be bait."

"Don't be ridiculous," Amai snapped, and Kazuchiyo was startled to hear even the strained attempts at humor gone from his voice. "We could have burned to cinders getting you out of that castle, and now you want to go out on the field? What will that even accomplish?"

"More than staying here!" Kazuchiyo noticed some faces turning their way, but Yagi was still a ways off, talking to Mahiro. "I survived on that hill after killing Waseba, didn't I?" he said under his breath. "I *took* Nodo Bridge. I can take care of myself—"

"I saved your ass on that hill, don't forget—"

"And I have to save *my brother*," Kazuchiyo finished. That silenced Amai for the moment. "Please. I can't sit safely behind this wall while everyone I care about is going out there because of me."

Amai was quiet for a moment, and then he gave another great snort. "Volunteering me again, are you?"

Kazuchiyo grimaced. "Amai—"

"We're going to have a conversation about what you just

said later," Amai talked over him as reached for Kazuchiyo's armor. "For now, take off that armor you're wearing. Right now."

Kazuchiyo blinked and, dumbfounded, began to help him loosen the cords. "What?"

"There's no point in you yourself being bait when it's already this dark out," said Amai. "Give me your hitatare. I'll go out first."

Kazuchiyo pushed Amai's hands off him. "No. That won't work."

"Why the hell wouldn't it? It's pitch dark and we'll be riding *away* from them." Amai gestured for him to get back to work. "Give me that fancy coat you have on and Mutsuyama will be none the wiser."

"But then he'll be trying to kill you," Kazuchiyo retorted. He would have said more if not for a pair of hands suddenly grabbing him from behind.

"He's got a point," said Chikakuni as he worked Kazuchiyo out of his armor ties. "From behind, there's no way to know it's you other than your clothing and your horse."

"Chikakuni?" Kazuchiyo tried to look at him, but then Amai grabbed him by the front to untie his thigh guards. He sighed in frustration. "You should be protecting Lady Dada."

"She's got her nagamaki guardians with her. If the castle is breached my sword won't make a difference against four thousand." He freed Kazuchiyo's shoulder and then gave it a pat. "I'm a closer match to you in stature anyway."

"What? No, that's—"

"I don't think you can capture his nuance," Amai told Chikakuni, "but he'll feel better if they're shooting at you than at me, so have it."

"That's not—" Kazuchiyo tried to push their hands off him, but by then his armor was loose at most of its seams, and there didn't seem to be any room for complaint. "Everything I've worked to achieve between Sakka and Jisu will be ruined if anything happens to you," he said quietly.

Chikakuni moved around him and began shedding his own armor with Amai's help. "Lord Kazumune," he said with a smirk, "if you really believe something bad is going to happen, that's just proof enough that you shouldn't be going out there as yourself."

Kazuchiyo's shoulders sagged in defeat. "Please be careful."

"You first."

The three of them fit Chikakuni into Kazuchiyo's light armor and then drew his handsome indigo hitatare over top so that the Aritaka crest on its back would be a clear target. It took a little coaxing to convince Hashikiri to accept the substitute, but once Chikakuni was seated and taking his place in the line, Kazuchiyo had to admit he looked fairly convincing. Even Yagi looked twice in momentary confusion. As Chikakuni explained their aim to Yagi, he seemed to calm significantly.

Kazuchiyo swallowed hard and had to tear his gaze away. "Amai," he said softly, "this doesn't change my mind."

Amai shook his head, but after a moment he sighed in resignation and handed him Chikakuni's violet chest plate. "Put this on."

They redressed Kazuchiyo in the Jisu armor. The captain Naoya had instructed to follow Kazuchiyo's orders brought them a horse, and Amai urged Kazuchiyo to climb up first. He then settled close behind him in the saddle.

"I'm only agreeing to this under one condition," Amai whispered hard against his ear. "If anything goes wrong, or if I have to jump off this horse for whatever reason, you keep riding east and don't look back."

"No," Kazuchiyo retorted as he guided their borrowed horse toward the front. "It won't come to that."

"Promise me," Amai insisted, hands fisting against Kazuchiyo's waist, "or I'll toss you off this horse right now."

"I'm not promising anything." Kazuchiyo motioned to a few of the Sakka soldiers among the riders to join them alongside the disguised Chikakuni. "I'm not charging across any rivers this year," he reassured Amai, "but I'm not going to flee at the first sign of trouble either. We'll know what has to be done when we're out there."

Amai growled under his breath. "You're so fucking stubborn." He reached into the spaces between Kazuchiyo's borrowed armor and tucked in what felt like Kazuchiyo's tanto. "Managed to save this from your things. Try not to need it, all right?"

"Thank you," Kazuchiyo whispered back. "I'm sorry."

Inside the storeroom, Rongi's soldiers removed several wooden planks from the floor to reveal a hidden set of pulleys. The remaining floor dropped down into the earth at an angle, making a plank that, as Naoya had said, was broad enough for two horses abreast to pass into the tunnel beyond. As a few soldiers hurried ahead to manage the exit, Yagi finally noticed Kazuchiyo among the gathered riders.

"Kazu," he said sharply, and Kazuchiyo's breath tangled in his attempt to come up with convincing enough words.

Amai came to his rescue once again, saying, "It's all right. I've got him." He wrapped his arm around Kazuchiyo's midsection as if to prove it. "Go kill that kamayari prick for us."

Yagi's brow furrowed intensely, and for a moment he looked as if he would protest, but then he nodded. "I will," he swore.

"Our small group will go first," Chikakuni said over his shoulder. "Wait only long enough for the enemy to give chase, then attack. All you need to do is convince them you're dangerous enough for them to fall back for a while so we can get our forces inside."

"What if they won't follow?" asked Purnima, one hand already on her sword.

"Then we'll ram our spears down their throats anyway," boasted Mahiro. She waved for them to carry on. "Go. We've got your backs."

Chikakuni smirked with appreciation and faced forward again. "Stay close, but not *too* close," he told Kazuchiyo, and with that he spurred his horse.

Six riders went out first, Chikakuni, Kazuchiyo, and Amai among them. The pounding hooves clattered down the hardwood slope, then dulled against the packed earth of the tunnel as the horses hurried them through the musty dark. There was no light to speak of for several long moments, until the path sloped upward again. Kazuchiyo caught only glimpses of the samurai who had gone ahead of them, holding open the great doors that had been laid open: their outside surface was decorated with hollow stones to avoid detection. Then they were outside the fortress and aimed at the east.

The cool evening air struck Kazuchiyo hard. Having gone from the crowded, stuffy banquet hall to the escape through the flaming keep, to the pulse-racing panic of the siege, he was unprepared for the thin chill of a late-summer night. The flat, gravel border around Rongi soon gave way to Kibaku's famous sloping fields, each emerald blade of grass bathed in gold from the flickering torchlights above. Kazuchiyo took in a deep breath. To his left, he could see the churning advance of the brown-clad army Amai had spoken of, which had just reached the northernmost wall. He could not make out any particular figure or banner, making them to his eye a flock of anxious vultures waiting to pick clean the shogun's kill. There was nothing to be done about them yet, so instead Kazuchiyo looked to his right.

Though only the easternmost flank of the Oomiyari's army was visible, it was more than enough to inspire fright. Their soldiers advanced in a tightly knit formation, spearmen at the front and archers firing over their heads. Huge, gold banners jutted out of each battalion, declaring their sovereignty.

My poor Kazuchiyo. All his life he had heard stories from Suyama and Sakka alike about the shogun's mighty army that slumbered in the west, stories that typically ended with sneers and disdain from the remote, country warriors whom the capital so contemptuously disregarded. For generations the eastern samurai, having sharpened their spears so faithfully against each other in near-constant warfare, believed themselves to be bettered through experience. They wore their badge of "uncivilized" with honor, while no one could rightfully say when last an army bearing the emperor's blessing had stepped foot outside its home province. No one would have believed that the failing Oomiyari could muster a great force comprised of anything more than farmers, bandit slayers, and samurai who had never seen the field.

And yet, from the moment Kazuchiyo spurred his horse outside of Rongi's walls, he felt the eye of that great army fall upon him, as heavy as the spear piercing the mountain on their banners. Almost immediately after spotting the retreating pack, a group of mounted Oomiyari broke away from the eastern flank to give chase. It was then that Kazuchiyo knew he had erred in provoking them.

"Here they come," said Amai.

"I know," Kazuchiyo replied, fingers white around the reins.

The riders shifted their formation, shielding Chikakuni and Kazuchiyo to the right and rear as best they could. Their horses grunted and huffed as if they were aware they had become prey. Kazuchiyo counted at least twenty Oomiyari in the chase, and before they had been free of the castle for a full minute of their escape, the soldiers at the front drew bows and fired.

The first volley fell short, but it chilled Kazuchiyo nevertheless. It would only be a matter of seconds before the capital's thoroughbreds drew their archers in close enough range for accuracy. He thought he could hear Mahiro's war cry, but he didn't dare turn in his saddle too far for risk of unsettling Amai. Just as he was contemplating telling Chikakuni to change their course, a second rain of arrows arched toward them. One caught a Sakka soldier in the back, not enough to kill him outright, but he cried out and lurched in the saddle. Another struck the rearmost horse in its flank. The poor creature fell with a terrible, braying shout and tossed its rider to the ground.

"Don't stop," Amai hissed in Kazuchiyo's ear preemptively, but then both flinched at the sound of a more familiar voice, raised not in pain but in fury, followed by a thud, a scream, and a man somewhere behind them hitting the ground.

Kazuchiyo turned then, and he was just in time to glimpse Yagi on horseback, wrenching his spear out of the back of the fallen Oomiyari. Several of their pursuers turned in alarm, and another was cut down before he could redirect his bow. Though the rear archers scattered to escape Yagi's wrath, those at the fore continued to fire at their target. An arrow struck Chikakuni square in the back of his helmet, and watching him pitch forward seized Kazuchiyo in a moment of breathless panic. But Chikakuni righted himself a moment later, cursing and grasping at the arrow lodged in his helmet.

"Chikakuni?" Kazuchiyo called.

"I'm fine!" Chikakuni wrenched the arrow free and cast it aside; Kazuchiyo couldn't tell if there was any blood on it. "Kibaku makes a strong—"

The horse next to him was struck, and as it and its rider crashed to the ground, Hashikiri startled and stumbled. Kazuchiyo's borrowed mare dodged admirably, but she swerved, off balance and struggling to stay upright with two riders clinging to her back. As Kazuchiyo fought to remain in control, they turned sharply to the north, and he was granted another look at the battlefield.

Yagi continued to tear through the Oomiyari's unprepared mounted archers. Several lay dead, and their formation fractured, with several curving off in different directions to avoid his spear. It was only then that Kazuchiyo realized Yagi was accompanied by only two men in Kibaku armor, who split from him with swords drawn to chase down the Oomiyari. The first of the Sakka men whose horse had been felled had even run back to claim a bow to aid in the fight, though his face was bloody from his fall and his legs shaky. As the odds swung in their favor, even Chikakuni and their remaining entourage turned back to give aid.

"Don't stop," Amai warned Kazuchiyo again, but by then he had turned fully about in search of his sister and the rest. Her telltale bellow he traced back toward Rongi, where she and Purnima were leading a furious charge through the Oomiyari's easternmost flank. Though it was difficult to judge in the dark and distance, they seemed to have planned their angle of attack perfectly: deep enough through the lines to create havoc and divide the flank, though shallow enough that their thunderous cavalry would not bite off a morsel too big to swallow. The foot soldiers streamed afterward, cutting off any who dared flee from Suzumekage's hooves.

Yagi cut the head clear off what must have been the leader of the Oomiyari's mounted archers, as the surviving four retreated quickly out of his range. They gathered together a few dozen meters away, and one felt bold enough to loose one more arrow at the snarling Yagi-douji himself. It struck him directly in his chest plate—the left eye of the oni insignia painted across it, in fact—but penetrated so shallowly that Yagi needed only to flex his shoulders for the arrow to fall to the ground.

"Yagi!" Kazuchiyo at last managed to calm his horse well enough to join the rest of the fractured unit as they regrouped behind Yagi. "Are you all right?"

"Fine," Yagi grunted, sparing only a quick glance back to assure himself that his two lovers were likewise uninjured before turning his attention in full back to the Oomiyari. "You should head back to the castle."

Kazuchiyo looked about at the state of the six of them: two of his men grievously injured, one dead from the fall from his horse. As Chikakuni yanked his helmet off, Kazuchiyo could see blood in the man's hair. Yagi and his Kibaku helpers had managed to kill over a dozen of the gold-clad invaders, but it seemed a pale victory considering the cost and the danger Kazuchiyo had put them through. He swallowed. "What about you? Are you going to the front?"

"Of course." When the same Oomiyari nocked another arrow, Yagi hefted his spear as if he might spur his horse at any moment, and the man thought better of firing. Yagi waited a moment longer to be sure before continuing. "After I finish off those four."

"It's a little late for us," said Amai, nudging Kazuchiyo hard in his side. "Look."

With a sick feeling, Kazuchiyo followed his prodding and looked back to Rongi. The brown-clad Nomino soldiers were advancing south along Rongi's eastern wall, their aim very clearly the secret entrance. Though the doors had been pulled shut, disguising themselves as impenetrable rock, there was no mistaking that the enemy had taken note of the fake retreat. Even if they took off at a full gallop then and there, there was no chance of them reentering the castle that way without putting its interior at further risk.

"Young lord, you should continue east," suggested one of the Kibaku soldiers. "There is a crossroads less than an hour's ride from here, and a small outpost. There are soldiers who would shelter you there."

"No," Kazuchiyo said immediately, and he reached behind him to squeeze Amai's thigh before he could offer any complaint. "No, I'm not retreating, not after having stolen from Lord Koedzuka his only means of escape. The rest of you should join Mahiro and Lady Purnima in the charge; General Chikakuni and I will stay close to the outer wall and join our troops, to help organize the retreat through the main gate."

"Oihata said he wouldn't open that gate," Yagi reminded him.

"He will if you can push the Oomiyari out of its range." Kazuchiyo looked again to the ongoing battle and was emboldened by Mahiro's progress; already he could see a shift in the shogun's ranks. Perhaps their strict formation and discipline were less experienced after all, he thought, thrown into disarray by Mahiro's enthusiastic barbarism. "There's no other choice to save our army and Rongi."

They took a moment to help the injured Sakka soldier onto a horse with his peer while the two Kibaku samurai tugged their helmets down and their shoulder guards forward. "Let us deal with those four archers," said one. "They don't deserve death by Yagi-douji."

Yagi snorted. "Go ahead then."

The pair charged ahead with swords raised, and though Kazuchiyo was anxious for them in the face of Oomiyari's skilled archers, Yagi was already motioning for them to hurry back to Rongi. "Stay on my right," he instructed sternly. "Their arrows aren't a match for my armor."

"And to think he used to hate it," Amai quipped close to Kazuchiyo's ear. Despite his teasing there was very little actual humor in his voice. "Not all of us are wearing armor that good, though, so let's get back behind the walls before our luck runs out."

Kazuchiyo nodded, and as they took off, he was sure to ride alongside Yagi as instructed. He was tempted to apologize to Amai again for insisting on this ploy; it did not seem to him then that they had accomplished much at all, save for a momentary distraction of the Oomiyari's east flank and twenty dead archers. As they drew closer to the true battle, however, he could see the golden banners moving back from the front line. The Oomiyari had stopped pressing the advance, and their ranks began to shift and tighten as Mahiro and Purnima readied another charge.

"It's working," Kazuchiyo said, almost breathless with relief. "We just need to buy more time."

Certainly once Yagi-douji had joined the counterattack, that time could be bought. Kazuchiyo allowed himself a moment to hope, until he noticed Chikakuni pointing into the enemy lines. One of the gold banners bearing the Oomiyari sigil was moving laterally along the rear of the vanguard, which then fell back after it. Someone was heading straight toward them at risk to the rest of their formation, daring even to unsettle their eastern flank further regardless of Mahiro and Purnima's carnage. As they broke free of the ranks, it became obvious that their armor was very fine, their helmets decorated with gleaming spearheads. They had come from the command unit, and at the head rode the kamayari general himself.

"Looks like they'd rather kill you than the thousand men outside Rongi," Chikakuni told Kazuchiyo. "You should be flattered."

Kazuchiyo grimaced. Though he had half a mind to steer around them and try to avoid a confrontation entirely, as soon as the Oomiyari were relatively clear of the battle, they stopped and spread out. With twelve men side to side, four on either end with bows already drawn, it did not seem possible that they could skate by unscathed. If the archers were any more skilled than the first twenty had been, they might have been in range already. After checking behind them to make sure the Kibaku samurai had taken care of the original stragglers, Kazuchiyo drew his mount to a stop. The rest of his comrades did the same, and their horses pawed the earth anxiously at the unexpected stalemate.

The Oomiyari general brandished his kamayari. He could not have been much older than thirty, but he carried himself with a stoicism beyond his years atop his sturdy, black horse that would have equaled Suzumekage were it half a hand larger. Thick, very straight, black hair hung down from beneath his helmet. "Aritaka Kazumune!" he called; his voice was full and very deep, like the lowest note of a biwa plucked deep within a cave. "By the shogun's decree, I, Oomiyari Jakusai, have come to carry out a sentence of death. You will, by the demands of your station and the will of the emperor, surrender yourself to me."

Goose bumps skittered across Kazuchiyo's skin, but before he could draw a breath, Chikakuni had thankfully beaten him to a reply. "Is it the shogun or the emperor who wishes me dead?" he shouted back, making a very serviceable attempt at mimicking Kazuchiyo's voice. "Anyone who is not Oomiyari knows well enough that they do not share a common interest."

General Jakusai motioned to one of his archers, who showed no hesitation in loosing his arrow. It passed so close by Chikakuni's left ear that as he jerked away, all could see the welt its fletching had drawn across his unguarded cheek. Yagi growled and hefted his spear, but a sharp word from Amai prevented him from charging outright.

"They're better than the last ones," he said, "and we're not all as well guarded as you. Be careful." Yagi ground his teeth but remained still.

"You will," Jakusai repeated, "by the demands of your station and the will of the emperor, surrender yourself to me."

"Come and get him yourself!" Yagi shot back. "I'll gut you and your horse together!"

Jakusai was given pause then, and Kazuchiyo felt the hairs on the back of his neck rise, as if Yagi's threat had sucked all temperature out of the air. As the Oomiyari looked to their general, he could not help but wonder if to them the grand, black gelding resembled Suzumekage's reputation as well as her size. They relaxed their bow arms as Jakusai climbed down from his mount and stalked forward with kamayari in hand.

Scowling, Yagi, too, dismounted to accept what was clearly a singular challenge. Kazuchiyo's stomach roiled as he watched them close the gap between the two small forces. Though Yagi seemed to have a slight advantage in height, Jakusai's build was just as strong, and Kazuchiyo had seen the swift and clever maneuverability of his half-cross spear. He could not stop himself. "Yagi!"

Yagi did not hesitate or look back, but Jakusai looked to him. His jaw tightened with anger and recognition—certainly he realized then that the fine indigo hitatare Chikakuni was dressed in did not belong to him. Kazuchiyo had faced a great deal of condemnation and disdain in his years serving Aritaka, but he found it difficult to remember a time when he had been fixed with such blatant and unrepentant hate as he was then.

"If you want him, you'll have to kill me first!" Yagi shouted, planting his feet in the earth as if once again facing down the bloody planks of Chibatake Bridge.

Jakusai halted and faced him. "You're the one they call

Yagi-douji," he said. "Which clan are you actually from?"

"It doesn't matter!" Yagi hefted his spear into a readied position. "I promised my lord I'd kill you for him, so come get it over with."

Jakusai's nostrils flared, but he did not bother to otherwise respond; he brandished his kamayari in a simple offensive stance and attacked.

Their spears clashed with an impact that resounded across the plain. Kazuchiyo's heart had no time to stumble back to its proper rhythm before they met again, each swing a test of the other's strength and defenses. The smack of the wood and the shrill clanging of metal had the horses up and down both lines squirming. After four bouts Yagi lunged, and with his full force against their crossed spears he threw Jakusai back.

For the barest of moments Jakusai's boot slipped against the grass in his attempts to brace himself. One can easily imagine the great shock it must be to any man who crosses spears with Yagi-douji for the first time, and learns then what strength itself is. But he recovered very quickly, and when next Yagi struck, he held his ground.

Kazuchiyo was so caught up in the spectacle that he barely noticed when Amai's hand snuck into his armor again to retrieve his tanto. It was when Amai slipped down from the saddle that he spared his attention. Amai shushed Kazuchiyo before he could question the shinobi on the matter and slipped forward to put himself in front of his horse.

Yagi and Jakusai each took a moment to breathe and reevaluate the other. "Who are you really?" Jakusai asked again. "Who was your father?"

"The king of hell," Yagi snapped back. "Now shut up!"

He swung with so much force that Jakusai was not fully able to retreat in time; the point of the spear tore a chunk out of his right shoulder guard and scraped along the top of his chest, scarring the lacquer of his cuirass. Though startled, Jakusai attempted to counter with a jab, but Yagi used the blunt end of his weapon to knock it aside. They clashed twice more, and each stepped back again.

"A shame," said Jakusai. He ripped the broken shoulder guard from his armor and cast it down. "The emperor could have benefited from a strength like yours, if only you had been properly bred and trained."

Yagi growled and charged. He jabbed toward Jakusai's now unguarded shoulder, though only shallowly—despite his rage, he had correctly judged the shedding of the armor to be a deliberate attempt at baiting his strike. As Jakusai countered with a powerful thrust, he feinted and attacked again. Their audience held their breath in anticipation of the blow that would sever the general's spear arm.

But Jakusai was prepared even for that. He twisted in mid-thrust, his right hand letting go of the end of his spear entirely as he twisted in place to avoid Yagi's blade. His thrust, which seemed to have swung wide, now proved to have been intentional; he twisted his wrist and pulled his arm back with all his might.

The jutting, sickle like blade of the kamayari caught the underside of Yagi's upper arm. It tore through the most vulnerable openings in the oni armor and split his flesh. In the shadowy dark of the night field, the blood looked black. Kazuchiyo could only stare in shocked horror as Yagi reared back with growled curses. Jakusai did not relent. With only a moment spared to retake his proper grip, he attacked again, this time swinging his spear laterally so that the shaft slammed into the wounded arm.

The sound it made was grotesque; the crunch of the iron scales, the sharp crack that might have been bone. Yagi howled like the hell beast he took his name from as his hand came off his spear. Sick with panic Kazuchiyo reached for his belt in want of a sword, as if he could draw his blade and send a wave of magic to drown their enemy as he had at Etsugo. He was unarmed, but his will raced to intervene nevertheless. Amai, whom Kazuchiyo had not seen move until he was already at Yagi's side, darted into the fray. With all a shinobi's speed and cunning, he skidded below Jakusai's spear and plunged Kazuchiyo's tanto into the man's thigh.

Jakusai made barely a sound as he stumbled back, but upon seeing who the attack had come from, a snarl of wrath twisted his features. Even Amai was not fast enough to escape the blunt end of the kamayari rushing toward him; he crumpled to the ground with one blow to his temple. He might have met his death then and there if not for Yagi in turn coming to his rescue. Brandishing his spear in only his left hand, Yagi threw himself on the shogun's dog, bellowing all the while.

The field fell to chaos. Several of the Oomiyari charged to their master's aid while others finally loosed their arrows. The Kibaku samurai rode to meet them while Chikakuni ducked behind his shoulder guard; it caught two arrows that otherwise would have taken his uncovered head. Kazuchiyo jumped down from his horse. With no plan in his head he rushed forward, dizzy with panic, and dropped next to Amai's fallen body.

"Please do something," Kazuchiyo prayed to the pair of beads strung so tightly against his wrist. "Please—"

Yagi kicked Jakusai in his injured knee; at last, the general surrendered a shout of pain as he retreated several steps. Only by planting his kamayari in the ground was he able to stay upright. Even with Yagi barreling toward him, despite his injuries, he seemed determined to hold his ground until two of his captains reached him.

"Sir!" one shouted. "Please let us—"

An arrow struck him straight through his right eye—an arrow fired by one of the Sakka samurai, who himself still had an arrow embedded in his back. As the Oomiyari fell from his saddle, Jakusai reassessed his odds. With one last hateful glare at Kazuchiyo, he dragged himself onto the horse.

"Don't you fucking run!" Yagi shouted, continuing to advance. When the second mounted Oomiyari moved into his path, Yagi forced his bloody hand to the grip of his spear and struck. Even wounded, his strength was great enough to sever the cords crossing at the samurai's ribs and into his chest; he, too, fell from his horse with a sick and raspy gurgle.

Jakusai turned his borrowed horse. "To Mutsuyama," he said to another of his approaching men through clenched teeth. Abandoning Kazuchiyo and his peers entirely, he whistled for his black gelding and then fled with his men back toward the eastern flank.

"Get back here!" Yagi hollered, and in rage he flung his spear at their retreating backs. Though it fell short, the Oomiyari quickened their pace and were soon far out of range.

"Yagi!" Kazuchiyo shouted, but Yagi was still yelling after them in wordless anger and wouldn't be swayed. Hands shaking, he checked Amai and was relieved to find him steadily breathing—knocked deeply unconscious, but alive. With a deep breath he stood. "Yagi, stop."

"Where's my horse?" Yagi spun about, seemingly oblivious to the nauseating way his injured arm swung at his side. It made Kazuchiyo want to vomit. "I'm going after him."

Kazuchiyo intercepted him. "Yagi, *stop*. Your arm…"

He reached for it, but Yagi pushed him back with his other hand. "Don't touch me!" he snarled, but when he took another look, his haze of anger briefly cleared. "Kazu." His eyes were wild, brow drenched with sweat. "Are you hurt?"

Kazuchiyo shuddered and reached for him again. "Let me see your arm."

"It's fine," Yagi grunted, pulling away again, but the movement only made the state of it clearer; his jaws clamped shut against a grimace and a hiss of pain. He looked down, and when confronted with the blood soaking his arm, his quivering fingers, a grave truth carved itself across his face. His eyes darting to Kazuchiyo's were full of dread.

Yagi swallowed. "Get back on your horse," he said, his voice raw. "You need to get back to the castle."

"Give me your arm," Kazuchiyo ordered, and that time Yagi did not fight as Kazuchiyo removed the rest of the ties on his broken spaulder. He did his best to hide his work from Chikakuni and the others as they regrouped, his shaking fingers tangling in the knots as they were slicked with blood. When at last he had a clear look at the damage, his heart dropped into his stomach.

The wound was deep. In the dark he couldn't be sure if it had cut to bone, but there was so much blood. Kazuchiyo measured his breathing as he yanked Yagi's bracer off and then ripped his sleeve to fashion into a bandage. "We all have to go to the gate," he said. "We *all* have to go. Their general is injured, they'll pull back. Oihata will open the gate. The physicians will take care of you."

"Kazu—" Yagi started to say, but Kazuchiyo drew the bandage tight, and he was forced to stop by a gasp of pain.

"They'll take care of you. We have to go." Kazuchiyo wiped his hands against his sleeves, over and over, trying to get the blood off them. "We have to go. Chikakuni?"

"Here." Chikakuni had dismounted and was gathering Amai up in his arms; there were arrows sticking out of his shoulder guard, and the back of his collar was stained with blood, but he moved without any sign of real injury. "Come on—I'll help you with him."

"Th-Thank you." Kazuchiyo shook himself and hurried over. Once he was back in his saddle, one arm around the unconscious Amai slumped in front of him, he at last looked over what remained of their small force: Chikakuni, climbing back into Hashikiri's saddle; Yagi, mounted and looking pale, his eyes wide and glossy; one of the Kibaku samurai holding Yagi's spear for him while the other lay dead; the last of his Sakka soldiers, breathing hard from the arrow still protruding from his back. Each looked to him.

Kazuchiyo took in a deep breath as he gathered up the reins in one hand. "Follow me," he said, and none objected as he spurred his horse and led them back toward Rongi.

CHAPTER TWENTY-TWO

Kazuchiyo and his small troop arrived at Rongi's doorstep amid one of the more incomprehensible front lines he had ever witnessed. The twin specters of Mahiro and Purnima along with their riders had carved a bloody path through the Oomiyari's eastern flank, and with that momentum the Sakka and Suyama soldiers positioned there were scrambling to take advantage. Their lines had begun to curve outward in defiance, as if peeling the shogun's men from Rongi's gate as one might a leech from a wound. The Oomiyari's vanguard, meanwhile, shifted continuously between order and disarray. With every bellow of their horns the commanders urged their samurai into ranks, only to have those ranks withdrawn or cleaved with every haphazard push from their trapped enemies. At ground level, there was no telling which had the advantage or would crumble first.

As they rode through the battered remnants of the camp, Yagi overtook Kazuchiyo at the head and motioned for the Kibaku samurai to return his spear. "Give me that," he ordered. "And get my lord back behind the gates. Mahiro and I will hold the retreat."

"Yagi, wait," Kazuchiyo said quickly, his heart already

pawing its way up his throat as he watched Yagi reclaim his spear with his left hand. His right he had wedged into his belt to keep his arm from too much movement. "Come with us. Mahiro has Purnima, but your—"

"*Go,*" Yagi demanded, with such heated intensity that Kazuchiyo shrank in his saddle. "Get behind that gate right now."

Kazuchiyo gulped. He couldn't speak, but he nodded. Once the Kibaku samurai had done the same, Yagi raced off to join the fray.

"Come on," said Chikakuni, drawing his horse close enough to give Kazuchiyo's elbow a tug. "There's nothing more you can do out here."

"But my..." Kazuchiyo peered into the mess of black armor jostling against the Oomiyari spearmen, but he could not spot General Zaiga's helmet among them, let alone any figure that might have been his brother. Then Amai's body shifted in his arms, and with a jolt he at last conceded. "All right. Let's hurry."

They followed the wall to Rongi's immense southern gate. By then Kazuchiyo could hear Yagi's telltale bellow above the cacophony, joined by Mahiro's enthusiastic war cries. Dozens of wounded men had already gathered just beyond the gate for hope that it would open for them; they gaped in amazement to see their lord riding to their aid. Though many must have mistaken Chikakuni for Kazuchiyo then, it mattered very little to their spirits, and several retook their weapons.

Once there, Kazuchiyo could see even less of the battle than before—only flashing spear points in the distance, and the horrible, hair-rising cries of furious and dying men. He craned his head up and could see Naoya where he had left him at the guard tower, now with bow in hand aiding the fight. Though he shuddered to think of what admonishments awaited him, he wet his lips and took a deep breath. "General Oihata!"

Naoya didn't hear at first, as he was too busy instructing his men on whom to next concentrate their fire. As Kazuchiyo shouted again, the soldiers around him began to call out and rattle their spears as well, at last drawing Naoya to lean over the rail. Despite the dark and the distance, Kazuchiyo was certain of the surprised and angry expression fixed on him then. Naoya swiftly drew back and began shouting new instructions to his men.

Amai jerked suddenly in Kazuchiyo's arms with a huge intake of breath. He struggled against Kazuchiyo at first, disoriented and slurring his words, until Kazuchiyo tugged him back against his chest.

"Amai! It's me." Kazuchiyo held him steady until it seemed he could sit up on his own. "Go slow. Are you all right?"

Amai hissed curses as he slipped one hand under his helmet to rub his doubtlessly sore head. "What happened?" He flinched. "Where's Yagi?"

Kazuchiyo scarcely needed to answer; Yagi's roar echoed down the line as if Amai had summoned it, with all the raw and beastly ferocity that had once shook even the battle-hardened Shimegahara. Though it was full of power and fight, Kazuchiyo shuddered. It had been a long time since he had heard his lover sound quite so hellish.

From above them came a shout, and all at once the battlefield was smothered in a blinding, white light. From Naoya himself a beacon erupted in furious glory; the Oomiyari recoiled, their eyes trained on the castle now turned against them. It was accompanied by the twang of hundreds of bows firing at once, and as their arrows rained down on the confounded fools, dozens fled or were cut down. Horses reared in panic and threw their riders, but not Suzumekage: as soon as the flash abated, Kazuchiyo heard Mahiro's gleeful wail, followed by screams of horror, and, then, a thunderous cheer.

Kazuchiyo rubbed his stinging eyes and again stared hard into the melee, but still he could make out very little. Soon enough, though, the clashing of spears faded in favor of pounding steps and hooves, and behind him, Rongi's gate began to creak.

"Stand back!" shouted the Kibaku samurai accompanying Kazuchiyo, and he and Chikakuni worked together to draw the wounded out of the way. As the castle entrance grew wider, he motioned for Kazuchiyo to go through.

"But—" Kazuchiyo started to protest, but Amai took the reins from him and spurred their horse inside.

Those soldiers within the walls moved to assist. They hurried forward to drag and carry the wounded, as already the blended armies of Sakka and Suyama had taken notice of the open gate and were racing to retreat. Lord Koedzuka himself came down from the western tower, where Naoya remained, to direct his samurai. As the ranks poured in, Kazuchiyo strained forward in search of familiar faces; he could still hear Yagi and Mahiro beyond the walls, and he had yet to locate any of his endangered family. As more soldiers were carried through the gates, sporting gruesome injuries, he began to despair, until at last he spotted a familiar helmet with red, looping cords.

"General!" Kazuchiyo jumped down from his horse. "Amai, I'll be back," he said, then ignored Amai's frustrated cursing as he pushed his way through the crowds. Among the ranks of black-armored Suyama troops, he at last spotted General Zaiga, limping from an arrow embedded in the back of his knee, his arm thrown over the shoulders of a shellshocked Shigeyuki.

Kazuchiyo choked on emotion as he rushed to them; he couldn't risk speaking at all when his brother's name was so heavy on his tongue. When Zaiga saw him, his pained expression crumbled into relief; Shigeyuki could only stare.

"General." Kazuchiyo took up Zaiga's other arm, propriety be damned, and helped them over to a small bench outside the stables. Though the arrow wound was grievous, it did not seem that Zaiga was otherwise injured, and Kazuchiyo quickly turned his attention to his brother. As soon as Zaiga's weight was lifted from him, the poor boy collapsed, despite Kazuchiyo's attempts to support him.

"He's all right," Zaiga said as Kazuchiyo crouched down

next to him. "He'll be all right."

He didn't seem so at a glance: Shigeyuki was trembling, blood-splattered, his eyes red with tears. On closer inspection, however, Kazuchiyo was elated to find no injuries worse than scrapes. Carefully he removed Shigeyuki's mask from him to better see his face. "Shigeyuki?" he whispered.

Shigeyuki gulped, but his eyes did focus then, and he stared at Kazuchiyo dumbfounded. "Brother?"

"Yes, it's me." Kazuchiyo leaned closer as Shigeyuki sagged into his shoulders. "Are you hurt?"

Shigeyuki shook his head as fresh tears collected in his eyes. Kazuchiyo put his arm around him, his heart breaking. He remembered very well those nights after *his* first battle, curled tight beneath his bedding as he shivered and cried. He supported Shigeyuki as best he could and hoped it was some comfort to him. "Uncle," he said quietly. "Your leg?"

Zaiga snapped the shaft of the arrow, though he left its point embedded. "It'll heal," he said, face and voice confidently at ease despite the gleam of sweat on his skin. "Don't worry about me—I've had worse."

Another flash of light caught the corner of Kazuchiyo's eye, and he raised his head as the archers again fired in unison. More and more soldiers in various colors of armor were streaming through the gate then, though thankfully none in gold or brown. As the wounded were carried off the main path, those that were still on their feet were pushed farther and farther into the compound to make way. At long last their mounted forces began to appear, and Kazuchiyo strained up on his toes to see.

"We're fine," Zaiga reassured him. "Go on."

Ginta came through next, leading his horse. There was no telling how much, if any, of the blood coating him was his own, but he bowed stoically to Kazuchiyo as they passed each other, looking very much like his father as he did. Chikakuni returned and was given a strained but heartfelt greeting by Lady Dada. Last to enter were Yagi, Mahiro, and Purnima. Each was an terrible but inspiring sight, splashed with gore and brimming with fiery defiance. Mahiro had tied a tall, oblong helmet to Suzumekage's pommel that doubtlessly still held its master's head, and though she laughed and beamed amid the soldiers' attentions, Kazuchiyo could see how exhausted and out of breath she was now that she was away from the fighting. It comforted him to see how closely Purnima was watching her.

But as we can readily understand, the bulk of Kazuchiyo's worry was saved for Yagi. He, too, was breathing hard, and so harshly that it seemed as though fire and ash might spew from his oni mouth at any moment. His fist trembled around the shaft of his blood-slick spear, and his eyes rolled back and forth like a hateful predator seeking its next kill. His skin was very pale beneath the blood.

Rongi's great gates closed with a heavy thud, and immediately Kibaku soldiers rushed forward with extra beams to strengthen the blockade. The archers all along the walls ceased their firing, and Naoya's voice fell quiet. The battle had ended. As everyone looked to each other, too weary and uncertain for any relief, Mahiro suddenly gave a great huff of laughter.

"Well, it fucking worked!" she crowed, and spotting her brother among the throngs, she rapped on the helmet tied to her saddle. "Their lead general turned tail before I could gut him, but I've brought you a gold-dusted head all the same! Let them rot outside these walls while we finish our feasting."

She nudged Suzumekage, who continued inside. The surrounding soldiers gazed up at the pair of them in confusion and awe. "You didn't think we'd leave you all to die out there, did you?" she goaded the crowd. "Mahiro the Iron Gate defends as well as she conquers! Whoever these invaders are, they were fools to step foot into lands under my protection. And don't forget the icy talons of the indomitable Lady Purnima, or the thousand-slaying oni, Yagi-douji!"

Yagi's horse followed instinctively behind Suzumekage, and Kazuchiyo fell into step alongside, latching onto Yagi's ankle. "Yagi?"

"I'm going to the keep," Yagi said, his eyes hazy but locked on the distant tower.

"All right." Kazuchiyo turned back but wasn't able to spot Amai, so he stayed at Yagi's side up the twisting path to the heart of the fortress.

"Rest up!" Mahiro continued to shout to the crowd as they went. "Lick your wounds, and then have a drink! We can outlast these cowardly fuckers who thought they could spoil our good time!"

A few cheered; a few nodded gravely. A few were too shocked to respond. But Mahiro was a monument to them all then, and Kazuchiyo was very proud to count her as family.

They reached the lesser keep first, where a retinue of Kibaku samurai had gathered to defend their lord's family hidden safely inside. Mahiro dismounted first, her only concern then to find water for Suzumekage. Purnima headed quickly inside to seek out Lady Anisha and confirm her safety. Yagi drew his horse right up to the engawa, and as he lowered himself from the saddle, Kazuchiyo finally understood his insistence: he took two steps into the building and then collapsed with a terrible thud.

The Kibaku samurai stared in shock as Kazuchiyo dropped to his side. "Yagi!" he cried, though he saw that Yagi hadn't completely surrendered consciousness. His half-lidded eyes sought Kazuchiyo dizzily.

"Didn't want them… to see," Yagi mumbled.

Tears surged to Kazuchiyo's eyes as he gripped Yagi's armor. "Help him!" he shouted at the stunned samurai around them. "Get him inside, and call for a physician—quickly!"

The men jarred to life. It took several to pull Yagi into the closest chamber, and there they set upon divesting him of his armor. Physicians came with water and salve and catgut. Yagi growled in and out of awareness as they washed, stitched, and bandaged the mangled wound, and Kazuchiyo helped prepare a broth of ginseng. In the candlelight, the laceration did not appear to Kazuchiyo's eye as horrific as it had on the field, but he couldn't stop thinking about the heart-rending crack that had followed. He couldn't stop his hands from shaking.

At last, Yagi lay cushioned on a futon, arm splinted and bandaged tight to his chest. Kazuchiyo managed to feed him a bit of the herbal tea, though Yagi seemed half conscious by then. As the physicians and samurai left, Amai appeared in the open doorway. He had shed his armor, and Kazuchiyo leaped to his feet at the sight of him. "Amai! There you are."

He rushed over. As he got close Amai put his hand to his chest as if to prevent him from closing the distance entirely, but Kazuchiyo did not understand and wouldn't be thwarted. He drew Amai close, eager for shared comfort and oblivious in that moment to the shinobi's squirms of protest . Amai's resistance soon crumbled, and he wilted into Kazuchiyo's enfolding arms.

"Oh, Amai, I'm sorry," Kazuchiyo whispered, feeling out the painful knot above his temple where Jakusai had struck him. "Are you all right?"

Amai shook his head against Kazuchiyo's collar, and he only stayed a moment longer before finally insisting on untangling them. He scraped his sleeve across his face and moved past Kazuchiyo to drop to Yagi's side. "Koedzuka's looking for you," he said.

Kazuchiyo looked between his two lovers, loath to leave either, and slowly realized that Amai refused to look at him. "Are you all right?" he asked again.

"*No*, I'm—" Amai caught himself and again scrubbed his sleeve across his face. "I'm fine. Knocked around, that's all. Go find Koedzuka. I'll stay with him here."

Kazuchiyo shifted back and forth, heart in his gut as he watched Amai's shoulders tremble. "I'll be back soon," he promised, and he took a moment to clean his own face as best he could before striking out of the keep.

Rongi's courtyards and outbuildings were stuffed to overflowing. Servants rushed from one soldier to the next, delivering water and fresh linen to the wounded, while each assisted the other as best they could. Horses milled about wherever there was room, anxious and dazed in the confusion. The archers along the walls had ceased firing, instead counting their arrows and mopping sweat from their faces. As Kazuchiyo made his way down the path, he turned to and fro to take it all in; by the time he had reached the storage hall they had made their departure from, he felt as if his head might spin from his shoulders.

Seeing a pair of familiar faces centered him: Beihou was reclined on a stool just outside the secret exit, drinking from a wine gourd, with Koedzuka alongside him. Kazuchiyo took a deep breath and approached the pair. "Lord Koedzuka!"

"Lord Kazumune," Koedzuka greeted him in kind, weary relief on his face. "It's good to see you unharmed." A bit of fatherly rebuke crept into his tone. "You gave General Oihata and me quite a fright, going outside the gate."

"I apologize," Kazuchiyo replied immediately, bowing his head. "It was not my intention to frighten anyone. I only hoped to distract some of the Oomiyari away from our soldiers."

"Even so," Koedzuka continued, "the lives of those soldiers would be no less endangered if you were killed in my care and Lord Aritaka demanded vengeance for you."

"Don't be too hard on him," said Beihou. "Just an hour ago you tried to scale a burning castle to save your family, and he's *much* younger than you." He offered up his gourd. "Take a drink, lad."

Kazuchiyo was not certain his stomach would appreciate the alcohol, but he accepted and took one small gulp. Koedzuka, meanwhile, released a sigh, and said, "We can speak about it later. For now—"

"No," Kazuchiyo interrupted as he handed the gourd back. "Excuse me, sir, but please allow me to make my apologies now." So saying, Kazuchiyo took a step back and lowered himself to his knees. To the surprise of the two men—and many others surrounding them, we must assume—he pressed his hands to the earth and lowered his forehead to them. "Lord Koedzuka, I must beg your forgiveness for drawing this enemy to your land.

It's only because of me that this attack took place." His jaw ached as he worked the words free. "When negotiating with General Umafusa of Tendo, I shared with him that you would leave Kibaku's capital to meet with us and Lady Dada. I believe that is what prompted the shogun to launch this siege."

A moment of quiet passed, and Kazuchiyo shivered beneath his sweat, until Koedzuka gently replied, "I know. General Oihata told me earlier. Please, stand up."

Kazuchiyo gulped and did so. Though Beihou was watching his lord with surprised curiosity, Lord Koedzuka's expression was only patient and kind. "When you spared my life last year, it was under an agreement: 'our enemies lie in the west.' At the time, I believed this war was my payment for that mercy. All of Kibaku has since then been prepared for it."

He took a step closer so he could set his hand on Kazuchiyo's shoulder. "But now you've helped save the lives of my wife and son," he said, emotion tightly restrained in his tone. "You risked your life for common soldiers instead of retreating. Your intentions and your character I will never underestimate again." He smiled grimly then and lowered his voice. "But as a daimyo to the man whom I may one day call lord, I beg you, put a bit more value on your own life. For all our sakes."

Kazuchiyo nodded, humbled and speechless. Koedzuka held him steady for a moment longer before stepping back. "Don't fear too greatly for Rongi," he continued. "General Sasahara here is as fine a samurai as he is a host."

"We were expecting to stuff the bellies of three whole armies for several more days of feasting," Beihou bragged. "If we ration carefully instead, we'll easily outlast anything the shogun's dogs brought with them, considering how many they brought. Even a small number of reinforcements will rout them once their bellies are empty."

"Reinforcements," Kazuchiyo echoed with trepidation. "Generals Rakuteru and Hosoda were guarding the borders north and south of here, but still the Oomiyari and even

Nomino were able to attack. Could they have been routed without us knowing?"

"We've had no word," Koedzuka confessed. "It may be wise not to assume they will come. Oihata may be able to get word to Ugarasu, though."

Kazuchiyo looked into the tunnel and considered the soldiers that sat around its entrance, spears in their laps. "Where are Nomino's soldiers now?"

"Retreated just out of range of our archers," reported Beihou with a snort. "They put some muscle into it, but even those old mountain goats retreated after we brought out the boiling pots. They're out in the field now, watching the Oomiyari to know when to try again."

Kazuchiyo nodded, trying to force aside his melancholy for more constructive thought. "I'm going to the gate," he said. "I'd like to confirm the Oomiyari's condition, whatever we may know of it, and make my apologies to General Oihata." He gathered himself. "By daybreak we should have a better understanding of what comes next and from where we might draw assistance."

Koedzuka and Beihou agreed, and they wished Kazuchiyo luck as he continued to the south gate.

The air there was even more tense. None of the archers had left their posts and were instead accepting fresh supplies, and soldiers sat in the center of the courtyard already in ranks. Kazuchiyo spotted General Zaiga to one side, counseling a group of Suyama samurai, but he thought better of going to him now that the initial chaos of the retreat had passed. It was safer and more appropriate that he approach Lady Dada, who remained positioned at the wall with the Kibaku archers, Chikakuni beside her.

"How's your head?" Kazuchiyo asked of Chikakuni once he had joined them on the scaffolding.

"Dreadful," Chikakuni replied, rubbing at the linen bandage wrapped tightly around his crown. "But it's still on my shoulders, so I can't complain." His manners sobered. "How is

Yagi-douji?"

"He's… resting."

Kazuchiyo intended to say more, but Chikakuni must have seen how tenuous his composure was because he quickly carried on. "Good. He looked awfully frightful when he came in—the soldiers won't stop talking about the three of them. Everyone says they fought like lions."

"Your sister took a general's head," Lady Dada added. "No one's quite sure whose, but the rumor is he's part of the shogun's branch family. It was quite a sight."

"You saw?" Kazuchiyo glanced to the open arrow slot they were resting beside. "Have you been fighting the whole time?"

"Of course," Lady Dada replied as if affronted. She tapped the bow leaning against the wall next to her. "If I had known we'd be entertaining the shogun's brood here, I would have brought my own."

Once again Kazuchiyo grew cold with shame. "I'm sorry," he said, again lowering his head. "I've brought you to terrible peril here."

"You mean what Oihata said? About the meeting?" Lady Dada waved her hand dismissively. "You would not have been in Jisu in the first place if not for me."

"Or my father's greed," Chikakuni added grimly. "So let's wait until all is said and done before we start apologizing to each other."

Though the relief tasted sour on Kazuchiyo's tongue, he nodded. "I'm very grateful to you both. Though please do find some chance for rest, before dawn. Who knows what the Oomiyari will have planned then."

They agreed, and at last Kazuchiyo climbed to the top of the guard tower that Naoya had staked as his post. He braced himself as best he could. "General?"

Naoya stood at the rail with a handful of men, each massaging their palms, weary from their bows. He turned at the sound of Kazuchiyo's voice and immediately took in a great breath, which he cautiously exhaled. He joined Kazuchiyo at the back of the tower. "Thank the heavens. Are you unhurt?"

Kazuchiyo's throat grew tight, but he nodded. "I'm fine. And I—" He had to pause for a breath before continuing. "As you already relayed to Lord Koedzuka and Lady Dada, I am to blame for this attack, and for that—"

"Please don't think my telling them that was any attempt to discredit you," Naoya said quickly. "My aim was only for them to understand the full circumstances."

"I understand. You were right to tell them. And I am sorry, for exposing your lord and your home to danger."

Naoya shook his head. "Danger we are well accustomed to. You, on the other hand..."

Kazuchiyo tensed at what he assumed would soon be a mighty admonishment, and Naoya must have seen as much, for he once again took a moment to rein in his temper before speaking. "Make no mistake: I am *furious* you acted so recklessly and against my advice," he said, eyes wet with emotion. "But it is done, and you are unharmed, and it may be that hundreds of my countrymen owe you their lives. So let us agree that we each had and have nothing but good intentions, and let that be the end of it."

"Yes," Kazuchiyo agreed. He would wonder later if these words of Naoya's were not some version of an apology for having so strongly delivered advice that, if followed, might have doomed several thousand men. At present, however, he could not have been more grateful for the reprieve. "Yes, I agree." He managed a shaky smile. "And please don't take it personally. I defied a lot of people's advice tonight."

"Fate is strange, Kazumune. We may never know if it was for good or ill." Naoya gathered himself up and gave another sharp exhale. "Now then, come see the situation—but be cautious. We still haven't pinned down that snake, Mutsuyama."

Kazuchiyo followed Naoya to the outer wall of the tower, fully on his guard. Only the barest hints of dawn glow showed on the eastern horizon, not nearly enough to provide decent illumination, so that the battleground below remained mostly in darkness. Kazuchiyo could make out the silhouettes of camp tents and crates of supplies on either side of the main road, now trampled and in tatters. Corpses littered the ground amid hundreds of arrows. Banners from five provinces lay stamped in the mud. Beyond that glowed the torchlights of the shogun's army—tiny, shining points that stretched out in either direction as if they were the camp's own fortress wall.

"From what I was able to determine, they came in three regiments," Naoya explained, and he pointed out where each had been positioned. "The command unit at the center, and two great flanks east and west. After Mahiro and Lady Purnima attacked the east flank, a portion split off from the command unit at the center."

"Oomiyari Jakusai," Kazuchiyo murmured, shivering with the memory of the man's hateful eyes on him. "He attacked us in the field east of here but was forced to retreat, injured." The confrontation was a dark and painful blur already in Kazuchiyo's memory, and he strained to remember just where Amai had struck the man, and how deeply. "Grievously so, I think."

"Jakusai," Naoya repeated gravely. "We only catch rumors of the shogun's family here in Kibaku, but I've heard the name. He may very well be the shogun's own nephew." He shook his head and continued. "The ranks had some difficulty keeping order after he left. Your sister, the lady Purnima, and Captain Ebara took advantage and pushed back the eastern flank. With that, I was able to distract them, and Lady Mahiro took that general's head. I believe he was from the Nokogiriha clan— extremely impressive." He nodded with appreciation. "Such an attack likely won't work again, but it was a fine kill, and they'll think better of trying to break these gates down if it means another Iron Gate is on the other side."

"I hope so." Kazuchiyo peered into the eerie dark, worrying his lip between his teeth. "General Sasahara is confident we can outlast them in here."

"We can, and we shall." Naoya looked to him quizzically.

"Unless you have some strategy in mind to repel them more directly?"

Kazuchiyo swiftly shook his head. "No, friend, I'm sorry. It's challenging enough to think straight at all right now." He stared at one of the distant torchlights and thought of Yagi back in the lesser keep, a single candle lighting the room. "We should organize a guard rotation and let the rest sleep as much as they can. Including you."

"I'm going to stay a while longer," Naoya insisted. "I daresay I wouldn't be able to sleep regardless, knowing that foul Mutsuyama remains at large." He touched his chest briefly, where his string of beads remained hidden beneath his robe. "If only I could draw him out, I might be able to determine how much magic he's still capable of."

"Is your..." Kazuchiyo frowned, glancing behind them at the Kibaku soldiers nearby. "How much magic are *you* still capable of?"

"Only enough to combat him singularly, I'm sure." Naoya's mouth twisted. "He's probably down there on the field now. Scavenging."

Kazuchiyo grimaced at the thought. He could not help but scan the bodies below, as if he might spot the old man bent over a corpse to feed. "Then... then I should give you this," he said, trying to keep his back to the surrounding soldiers as he tugged up his sleeve to reveal his two beads. "The hermit said it was almost entirely full, and..." Frustration made his fingers stumble over the knot, and he sighed sharply. "It did me no good out there when I needed it. You may as well—"

Naoya's hand fell over his; Kazuchiyo startled and then held still as Naoya retied the ribbon. "Keep it for now," he said quietly, though the words seemed to pain him. "There's still a chance Mutsuyama does not know you have it, which could prove a boon to us." He clasped Kazuchiyo's hand in both of his for a moment, as if imparting a great trust—and a greater burden. "Be careful with it."

"I will," Kazuchiyo promised, and he bowed his head.

He stayed for a few minutes afterward, discussing with Naoya the possible strategies the Oomiyari might deploy against them come daylight. It was just as he was beginning to forget his exhaustion that a shout arose from deep within the fortress: the heart-rending demon wail that Kazuchiyo knew so well. Even from as far away as the lesser keep, it turned the head of every soldier. Naoya himself startled and grew pale. Before any could assume the assault had resumed, Kazuchiyo quickly moved toward the tower ladder.

"It's all right," he said. "Everything's all right, but I must go to him. Naoya, please send someone for me at the first sign of attack."

"Of course," Naoya said, though he watched the lesser keep with apprehension. As Kazuchiyo climbed down, he could hear Naoya rally himself and order his men back to their posts.

Kazuchiyo hurried back the way he had come. Up and down the different baileys samurai, servant, and foot soldier looked to the keep in confusion and alarm. Only a handful of those from Sakka recognized the oni's fever dreams for what they were. And then, the cries died out. Kazuchiyo quickened his pace, the silence frightening him more than the shouts had. He pushed past a group of servants huddled in the corridor outside Yagi's room and dashed inside.

Yagi was asleep—fitfully so, but breathing steadily—and curled very tightly against him was Amai. Kazuchiyo relaxed somewhat as he closed the panel behind him and at long last began removing his borrowed armor. "Amai," he said gently, and when he was free of the metal plates, he kneeled beside him. "What happened?"

Amai shook his head and pressed his face into Yagi's collar rather than answering. When Kazuchiyo put a hand to his shoulder and found it shaking, he gave him some time; he checked Yagi's arm to make sure the bandages had not been disturbed and then rubbed Amai's back as he gradually calmed.

"I'm fine," Amai said finally, though his voice was hoarse. Kazuchiyo scooted back so he had room to sit up, which he did so gingerly, rubbing his head. "He just started screaming like that out of nowhere—scared the life out of me."

Kazuchiyo looked again to Yagi, whose eyelids continued to twitch, and whose voice roiled and grumbled in his sleep. "It's been some time since his nightmares were this bad. I'm sorry I wasn't here."

Amai scoffed quietly. "What did Koedzuka have to say?"

Kazuchiyo wound his fingers in his hakama. "I know you're upset with me."

Amai sighed and rubbed his temple again. "I don't think we should talk about it now."

"I didn't intend for either of you to get hurt," Kazuchiyo carried on regardless. "But I couldn't sit by and do nothing."

"I know," Amai said, still refusing to meet his gaze. "I know that."

Kazuchiyo told himself to stop. Amai was obviously still in pain, and it would do neither of them any good to argue in such weary states. He told himself that and kept talking anyway. "I wish I could have come up with a better plan, one that didn't put you both in harm's way. You know I would have taken your wounds myself if I could have."

"I know that!" Amai grumbled in frustration as he scrubbed at his face. "Kazu, I wish I could make you feel better about this, I really do. Maybe you were right to go, maybe Yagi would have gone straight to the front if it was just Chikakuni in danger instead of you. Maybe that bastard would have beaten him in front of everyone, and he'd be dead—maybe we'd *all* be dead. I don't know!"

He at last turned to face Kazuchiyo, his eyes red with anger and exhaustion. "I just know that I asked you not to, and you went anyway."

Kazuchiyo tried to swallow down the great lump in his throat. "I'm sorry," he said. "But you know I had to."

"I know, but no you *didn't*," Amai retorted. "You're too important."

"No." Kazuchiyo shook his head. "No, I'm not more

338

important than him or—"

"You are, though!" Amai snagged Kazuchiyo's hands; his palms were clammy with sweat. "I know you wanted to help your family," he said in a hard whisper, "but Yagi and I—I don't know what that means. I don't have family anymore. I just have the two of you. And you promised you'd—"

"I didn't promise anything," Kazuchiyo replied reflexively, before he had absorbed any of Amai's meaning. He immediately regretted it, but even that was too late. Amai let him go. "Wait, Amai—"

"Fuck this," Amai muttered, and he clawed to his feet before Kazuchiyo could snag him.

"Amai, wait!" Kazuchiyo gave chase. When Amai paused to open the chamber's panel, Kazuchiyo took his arm. "Please don't."

Amai shoved his hand off and darted outside. When he stumbled over his feet Kazuchiyo was able to catch him again, and again he yanked free. "Get off me!" he snapped, and without looking back he broke into a full sprint toward the rear of the keep.

Kazuchiyo followed, but Amai was too fast for him. The little beast threw himself into a different chamber, and when Kazuchiyo rounded the turn, all he could see were Amai's feet as he climbed into the ceiling of an open closet. He ran to the opening, palms smacking against the wall as he halted. "Amai!" he shouted after him, angry and distraught, but Amai was already in the castle's bones and swiftly gone.

Kazuchiyo sagged in defeat, and he had little choice but to return to Yagi's small chamber. As he lowered himself to his knees alongside his lover, quivering in frustration, a tug to the leg of his hakama startled him.

Yagi was peering up at him with one half-lidded eye. "What's he so mad about?"

"It's... nothing." Kazuchiyo wiped the tears from his eyes in the hopes that Yagi hadn't seen them, and then lay down beside him, where Amai had been just minutes ago. "He'll be fine. Go back to sleep. You need it."

Yagi grumbled something and closed his eye. He was very quickly unconscious again, and Kazuchiyo stayed at his side through to morning.

CHAPTER TWENTY-THREE

Kazuchiyo awoke to the sound of a very quiet, very timid, "Excuse me?"

He sat up and checked on Yagi first: asleep still, though uncomfortably so. He took a moment to compose his appearance as best he could and moved to the chamber's sliding panel. "Yes?"

"Excuse me," the voice said again, and Kazuchiyo opened the screen to reveal little Danmaru, one hand clutching his mother's kimono, the other fastened around a small sheet of paper.

"Sorry to disturb you," said Lady Anisha. Though she had changed into new clothes and cleaned the soot from her face, Kazuchiyo could still smell the fire on her. A pair of Kibaku samurai stood guard a few steps behind. "My son wanted to give you something, from the two of us."

She touched the top of Danmaru's head, and he gingerly held up the paper. Though mystified, Kazuchiyo accepted and unfolded the gift. On it in very simple, childish brushstrokes was written the character for gratitude.

Kazuchiyo smiled, though the expression felt pained. "I should thank *you*," he said as he refolded the paper and tucked it into his robe. "You showed great courage last night. It inspired me to be courageous too."

Danmaru ducked shyly into his mother's side. Anisha smiled as she stroked his hair. "That's kind of you to say, but we thank you all the same. Not only for your efforts on our behalf, but for every soldier now in this fort."

Kazuchiyo tried not to let show the pang of guilt and grief her well-meant words caused him. "I only did what I felt I must."

"There's a private room available to you upstairs if you need it," Anisha offered. "Not everything of yours could be salvaged from the great keep, but there's fresh clothing and clean water."

It was only then that Kazuchiyo realized he was still clad in his underrobe, hands and hair stained with ash. He tightened his belt in embarrassment. "Yes, thank you. If you'll excuse me, I think I'll go there now."

"I'd be happy to show you the way."

She did so, and there she and Danmaru bowed their heads in gratitude one more time before leaving Kazuchiyo to his privacy. He wiped as much of the soot and dirt from his skin as he could, combed it from his hair, and redressed in a clean, blue hitatare and hakama.

He then spent a few minutes more in the chamber alone, composing himself for whatever might come next.

A strained and weary aura had fallen over the lesser keep. Other than the few small rooms set aside for the lords, ladies, and generals, every other chamber was crammed full with wounded soldiers and those tending to them. They spilled out into hallways and crowded the porches and balconies. Kazuchiyo headed out into the courtyard seeking fresh air, only to find those whose injuries were less severe gathered on every path and stretch of grass. Storage huts and even the fortress's small shrine had been converted to barracks and triage. The sun was still not very high, casting long, gray shadows over the exhausted armies. To one side, a man from Sakka fastened his indigo headband around the wounded forehead of one of Jisu's nagamaki wielders, and to another, a Kibaku samurai still in his armor instructed Zaiga's Suyama troops in replacing their worn and severed cords. Kazuchiyo recognized this man as one of the two who had ridden to his aid alongside Yagi in the field.

Kazuchiyo approached, and the man paused in his work to offer him a deep bow. "Lord Aritaka."

Kazuchiyo bowed his head. "Sir, forgive me for not knowing your name, but I wanted to thank you for your service last night."

The samurai was at least twice his age, and he seemed a bit embarrassed by the attention. "My name is of no consequence. It was my honor to serve."

"There was a man from Sakka who made it back with us, wounded by an arrow. Do you know where I might find him?"

The samurai looked confused at first, but as he seemed to realize that Kazuchiyo's intentions came from concern, a grave sincerity overtook his features. "Lordship, he died in the night from his wound."

"Oh." Kazuchiyo's shoulders fell. "I see. Thank you."

He started to turn, but then the Kibaku samurai cleared his throat, and he looked back. The man bowed to him again. "He would have been honored by your care," he said, and the other young soldiers watching them bowed their heads in respect.

Kazuchiyo swallowed and was not certain what to think. He returned the courtesy and then continued on.

He soon learned that the Oomiyari and their allies had not attempted any further attacks during the few short hours he had spent asleep. In the light of day the enemy's numbers were more certain—nearly six thousand between the two armies, who were now setting up camp in preparation of a long siege. Naoya had yet to leave his post, though he had still taken Kazuchiyo's advice: he sat in a corner of the guard tower, asleep.

After touring the grounds to reaffirm the situation, Kazuchiyo returned to the lesser keep. His fingers tingled restlessly and he considered over and over where he ought to apply himself, with everyone else working so diligently. But he could not devote himself to any task without checking again on his injured lover. He entered Yagi's small room and was surprised to find Purnima there, gently laying a sleeping Amai down on the mat next to Yagi.

"I found him asleep in the walls when I was looking for more spies," she said quietly. "I did not want him to wake up alone like that."

Kazuchiyo grimaced; he did not necessarily agree that Amai would think the same. "Thank you," he said anyway. "Let's speak outside so we don't wake them."

Purnima followed him back outside the room. He expected that she would immediately take her leave, but she stayed for a moment, and he took the opportunity to ask, "Are you all right? Everyone said you fought like a lion last night."

"Shuyun people have never seen lions," Purnima replied, gathering herself up proudly. "Your sister and I fought like *tigers*."

Kazuchiyo smiled. "You always do. Do you know where Mahiro is now? I'm embarrassed that I didn't check up on her as well."

"She was sleeping when I left," said Purnima, but then her cheeks reddened. Though she was no longer in her armor, she was still dressed in her attire from the dance the night before, and she tugged the collar of her blouse up to try to hide her face. "She will need it when we fight back."

Kazuchiyo's fond amusement was cut short by her choice of words. "Fight back?" he echoed. "I'm not certain we will. Lord Koedzuka and General Sasahara are confident we can outlast them in a siege."

"We can," Purnima agreed begrudgingly. "But what a waste. Their army is big, not strong."

Kazuchiyo thought of Oomiyari Jakusai atop his great, black steed and suppressed a shudder. "Some of them are plenty strong. They're from the capital—please don't underestimate them."

Purnima shook her head with disdain. "Their army is a saucer of wine," she said, holding her hand in front of her, palm up. "It looks still and strong, but with one general dead"—she flicked the side of her hand with the other and then wiggled her fingers for effect—"it sloshes."

Kazuchiyo frowned pensively. "If only killing their generals was so simple."

"Mahiro had help from my lord last night. Next time, I'll take the west flank myself. Trust me."

"I would never doubt you, but I'm not sure we can even get outside the castle as things stand now." Kazuchiyo sighed, but he did offer her a reassuring smile. "Thank you, Lady Purnima. I'll keep your counsel close to heart."

Purnima nodded, satisfied, and she moved on to her duties just as a familiar trio approached from the courtyard: General Zaiga, with his old captain and Shigeyuki in tow. As they bowed to each other, Kazuchiyo braced himself for another scolding.

"Excuse me, lordship," said Zaiga, and already Kazuchiyo could hear the fatherly concern in his tone. "It's not my place to check up on you, but I was hoping you wouldn't mind if I did, all the same."

"I thought you might," replied Kazuchiyo. "Though let me first ask if the three of you are well. It was a hard-fought battle outside the gate."

Shigeyuki lifted his head. He was still in his armor, but it looked as though he had made an effort to clean it, and his face, though still weary, was more alert than it had been a few hours before. "Your lordship is very kind to ask," he said with practiced manners. "We are very well."

"I'm glad to hear it." If only they had better privacy Kazuchiyo would have liked to offer some greater comfort, but he hoped the sincerity of his voice was enough.

"He is my son and heir, and his safety is my personal responsibility," said Zaiga. Now the quiet sternness came into his face, which Kazuchiyo remembered so well from his boyhood. "As is yours."

Kazuchiyo swallowed. "Excuse me, General, but will you walk with me? There are many soldiers at rest here in the keep, and I don't wish to disturb them."

Zaiga nodded, but before he and Kazuchiyo could move away, Shigeyuki cleared his throat. "I was hoping to congratulate Yagi-douji on his prowess last night," he said. "Is he here?"

"He... yes, but he still sleeps." Kazuchiyo hoped his smile was not too much like a grimace. "He's earned it, so please leave him be a while longer."

Shigeyuki and the captain bowed with understanding and respect, and Kazuchiyo and Zaiga continued on. Kazuchiyo did not trust even the private room upstairs with walls so thin, and so they walked together along the keep's outer engawa, like two samurai of command surveying the troops.

"I know what's on your mind," Kazuchiyo preempted his uncle. "You must have heard that I was outside the walls last night."

"I did. You must also know what I have to say about it."

"I do." Kazuchiyo forced himself to keep his chin high. "I did what I felt I must, same as you did when *you* went over the wall."

Zaiga frowned at him. "I have always been ready to lay down my life for the dragon banner. That is my duty. Staying alive is yours."

After the words he had shared with Amai the night before, Kazuchiyo's heart didn't have the strength for another argument on that front, and he quickly relented. "I know, and I'm sorry that I caused you concern, even after the fact. I've learned my lesson."

"Good." Zaiga sighed with relief. "I am glad to hear it. The Oomiyari will give up on this siege before long. There's no need for you to put yourself in any further danger."

It was Kazuchiyo's turn to frown. They were opposite the main keep now, a handful of servants still moving in and out as they took stock of what could be salvaged and how much reconstruction would be necessary. "I worry, though," he admitted. "Even if Master Mutsuyama marches his entire army home again for the season, without my head they won't have accomplished their goal. They will try again."

"Even the shogun's spies will have a difficult time infiltrating so far into the east once we've quit this place. We will be ready for them if they try."

"That's not entirely what I mean." Kazuchiyo paused then, watching as a pair of young women met outside the blackened entrance to the keep. One was trying to comfort the other, who was splashing her eyes with water from a gourd, as if to dislodge ash. "They will certainly get revenge on Jisu for rejecting their magistrate, who may still be vulnerable come spring. Izuho and even Kibaku will still be targets for the shogun's ire. If only there was some way to finish this more decisively, to help safeguard them from another attack as soon as the winter thaws…"

He realized then that Zaiga was watching him very closely, concerned and perhaps also disappointed. "That you have such care for your allies is admirable," Zaiga said gently. "However, they have lived in the capital's shadow for a long time. It is not up to you to decide their fates."

"Isn't it?" Kazuchiyo replied, fresh turmoil stewing within his ribs. "I've brought war and ruin on them in Aritaka's name, but still…" He shook his head. "I can't wash my hands of all this, not now."

"I'm not asking you to." Zaiga stepped even closer so he could lower his voice. "But your first duty is to your homeland," he reminded Kazuchiyo gravely. "It's important that we conserve our strength and our soldiers here—and your safety most of all. Once we've retaken Suyama, we can rid ourselves of Aritaka and have peace at last. The kind of peace your father hoped for."

"Peace," Kazuchiyo echoed, watching the two women again as they each took a deep breath and then returned to their work. "Maybe he was naive to think it could be that easy."

"Young lord," said Zaiga, the admonishment in his tone

much clearer now. "I know you have been through a great deal recently, but I won't hear you speak ill of your father's convictions like that."

Kazuchiyo lowered his eyes. All he could think of in that moment was his father's hand trembling around the grip of his spear. He knew better than anyone the limitations of his father's conviction. "Uncle, forgive me," he said. "I will of course always strive to do what's best for our home. But I'm not my father." He faced Zaiga seriously. "I will have to find my own path toward peace."

Zaiga was quiet, but he nodded, and then he took a step back again so he could bow at the waist. "I understand."

They parted, and with a strange kind of conviction, Kazuchiyo returned to the small room in the keep Anisha had offered him. Though he could not say his heart was quiet, as I had suggested, it was laid open and desperate. Perhaps this was the next best thing. He sat down in the center of the room and untied the ribbon around his wrist. He closed his eyes as he rolled his two beads around in his hands and at last clenched one in each palm. He took in a long, slow breath.

The rest of the keep was a tumultuous backdrop unfit for concentration: the moans of injured soldiers, the patter of socked feet up and down the wooden halls, and the continuation of battle preparations outside all threatened his concentration. Even so he held my counsel close to heart and imagined each of his closed hands as weathered brass vessels, and the bead in each a small, black coal. He remembered the heat spreading up his arm when he slew Nanpa, and again when he drew his sword at Etsugo to save Yagi's life. He remembered the many times he had watched Naoya cast a spell or prepare a message, and the fire bursting from Mutsuyama's arrows. But no matter how clear those recollections were, and no matter his determination, he could not honestly sense any particular warmth from either bead.

Frustration began to settle in, but Kazuchiyo shook his head, loosened his fists, and tried again. He thought instead of Master Iomori's cold hand strongly clasping his wrist. How easily she had drawn the past from his bead, images and knowledge flashing between them both. Each of the small beads he clasped bore histories within them, and he tried to picture each departed soul as brushstrokes on a page, just as I had described them.

That concentration faltered when he was reminded of the careless words Amai had spoken while descending the hill, and those musings that had, at the time, seemed so disturbing overtook his fragile curiosity. All at once the heat rushed up from his palm, and across the black of his closed eyelids, he glimpsed a memory that wasn't his: Yagi-douji barreling down on him, the cross-blade spear racing toward his face. He felt the metal shatter his teeth and carve across his cheeks a bloody smile, and reflexively he let go with his right hand. The black bead bounced to the tatami.

Kazuchiyo stared down at it, his heart pounding fiercely. He had seen Yagi enraged plenty of times, but it was another experience entirely to be on the other end of his spear. As he took a few breaths to calm himself, he was encouraged to realize that he had let go of the correct bead: his own red stone he still clasped in his left palm.

Wondering if that was enough to prove some measure of talent, Kazuchiyo gulped and then collected the bead. He closed his eyes and again passed the two beads back and forth between his hands until he could no longer be positive which was which. With that uncomfortable memory still close in his mind, it took very little effort for him to identify that the bead that held it now sat in his left palm. Deciding to let it be for the moment, he focused instead on the other, curious to see what vestiges lay at the bottom of his shallow well.

His mind's eye seized almost immediately on another too familiar image: Oomiyari Jakusai atop his horse, the blade of his kamayari slicing forward. He thought at first that painful recollections were intruding on his concentration again, only to be awoken from that concern by the feeling of cold steel stabbing into his unprotected armpit. The strength flooded out of him as Jakusai raked his weapon downward, splitting his armor open at the seams, along with several ribs.

This time, Kazuchiyo forced himself to retain his grip on the bead. He followed the memory through to its end: poor old soldier Mizutane succumbed so quickly to blood loss and suffocation. As obvious as it should have been, Kazuchiyo was still shocked to see himself through the man's eyes. He shivered through the old man's memory of encroaching demise, of his anguish at not being able to finish speaking his full name before his lord. He experienced death more closely than a mortal man is meant to more than once.

Kazuchiyo shook, but he was determined to finish what he had started; he had promised the old soldier that his family would be tended to, and after so much heartache and guilt, a small chamber in his heart was desperate to not fail in that as well. His own recollections leading up to that tragic sacrifice helped him in reconstructing that night: the pride Mizutane had felt in earning his place alongside Captain Nishigame, to fight alongside Yagi-douji after so many years of wielding his spear among the foot soldiers; the horror and awe of witnessing the battle at Chibatake Bridge the year before, granting Kazuchiyo his only glimpse of Yagi as he had been then, howling across the worn planks at Kibaku troops outnumbering them three to one; even the rainy plains of Shimegahara, just as Kazuchiyo had once wondered, where Mizutane fought for Aritaka for no reason other than survival for himself and his family, with no idea of the significance of the battle beyond that.

His family: a wife, a son, a daughter-in-law, and grandchildren. They lived together in a small village close to Ninari Castle, where his son worked as a blacksmith, and their wives wove baskets and hats for those in the fort. His daughter-in-law had been with child, last he heard. She was a bit old to be giving birth, and he worried for her. He hoped for a grandson, a strong, young boy who would be known as Mizutane, as he was.

Kazuchiyo opened his eyes and his hand, and he gazed down at the tiny bead that held so much. A stranger's entire history lay in his palm, and in the other, hundreds like it. He sat there quietly for a long time, humbled by the weight of such a simple little thing. To those of the strongest character, it is a revelation that never truly fades.

As time passed, however, that melancholy and awe were replaced by a strangling anger. Their enemy was a powerful onmyouji, who clearly had been employing his necromantic arts for many years. He wielded the lives of his countrymen with more careless violence than an archer spends his quiver. He had manipulated lords against each other and their own best interests, attacked civilians with fire in the dead of night, and, most painful to Kazuchiyo, turned his own hopes for unity and peace against him. Here was a snake he did not fully know, who nevertheless had read his intentions with ease and was poised to take everything away from him.

And this villain, sent forth by the shogun, Oomiyari Ryousai himself. What callous beast sat in the great halls of the capital who could feel no shame in unleashing such a tyrant? Did such a ruler deserve the blessing of an emperor and the loyalty of his people? Kazuchiyo remembered the hate that Jakusai had fixed on him, and he felt that hate himself in equal measure.

An hour later, he climbed to the top of the tower for a proper meal. Lord Koedzuka, Beihou, and Lady Dada met with him there, sharing reports of casualties from the night before as well as the state of their rations. Once again, Beihou voiced his confidence that they could outlast the Oomiyari in a siege.

As they finished the meal, Kazuchiyo nudged his tray aside and said, "I think we should consider assassinating the onmyouji, Mutsuyama."

Koedzuka and Beihou stared back at him, incredulous, while Lady Dada gave an amused snort. After a moment had passed, Koedzuka gathered himself and asked, "How?"

"I don't know yet," Kazuchiyo admitted, "but it's an avenue

351

we should consider. Lady Purnima described the Oomiyari's army as a filled cup: larger than ours, but easily disturbed. They could have overwhelmed the gate last night, if not for Mahiro taking the general's head being so effective in routing them. If they lose Mutsuyama, they may abandon the siege."

"At least Naoya would finally be able to get some sleep then," said Beihou. "But I imagine it's easier said than done."

Koedzuka frowned, seeing how serious Kazuchiyo was. "The ladies Purnima and Mahiro are formidable, but we are completely pinned down now. We have no way to mount an attack, and only General Oihata has the means to combat Mutsuyama's magic." His voice hardened. "I will not risk him, not when we can just as easily wait them out here."

"Yes. We can wait." Kazuchiyo's gaze darted to Lady Dada, who seemed to already perfectly understand his meaning. "But I worry what it will mean for you come spring. Once our armies have returned to Sakka, we won't be able to return until after spring planting. That will leave the shogun plenty of time to try his hand against you before we can support you."

"They won't catch us unaware again," Beihou promised.

"Of course they won't," spoke up Lady Dada. "You'll have plenty of warning as they're chewing through Jisu."

Koedzuka and Beihou exchanged a look, but she continued before either could interrupt. "I agree with Lord Kazumune. We must make more of a stand here than simply waiting for them to leave, or else we will each face the same crisis again. Killing their onmyouji will send the message that we are not to be trifled with."

Koedzuka stroked his beard, still appearing unconvinced. "We don't have the means. Even with our spies and Oihata's magic, we can't hope to sneak an assassin into a camp of that size. And, as I understand, we may not be able to depend on the brute strength of Yagi-douji either."

Kazuchiyo swallowed. "No, I don't think we will. But I don't think going to Mutsuyama in his den is the answer."

Each caught on immediately; Beihou fixed Koedzuka with

a lopsided smile. "I don't think he's taken your advice to heart after all."

"I will not make you into bait," said Koedzuka firmly.

"I'm not leaving the castle again," Kazuchiyo reassured him. "There may be another way." Before Koedzuka could protest further, he added, "I don't have much of a plan yet at all. But I *am* trying to think of how it can be done. I'm asking that you all aid me."

Though Koedzuka and Beihou still looked hesitant, Lady Dada nodded with conviction. "I'm with you. After what that creature did to Agarigumo Temple, he deserves death and worse."

Koedzuka sighed, shaking his head. "I will speak to Oihata. For now, it's more important that we consider there'll be another attack tonight. There's no guarantee that the Oomiyari are planning to wait us out either." He hesitated a moment and then added, "But yes, we will try to think of some method of eliminating Mutsuyama, if we can."

"Thank you," said Kazuchiyo, bowing his head. "We'll speak again tonight."

Everyone agreed, and they separated to continue preparations.

Once again, Kazuchiyo returned to Yagi's room at the base of the keep. As he approached the closed door panel, he could hear Yagi's voice, and his heart skipped with relief and, shamefully, some trepidation. He had yet to come up with any reliable way to address his lover in the aftermath of all that had happened. Still, he could not bear to hesitate and rushed inside.

Yagi was sitting up on his own power. He looked pale in the room's poor lighting, and his face was drawn tight with strain. Amai sat beside him, and he flinched when Kazuchiyo entered. He kept his attention on Yagi, saying, "Well, he's already here. Do you want me to stay?"

Yagi's brow furrowed more deeply, and Kazuchiyo stood frozen in the doorway watching them, sick with curiosity to know what their conversation just then had been. "Thanks, but no," Yagi said at last. "Do you mind giving us a minute?"

"Sure."

Amai stood. He avoided Kazuchiyo's gaze as he headed for the door, looking more embarrassed than angry, and Kazuchiyo had no idea how to approach him either.

"Amai," he said, and he started to reach for him but then stopped himself.

Amai continued to avoid his eyes, but he did pause in the doorway. "Um. We'll talk later, okay?"

"All right." Kazuchiyo gave him a wide berth, reminding himself how he perhaps ought to have respected Amai's wishes the first time. Though he hated to watch him leave, he closed the panel behind him and then moved to Yagi's side.

"Yagi..." Kazuchiyo kneeled down next to his lover's right arm, which he was holding close to his chest. Though the bandages looked to have been recently changed, it was clear that the wound had swelled overnight, with terrible bruises stretching out beyond the bounds of fabric. Kazuchiyo ached with sympathy. "It's good to see you up," he said. "How are... how bad is it?"

"It hurts," Yagi admitted, and Kazuchiyo hated to see how clearly that pain was carved into his face. There was already sweat on his brow from the strain. "A lot. But at least it's still attached."

"Yes." Kazuchiyo shuddered and looked to Yagi's right hand cradled in his lap. "Can you..."

"Yeah, they still work." Yagi wiggled his fingers weakly. "But that hurts, too, so I'm trying not to move them either."

"No, that's... of course." Kazuchiyo swallowed, hating how timid and frightened he sounded. He was supposed to be taking care of his lover when he needed him most. "Do you not want me to be here?" he found himself asking anyway. "If you want me to leave—"

"No," Yagi said quickly, and unlike Amai he sought and held Kazuchiyo's gaze. "Don't go. That was…" Yagi's nose scrunched with distaste. "I was just telling Amai I didn't know what I'd say to you when you came back."

Kazuchiyo wanted to be relieved that at least Yagi wanted him to stay, but it was difficult to indulge in the emotion when there was still so much difficulty ahead. "I'm not entirely sure what to say either," he admitted. "But I want you to know, I'm—"

"I'm sorry," Yagi interrupted him, and he lowered his eyes. "I told you I'd kill him for you, but I couldn't."

"What? No." Kazuchiyo leaned forward to take Yagi's hand, though gently. "No, *I'm* the one who should apologize. It's only because of me that you were in that position."

Yagi shook his head. "We talked about that too," he said, making Kazuchiyo wish all over again he had managed to eavesdrop on some of that conversation. "None of that matters because I was *supposed* to beat him. I didn't. I don't want to hear you apologize about it."

Kazuchiyo wilted. He wanted to say something reassuring, whatever it might have been that Yagi wanted or needed to hear, but his confidence in this arena was still so much less than it had once been. "All right," he said. "Then I don't want to hear you apologize either. Only our enemies are to blame."

Yagi's frown deepened. Perhaps he wasn't ready to accept that much. So Kazuchiyo licked his lips and tried again. "Is there anything I can do for you now?"

Yagi considered that for a moment and then gestured with his other hand. "Come on this side."

Kazuchiyo did so, and as soon as he had settled, Yagi twisted his good arm firmly around his back. Though Kazuchiyo tried to be cautious in embracing him in return, Yagi drew him so tight and close it was difficult to breathe at first. "Oh, Yagi," Kazuchiyo murmured, though he managed to catch himself before offering more apologies. He drew Yagi's head to his shoulder, stroked his hair, and rubbed the back of his neck. "It'll be all right. All you need to worry about now is getting your strength back. You lost so much blood."

Yagi's greater frame wilted into him. "I don't remember much... after," he confessed into the collar of Kazuchiyo's robe. "I'm sorry I didn't protect you."

"You did, though," Kazuchiyo rushed to assure him. "If not for you and Amai, I'd be dead. Hush now." Kazuchiyo's voice grew rough with emotion, but he fought not to let it get the better of him. "You protected *everyone*. You did enough."

Yagi went quiet for a moment, though his grip remained tight and shaky. "It's broken."

"It might not be," Kazuchiyo replied automatically. "I'm sure it hurts, but—"

"It's broken," Yagi repeated. "Not completely, but I felt it." Yagi stretched his shoulders but then had to stop, grimacing with pain. "It's not my first broken arm."

Kazuchiyo fell quiet, stunned, as he tried to make sense of those words. He had known all about Yagi's scars before knowing the man himself, but he couldn't remember if Yagi had ever admitted to having broken a bone before. "Then it won't be your first time healing from a broken arm," he said once he had his composure back. "Be gentle with it for now. It'll be all right." Deciding to trust his instincts after all, he turned his lips close to Yagi's ear and said, "I love you, and I'm going to take care of you. It'll all be all right."

Yagi shuddered, and he nodded against Kazuchiyo's neck as if not trusting himself to speak. Kazuchiyo held him tight, soothing him with tender murmurs and wordless sincerity as best he could.

CHAPTER TWENTY-FOUR

Kazuchiyo spent the rest of the morning with Yagi, tending to and encouraging him. By afternoon, however, Yagi started to become anxious and asked to be left alone for a while. Kazuchiyo could tell he was worried about who might see him in the state he was in, as time drew on and his and his lord's absence became noticed. Though Kazuchiyo hated to do it, he kissed Yagi's forehead one more time and let him be.

He stood out in the courtyard for a while, once again watching the soldiers and workers bustle about their duties. Mahiro was out and about by then, back in her armor and guiding their efforts. "Get those spears tightened!" she shouted to young samurai gathered around the armory. "Fill those quivers! You think those gold-dusted buffoons are going to sit on their asses while we feast? When they come pounding on our gates, I don't want to hear one complaint that we weren't ready for them!"

Kazuchiyo silently thanked fate for blessing him with such an enviable sister. Her cheerful badgering put everyone to work more efficiently than threats or fear would have. As he watched, another familiar figure emerged from the armory: Chikakuni in his armor, carrying a handsome longbow. He spotted Kazuchiyo and moved to join him.

"My lady asked me for the heaviest longbow in the fort," he said. "I hope this will do the trick."

Kazuchiyo looked the weapon over, impressed; he certainly could not have drawn it himself. "I can't imagine anything else here would outdo it. Let's hope Mutsuyama isn't hiding at the very back of their army, but even if he were, she could hit him with that."

"I imagine that's the idea." Chikakuni gave him a quick look-over. "How're you holding up, if you don't mind me asking?"

"I'm..." Kazuchiyo hesitated, unsure. He felt raw, jagged, and angry, like a fevered wound. "I'll be ready when the time comes," he settled on. "Though Lady Dada is a step ahead of me, it seems. I don't even know yet what my weapon will be."

Chikakuni straightened up. "Ah, that reminds me. Come here; there's something set aside for you."

He led Kazuchiyo to a small storehouse near the main keep that had remained mostly untouched by the fire. "Apparently most of the damage to the main keep was on the upper levels. Not many of yours or Lady Dada's personal effects survived, but they did find some items from your room that had been stuffed through a hole in the alcove floor. The place is crawling with shinobi tunnels, and they protected a few things."

"Amai..." Kazuchiyo gulped. "You haven't seen him lately, have you?"

"Not since last night." Chikakuni brought them to a halt next to one of the shelves, where various items from the keep had been stowed as they were recovered. "Is he all right? That was quite a hit he took."

"It was," Kazuchiyo said, ill with the memory. "But yes, I think so."

"Good." Chikakuni pulled a sword off the shelf and offered it up. "You probably have him to thank for saving this."

Kazuchiyo accepted the katana, brow raised in surprise. "Itogiri. I'd almost forgotten about it." Though the scabbard had a few soot stains and the cords were singed, when he clicked the blade out, it appeared undamaged. He sheathed it once more and threaded it through his belt. "Its previous owner seemed to think it was worth boasting over. I wonder if it was fate as much as Amai that rescued it."

"It's a fox's nature to hoard valuable things." Chikakuni smirked, then reached back onto the shelf for one more item. "There was this too."

It was a narrow, lacquered case, blackened by fire, but when Kazuchiyo opened it, the contents were again mostly unharmed: his bamboo flute. Kazuchiyo held it in both hands, momentarily overcome with emotion. That Amai would take the time to secure his belongings, in a burning castle surrounded by the shogun's assassins, made him ache more than ever to find and reconcile with him. "Thank you," he said, discarding the case and tucking the flute into his sleeve. He bowed his head.

"It's not me you should thank," said Chikakuni, and the two of them left the storeroom. "But if you must, why not make it into a song? We heard some of your playing at Etsugo. I'm sure the soldiers here would appreciate it too."

"Yes," Kazuchiyo said distractedly. "Yes, I think I will."

He made his way to the top of the lesser keep, where a small but handsome room lay open. Judging by the poetry adorning its walls, it appeared to be Naoya's dedicated guest chamber. Kazuchiyo hoped he would not mind the intrusion and opened the window so he could climb out onto the rooftop. There he took a deep breath and looked out over the fortress.

From so high up, the precarity of their situation became even more clear to him. The walls were manned with guards that had been rotated for regular breaks, and soldiers occupied every available space within the baileys, and yet he could not banish a feeling of ill ease. Beyond their gates to the south and east, their enemies in their camps spread out in terrifying numbers. It reminded him of something Waseba Yuuichirou had once said to him when overlooking his hillside battleground.

"Watch, as the wave breaks on the shore," Kazuchiyo

quoted with apprehension. He wondered if Waseba's black soul resided somewhere deep within his bead as well, or if perhaps it had already been spent, disintegrated like ash.

Somewhere far below in that camp, Mutsuyama was likely plotting another attack. Amai's blow to Oomiyari Jakusai may or may not have claimed his life, but either way, he would not suffer the shogun's enemies to escape with such a victory to their names. To wait for his sense or his mercy to break the siege was no option in Kazuchiyo's mind. He thought of Yagi wilting against his chest, despite all his bravery feeling in that moment as small as young Danmaru had. He thought of Amai crumpling beneath the butt of Jakusai's spear, of a bold Sakka warrior firing into the shogun's men, even with the arrow that would later kill him embedded in his back. The quiet anger in Lady Dada's voice when she spoke of Agarigumo Temple, and the piles of charred, innocent bodies Mutsuyama had likely used as fodder for his magic. Chikakuni's father buried in Chouwa Valley, and General Umafusa's head tumbling from its shoulders. His brother's haunted face as he stumbled away from his first battlefield, so terribly reminiscent of another brother taken from him too young.

Kazuchiyo pulled the flute out of his sleeve, took a deep breath, and began to play.

He started slow. Each note he drew out almost as long as his breath would hold, clear and strong and patient. It was the kind of disciplined, elegant music that he had been raised to believe the capital enjoyed, with all its structured refinement. Simple notes each played to a striking, pretentious perfection. Having once been a member of that courtly setting, I can attest these impressions of his were quite correct, and there can be no doubt that Mutsuyama immediately recognized each was meant for him.

But over time, Kazuchiyo's tempo quickened. He began to sculpt his notes into melody, an ancient ballad that, like much courtly music, had been written to follow the meter of poetry. Deep into his memory he reached, calling forth the musical tales of his youth, which lived in the hearts of any born in the Dragonlands of the east. It was a song of old Touyun, from a time even before the emperor when the territories of eastern Shuyun were ruled by one powerful warrior. Touyun no Kami they had called him in death, its lord and its guardian, descendant not of the gods but of the land and its people. Even after the emperor had claimed dominion over Suyama and its neighbors, and after the shogun claimed authority in his name, never had the warriors of the east forgotten those days when they ruled only themselves.

Kazuchiyo summoned forth those lullabies from his youth, filling each note with pride and defiance. His song twisted and swirled down from the roof of the lesser keep, lifting and falling like a serpent's spiraling flight. Though his gaze never left the gold banners on the horizon, we can well imagine the faces of the samurai below turning up toward him in inspiration and wonder. Four armies, which had only the year before been bitter armies, or else even more bitter servants, now joined in survival against the ruthless vanguard of a vain and craven ruler. Several thousand ears belonging to friend and foe attuned to Kazuchiyo's flute, each sensing from its rising, racing music a powerful declaration of war.

The song ended sharply, definitively, and Kazuchiyo lowered his flute to catch his breath. He glared into the Oomiyari camp and dared even one banner to move.

"Sure sounds like you've made up your mind this time," said Amai.

Kazuchiyo turned so sharply that his foot slid against the roof tiles; though there was little danger of him actually losing his balance, Amai's hand shot out through the open window to snag his belt, steadying him. He smiled sheepishly. "Sorry."

"Amai…" Kazuchiyo held very still even after Amai had let him go, fearing that any sudden or unwise movement would startle the creature away. He watched as Amai climbed up to sit in the open window sill, looking for all the world as casual as you please, as if no hardship had passed between them at all.

"I haven't heard that one before," Amai continued easily, "but even I could tell what it meant. Mutsuyama won't be happy."

"Good." With one moment more to steel his courage, Kazuchiyo tucked the flute back into his sleeve and joined Amai. Just like they had many nights ago when first arriving at Rongi, they sat together in the window, their knees bumping.

"I think I have you to thank for saving my flute, among other things," Kazuchiyo said.

"Yup, that was me." Amai shrugged. "I couldn't get up to Koedzuka's room at first, so I circled back to yours, thinking maybe some of the shogun's spies might look for you there. I managed to save a few things." His lip quirked. "I'm sure you're not *too* upset about losing Aritaka's armor."

"Not at all. Thank you." Kazuchiyo frowned, all the courage he'd built for himself through his music beginning to slip away when faced with just how nonchalantly Amai was approaching their first conversation in some time. "Amai, I—"

"I'm sorry," Amai interrupted. He gave another shrug. "I shouldn't have run away from you like that. That was"—he sighed, eyes rolling away in embarrassment—"pretty childish, I guess."

"No, you were right." Kazuchiyo reached down; they were forced so close together within the sill that he was able to find and grip Amai's ankle, like a tether. "I should have listened to you when you said not to talk about it then. I'm sorry."

"You weren't wrong, I just knew it wasn't going to end well. I wasn't..." Amai paused, frowning around the words. "I wasn't ready," he concluded, and in fact he did not look any more prepared then, his guise of carelessness beginning to slip. "I knew..."

He stopped again, staring off into the distance. Kazuchiyo held his breath and bit his tongue, determined this time to be patient, and at last it paid off. "I knew something was going to happen," Amai continued, running his fingers back through his hair. He was still trying not to let sentiment get the better of him, and beginning to fail at it. "From the moment you all showed up at the east wall, I just knew you were going to do something foolish and get yourself killed. I could *see* it. An arrow through the head or the back, or... I'm not usually like that, but it felt like a bona fide premonition."

Kazuchiyo moved his fingers gently against Amai's ankle, not trusting himself to speak but eager to bestow what little comfort he could. Amai's lips twisted in a tiny, brief smile. "Then that kamayari asshole showed up. As soon as he got off his horse, I realized... it wasn't you in my premonition. It was *him*." His smile deepened and grew crooked. "I was so worried about you, it didn't occur to me that I should have been worried about Yagi too. *He* was the one my gut was warning me about."

Kazuchiyo licked his lips, remembering how Amai had dropped down from the horse at the start of Jakusai and Yagi's duel. "You knew from the first hit he was going to lose, didn't you?" he asked quietly.

Amai nodded and then kept his head down, glaring at his own hands in his lap. "I guess I just wasn't ready for that."

"It was shocking for me, too—for everyone. He's never lost like that before." The memory shoved emotion up Kazuchiyo's throat, but he swallowed it back; he was determined to focus on his lover in front of him. "We were all scared."

Amai's faced screwed up briefly, and he gave a short shake of his head. "It wasn't just that. I felt *guilty*. Why *wasn't* I more scared for him? It's been the three of us all this time, but I was so busy trying to make sure the two of you were getting along, I guess I didn't realize... Fuck."

Amai twisted, tugging his ankle out of Kazuchiyo's hand as he let both legs dangle inside the room. Kazuchiyo snagged his robe, afraid he was about to bolt again, but Amai only leaned over his knees and scrubbed his face with both hands. "I hate this," he complained as Kazuchiyo moved to sit next to him. "It's so stupid."

Kazuchiyo rested his hand against Amai's back. "You didn't realize how much he meant to you too?" he supposed

363

gently. "You love him."

Amai let out a long sigh. "Yeah," he muttered, rubbing his stomach. "Pretty fucking dumb, having to admit that now, after all this time, huh?"

"Of course not." Kazuchiyo wrapped his arm around Amai's slender shoulders and tugged him closer, a strange feeling of relief washing over him to see Amai, teasing little scamp that he was, so emotional over the lover they shared, then relieved even more when Amai leaned gratefully into him. "I've loved Yagi from the moment I laid eyes on him, I think. But you..." He chuckled into Amai's hair. "It took me a long time to admit to myself that I love you."

Amai shuddered and seemed to shrink beneath Kazuchiyo's arm. His breath hitched. Kazuchiyo held him tighter, saying, "But to be fair, you did almost assassinate me once."

Amai did not seem to appreciate his glibness turned against him at all; he tried to laugh, a frail and unconvincing sound, but his breath soon choked. Though he tried to hide beneath his hands, there was no disguising his tears. Kazuchiyo slid from the window so he could wrap Amai up with both arms and welcome him against his chest; feeling Amai wilt against him, cling to him, almost overwhelmed him with emotion of his own. But he held fast, stroking Amai's hair and reassuring himself that their argument had passed.

In time Amai collected himself and urged Kazuchiyo back so he could stand. "To be fair," he said, smirking even as he wiped his eyes with his sleeve, "I was going to be paid a lot of gold for that."

"Fair enough," Kazuchiyo agreed, and once Amai's hands were out of the way, he held him still for a kiss. Amai wilted into that, too, and he blushed in embarrassment once Kazuchiyo let him go. But even after that, Kazuchiyo cradled his cheeks, determined to have the final, serious word. "Thank you, Amai, for all the times you've saved my life. And Yagi's. Please don't feel guilty about anything you felt out there, because all that matters now is that we all survived thanks to you."

Amai squirmed, trying to shy away from that much sincerity being pinned to him. "Yagi said that, too, but neither of us actually remembers what happened after he got hurt. We think you made it up to make us feel better."

"You don't?" Kazuchiyo felt out the tender lump still healing near Amai's temple; he winced but held still. "You don't remember this?"

"No." Amai pushed Kazuchiyo's hand away so he could rub the welt himself. "I remember hearing Yagi's arm break," he said, face a little green. "And I felt my body move, but... that's it, until I woke up on the horse."

"You took my tanto and stabbed Oomiyari Jakusai in the thigh," Kazuchiyo told him without hesitation. "He and his men had to retreat. You very well might have killed him."

"Really?" Amai perked up, his brow furrowing as he tried to remember. He shrugged. "Well, at least I can feel better about that. Though we should probably go, before Oihata finds us trespassing in his room."

Seeing his desire for escape so blatant, Kazuchiyo nodded. He was pleased with the honesty he'd wrung from his ever-slippery companion and understood how raw it had left him. "Yes, you're right," he said, and he gave Amai one more kiss before letting him go. "I should rejoin our soldiers, but you ought to get more rest. Maybe stay with Yagi to keep him from getting too despondent?"

"Fine by me." The pair of them closed up Naoya's window and then headed out together. "He wouldn't talk about it too much yet, but I'm sure he's worried you'll leave him behind if he can't fight again."

"That's absurd," Kazuchiyo replied quickly, as much to Amai as to the frightened little impulse at the back of his mind. "I've told him before, my affection for him does not depend on his usefulness to me as a soldier."

"Yeah, but it's different now that it's actually a possibility that he's been crippled."

"He'll get better." Kazuchiyo led the way down the stairs,

ears alert for any soldiers that might be nearby. He wasn't certain yet how many knew the full extent of Yagi's injuries; better that it be kept to as few as possible, as long as the siege was underway. "He's healed from similar injuries before, he said so himself."

"Right, but…" Trailing behind, Amai took in a huge breath. "No, you're right. He'll get better. He always does."

They made their way down the keep, but just before reaching Yagi's room, Amai gave Kazuchiyo a tug. "Hey," he said, once again trying to cover his embarrassment with glib charisma. "How did you dig me out of the wall, anyway?"

"It was Purnima. She was hunting for shogun spies and found you, she said."

"Oh." Amai pulled a face. "Guess I'll never hear the end of that, then." He stepped past Kazuchiyo to reach the sliding panel that led into Yagi's room. "Go on and look pretty for the soldiers," he said, shooing Kazuchiyo on. "I'll let you know if he says anything important, or if we need you for something."

"Thank you," said Kazuchiyo, and before Amai could slip inside, he added, "And I really am sorry."

Amai hesitated, a smile forming and then cracking a little on his lips. "Me too," he replied, and he hurried on before emotion could get the better of him again. Feeling much the same way, Kazuchiyo headed outside.

He had barely made it into the courtyard when a young soldier in green Kibaku armor came racing up the path toward him. "Lord Aritaka!" he called, and he all but skidded into a bow in front of him. "Lord Aritaka, General Oihata has requested you at the wall! We've spotted movement within the enemy camp."

Kazuchiyo straightened, suppressing a shiver of dread at the thought that his provocations to Mutsuyama had been answered so swiftly. Reminding himself that a reaction had been his intention all along, and that he was equipped to meet the vile snake in kind, he nodded to the soldier. "I'll be there soon," he promised, and as the messenger scurried off to spread his news, Kazuchiyo sought out his men for fresh armor befitting a lord.

CHAPTER TWENTY-FIVE

By the time Kazuchiyo reached the southern gate, soldiers of all colors had sprung into action. Unlike the anxious bustle of the night before, however, each took to their tasks and positions with determined poise. There was no being caught off guard this time. In the center of the lower bailey, General Beihou had constructed himself a command post with banners flying, where he relayed orders with vigor to eager soldiers. Samurai formed ranks while weary archers relinquished their spots along the walls to fresher men. Junior ranks carried quivers full of arrows and gourds full of water up and down the scaffolding while iron pots full of oil were hoisted up to the guard towers. Every heart and mind was hardened for the coming siege.

Kazuchiyo approached Beihou flanked by half a dozen Sakka guards, who were now determined not to let him too far out of their sight. "General," he greeted the man, and he bowed. "What is the situation?"

"Too soon yet to tell," Beihou admitted with a grim smile. "Our scouts reported movement from both enemy camps. Either they're keen to throw themselves on my walls for sport, or they just want to position themselves closer to keep us from feeling too comfortable." He raised an eyebrow at Kazuchiyo. "Or maybe your audience just wanted a closer seat."

Kazuchiyo gathered himself up to his full height, fueling himself with the same conviction that had inspired his playing. "If so, I'm happy to play for Master Mutsuyama again, though I doubt he'll like it any more the second time."

Beihou laughed, and despite unhappy looks from Kazuchiyo's retainers, he stepped forward to thump Kazuchiyo heartily in the side. "No, I don't think he will! Not any more than he will like what we have to perform for him." He gestured toward the guard towers, where fires were already being stoked to heat the oil. "It'd take an army three times their size to tear these walls down. The sooner they tire themselves out trying, the sooner they run out of supplies and will be forced to retreat."

"I certainly hope so," Kazuchiyo replied, disguising his doubt. He looked to the tower west of the gate, where Naoya was up and about again, coordinating the soldiers there. "I'm going to take a look for myself, if you don't mind."

"Even if I did, I doubt it would dissuade you." Beihou bowed his head. "Be my guest."

Kazuchiyo thanked him and proceeded toward the tower. As he approached the gate, he took note that a larger number of Jisu's violet-armored archers had taken over a portion of the wall, Chikakuni among them, who waved to him from the scaffolding. Just as Kazuchiyo was wondering if he ought to check in with the man again, another group approached laden with arrows, headed by Lady Dada herself. She was dressed again in her full armor and carrying the heavy longbow that Chikakuni had ferreted out for her.

"Lady Dada," Kazuchiyo greeted her. "It's good to see you're again willing to defend the walls of Rongi."

"As if there's much choice," she replied coolly. "If those walls fall, our heads will line up very nicely at Mutsuyama's next meal." She hefted the bow. "Draw him close for me, and I'll take his head instead."

"I'll do everything in my power," Kazuchiyo promised,

and as she joined Chikakuni on the scaffolding, he joined Naoya in the tower.

"Don't feed it too hastily," Naoya was scolding one of the soldiers tending to the brazier at one end of the tower. "It will take them over an hour to reach us at this rate, and that wood will have to last the night. Be mindful."

Kazuchiyo moved to the forward rail, taking a moment to look over the scene for himself while Naoya was distracted. As the scouts and others had reported, there was definitely movement from the Oomiyari camp to the south and the Ba'nyuunuma camp to the east; banners that had once stood at the outskirts were now hoisted and moving onto the field for troops to form ranks around. They did not seem to be in a spectacular hurry, but already Kazuchiyo could feel tiny vibrations through the earth as thousands of soldiers began moving into position. He hoped very much that, somewhere among them, Mutsuyama was seething.

"Kazumune!" Having noticed him at last, Naoya hurried over. He was still in his robe from the night before, though now with his armor over it, his full, fiery righteousness holding exhaustion at bay. "It looks as though the shogun's mules are straining their yoke," he declared. "Well, they won't catch us off guard again! With all our men behind the walls, all they can do is fire arrows over top and hope for a few casualties while we pick them off from above."

"Yes, so it would seem," Kazuchiyo cautiously agreed. Though he hoped that Mutsuyama's temper had been roused so well that he was wasting his army's vigor and resources for pride's sake, he reminded himself that he did not know his adversary all that well. Certainly not as well as Mutsuyama had measured him. "Any man can see the strength of Rongi. He must know we intend to wait him out, and so will attack again at night to exhaust our soldiers and weaken our resolve."

Naoya scoffed. "Kibaku's resolve is without measure. All he will accomplish is demoralizing his own troops."

Kazuchiyo nodded, but as he stole another glance at Naoya,

he could not help but frown. It may very well have been true that no army, imperial or otherwise, could topple the stout-hearted Rongi through force, but it had taken only one master onmyouji to wreak havoc on its occupants. If the serpent lay rested while Kibaku's best defense stood ragged, breaching the walls may not be the only path to Kibaku's destruction.

Naoya caught him staring, and perhaps he saw through him as well, as some of that concern showed in his face. "Trust me, Kazumune," he said firmly regardless. "They will not shake noble Kibaku."

"I trust you," Kazuchiyo reassured him. "And I will assist however I can."

The Oomiyari took their time in preparing for the second night of the siege. From afternoon into evening they formed their ranks and beat their drums and waved their banners. As their tactic to stall for nightfall became ever clearer, Kazuchiyo convinced Naoya to share a light meal with him to keep their strength up. Naoya agreed, despite refusing to step down from the tower. As the hour dragged on, the energy within the castle grew tighter, each soldier's determination straining beneath so much time spent in suspense.

At long last, the general march began. The Oomiyari set out from their camp again in three regiments, just as Nomino's Ba'nyuunuma clan advanced on the east wall's no longer hidden entrance. As their footsteps rumbled along the rolling plains, they were joined by a cheer from further within Rongi's compound, and Kazuchiyo turned to look.

"Make way!" shouted Mahiro. She was once again in her armor atop mighty Suzumekage, fresh, white horse hair pouring down the back of her helmet. She brandished her naginata before her as soldiers parted gladly. "Make way! Where else does the Iron Gate stand if not at the front? Let even one little yellow worm crawl into this fortress, and by the god of war I swear to make even their ancestors regret it!"

The soldiers were all too eager to clear a path, though as Mahiro made her way to the main courtyard, it soon became clear that she was accompanied by two others on horseback: Purnima, back in her proper armor and full-moon helmet, and Yagi.

"I'll be right back," Kazuchiyo heard himself say, and he hurried down from the tower.

By the time Kazuchiyo was able to intercept them, the trio had already reached the forward regiment. Mahiro and Suzumekage took the lead position facing the gate, with Purnima and Yagi on either side, and behind them an entourage led by Captain Nishigame and General Zaiga stood as loyal sentinels. Kazuchiyo glimpsed his brother Shigeyuki carrying Yagi's spear for him and Amai in light armor next to his horse, but the bulk of his anxious focus was on Yagi himself: back in his oni armor, with a repaired right spaulder and bracer that were a bit too large in hopes of disguising his swollen, bandaged arm. A broad, emerald sash had been strung from his shoulder bearing the embroidered title of "Champion," which he was inconspicuously using as a sling. Though he stood tall in his saddle and few would think twice about the hard grimace on his face, as Kazuchiyo drew closer, he could see that Yagi was pale and sweating beneath his helmet, eyes hazy from pain.

"Brother!" Mahiro leaped down from Suzumekage before he could take a breath to speak, and tossed the reins to Purnima. "Tell me it's true," she declared. "Let me hear that the shogun's whipped pups have come back for another thrashing!"

Kazuchiyo gulped, unable to stop his eyes from traveling back to Yagi. "It's true," he said. "I know you're probably hungry for the field again, but our only option now is to hold the gate and the walls."

"Pah! Who knows that better than me?" Mahiro clapped his shoulder guard, startling him and resettling his attention on her. "Tonight is when I outshine this cumbersome oni, and his supposedly infamous holding of the bloodstained bridge. No one steps inside this courtyard while *I* hold the wall."

She leaned closer then, lowering her voice so that only Kazuchiyo would hear. "He needs to be here. The soldiers need to see him."

Kazuchiyo blinked, caught off guard by her concern. He looked again to Yagi, and despite the pain it caused him, he nodded. "I know. But if he's made to fight—"

"If they come through the gate we're all dead anyway. You'd rather he die at your side than alone, half naked in the keep, right?" Mahiro gave him another thump and then straightened up. "Lady Purnima!" she called. "If even one slithery imperial gets past me, let loose Suzumekage! She'll stamp the little beasts to blood!"

"With pleasure," Purnima replied, and Mahiro beamed as she turned back to Kazuchiyo.

"I want a better look at them. General Oihata had better make room for me up there!" She winked at her brother and then marched forward to scale the tower.

Kazuchiyo could not leave as easily as that. He moved in front of Yagi and bowed his head just enough in greeting. "Captain Ebara," he said. "I hope we won't have much need for infantry in this fight, but… it's good you're here."

Yagi's jaw worked as he glanced around at their audience. "I'll do whatever's necessary," he promised, and Kazuchiyo was sure he heard a *Don't worry about me* in the words as well. Standing alongside him, Amai offered a nod as if to say the same.

There was nothing Kazuchiyo could do but trust the two of them to look out for each other. After receiving determined looks from Zaiga and Shigeyuki as well, he followed Mahiro back up the guard tower.

"I'll swing straight down from this tower and decapitate him myself!" Mahiro was insisting to Naoya as Kazuchiyo rejoined them. "Just hold on to the back of my mane, General. We can end this fight in one swoop!"

"Don't be preposterous," Naoya sputtered. "This is going to take precision and endurance, not theatrics."

"It was theatrics in Izuho that won that fight," Kazuchiyo reminded Naoya, moving to stand between them at the tower rail. "Though I can't say I'm encouraging you to move even one hand's width outside these walls, Mahiro. You're our best defense."

"Oh yes, I know." Mahiro thumped the butt of her naginata against the wooden floor. "And my blade is so sharp, all I have to do is hold it out for the little fish to skewer themselves."

The sun had begun to set by the time the Oomiyari reached the field beyond Rongi's gate. They spread their three regiments wide across the remnants of their enemy's former camp, far enough away that even archers firing from the relative height of the fortress walls would lose their effectiveness. The Ba'nyuunuma were a bit bolder, creeping into Rongi's own long shadow, rattling their spears in eagerness for the assault. It had all the markings of a show of strength rather than the expression of it; fresh soldiers lined up to harry their surrounded enemy out of much-needed rest. Such tactics would likely stretch the siege out for many days.

"Cowards," Mahiro grumbled. "They think if they keep us on our toes long enough, we'll just give up?"

Naoya scoffed; for once the pair of them seemed to be in perfect agreement. "Never. Our stores are stocked and our wells run deep, and the samurai of Kibaku will never surrender."

Kazuchiyo remained quiet; he scanned the Oomiyari line for any breaks or weaknesses, any indication that their formation was suffering from the lack of General Nokogiriha. Though the failing light made it difficult to tell, this did not seem to be the case.

A group of riders came forward from the command unit, banners hoisted at the fore to indicate a messenger. Half a dozen would have sufficed, but nearly thirty horses came forward in a parade-like presentation. Mahiro continued to grumble about the theatrics, but Naoya took their advance seriously, passing orders on to his captains for all archers to be on high alert. Kazuchiyo soon spotted the reason for his caution: Mutsuyama, leading the procession alongside Oomiyari Jakusai.

Kazuchiyo ground his teeth. However poorly Amai

remembered the encounter, he was certain his eyes and memory were sound: Jakusai ought to have died from his wound, or at least have been as incapacitated as Yagi. Even so, he showed very little evidence of discomfort let alone injury as he strode forward atop his black steed, glaring up at Rongi in angry defiance.

"You said that if Mutsuyama comes close enough, you might be able to determine how much magic he's still capable of," Kazuchiyo said to Naoya. "How close must he be?"

"Closer than he's likely to come," Naoya admitted. "Unless he's intent on breaching us tonight."

The formation did not make it seem this was the likely course, but all remained vigilant as the envoy came to settle just beyond Rongi's gate. Mutsuyama and Jakusai came forward, flanked on either side by armed samurai in ornate armor. As the dusk-light finally failed, only their blazing torches lit the scene for those above.

"I am Oomiyari Jakusai," the man declared. "Dispatched by my uncle, Shogun Oomiyari Ryousai, commander of the imperial armies and guardian of all Shuyun. On orders from the exalted emperor himself, my singular purpose is to retrieve the head of Aritaka Kazumune, who stands guilty of treason. If the lord of Rongi will not surrender him, then all of Kibaku, too, shall be considered traitorous and share his fate."

Kazuchiyo clenched his fists tight, but Naoya was quick to reassure him, saying, "Worry not, Kazumune. Lord Koedzuka thinks too highly of you to give you up, and his honor would not allow it regardless."

"I never doubted," Kazuchiyo replied in kind.

Mahiro gave a great snort. "As if they would simply leave, even if we threw our heads at their feet." She pounded her naginata against the tower floor. "No one here believes His Exaltedness the emperor would have sent such a sorry-faced lot of wormy cowards!" she bellowed down at the pair. "Just admit you're too scared to fight and slink on home!"

Jakusai bristled with fury. "Name yourself!"

"Gladly!" Mahiro pounded her naginata again, and the samurai with them in the tower stomped their feet, swept up in her bravado. "I am Aritaka Mahiro, daughter of Shuyun's great northern bear. I am the Unyielding Iron Gate! As long as Rongi is under my protection, no yellow coward from the west will take one step past this wall!"

Jakusai looked ready to respond, but Mutsuyama held up his hand, and he quieted. "Your threats mean nothing to me, Aritaka Mahiro," Mutsuyama called to her. "I have already been past your walls. I can do so again whenever I like, regardless of the presence of General Oihata there."

"Then come and try it now!" Mahiro goaded as Naoya glowered. "I'll pluck out all that old hair of yours, and sit your head next to your general's at my supper!"

Jakusai hissed something that could not be made out across the distance, and Mutsuyama nodded. Not wanting them to have too much time to confer, Kazuchiyo at last spoke up. "Master Mutsuyama," he shouted down from the tower, "we all know how this conflict will end. You have your orders, but we have our resolve, and the shogun's will alone will not topple Rongi. Let your men go back to their fields for the harvest. There will be plenty of time for you to take my head without risking famine at the capital."

Mutsuyama regarded him smugly in return. "Resolve, however bold, is not enough to defend a fortress with either," he replied. "If you are so concerned about the harvest, tell Lord Koedzuka to mind his own. Who will tend his famous rolling fields if he and all his citizens are dead?"

"Unbearable swine," Naoya growled. "As if I would ever allow it." Unable to further rein in his temper, he leaned forward against the rail. "The samurai of Kibaku will never fall to honorless dogs! We need only outlast you to be victorious. Will you slink back to your master with starving men unable to tend rotten crops? Your arrogance will be the end of your line!"

Mutsuyama gave a short, bitter laugh. "It may indeed. But for arrogance, you need only look to your left." He stared up at

Kazuchiyo. "Young Lord Aritaka, earlier you relayed a message that I believe was meant for me. Allow me to share with you my answer."

He reached into his robe, and the soldiers manning the tower tensed in readiness. Mahiro hefted her naginata, and Naoya put his hand to Kazuchiyo's chest, ready to shove him back. What Mutsuyama drew from his sleeve was only a folded shiki, which he tossed into the air. Its paper wings beat swiftly, propelling it up toward the tower. Though all remained on guard, when the message drew within range Kazuchiyo extended his hand. He accepted the shiki and unfolded it.

The parchment used was very fine, and the calligraphy gracing its pages in dark ink even more so. It was addressed to him, but Kazuchiyo was only able to make out that much before the letters began to ooze. The paper blackened and reeked of a nauseating, rotten odor like old meat. Just as Kazuchiyo feared the terrible stench would overwhelm his consciousness, Naoya clapped both hands around the shiki. Kazuchiyo felt the rush of heat that had accompanied most magic he'd experienced, but also that terrible, biting cold gained from the last memories of poor Mizutane. His stomach turned over as the paper disintegrated into ash.

Naoya let go and immediately shed his gloves, which Kazuchiyo realized were charred black. Their eyes met. Naoya's expression was furious, but his cheeks were very pale, and it took no words between them for Kazuchiyo to intuit how close he had been in that moment to a swift and painful death. Moreover, and nearly as distressing, he could see another ruinous truth: that in dispelling the curse, Naoya had expended the last of his magic.

"What was that?" Mahiro demanded, pointing her weapon at Mutsuyama. "You gutless vermin, what did you just do?"

"We have twice your number in soldiers!" Mutsuyama declared, his gaze sweeping the wall. "You cannot defeat us on the field! We have ransacked your villages; we have slaughtered your two thousand reserves to the south! You cannot hope to outlast or resist us! Kibaku's only hope for survival now is to surrender the head of Aritaka Kazumune, and receive His Excellency's pardon!"

His eyes ended on Kazuchiyo, daring him to speak. A hot shudder passed through Kazuchiyo's body as he saw very clearly what the next several days would entail: the Oomiyari marching their soldiers to the field to wave their banners and rattle their spears, keeping all of Rongi anxious and depleted; more attacks in the night, fire arrows and maybe even more shinobi sent to pick off their higher officers; Mutsuyama himself sneaking past the wall when it was least expected. All it would take was one lapse in an exhausted guard rotation for him to open the gate from within. Even if the samurai of Kibaku proved as robust as they boasted, Kazuchiyo could not bear to suffer those long days of stress and uncertainty at such cruel hands.

"You can expect no reinforcements!" Mutsuyama continued to shout, and almost without realizing it, Kazuchiyo took hold of his sword. "You have no avenue of retreat! If it is a swift end to this stalemate you seek, cast the traitor down, or let us in and accept your shame!"

"Mahiro," said Kazuchiyo, "show me how *you* would have done it at Izuho."

"Gladly," Mahiro snarled, and she tossed her naginata in the air so she could recapture it in a javelin stance. With a bellow of fury she launched the blade directly at Mutsuyama.

Mutsuyama raised his hand, and a heavy gust of hot wind diverted the whirling naginata just enough that it spiraled aside—into the chest of one of Mutsuyama's guards. Mutsuyama paid him no notice as he screamed. In that moment his sleeve fell back, revealing the string of beads tied around his wrist, just as I had worn during our meeting in the temple. Obeying his most primal instincts, Kazuchiyo struck; he drew Itogiri with all his strength and focus, like he had against Tendo to save Yagi's life, and against Nanpa before that. His spell arched forth in an invisible blade that severed Mutsuyama's forearm and sent his hand careening through the air. His beads glinted in the light of the torches and scattered.

Mutsuyama sat in his saddle, shocked, blood spurting from his stump of an arm. He did not see the arrow fired from Kibaku's heaviest bow until it was lodged in his throat.

"Master Mutsuyama!" Jakusai grabbed the old man's shoulder to keep him upright, aghast at the blood pouring down his arm and neck. He glared at their surrounding men. "Kill them!"

The soldiers fired arrows up at the walls; Kazuchiyo and his companions ducked behind the rail as their archers returned fire. But Kazuchiyo could not bear to miss whatever happened to Mutsuyama, and he cautiously raised himself enough to see.

Mutsuyama was still atop his horse, thanks to Jakusai's support. Gagging and wheezing, he gripped the shaft of the arrow still embedded in his throat and ripped it free. To Kazuchiyo's confusion and shock, he then stabbed it directly through the eye of his horse.

The unfortunate beast cried out and collapsed, Mutsuyama with it. By then the soldiers had spurred their horses forward, blocking him with their bodies and banners. Kazuchiyo lifted himself higher, trying to get a better view even as an arrow impacted the wood close to him. He had to see the man's fate with his own eyes. His heart pounded in those long seconds, and then fell when he saw Mutsuyama climbing up behind one of his soldiers in his saddle. Though blood still coated his robes, the hole in his neck had closed over and he was still alive.

From the darkened hills to the east came the piercing shout of an oxen horn. Kazuchiyo and Mahiro bolted upright at once at the familiar cry and stared into the dark horizon. Torchlights appeared along the hills by the dozens, stretching far to the north and south. Each illuminated tall banners bearing two different family crests, both of which were familiar and very welcome sights.

"It's Rakuteru!" Mahiro shouted gleefully, pounding her fists against the rail. "Ride the bastards down!"

"Rakuteru," Kazuchiyo breathed with relief. "And...

Watarizume?" He blinked at the white flags with their black, jeweled emblem in shock. Though their torchlights gleamed in the south for half a mile, he knew the fledgling province of Izuho could never have produced such numbers. "But how?"

Another blow from the ox horn sounded the charge, and some eighty riders came pounding down the hillside. Having learned much from Kibaku's use of cavalry, they aimed their spears straight ahead and quickly took shape into two arrowed points. The larger of the two veered to the north, and shouts echoed out from the Nomino samurai as General Rakuteru himself led the charge across their rear flank. Though Kazuchiyo could not see the outcome of that attack from his vantage, he could hear the twang of Kibaku bows aiding it, and the furious shouts of men in retreat.

The second of the two forces aimed directly at Mutsuyama and his thirty riders. Though the banners jutting from their armor were of Izuho, Kazuchiyo recognized a folded straw hat among those at the front. His hunch was confirmed when the rider gestured with one hand, and each of the Oomiyari's golden banners burst into flames.

"Iomori," Kazuchiyo murmured, amazed, as the Oomiyari's horses startled and turned. Jakusai ordered a retreat, though he spared one last, hateful look for Kazuchiyo before turning his horse. Then they raced back toward the Oomiyari's main force with Iomori and two dozen Izuho samurai on their heels. All along the walls samurai from four provinces cheered and stomped at the sight of the shogun's best in full flight. Iomori was too clever to follow too far, though; she and the riders turned back before putting themselves in range of archer fire. They turned to the gate and a welcoming cheer.

"Young lord!" Iomori called up to the tower, tilting her hat back. She looked very much like Kazuchiyo had seen her last, in her green kariginu, with her long hair tied back. "How fare your forces inside the castle?"

"Over three thousand who can still fight!" Kazuchiyo replied. "And stores enough to last several days."

"Lend me half your soldiers, then! My beacons won't fool them for long."

"Fool them?" Kazuchiyo echoed, and he looked again to the hillside. To his eye the torches and banners still appeared genuine, though he knew then that could not be the case. Rakuteru had left with a thousand men, but Watarizume could not have produced even a quarter of that number in so short a time.

"Illusions," confirmed Naoya. "But if we position half our troops to the southeast, we can flank any attempt from Mutsuyama to assault the gates again."

"Leave it to me!" crowed Mahiro, and she pushed away from the rail. "We can make it if we're quick!"

"Go," said Kazuchiyo, and without needing any further encouragement Mahiro climbed down from the tower, already shouting for Suzumekage and a new weapon.

Kazuchiyo remained in the tower as the gates ground open. He watched the soldiers pour out of Rongi with Mahiro and Purnima at the head and Ginta close behind, but he did not see Yagi, Zaiga, or his brother among them. Just to be sure, he crossed to the interior and was relieved to find that the three of them and Amai had remained with the soldiers inside to guard the gate.

"This will work," he said, his energy renewed as he rejoined Naoya at the head of the tower. As Mahiro and their soldiers raced to join Izuho's reinforcements on the hill, the Oomiyari remained at a distance, seemingly bewildered by the new army and the damage done to their commanders. "If Mahiro can form a line far enough away, the Oomiyari won't be able to advance without being caught between her and the castle. And Nomino." Kazuchiyo strained up on his toes to try to see anything from the eastern gate; he could still hear great shouting and pounding, but the geography of the fortress made it impossible to see. "Ba'nyuunuma brought no more than two thousand men. If Rakuteru can push them far enough north, they'll be cut off from the Oomiyari and won't be able to coordinate their attacks."

"If he came from the north, he must have planned his approach very carefully," said Naoya with appreciation. "Swung very wide so he could attack from the southeast. That will make Ba'nyuunuma's decision to return home much easier, should the siege swing against their favor." He let his breath out in a long sigh. "You're right: this may prove the end of this."

Kazuchiyo nodded, though it was difficult to relax even then after having watched Mutsuyama escape. "Is your magic now spent?" he asked bluntly.

"Yes," Naoya admitted, grimacing. He rubbed his palms together as if remembering the sting from Mutsuyama's curse. "I should have known he was capable of cowardly magic like that," he said quietly. "He must still have many stones in reserve if he was willing to expend so many."

"You saved my life," Kazuchiyo told him sincerely. "You have my thanks."

"You would have done the same for me if you had the skill." Naoya frowned, seeming to understand the implication behind his words. "Your spell was equally well cast."

Kazuchiyo only realized then that he was still gripping Itogiri, unsheathed. He slid the blade back into its scabbard. "I don't know how much good it did. He still survived."

"At great personal cost." Naoya glared into the Oomiyari's distant line with disgust. "Separated from his stones, he could only resort to his horse's life to spare him. But as I cautioned you before, such actions change a man."

Kazuchiyo lowered his gaze to the field below, where the body of Mutsuyama's horse remained, the arrow sticking out of its skull. "A horse's soul," he murmured, his mind whirling with new possibilities. "I hadn't considered that was even possible."

"A powerful enough onmyouji can employ means beyond a normal man's imagining. We cannot afford to underestimate him." Naoya looked to him and took in a deep breath. "The two of us together, however, can best him without resorting to such depravity. And we will."

Kazuchiyo nodded. "We will."

Each then turned their gaze forward, eager to watch the conflict through to its now inevitable end.

CHAPTER TWENTY-SIX

The gates swung closed again. With Mahiro at the head, the combined soldiers made good time across the field and up the hill alongside Iomori's reinforcements, lending even more torches and banners to the illusions that remained in place. As they settled into ranks, their voices even raised in a raucous song, and the commotion from the east gate ceased. Kazuchiyo and Naoya remained watchful in the tower, though within the hour it became clear that the Oomiyari's large force was uncertain how to proceed. Though their numbers remained superior, they had suddenly found themselves out-positioned and facing a powerful new foe. Even arrogant Mutsuyama must have felt some apprehension about contending with another onmyouji fresh to the field, with no insight as to her skills and reserves. A night siege under such circumstances would have been the height of foolishness, but to retreat would mean surrendering all momentum.

At last, with the moon high and waxing, Chikakuni climbed the tower with news. "Ba'nyuunuma's retreated to the north wall," he said with weary relief. "They've taken up a defensive position. It looks like they're honestly worried about Rakuteru and are settling in for the night."

"And Rakuteru?" Kazuchiyo asked.

"Outnumbered but holding. His riders are well positioned. One of their captains approached the east gate to let us know that they've sent riders east and north to call for reinforcements. Nomino sent some of theirs to pursue the man headed north, but the eastern messenger is long gone."

"Then we can expect reinforcements from Ugarasu before the week is out," Naoya said. "And maybe Castle Tettsu as well. My brother will certainly send our reserves if he's made aware of the situation." He sighed, and Kazuchiyo could see his long-held exhaustion making itself ever more known. "Unless Mutsuyama is keen to draw this out at least twice as long as he expected, we may have truly settled this."

"I'm not leaving this post until we're certain," Kazuchiyo told him. "By first light, we should be able to tell." He turned back to Chikakuni. "Tell your lady that her arrow was well struck, even if the snake managed to wriggle free. She has all our gratitude."

"I'll wait until it's over," Chikakuni said with a half smirk. "She's still very put out that it didn't kill him. But what can humans do against demons, hm?"

Kazuchiyo frowned as Chikakuni climbed down from the tower. He touched the beads tied so close to his wrist and thought he could still feel the heat lingering around them, like two tiny coals.

As expected, the stalemate dragged on until dawn. Every hour Mahiro would lead their soldiers in another round of singing and stomping and hollering that echoed across the fields. By the first light of morning, Kazuchiyo could no longer fathom how she kept up the energy, but they never faltered, unlike their opponents. The rising sun cast long shadows of her line across the grass, and at last, the Oomiyari returned to their camp, hoots and cheers chasing them back.

Lord Koedzuka climbed the guard tower then, still in his full armor. "We shot a messenger arrow down to the Nomino army an hour ago," he reported to Kazuchiyo and Naoya. "I offered that we would allow them back into their camp to gather their supplies if they would abandon the siege. Their general just sent back word that he agrees."

"My lord," Naoya said carefully, "I beg you will excuse my impropriety, but is that wise? They may reclaim their camp and resettle. Can we not wait for our reinforcements to arrive and drive them home in shame?"

"We probably could, but there is a chance that they could also draw reinforcements in that time. It will do us all good to seek the swifter end." He nodded to Kazuchiyo. "And it may prove a boon to you someday, young Lord Kazumune, that they were shown mercy here."

Kazuchiyo bowed in gratitude. "Your foresight is greatly appreciated, Lord Koedzuka. With Nomino gone, hopefully the Oomiyari will rethink their own odds."

His words would soon prove true. As the sun rose on first day of the tenth month of 1488, General Rakuteru pulled his troops back a respectful distance so that the Nomino soldiers could reenter their camp. Though tensions remained high, it was soon apparent that they meant to make good on their word of abandoning the siege. As they packed their equipment and rations into carts, so, too, did Rongi ferry supplies to its allies on the hill, where Mahiro insisted on staying vigilant over a camp of her own. Seeing this only helped to quicken Nomino's pace, and another message was shot by arrow over the wall. Now down in the courtyard at Yagi's side, Kazuchiyo read the note over with General Sasahara.

From one northern beast to another, no hard feelings, it read in its entirety. Though Beihou scoffed mightily, Amai found it far more genuinely amusing.

"I'm looking forward to us meeting this general someday," he said, and despite the circumstances, Kazuchiyo had to admit that so did he.

The Ba'nyuunuma retreated deeper into the north, and as their figures grew smaller against the horizon, another messenger procession came forth from the Oomiyari camp.

Only half a dozen approached this time. Master Mutsuyama and Oomiyari Jakusai were not among them. A man in gold armor announced his name and requested an audience with Kazuchiyo, who agreed, though only insofar as he retook his place on the tower.

"I bear a message from my lord, Master Mutsuyama," he declared. "He has agreed with your earlier proposition that he shall take your head another time." Lady Dada put an arrow through his eye, and his peers fled back to their camp with twanging bows at their heels. Soon after, it became clear to all that the Oomiyari were breaking down their camp. After a mere two days, the siege had ended.

The night that followed passed in an exhaustive blur. Kazuchiyo insisted that Yagi return to his small quarters to rest, and though it took some convincing, he finally agreed, taking Amai with him. Kazuchiyo himself remained, presiding over the watch for as long as his stamina would carry him. He even convinced Naoya to at last return to his chamber atop the lesser keep for a proper rest. Rongi's soldiers remained on edge, some refusing to leave their posts while others paced about restlessly. All eyes were drawn continuously to the movement within the Oomiyari camp. By the third dawn since their initial attack, the Oomiyari were on their way back into the west, and Kazuchiyo was sinking to the mattress between his lovers.

"I'm sorry I couldn't help you," Yagi mumbled as Kazuchiyo stretched out alongside him. "But it didn't seem like you needed us this time anyway."

"Don't be ridiculous," Kazuchiyo replied, scooting closer as he drew Amai to him. "I couldn't have done any of it without you both."

"Oh, we know," said Amai, and he kissed his shoulder. "We know."

CHAPTER TWENTY-SEVEN

Only after the last member of the shogun's brood had disappeared into the west did Rongi loosen its cords.

Celebrations were muted. Mahiro's camp on the hill was rebuilt larger and with finer tents, as the fortress, which had already been overflowing with soldiers, now had even more guests to accommodate and only one keep safe for the lords and generals. Whispers of amazement passed from one soldier to the next as they began the slow process of rebuilding and recollecting their armies, and rumors abounded. Many were unclear as to how the shogun's ire had fallen on them so intensely and how it had dissipated just as quickly. Some claimed that it had been Mahiro's naginata that ripped Mutsuyama's hand from his arm while naturally most of Kibaku insisted it was the work of their proud General Oihata. So, too, did rumors swirl around Yagi-douji, spreading from those who had witnessed his collapse, yet this gossip was opposed by his staunch supporters among Nishigame's company.

There was, however, one matter that all could agree on: that the young heir to the east had stood up against the will of the emperor himself, and he had won.

The path now clear, Kazuchiyo rode out with Naoya and

a group of samurai to see what had become of the temple village south of Rongi. The stench reached them long before they arrived, that of burnt wood and cooked and rotten flesh. Kazuchiyo's heart ached as they came upon the tragic sight: the village destroyed, its homes and markets blackened and hollow from Mutsuyama's horrific fire, piles of corpses strewn on doorsteps and in the streets. The temple that stood at the center of what had once been a charming town had been looted and burned, its shrine desecrated. Adults and children both had been cut down by blades and arrows, the few bearing any kind of armor ripped open. As Kazuchiyo toured the ruins, he spotted more than one unfortunate soul split open at the armpit just as old Mizutane had been, likely a victim of Oomiyari Jakusai's loathsome kamayari.

Naoya wept, furious and inconsolable. His soldiers pried open homes looking for survivors, but they found none. Kazuchiyo looked out over the devastation from atop the anxious Hashikiri, a fist clenched tightly to his chest. The stench of bodies reminded him very clearly of the curse that had almost claimed his life the night before, and he became convinced that it was precisely these slain villagers that Mutsuyama had employed when attempting to murder him. His blood seethed in his every vein, and he knew he had no hope of turning his back to the west now.

The shogun and his dogs he had always known to be selfish and neglectful, undeserving of their titles and power. With this added brutality there could be no question that the Oomiyari's rule was meant to end. However, as Kazuchiyo surveyed the corpses offered in sacrifice, he was equally convinced that Aritaka in the same position would have behaved no more nobly. Our beautiful Shuyun and its people deserved better than these greedy cowards, and there was no one better positioned to answer its desperate need.

In the evening, Kazuchiyo climbed to the top of the lesser keep, where an assembly of lords, ladies, and generals had gathered to share a celebratory drink. It was there that he was finally able to greet General Rakuteru, Lord Watarizume, and Master Iomori. It may well be that Rongi would have survived the siege thanks to Mutsuyama's injuries alone, but their well-timed arrival was still a boon to be commended. Kazuchiyo bowed low to each, and they to him.

"It's very good to see you well, General," said Kazuchiyo as he joined the assembly with Koedzuka, Beihou, Lady Dada, and Chikakuni. "When we heard Nomino had come from the north, we feared the worst for you and your men."

Rakuteru released a heavy sigh as he took his seat. "It shames me to admit it, but you had every reason to," he replied. "That blasted Ba'nyuunuma took us by surprise, forced us north, and pinned us down for a time. It was thanks to the Jisu samurai we discovered that we were able to make our way east without them pursuing, where we met with Lord Watarizume. Took longer than I would have liked." He bowed to Kazuchiyo. "For that, I offer my apologies, and my life."

"That's not necessary," Kazuchiyo replied quickly. "Your arrival was so perfectly timed, I would rather have scolded you for coming any earlier." At his gesture, Rakuteru straightened up again, and Kazuchiyo looked to Lord Watarizume. "You are very welcome as well, my lord."

Watarizume shifted self-consciously. He was dressed in his white armor robes, as if he had left Izuho in such haste that he had not had the time to prepare a lord's full attire for this meeting. His long hair and mustache were only roughly combed. "When I agreed to offer my soldiers in exchange for your aid, I did not expect it would be so soon," he said. "But once Master Iomori alerted us to the situation, I knew we had to act." He looked to Koedzuka and Beihou: the former was calm and impassive, Beihou smiling but tightly. He bowed his head. "Despite our disagreements earlier this year, I am still a man of honor, and I hope that with this Izuho can make amends."

"You came to us when we were in need," Koedzuka said graciously. "As long as we can come together now and agree on where each of our borders lie, I see no reason why we can't or shouldn't be allies going forward."

Watarizume nodded gratefully, but Beihou remained not quite convinced, saying, "If you left Shihomi only *after* hearing that the Oomiyari were at our door, you must have made excellent time."

"We brought only riders and took the surest path in order to achieve exactly that. Master Iomori insisted."

All eyes turned to Iomori, who was sipping from her saké cup. She was in no hurry to answer. Though it had not been overly long since Kazuchiyo had seen her last, he had gained so much knowledge of the machinations of her magic that he could not help but view her in an entirely different light. She set her cup down and lifted her head, and he watched closely, hopeful he could at last glean more of her motives.

"I was on my way here from Shihomi to fetch my lord when I came across refugees from a small village," she explained, and Kazuchiyo's heart again grew heavy at the memory. "Only a few had escaped slaughter at the Oomiyari's hands. Hearing this, I thought to draw reinforcements." She glanced sideways at Watarizume, who seemed uncomfortable beneath her eye. "His soldiers were still gathered at Shihomi following what was nearly a siege. Most convenient for us."

"Convenient for me as well," replied Watarizume, though stiffly. He was obviously not yet well versed enough in daimyo politics to speak with confidence. "It gave me the opportunity to prove my word to Lord Aritaka here. And to prove to the shogun's men that we will, in turn, have his protection in the future."

"And the refugees?" asked Chikakuni.

"General Oihata was able to catch up to them," said Kazuchiyo, heart heavy with the memory. "They will be sheltered at Mitake until the village can be rebuilt."

"There is much else that needs to be addressed," spoke up Lady Dada. "My uncle and his men to the south are still unaccounted for, as are some two thousand of Sakka's. I'm certain all our soldiers are eager to return home for the season, but I cannot in good conscience return to Etsugo without confirming what Mutsuyama said, about them having been wiped out."

"Yes, indeed," said Koedzuka. "There is still a great deal left to do. Rongi's hospitality may only be able to bear you all a while longer, but arrangements will be made." He reached for his cup. "The dead deserve their homecoming too."

Everyone agreed, and they lifted their saucers to toast the fallen. Before the assembly could part, Kazuchiyo gathered their attention to him one last time.

"I want to thank you all," he said, and though a surge of emotion threaded through his ribs, he sat tall, and his voice did not waver. "I am not so arrogant as to believe our victory here was for my sake alone, but I am very aware of what all of you have sacrificed, which you might not have been made to do if not for me. Because of my actions and my choices and my words. I intend to prove through these that your faith in me shall never be proven false, nor taken advantage of."

He took a deep breath. "Together, we can stand against Shogun Oomiyari's cowardice and cruelty. When we take the capital, we will restore strength and dignity to the title so that never again will the will of the emperor be wielded so falsely. Will you aid me?"

Each of them bowed their head low in answer. "Yes, lord."

They departed from the chamber, and as Kazuchiyo made his way out of the keep, he kept Rakuteru beside him. "Our men are exhausted," he said. "We need to start sending them home, but we must take volunteers to linger a while longer, so that we can uncover the whereabouts of General Hosoda."

"He's dead," Rakuteru reported grimly. "Come with me."

Kazuchiyo followed Rakuteru into the courtyard. Ginta was there waiting for the meeting to adjourn, and with him stood a familiar soldier—young Tomoto, still dressed in armor stained with blood and dust. His helmet had been damaged so badly that it sat askew, and Kazuchiyo could see linen bandages rusty with blood poking out from beneath it. Kazuchiyo's heart sank; Tomoto was gripping Hosoda's cracked war fan in both hands.

Upon seeing Kazuchiyo, Tomoto lowered himself to his knees and bowed. "My lord," he said, voice hoarse. "I wanted to... to present this to you." He lifted the wooden war fan, its lacquer scratched and a crack running down one side. "It's all I could spare of General Hosoda."

Kazuchiyo accepted the fan from him and cradled it gently. "Thank you, Tomoto. I am deeply sorry for your loss."

Tomoto's shoulders hitched, and he took a moment to scrub his eyes. Ginta took over for him, saying, "Apparently the Oomiyari ambushed them while General Hosoda was meeting with us in Kanrei Temple, and caught him on his way back. Only a very small number survived, trapped behind their lines. It was only when General Oomiyari moved their army to surround Rongi that Tomoto here was able to lead their way back."

Kazuchiyo spread the map across his mind, trying to calculate the timing of such an attack. It sickened him to think that while they were feasting at Rongi, unaware, so many souls had fallen to the shogun's vile dogs. He wondered, too, if any of them, perhaps even Hosoda himself, had been employed by Mutsuyama at the battle. It was becoming ever clearer to him why Naoya had thought to hide the truth of magic's origins from him.

"You've done very well to return this to me," Kazuchiyo told Tomoto softly. "General Hosoda was a good man and a good soldier. He will be honored." His grip tightened around the fan. "And avenged."

"Thank you, my lord," said Tomoto, still bowed.

Kazuchiyo and Rakuteru moved away to converse in private while Ginta tended to Tomoto. "Even so, we must recover his remains," Kazuchiyo insisted. "I won't leave our men to rot in a foreign land, nor leave them for Jisu when they already have their own dead to bury."

"We're in agreement," Rakuteru said gruffly. "Though before you divide our forces too hastily, you'll have to talk it over with *that* one."

He motioned with his chin, and Kazuchiyo turned to look over his shoulder. Iomori was approaching. It was only then that Kazuchiyo remembered her words from the assembly, and he gestured her forward. "Master Iomori, what news is there from my father?"

"He has summoned you to him," Iomori replied as she joined them. "Though he wasn't aware of the siege here when he ordered it, his command is that the army be disbanded back to their homesteads while you and your retinue join him."

Kazuchiyo's skin prickled with apprehension. "Your last message indicated that he had left Gyoe. Where shall I meet him?"

"Suyama," Iomori replied crisply, and Kazuchiyo's pulse raced into his ears. "We are to meet him at Suyama's capital, Tengakubou, as soon as possible."

"Tengakubou," Kazuchiyo repeated, struck all but senseless by the mention of it. He had not glimpsed the seat of his home province's rule since he was a foolish young boy, riding out with his father the Red Dragon, seeking war. "You're certain?"

"Absolutely so. Your father's brother, Lord Sourei, has invited you both to celebrate the harvest there."

Rakuteru raised his eyebrows but said nothing. It took Kazuchiyo a moment more to reclaim his wits, but when he did, he seized them with greater conviction than he had been in possession of at the start of his campaign. He gathered himself to his full height. "In that case, I look forward to it," he said, and he turned to Rakuteru. "Please spread the news to our commanders. I'd prefer if you stay yourself, General, with men of your choosing, to tend to the dead. Commander Nishigame will lead the rest of Sakka's troops home. My entourage can go with them; I'll have all the security I need traveling with General Zaiga back to Suyama."

"Of course." Rakuteru bowed shortly, and when he rose, Kazuchiyo was certain he glimpsed a very similar conviction in his face as well. "Please do not hesitate to call on me and my men if it is needed."

"You can depend on it, General." Kazuchiyo took a step back and looked expectantly to Iomori. "If you'll join me for a little longer?"

"Certainly."

The pair of them continued on through the courtyard, heading down the winding path that led to the main gate. Feeling ever more emboldened, Kazuchiyo spoke his mind. "I won't be coy with you. I know now how magic works."

Iomori did not seem surprised, and Kazuchiyo had to wonder if she had seen his spell cast against Mutsuyama. "I am impressed that Oihata trusted you with that knowledge. He and I don't know each other well, but I had thought he wasn't inclined to share."

Wisely, Kazuchiyo decided not to correct her; *how cross I would have been with him, had he revealed me to her then!* "General Oihata and I have had our disagreements over it, but we have come out stronger," he said. "He trusts me with it." He cast Iomori a sideways glance. "I don't yet know if I can trust *you.*"

Still, Iomori's face betrayed no recognizable reaction. "You offend me, Kazumune. Have I not been a champion of your well-being all this time?"

"You've intimated to me several times that you have visions of the future," Kazuchiyo said, though he was mindful not to let his volume rise too high with so many loose ears about. "That you saw in me a great fate."

"I do, and I did."

"I know now that magic is not capable of that."

"Not literally, no." At last, a sliver of a grin pulled her thin lips. "But to claim as much has done wonders for your father's faith in me. I'm certain that you can understand why I, like Oihata, have been very careful about whom I share *my* knowledge with."

Kazuchiyo frowned; it did not take much imagination at all to picture what a man like Aritaka Souyuu would do if given the truth. "I do understand. But I also have so many questions."

"I wasn't lying to you," Iomori continued more seriously after they had passed a group of soldiers. "When you were still a boy, I did see in you a great fate, which I fought to protect. Not one shown to me by little stones painted like beads." She tugged her sleeve up to give Kazuchiyo a fleeting glimpse of her collection. "Age and experience can teach a woman much. The experience of innumerable human lives, even more so. After a time, experience becomes instinct, and instinct becomes foresight."

Kazuchiyo continued to stare at Iomori's wrist even after she had tugged her sleeve down again. "When you gave me my bead, was it because you hoped I would use it?" he asked. "Or were you hoping to collect my soul if I died?"

"Both," Iomori said with an airiness that betrayed the gravity of such an admission. "I'm certain you're wondering also if I gave you that bead in Sabi so that I could harvest the mountains of dead slain by Yagi-douji."

Kazuchiyo's heart skipped. He couldn't help but remember the tiny glimpse he'd gotten from his own bead of Yagi charging forth in fury, the cross-blade spear filling his sight. He gulped and shuddered. "Did you collect my father's soul at Shimegahara?"

Iomori fell quiet then, ignoring Kazuchiyo's hard stare. After a time, she at last said, "Come with me, Kazumune."

They had reached the main gate. It was thrown open then, with soldiers moving in and out with supplies. The guards snapped into bows as Kazuchiyo passed, but he was barely able to acknowledge them; he was only watching Iomori. They left the fortress together and followed the road a short way, to roughly where Mutsuyama had stood during their final confrontation. There was still blood smeared in the dirt, from Mutsuyama, his soldier, and his horse. Iomori then moved a little farther on and crouched down on the balls of her feet. She picked something up out of the grass.

"Mutsuyama no Shishio," she said thoughtfully, and she showed to Kazuchiyo the small, gold bead. "We've known of each other for some time. He is powerful, but he is also arrogant and wasteful. He will not hesitate to kill by the hundreds to feed his talent. It's likely he'll one day be consumed by it, as many of our kind are." She offered the bead to him. "You shouldn't look too deeply into these beads, Kazumune. They will change you if you're not careful."

After some hesitation, Kazumune accepted the bead into his palm. It was warm to the touch from the morning sun. "Master Iomori, please. Did you or not?"

Iomori sighed. "Your father died at Shimegahara," she said firmly. "His soul is not here." She leaned closer and lowered her voice. "His will only lives on in you now. How you wield it is up to you."

She straightened up again and turned back toward the fortress. Kazuchiyo let her go. He looked to the bead in his hand and then into the east, where the sun gleamed a welcoming morning. With a gentle breeze buffeting him from behind, he tied Mutsuyama's golden bead into the same ribbon around his wrist that bore his other gifts.

Kazuchiyo and his soldiers remained in and around Rongi for another three days after that, resting and preparing for the journey home. He spent most of his time split between tending to his lovers and discussing terrain with the different provincial lords. Each shared with him as much knowledge of their homelands as they were able, with his promise that he would return to them during the next campaign season ready to defend them should Shogun Oomiyari flex his muscles again. His mind, however, was continuously drawn to the east, and the father who awaited him there.

Lady Dada was the first to depart. She and Kazuchiyo bid their goodbyes in the bailey just within the main gate, with Chikakuni at her side and her soldiers accompanying them. "Next time, it will be Jisu who rides to your aid," she promised Kazuchiyo. "Until then, we will hold your border against Tendo and the Oomiyari."

"Though we do hope you'll coax Ba'nyuunuma to your side before too long," added Chikakuni with a smirk. "Enemies on three sides is a bit much, even for us."

"You can count on it," Kazuchiyo reassured him. "Stay safe, and I'll be by your side again before long."

Watarizume and his retinue left next, his white coat now finally showing a bit of wear. Rakuteru, who was to remain, shared with Kazuchiyo only a brief farewell, though full of the same stoic gravity that Kazuchiyo had sensed from him before. Then it was time at last for Kazuchiyo to take his leave. He shared one last drink with Naoya, who was naturally quite teary-eyed over the affair, and embraced him as a brother with promises that they would meet again in due time.

"I am sorry that I wasn't a more pleasant guest," Kazuchiyo offered to Koedzuka and Beihou both. "I will repay you someday for the generosity and loyalty you've shown me."

"You saved my son's life," Koedzuka reminded him. "You will owe me nothing ever again."

Mahiro's farewell to Purnima took place off to one side of the bailey, though they did not escape Kazuchiyo's notice. It seemed to involve some laughter and some shoving, and then Mahiro bounded back to Suzumekage. "Let's go already!" she roared. "I'm taking the fore!" Without waiting for permission from anyone, she spurred Suzumekage to the front of the line.

Kazuchiyo took his place atop Hashikiri among the command unit. Yagi was already atop his horse beside him, once again depending on Kibaku's victory sash as a sling for his injured arm. Though he had managed to rest well in the days after the siege, he still looked pale to Kazuchiyo and travel would not be kind to him. Kazuchiyo vowed to keep a close eye on him and was relieved to see that Amai had snuck in among the unit, taking the place of a guard to lead Yagi's horse.

Mahiro sounded the advance, and the army departed from Rongi just before midday. At last, the summer heat had broken, leaving only clear, blue sky and a gentle wind to accompany their march. Kazuchiyo glanced back only once to bid farewell to stout-hearted Rongi. He hoped he would see it again someday, when its grand keep had been restored to glory.

As the procession moved on, General Zaiga moved his horse closer. "My lord," he greeted Kazuchiyo, and though his face was as ever calm and thoughtful, Kazuchiyo thought he detected a sharpened eagerness beneath his eyes and tone. "It is true, isn't it? That you will be joining us all the way back to Tengakubou?"

"It is. I hope you will help guide me, General, as I no longer remember the way."

"I shall," Zaiga replied with determination, and as he put a respectful distance between them again, Kazuchiyo could see Shigeyuki draw his horse close beside him. The pair continued to converse in low tones as they marched on.

"Tengakubou," said Amai wistfully. "I hope it's as grand as the stories claim."

"More so." Kazuchiyo stared into the east, very eager to fit an image of his home to his hazy memory of it. "It's not far from the ruins of the ancient palace where Touyun no Kami once ruled, almost a thousand years ago. When the east was all one kingdom, unified under his banner."

"It's going to be again, isn't it?" asked Yagi. "You've got almost all of them now." He frowned thoughtfully, lowering his voice. "Have you made up your mind?"

"Yes," Kazuchiyo said, and he straightened his back proudly, his gaze fixed ahead. "But first, I have to face my father."

And on Kazuchiyo rode, his path laid into the east, where the Dragonlands waited to welcome their master home.

Thank you for reading KAZUCHIYO: The Breaking of the Siege! The adventures of Kazuchiyo, Yagi, and Amai will continue in book 3.

Please visit MelanieSchoenBooks.com to purchase your copy and get information on my other books.

ABOUT THE AUTHOR

Melanie Schoen is an indie author born and raised in Michigan. From a young age she enjoyed crafting stories, particularly those featuring historical settings with diverse characters, full of adventure and drama. After studying Japanese language and culture and earning a bachelor's degree in East Asian Language and Studies, she spent several years translating manga for various American publishers. These days she works an office job to lend more time to her passion for her personal fiction, marrying her love of history with a desire for more progressive narratives.

In addition to Kazuchiyo, Melanie is publishing graphic novel *Bang! Bang! BOOM!* along with its prequel novel, *Bang! Bang! BOOM! [NEW YORK]*, a jazz era adventure series featuring LGBT gangsters and magic. For updates, other news, and information about all current projects, please visit MelanieSchoenBooks.com